N I C K
C U T T E R

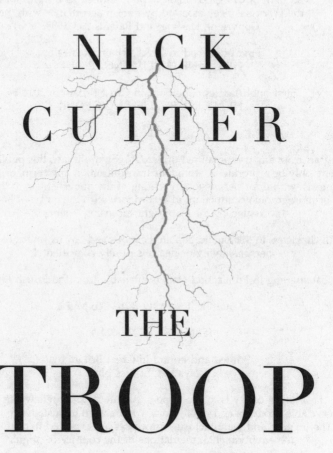

THE
TROOP

headline

First published in Great Britain in 2014 by
HEADLINE PUBLISHING GROUP

First published in paperback in Great Britain in 2014 by
HEADLINE PUBLISHING GROUP

1

Cataloguing in Publication Data is available from the British Library

Interior design by Ruth Lee-Mui

ISBN 978 1 4722 0624 4

Printed and bound in Great Britain by
Clays Ltd, St Ives plc

Headline's policy is to use papers that are natural, renewable and
recyclable products and made from wood grown in sustainable forests.
The logging and manufacturing processes are expected to conform to
the environmental regulations of the country of origin.

HEADLINE PUBLISHING GROUP
An Hachette UK Company
338 Euston Road
London NW1 3BH

www.headline.co.uk
www.hachette.co.uk

For my brother,
Graham

Part One

THE HUNGRY MAN

THE HUNGRY MAN OF PRINCE COUNTY!

By Huntington Mulvaney

Fearsome news, dear readers, from one of our loneliest outposts—the tiny fishing community of Lower Montague, Prince Edward Island. A forlorn, foreboding spike of rock projecting into the Atlantic Ocean.

The perfect location for devilry, methinks? Thankfully for you, we have eyes and ears everywhere. We see all, we hear all.

Sadie Adkins, waitress at the Diplomat Diner in Lower Montague, had her late-model Chevrolet truck stolen from the restaurant's lot last night by an unnaturally emaciated thief. Adkins placed a call to our toll-free tip line after her entreaties to local deputy dawgs were cruelly and maliciously rebuffed, deemed—and we quote—"ludicrous" and "insane."

"I know who stole my damn truck," Adkins told us. "Starvin' Marvin."

An unidentified male, with close-cropped hair and baggy clothing, entered the Diplomat at 9 p.m. According to Adkins, the man was in a severe state of malnourishment.

"Skinny! You wouldn't believe," Adkins told our intrepid truth-gatherers. "Never in my life have I seen a man so wasted away. But *hungry*."

Adkins reports that the unidentified male consumed five Hungry Man Breakfast platters—each consisting of four eggs, three buttermilk pancakes, five rashers of bacon, sausage links, and toast.

"He ate us out of eggs," Adkins said. "Just kept shoveling it in and asking for more. His belly must have swelled up tight as a drum. He . . . well, he . . . when I came back with his third platter, or maybe it was his fourth, I caught him eating the napkins. Ripping them out of the dispenser, chewing and swallowing them."

The unidentified man paid his bill and left. Shortly thereafter Adkins went outside to find her truck stolen—yet another malicious indignity!

"I can't say I was too surprised," she said. "The man seemed desperate in every way a man can possibly be desperate."

She fell silent again before adding one final grisly detail:

"I could hear something coming from inside him—I'm saying, under his skin. I know that sounds silly."

The unidentified man remains at large. Who is he? Where did he come from? The people who *know*—and longtime readers know who we're talking about: the government, the Secret Service, the Templars, the Illuminati, the usual shady suspects—aren't forthcoming with info . . . but we're beating the bushes and scouring secret files, investigating every legitimate tip that arrives at our tipline.

Something evil is afoot in sleepy Prince County. No man can be *that* hungry.

IF YOU LIKED THIS ARTICLE YOU MAY ALSO ENJOY:

- **CHEESEBURGER KILLS SPACE ALIEN!**

- **BEEZLEBUB CAPTURED BY GI'S IN IRAQ!**

- **HELLSPAWN BABY RUNS AMOK IN TUPELO!**

- **EL CHUPACABRA DRAINS TODDLER'S BLOOD IN PUBLIC PARK!**

Chapter One

Eat eat eat eat

The boat skipped over the waves, the drone of its motor trailing across the Gulf of Saint Lawrence. The moon was a bone fishhook in the clear October sky.

The man was wet from the spray that kicked over the gunwale. The outline of his body was visible under his drenched clothes. He easily could have been mistaken for a scarecrow left carelessly unattended in a farmer's field, stuffing torn out by scavenging animals.

He'd stolen the boat from a dock at North Point, at the farthest tip of Prince Edward Island, reaching the dock in a truck he'd hotwired in a diner parking lot.

Christ, he was hungry. He'd eaten so much at that roadside diner that he'd ruptured his stomach lining—the contents of his guts were right now leaking through the split tissue, into the crevices between his organs. He wasn't aware of that fact, though, and wouldn't care much anyway in his current state. It'd felt so good to fill the empty space inside of him . . . but it was like dumping dirt down a bottomless hole: you could throw shovelful after shovelful, yet it made not the slightest difference.

Fifty miles back, he'd stopped at the side of the road,

having spotted a raccoon carcass in the ditch. Torn open, spine gleaming through its fur. It had taken great effort to not jam the transmission collar into park, go crawling into the ditch, and . . .

He hadn't done that. He was still human, after all.

The hunger pangs would stop, he assured himself. His stomach could only hold so much—wasn't that, like, a scientific fact? But this was unlike anything he'd ever known.

Images zipped through his head, slideshow style: his favorite foods lovingly presented, glistening and over-plumped and too *perfect*, ripped from the glossy pages of *Bon Appétit*—a leering parody of food, freakishly sexual, hyperstylized, and lewd.

He saw cherries spilling from a wedge of flaky pie, each one nursed to a giddy plumpness, looking like a mess of avulsed bloodshot eyeballs dolloped with a towering cone of whipped cream . . .

Flash.

A porterhouse thick as a dictionary, shank bone winking from fat-marbled meat charred to crackly doneness, a pat of herbed butter melting overtop; the meat almost sighs as the knife hacks through it, cooked flesh parting with the deference of smoothly oiled doors . . .

Flash.
Flash.
Flash.

What *wouldn't* he eat now? He *yearned* for that raccoon. If it were here now, he'd rip the hardened rags of sinew off its tattered fur; he'd crush its skull and sift through the splinters for its brain, which would be as delicious as the nut-meat of a walnut.

Why hadn't he just eaten the fucking thing?

Would they come for him? He figured so. He was their failure—a human blooper reel—but also the keeper of their secret. And he was so, so *toxic*. At least, that's what he overheard them say.

He didn't wish to hurt anyone. The possibility that he may already have done so left him heartsick. What was it that Edgerton had said?

If this gets out, it'll make Typhoid Mary look like Mary Poppins.

He was not an evil man. He'd simply been trapped and had done what any man in his position might do: he'd run. And they were coming for him. Would they try to capture him, return him to Edgerton? He wondered if they'd dare do that now.

He wasn't going back. He'd hide and stay hidden.

He doubled over, nearly spilling over the side, hunger pangs gnawing into his gut. He blinked stinging tears out of his eyes and saw a dot of light dancing on the horizon.

An island? A fire?

NATURAL RESOURCES CANADA
GEOGRAPHICAL SURVEY REPORT
Falstaff Island, Prince Edward Island

Situated fifteen kilometers off the northern point of the main landmass. Highest point: 452 meters above sea level. 10.4 kilometers in circumference.

Two beachheads: one on the west-facing headland, one on the northeastern outcrop. A granite cliff dominates the northern shore, dropping some 200 meters into a rocky basin.

Terrain consists of hardy brush-grasses, shrubs, jimsonweed, staghorn sumac, and lowland blueberry. Vegetation growth stunted by high saline content in the island's water table. Topsoil eroded by high winds and precipitation.

Home to thriving avian, marine, mammal, reptile, and insect life. Pelicans, gulls, and other seafowl congregate on the northern cliffs. Chief stocks: salmon, cod, bream, sea bass. Sea lions bask off the island in the summer, drawing pods of orcas. Small but hardy indigenous populations of raccoon, skunk, porcupine, and coyote. These specimens are likewise smaller and leaner than their mainland counterparts.

A single winterized dwelling, government-owned and -maintained, acts as an emergency shelter or host to the occasional educational junket.

Absent of full-time human occupation.

Chapter Two

Tim Riggs—Scoutmaster Tim, as his charges called him—crossed the cabin's main room to the kitchen, fetching a mug from the cupboard. Unzipping his backpack, he found the bottle of Glenlivet.

The boys were in bed—not *asleep*, mind you; they'd stay up telling ghost stories half the night if he allowed it. And often, he did allow it. Nobody would ever label him a killjoy, and besides, this was the closest thing to a yearly vacation a few of these boys ever got. It was a vacation for Tim, too.

He poured himself a spine-stiffening belt of scotch and stepped onto the porch. Falstaff Island lay still and tranquil under the blanket of night. Surf boomed against the beachhead two hundred yards down the gentle grade, a sound like earthbound thunder.

Mosquitoes hummed against the porch screen. Moths battered their powdery bodies against the solitary lightbulb. The night cool, the light of the moon falling through a lacework of bare branches. None of the trees were too large—the island's base was bare rock pushed up from the ocean, a sparse scrim of soil on its surface. The trees had a uniformly deformed look, like children nourished on tainted milk.

Tim rolled the scotch around in his mouth. As the sole doctor on Prince Edward Island's north shore, it wasn't proper that he be caught imbibing publicly. But here, miles from his job and the duty it demanded, a drink seemed natural. Essential, even.

He relished this yearly trip. Some might find his reasoning strange—wasn't he isolated enough, living alone in his drafty house on the cape? But this was a different kind of isolation. For two days, he and the boys would be alone. One cabin, a few trails. A boat dropped them off with their supplies earlier this evening; it would return on Sunday morning.

It almost hadn't happened. The weekend forecast was calling for a storm; weather reports had it rolling in off the northern sea, one of those thunderhead-studded monsters that infrequently swept across the island province—half storm, half tornado, they'd tear shingles off houses and snap saplings at the dirt line. But the latest Doppler maps had it veering east into the Atlantic, where it would expend its fury upon the vast empty water.

As a precaution, Tim had ensured that the marine radio was fully charged; if the skies began to threaten, he'd radio the mainland for an early pickup. In truth, he disliked the necessity of the shortwave radio. Tim had strict rules for this outing. No phones. No portable games. He'd made the boys turn out their pockets on the dock at North Point to ensure they weren't smuggling any item that'd link them to the mainland.

But considering the weather, the shortwave radio was a necessary evil. As the Scout handbook said: *Always be prepared*.

A bark of laughter from the bunkroom. Kent? Ephraim? Tim let it go. At their age, boys were creatures of enormous energy: machines that ran on testosterone and raw adrenaline. He could barge in there, shushing and tut-tutting, reminding them of the long day ahead of them

12

tomorrow—but why? They were having fun, and energy was never in short supply among that group.

Fact was, this trip was as necessary for Tim as it was for his charges. He was unmarried and childless—a situation that, at forty-two, in a small town harboring precious few dating prospects, he didn't expect to change. He'd grown up in Ontario and moved to PEI a few years after his residency, buying a house on the cape, learning how to string a lobster trap—*See? I'm making a genuine effort!*—and settling into the island rhythms. Hell, his voice had even picked up a hint of the native twang. Yet he'd forever be viewed as a "come-from-away." People were unfailingly friendly and respectful of his skills, but his veins swam with mainlander blood: he bore the taint of Toronto, the Big Smoke, the snobby haves to PEI's hardscrabble have-nots. Around here, it's as much a case of *who* you're from as *where* you're from: bloodlines ran thick, and the island held close its own.

Mercifully, his Scouts didn't care that Tim was a "come-from-away." He was everything they could possibly want in a leader: knowledgeable and serene, exuding confidence while bolstering their own; he'd learned the native flora and fauna, knew how to string a leg snare and light a one-match fire, but most crucially, he treated them with respect—if the boys were not quite yet his equals, Tim gave every impression that he'd welcome them as such once they'd passed the requisite boyhood rituals. Their parents trusted Tim; their families were all patients at his practice in North Point.

The boys were tight-knit. The five of them had come up together through Beavers, Cubs, Scouts, and now Venturers. Tim had known them since their first Lodge Meeting: a quintet of five-year-olds hesitantly reciting the Beaver pledge—*I promise to love God and take care of the world.*

But this would be their last hurrah. Tim understood why. Scouts was . . . well, *dorky*. Kids of this generation didn't want to dress in beige uniforms, knot their kerchiefs, and earn Pioneering badges. The current movement was over-populated with socially maladjusted little turds or grating keeners whose sashes were festooned with merits.

But these five boys under Tim had remained engaged in Scouting simply because they *wanted* to be. Kent was one of the most popular boys in school. Ephraim and Max were well liked, too. Shelley was an odd duck, sure, but nobody gave him grief.

And Newton . . . well, Newt was a nerd. A good kid, an incredibly smart kid, but let's face it, a full-blown nerd.

It wasn't simply that the boy was overweight; that was a conquerable social obstacle, no worse than a harelip or pimples or shabby clothes. No, poor Newt was simply *born* a nerd, as certain unfortunates are. Had Tim been in the delivery room, he'd've sensed it: an ungrippable essence, unseen but deeply felt, dumping out of the babe's body like a pheromone. Tim pictured the obstetrician handing Newton to his exhausted mother with a doleful shake of his head.

Congratulations, Ms. Thornton, he's a healthy baby nerd. He's bound to be a wonderful man, but for the conceivable future he'll be a first-rank dweeb—a dyed-in-the-wool Poindexter.

All boys gave off a scent, Tim found—although it wasn't solely an olfactory signature; in Tim's mind it was a powerful emanation that enveloped his every sense. For instance, Bully-scent: acidic and adrenal, the sharp whiff you'd get off a pile of old green-fuzzed batteries. Or Jock-scent: groomed grass, crushed chalk, and the locker room funk wafting off a stack of exercise mats. Kent Jenks pumped out Jock-scent in waves. Other boys, like Max and Ephraim, were harder to define—Ephraim often gave off a live-wire smell, a power transformer exploding in a rainstorm.

Shelley . . . Tim considered between sips of scotch and realized the boy gave off no smell at all—if anything the

14

vaporous, untraceable scent of a sterilized room in a house long vacant of human life.

Newton, though, stunk to high heaven of Nerd: an astringent and unmistakable aroma, a mingling of airless basements and dank library corners and tree forts built for solitary habitation, of dust smoldering inside personal computers, the licorice tang of asthma puffer mist and the vaguely narcotic smell of model glue—the ineffable scent of isolation and lonely forbearance. Over time a boy's body changed, too: his shoulders stooped to make their owner less visible, the way defenseless animals alter their appearance to avoid predators, while their eyes took on a flinching, hunted cast.

Newton couldn't help it. A trait burdened to his DNA helix, inexcisable from his other attributes—which, Tim gloomily noted, were numerous but not valuable at his age: Newton was unfailingly kind and polite, read books, and made obvious attempts at self-betterment—the equivalent of an air-raid siren blaring in a tranquil neighborhood: *NEeeeerd-AleeeRT! NEeeeerd-AleeeRT!* Tim felt incredibly protective of Newton and was saddened by his inability to help . . . but an adult protecting a boy only opened that boy up to further torments.

Tim stepped down from the porch to turn off the generator. Mosquitoes zeroed in; he felt them at the back of his neck like drunks at the bar set to guzzle their fill. He slapped them as he walked around the back of the cabin, his fingers brushing the log wall for balance—he'd drank that scotch too fast . . .

Here they came, the mosquitoes alighting on every bare inch of skin, sinking in their proboscises and injecting itchy poison. He stumbled upon the generator, barking his shin on its metal housing, fumbling for the switch while swatting at the hovering bloodsuckers; after an increasingly distracted search—he paused to wave at what felt like a massing sheet of insects—he thumbed it off.

The porch light dimmed. In the new darkness, the mosquitoes seemed to multiply exponentially; Tim felt them everywhere, their bloodless legs dancing on his flesh, the maddening whine of their papery wings filling his ears. He slapped wildly, barely tamping down the sudden yelp that rose in his throat. A semisolid wall pulsed on every side—a buzzing, biting, poisonous shroud. In his ears, tickling his nose, fretting at the edges of his eyes.

"Bloodthirsty bastards . . ."

Grasping blindly for the door, Tim flung it open and staggered into the screened-in porch. He slapped himself down the way a ranch-hand whaps the dust off after tumbling from a horse, relishing the soft crumple of the mosquitoes' bodies.

Tim let out a ragged exhale that ended as a mirthless laugh. His hands were sticky with pulped insects. He thought about Gulliver tied down by thousands of Little People—a scene that had never stirred fear in him until now. The prospect of being beset by thousands, *millions*, of tiny assailants was actually quite terrifying.

In the new silence, he heard a steady drone rolling across the water—the sound of an outboard motor. An emergency on the mainland? No. Someone would have radioed him first.

He went inside and checked the shortwave radio. It gave off a low hiss that indicated a functioning frequency. Outside, the motor's burr intensified.

Tim lit a Coleman lamp and sat on the porch. He clawed at the whitened bumps on his neck, wrists, and hands. A shiver rolled up his legs and through his gut, which clenched painfully as gooseflesh broke out on his arms. He laughed—a confused, gooselike *whoonk!*—and smoothed his hands over his skin, which was pebbled like orange rind. His bladder tightened with piss as the pleasant scotch taste soured in his mouth.

It is a fact that cannot be denied: the wickedness of others becomes our own wickedness because it kindles something evil in our own hearts.

Carl Jung. Undergrad psychology. Jung, Tim would later conclude, was a blowhard and a crank and anyway, his theories were of limited value to a small-town GP whose day-to-day consisted of administering flu shots and excising ingrown nails from the toes of windburnt fishermen. As such, Tim had forgotten the name of Jung's book and the name of the professor who'd taught it—but the quote came to him whole cloth, the words leaping from a dark cubbyhole in his memory.

The wickedness of others becomes our own . . .

Tim Riggs stood in the screened patio, vaguely uneasy for no reason he could lay a finger on—the wind called a mordant note through the sickly trees while other, less explicable sounds scraped up the beachhead toward him— waiting for that unknown wickedness to arrive.

Chapter Three

Eat eat—

Dark. So dark.

Empty.

Before, there had been light. He'd been following it. Moth to a flame. Now it was gone. Just this insane eye-clawing darkness . . . and the hunger.

The man crawled up a stony beach, skidding on the water-smooth pebbles. The rocks were slick with cold, snot-like algae. He scooped it up and shoveled it into his mouth, sucking the dark green strings through his lips like a child slurping egg noodles.

There! Skittering along, its exoskeleton glossed in the moonlight. A sand crab. His hand closed over it—its ocean-coldness wept into his flesh—and stuffed it between his lips. He felt it dancing along his tongue with its hairy little legs. He bit down. A gout of salty goo squirted in his mouth. Its pincer snipped the tip of his tongue in a death spasm, bringing the penny-bright taste of blood; he swallowed the twitching bits convulsively, the spiny exoskeleton tearing into the soft tissues of his throat—which felt so *thin* now, nothing but a fleshy drainpipe, the skin stretched tight as crepe paper over his esophageal tube.

A path materialized, tamped down through the waist-high grass. A black-bodied spider sat on a blade of grass. He pinched it between his fingers before it could get away and ate it up. Very nice, very nice. Succulent.

He squinted. A box sat angled at the hillside, its shadow tilting against the shapeless night. Its geometries were too perfect for it to be anything but man-made.

A feeble pinprick of light emanated from within.

Chapter Four

"You guys ever hear about the Gurkhas?"

Ephraim Elliot's face hovered in the flashlight's glow like the disembodied head of a sideshow oracle. The other boys lay propped up on their elbows, listening intently.

"They're these elite soldiers, right, from Nepal? Little guys. Five foot tall. Munchkins, practically. Crazy buggers. They're trained from the time they're infants to do one thing and do it well—to *kill*. The Gurkhas are crack-shots with a rifle. They can peg the pollen off a bumblebee's ass at a hundred yards. They are masters with the kherkis, too—a long curved knife they keep wicked sharp. They can split a human hair with their knives . . . split it into *thirds*."

"Seriously, Eef?" said Newton Thornton, his pillow-messed hair sticking up in tufts.

"You bet," Ephraim said soberly. "What hardly anyone knows is that a planeload of Gurkha warriors went down off the coast. They were on their way home after a very hairy mission—trench warfare, heads spiked on sticks, that sort of thing. These guys were driven half-crazy by the blood, right? The government of Nepal would probably have locked them up in a funny farm so they wouldn't kill and maim anybody . . . but they never made it home. The plane went down over the ocean right around here."

20

Shelley Longpre listened intently. The usual gray of his eyes—which most often resembled chunks of dirty ice—were now hard and bright with interest.

Ephraim said, "They could even be *here*. This island. It's isolated, quiet. Hardly anyone comes to Falstaff Island except the odd fisherman or, well . . . us. The scouts of Troop Fifty-Two."

Max Kirkwood raised three fingers of his right hand and recited solemnly: "I promise to do my best, to do my duty to God, the queen, and to obey the laws of the Eagle Scout troop."

"Their bodies were never found," Ephraim said, smiling at Max. "If they're still alive, they would be total batshit madmen by now. But even if they *were* here, stalking this island, there's a way to save yourself. The Gurkhas attack at night, okay? *Always*. They sneak into your cabin silent as death. They hover over your bed and feel your bootlaces. If they're laced over and under . . ." Ephraim drew his thumb across his throat, a slitting motion. "But if they're laced straight across, same way the Gurkhas lace them, they'll let you live." He yawned. "Well, good night, guys."

His flashlight snapped off. Soon afterward, a body thumped onto the floor. Ephraim's flashlight pinned Newton in a halo of stark light, lying in a heap beside his boots.

Ephraim said: "I knew you'd crack, Newt!"

Newton sat up awkwardly, rubbing his knees. His skin was even pinker than usual in the flashlight's glow: piglet-pink.

"Jeez, well . . ." Newton bowed his head, rubbing his eye sockets. "You ought to be ashamed, Eef, telling that creepy stuff . . ."

Kent Jenks cried, "Newt, you bed-wetter!"

Shelley merely watched with an owlish expression, large yellow-tinted eyes staring from the milky oval of his face.

Not smiling or laughing with the others—a blank test pattern of a face, expressive of nothing much at all.

"Boys, hey! Come on, now," Scoutmaster Tim said, stepping into the room. "It's all fun and games until someone falls out of bed. What say we call it quits for the night, okay?"

Newton stood, still rubbing his eyes, and heaved his bulk into the top bunk—but not before checking his bootlaces to make sure they were laced straight across.

"Go to sleep, fellas," Scoutmaster Tim said. Newton thought he could glimpse signs of strain on his Scoutmaster's face: a vaguely panicked cast to his eyes. "Big day tomorrow."

The door shut. Wind raced over the sea, howling around the cabin's edges. The logs groaned, a melancholy note like the hull of an old Spanish galleon buffeted by ocean waves. The boys lay in their bunks, breathing heavily. Ephraim whispered:

"Gurkhas gonna get you, Newt."

Chapter Five

Tim heard the man before he arrived. Heard him coming at a tortured shamble like a disoriented bear stirred from hibernation.

By nature, Tim was calm and unflappable—a valuable personality trait for a doctor, whose day could swing from soothing and treating a boy with a simple case of measles to inserting a tracheal stent in the throat of a girl who'd gone into anaphylactic shock following a bee sting. He'd spent nearly a year in Afghanistan with Doctors Without Borders—had he been rabbity by nature, there was no way he'd have lasted that long. His mind naturally gravitated to the most likely causes, and from there coolly cataloged the possible effects.

Fact One: a boat had arrived. Could be one of the boys' parents—had Newton forgotten his asthma inhaler? Likely not, seeing as Newt rarely forgot anything. Could be a ship had gone down—had a trawler capsized while netting pollack in the westerly seas?—and the boat contained its bedraggled survivors.

Tim's mind snapped into triage mode: if that were the case, they'd need medical attention; he'd stabilize them here, on the beachhead if need be, and radio for a medevac chopper.

Or it could be a drunk from the mainland who'd lost his way on a night-fishing jaunt. Unlike the drunks in Tim's hometown who'd hit the fleshpits once the bars shut down, the good ole boys around here hit the water. Slewing across the ocean in open-motor skiffs, bellowing like bulls as they skipped across the waves—that, or they'd drop a fishing line and low-cycle the motor, trawling at a leisurely pace. A few years ago, a winebag named Lester Hamms froze to death on his boat; Jeff Jenks, North Point's chief of police, discovered Lester seven miles off the cape, skin crystalline with frost like a piece of unwrapped steak in a freezer, his ass ice-welded to the seat, a pair of frozen snot-tusks poking out his nostrils. Lester's boat was still puttering along; before long it would've hit the tidal shelf and been carried out to sea—Tim pictured his frozen corpse bumping along the shore of Greenland like a grisly bit of driftwood, a polar bear giving it a curious sniff.

Whoever it was, Tim was sure he or she posed little threat . . . ninety-nine percent sure.

Fact Two: he and the boys were on an isolated island over an hour from home. No weapons other than their knives—blades no longer than three and a half inches, as outlined in the Scout Handbook—and a flare gun. It was night. They were alone.

Tim eased the porch door open with his boot. It issued a thin squeal—*eeeee-ee-eee*—like a rusty nail pried out of a wet plank.

He edged around the cabin, heartbeat thrumming in the veins down his neck. Mosquitoes wet themselves in his beading sweat. He should've brought the lamp, but a signal broadcasting from deep within his reptile cortex said: *No light. Don't make yourself visible.*

Unsheathing his Buck knife, he pressed it flat along his thigh—his sensible self thinking: *This is ridiculous; you're*

24

being idiotic, totally paranoid. But the primal and instinctive part of him, the part ruled by the lizard brain, issued only a mindless buzz like a hive of Africanized bees.

Wind howled along the earth, attaining a voice as it gusted around the rocks and spindly trees: a low muttersome sound like children whispering at the bottom of a well. It whipped up the back of Tim's legs, icy tongues chilling him to the core. He squinted at the tree line, sensing something, the shadows coalescing to attain a certain weight and permanence.

A shape materialized from the tangled foliage. Tim inhaled sharply. By the light of an uncommonly bright moon, he beheld a creature stepped fully formed from his blackest childhood nightmares: a rotted monster who'd dragged itself from the sea.

It wasn't much more than a skeleton lashed by ropes of waterlogged muscle, its flesh falling off its bones in gray, lace-edged rags. It lumbered forward, mumbling dully to itself. Tim's terror pinned him in place.

The thing shambled through a shaft of moonlight that danced along the tall grass; the light transformed the nightmare into what it truly was: a man so horrifyingly thin it was a miracle he was still alive.

Tim stepped from cover without thinking, driven by the instinctive urge to offer aid. "Hello? You all right?"

The man turned his brightly burning gaze on him. It was a gaze of mindless terror and desperate longing, but what really spooked Tim was its laserlike focus: this man clearly *wanted* something. *Needed* it.

The stranger shuffled closer, pawing down the buttons of his shirt, running a quaking hand through his greasy pelt of hair. Tim suddenly understood: the man was making token efforts to render himself presentable.

"Do you have anything . . . to eat?"

"I might," said Tim. "Are you here alone?"

The man nodded. A quivering string of drool spooled over his lip, hung, snapped. His skin was stretched thin as crepe paper over his skull. Capillaries wormed across his nose, over his cheeks, and down his neck like river routes on a topographical map. His arms jutted from his T-shirt like Tinker Toys. The skin was shrink-wrapped around the radius and ulna bones, giving his elbows the appearance of knots in a rope.

The man said, "Are *you* alone?"

It was safer to let the stranger think so. "Yes, I'm doing some geological surveys."

The man picked up a handful of coarse soil and stuffed it in his mouth. To Tim, it looked like an involuntary reflex action, same as blinking your eyes.

"Whoa! Hey, you don't have to . . . to eat that," Tim said, struggling to maintain his calm. "I have food."

The man smiled. A death's-head grimace. His lips were thin bloodless fillets. His gums had receded severely, making his teeth look like yellowing tusks clashing inside his mouth, dark soil lodged in their chinks.

"Food, yes. So nice. Thank you."

As a doctor, Tim had dealt with the human form in all its revolting variations. He'd emptied colostomy bags. Seen throbbing tumors pulled out of stomachs. But this man was sick in some unnatural way that Tim had never encountered. It sent a spike of pure dread down his spine.

Unclean, his mind yammered. *This man is unclean . . .*

The man's stink hit Tim flush in the nose. A high fruity reek with an ammoniac undernote. Ketosis. The man's body was breaking down its fatty acids in a last-ditch effort to keep its vital organs functioning. When burnt, ketones released a sickly sweet smell—the desperate reek of a body consuming itself. The stench coming out of the

26

man's mouth was like a basket of peaches rotting in the sun.

Tim tried not to inhale, certain that it would trigger his gag reflex; the man swooned, equilibrium failing, and Tim impulsively wrapped a steadying hand around the guy's waist . . .

He reared back. When his hand slipped under the man's shirt, over his stomach, he'd felt *movement.* Something stirring under his skin.

That's absurd, he told himself. *It was just gas. Maybe even a section of herniated intestine. God only knows what's wrong with him.*

Despite these rational protestations, he couldn't shake the feeling. It lingered on his fingertips: a sly *flex* beneath the skin, as though something had reacted to his touch before settling again.

The man shuffled toward the cabin and its burning lamp with mothlike determination. His moonlight-glossed eyes were a pair of blown fuses screwed into the fleshless mask of his face. Tim stuck his arm out, palm up, stopping him—a purely instinctive gesture.

He didn't want this man in the cabin with the boys. Not yet, maybe not at all.

"Wait a sec, hold your horses," he said, addressing the man as he might a hyperactive child. "Are you lost? Do you even know where you are? I've never seen you around."

The man pushed his body against Tim's palm, rocking slightly so the pressure intensified, slackened, intensified again. Tim got the sense the man knew it must've revolted Tim—the fluctuating contact, the man's skin weeping oily sweat like the residue on an ancient crankcase. Tim laughed as if this were all a joke, some weird misunderstanding; but there was a brittle glass-snap edge to his laughter that transformed it into a loony cackle.

"I'm lost," the man said. "Lost and . . . un*well*. Just a night. I'll leave in the morning. Please—*feed* me."

"Do you have a family?" Tim couldn't explain why this seemed crucial: Was this man missed by anybody at all? "Is anyone looking for you?"

The man only repeated himself: "Just one night. *Food*. Please."

Tim debated leaving him. He could bring food out, let him feed in the woods (his word choice puzzled him, yet it felt right: this wasn't a man who wanted something to eat—this was a man who needed to *feed*). Tim could restrict the boys to quarters, even, eliminating all contact. Leaving the man out here went against just about every tenet of the Hippocratic Oath, but an aspect of good doctoring was triage. You couldn't save everyone. Sad fact of life. So you saved the youngest, or the ones with the best hope of survival.

"Please."

The man offered the most wretched smile. Could Tim possibly leave him alone and starving a few feet outside the cabin? Could he live with that stain on his soul?

No. He could figure this out. He must take every available precaution, but it could be managed. The man's eerie thousand-yard smile persisted. Was it some kind of ailment Tim was unfamiliar with—a wasting-away disorder? Or just a commonplace malady run amok?

"You'll do exactly as I say," he told the man in his no-BS GP voice.

"Ugn," the man said.

"If you don't, you can't come inside."

The man's body butted Tim's palm—the hardness of bone through the thinnest veneer of flesh; to Tim, it felt like a plastic tarp draping a pile of shattered bricks.

"Come on, then."

Chapter Six

Tim instructed the man to lie on the moth-eaten chesterfield and retrieved the lamp from the porch.

The man looked worse in the lamplight. His skin washed of pigment. Tim's mind conjured a weird image: the last few sips at the bottom of a Slurpee cup, the color all sucked out, only the tasteless ice crystals left.

The guy's pants were inexplicably cinched with an orange extension cord. How much did he used to weigh? Tim turned the man's T-shirt collar out. XL, the tag read. Lord. His clothing appeared to be draping a heap of jackstraws in the rough shape of a human being.

The bottom of his shirt rode up. The skin of his stomach was folded over on itself, reminding Tim of a shar-pei dog. People who had undergone lap-band surgery followed by drastic weight loss looked much the same. They often opted for a dermal tightening procedure: a plastic surgeon hacked a sheet of skin the size of a dish towel off their midsection and stitched the loose ends back together.

Low murmurs from the bunkroom. The boys must've woken up. Tim needed to get a handle on the situation; he didn't fancy the idea of five groggy boys rubbing sleep-crust out of their eyes while gazing at the human boneyard on the chesterfield.

"Boys, listen up," he said, easing the door open and closing it swiftly to maintain that barrier. "Something's come up. It's nothing major"—*was it?*—"but it's best you stay here, in your beds."

"What's wrong, Tim?"

This from Kent, who'd taken to calling him "Tim" of late. He'd dropped the Scoutmaster part. Kent sat on the edge of his bed, hands clasped, shoulders rounded like a wrestler awaiting his call to the mat. *Kent*—even the name had a pushy, aggressive quality. An alpha-male moniker, of a piece with Tanner and Chet and Brodie, names parents bestow upon a boy they've prefigured as a defense attorney or a lacrosse coach. No parent harboring the hope for a sensitive, artistic child names that child *Kent*.

"It's a guy," Tim said. "Nobody from around—I've never seen him. He just showed up."

"Does he have a tent?" Newt asked, his thick chin flattened across the mattress. "Like, a hiker or something—an adventurer?"

"Not that I can see." Tim knelt in the ring of boys. "He seems sick."

Ephraim whispered, "Sick how?"

Tim sucked in his lips, thinking. "Sick like a fever, something like that. He's very thin. He's been asking for food."

"Maybe he's a Gurkha," said Shelley, the words hissing between his teeth.

"He's not a Gurkha," Tim said, jaw tight to hold back a mounting queasiness—the man's funk was seeping under the door, perfuming the room with its rotten-peach stink. "He's . . . it could be a lot of things, okay? He could've been in some other country, some other part of the world, picked up a virus and carried it back with him."

Kent said: "We should call the mainland, Tim."

Tim gritted his teeth so hard that his molars squeaked in their gum beds.

"Yes, Kent. I've thought about that, and yes, I'll do it. In the meantime, I need you boys to stay here. Is that clear?"

"You don't need help?"

"No, Kent, I don't," Tim went on. "I'm a doctor, yes? I'm this guy's best chance right now. But we don't know what's the matter yet, so this is the safest place for you."

Tim opened the door. The frail light of the lantern fell upon a quartet of pinched, anxious expressions—all except Shelley, who stared listlessly at the canopy of cobwebs on the ceiling. He closed the door, debated a moment, then tilted a chair and jammed it under the doorknob.

Tim crossed the main room to the shortwave radio and clicked through the frequencies in search of the mainland emergency band. All he had was a tricked-out medical kit with a few more bells and whistles than your standard wilderness survival kit—items plucked from his own private stockpile. But if he radioed it in, they could send the medevac chopper in from Charlottetown and—

"*Reeeeaaagh!*"

The man staggered up, careening toward Tim like a sailor on a storm-tossed boat. With one swift motion he ripped the shortwave radio off the table, raised it above his head, and brought it down. It smashed apart in a squeal of feedback. A string of sparks popped inside the busted casing, issuing forth gouts of stinking electrical smoke.

The man brought his foot down on it, stomping with crazed strength. Tim put his arms out to stop him, tipping the lantern over and extinguishing the flame.

He grappled with the man in the dark. It was like wrestling a bag of snakes or steel cables coated in granular grease: cold, oily, and revolting.

"Goddamn it! Stop!"

The man snarled, a cruel silver sound that ripped through the dark like a band saw blade. He coughed something up; wet warmth splashed Tim's face. Tim squealed thinly—he couldn't help it—and wiped furiously at his cheek.

The man's body suddenly went slack. Tim fought the urge to drop him, the way you might a fat-smeared tackling dummy.

Unclean! UNCLEAN!

The bunkroom knob squeaked, followed by a sequence of jarring *thumps* as the door shuddered against the chair. Tim pictured Kent hammering his shoulder against it, aiming to splinter it to pieces.

"Tim! Tim, open this door!"

Navigating clumsily in the dark, Tim guided the man back to the chesterfield. He felt around for the lamp, found it, relit it. Fetched the medical kit. He tore open packets of sterile wipes and furiously swabbed down every place the man had touched him, specifically his face. Whatever he'd spat up lingered on Tim's skin—he could feel the dissipating sting, his flesh flushed red as if he'd been slapped.

"Tim!" Kent bellowed. "Open this door *right now*!"

"Stay *inside*!" Tim yelled—screeched, more like, his voice elevating to a teakettle shriek. "Try to open that door again, Kent Jenks, and I'll make damn sure your father hears about it."

Kent's sullen footsteps retreated; the bedsprings squeaked as he slid back under the covers.

Tim filled a hypodermic needle with 100 mg of doxylamine. The man's veins were easy to locate: a rail yard's worth of blue tubes snaked at the crook of each elbow. After the injection, the man's breathing normalized.

Greenish matter oozed out the side of his mouth. Is that what he'd spit up? Had he actually been eating rock slime?

Algae. Okay, it's just algae. Algae's not infectious. Algae's just . . . gross.

Tim's hand dropped to the man's stomach—he felt it again. A subtle movement like an adder resettling itself under a warm blanket.

It's just peristalsis. The man has a severe blockage in his intestines; all you're feeling is a protracted flex as he tries to pass whatever it is.

Tim's testicles drew up. He swooned with sudden unexplainable fear, his belly packed with cold lead. Who *was* this man? What in God's name was the matter with him? Why the hell had he thought it right or appropriate to let him in here? Private hospitals can refuse treatment if a person's condition is deemed a threat to others—what in God's name had he *done*, turning a cabin on an isolated island into a trauma ward?

He reached for the man's T-shirt, guided by a horrible impulse: pull it up. But even his morbid sense of curiosity resisted it. He didn't *want* to see. Not now, at night, alone in this dark.

Except he wasn't alone, was he? He swung the lamp toward the bunkroom door, the chair still wedging it shut.

"It's okay," Tim said, after moving the chair aside and stepping softly inside with the boys. "Please go back to sleep."

"Who is that?" Kent's voice had forfeited its thunder: he asked as a boy who was scared and too far from home.

"Like I said—a stranger. Someone who needed help, so I'm giving it to him. I don't know where he's from. He couldn't even give me his name. He can barely talk. He's asleep now."

Tim saw his answer only intensified their worry, but found it impossible to offer anything more concrete. It was like one of those TV medical dramas where patients roll into the ER with mysterious ailments—the towheaded boy who weeps tears of blood; the high school prom queen whose head swells up like a beach ball—and only the brilliant pill-popping MD can suss it out: a hairline rip in the aqueous humor; the remains of a parasitic twin resting deep in the thalamic folds. Problem being, Tim was just a small-town sawbones, unremarkable and generally unambitious—none of which had been a problem until now.

Max said: "Well, how sick is he?"

Tim found it difficult to meet their searching eyes—fact was, he had no earthly idea. But he was the adult here, the authority—moral and otherwise—and it was his responsibility to tell them *something* if only to allay their fears, even as his own mounted.

"He seems manageable, guys. I've seen worse." This lie came so smoothly that it shocked him. "We'll get him to a hospital and let them deal with it."

"The radio?"

"I can't see right now," Tim told Ephraim. "It may be broken."

Kent said: "How did that . . . ? It's our only—"

"He got here in a *boat*, okay? If we need to get back to the mainland, we'll take that. Now . . . go . . . to . . . *bed*."

Tim turned and shut the door. The man breathed tortuously off to his right. His face radiated an unearthly light all its own, as if his veins ran with phosphorus. His features gave off the sick light of those poisonous mushrooms that grew in dank island caves.

An image came to Tim, plucked from the deepest recesses of his memory. A man's face in a parking garage. Tim's mother had taken him grocery shopping. He was five. The underground lot was nearly empty. They'd passed a huge cement stanchion, the load-bearing ones that kept the supermarket from collapsing, burying them under shelves of creamed corn and Frosted Flakes. A shape leaned against it. A pile of water-fattened trash bags? The pile stirred, shifted, and a face materialized. Tim told himself—he told himself *today*—that the man must've fallen prey to the commonplace decays, drink and drugs and disease . . . but his younger eyes, his boyhood eyes, had seen something else entirely.

The man's face had been black, but that was not its birth color: it was the lumpen, withery, rotted black of a banana forgotten at the bottom of a fruit bowl. Had he touched that face, Tim was certain his fingers would've sunk into it. The man's nose looked as though it had been subjected to enormous pressures, or else eaten away by something: a caved-in pit above his lips, which were cracked and bloated and coated in unknowable glaze.

Tim's breath had locked in his lungs, his upflung eyes finding his mother—who was obviously scared, too, a fact that deepened his own fear.

The man had been sick in a way that didn't seem possible—nothing on this earth, not disease nor the elements nor the tortures of mankind, could *do* that. He looked like a man who'd been abducted by a vengeful alien race who'd done terrible things, reduced him in some unspeakable way, then delivered him back to earth in order to examine how the rest of his species would react.

He's seen hell, was Tim's childish thought.

Worst of all were the man's eyes—always the eyes, wasn't it? A calm ongoing shade of brown, and the most awful part was that something continued to live in them—because normally there'd be nothing, right? Defeated and foggy and unthinking, to match the body. But these eyes harbored a remote intellect, a keen awareness. Which was the scariest part: this man had to confront the devastation of his body. He was cognizant of his own ruin. How could he possibly cope with that?

The man didn't ask for anything. He simply watched, those coolly considering eyes socked in that tragedy of a face, until they passed from sight.

As he remembered this, the veil of disquiet that had settled over Tim shifted and something terrible peered through from the other side—the squirrelly, squealing face of terror. That man's nightmarish face. Then it was gone.

Tim slipped into an uneasy sleep. Sometime before dawn and without quite realizing it, he rose out of the chair and stumbled to the cupboards.

News item from the Montague (PEI) *Island Courier,*
October 21:

MILITARY CORDONS OFF NORTH POINT WHARF, ESTABLISHES NO-FLY, NO-WATERCRAFT ZONE

The military descended upon the tiny town of North Point (pop 5,766) early this morning. Residents awoke to Armored Personnel Carriers rumbling down their sleepy streets.

"They chewed right through the pavement," said Peggy Stills, owner of the Island Cafe on Main Street. "The street's full of holes."

The convoy made its way to the North Point dock. A barrier was swiftly erected, encompassing the waterline and outlying areas. A pair of Apache helicopters were spotted sweeping the waters off North Point.

Shortly after 10 a.m. an official dispatch was released, stating that traffic on the waters north of the island was strictly prohibited. A message was sent over the emergency nautical broadcast channel alerting watercraft; the waters off North Point are trafficked by commercial fishing vessels and the occasional ocean liner.

Requests for information from on-site military personnel were rebuffed. The *Courier* has attempted to contact a military press agent, but to this point this reporter's calls have gone unanswered.

Chapter Seven

The boys rose with the drowsy half-light of dawn. The moon hung in its western altar like the last melancholy guest at a dinner party, who was too lonely to leave.

None of them had slept well. They'd heard Scoutmaster Tim come inside with the man—the man hadn't spoken, but they could smell him: a syrupy foulness like the juice at the bottom of an amusement park trash can. As the Scoutmaster busied himself beyond the bunkroom door, Kent had sat up on his elbows.

"I better check it out."

Kent Jenks *always* had to check "it" out. Made no difference what "it" happened to be; Kent was suffused with the unshakable conviction that things would be better if he intervened—as if, by dint of his presence, the situation would come under control. He'd been this way since Beavers, and because Kent was bigger and carried an air of prepossession that could come off as menacing, the other boys typically bowed to his will.

It was the same at school. Kent was the kid who'd butt in front of you at the water fountain—*literally* butting, a solid hip-check that'd send you flying—saying *I got cuts* with a chummy backslap, his voice a full octave lower than anybody else's. The boy who'd grab your sandwich off the waxed paper your mom wrapped it in, take a humongous bite, and go *You mind?*, flecks of egg salad spraying between his lips. He wasn't truly mean-spirited, though. Max thought of him as a Saint Bernard: big and slobbery, a bit dumb and oblivious to his own strength, but his heart was usually in the right place. Kent constantly threw down these gauntlets, though, and dared you to run them. Most days it was easier to surrender your spot in line or bite of sandwich.

Lately Kent had been testing how far he could challenge adults. He'd raise his hand in class, grinning sunnily while asking the teacher: *Are you suuure?* He'd started to call teachers by their first names, too. It wasn't Mr. Reilly in homeroom anymore—it was Earl. The boys were waiting for the day when Kent sauntered into the teachers' lounge, took a bite of the gym teacher's lunch, and said, *You mind, George?*

When Kent had gotten out of bed and crossed the bunkroom to the door, only Newton had spoken up.

"Better not, Kent. The Scoutmaster—"

"Shut up, flapjack," Kent had shot back, so casually that you couldn't even call his tone dismissive: more like how you'd shush a yappy dog. "If I wanted your opinion, I'd—"

"For real, bro," Ephraim had said. "Don't go out there."

Kent blinked, his head cocked at an inquisitive angle. Ephraim was the only boy who worried him—there was something a bit crazy about Eef, this jittery powder-keg quality that made Kent uneasy.

"Gimme one reason why not, man."

Ephraim just said: "Because."

"That's it? That's the reason—*because*?"

"Yep," Ephraim had said.

"Thanks, Eef," said Newt.

Ephraim said: "Shut up, pork chop."

Next Scoutmaster Tim had entered the bunkroom and

told them that their asses better remain in bed. Soon after came the commotion: the stranger's scream—*"Reeeeaaagh!"*—followed by a scuffle, a crash, and the acrid smell of smoke wafting into their room, mingling with the sweetly rotten stench.

Kent had leapt out of bed, attacking the door with savage shoulder-butts; it wouldn't budge, but Kent kept flinging his body at it, the way he always did—hurling his unthinking bulk at any obstacle with the ironclad surety it'd eventually buckle. He'd only quit when the Scoutmaster threatened to tell his father; Kent stepped away from the door breathing like a bull, his wide-set and faintly bovine eyes reflecting dull smokeless hate.

Around four in the morning, Newton had sat bolt upright in bed. He'd been awoken by the noise of cupboard doors opening and slamming shut. Next had come . . . crunching sounds? Monotonous, plodding, softly grinding.

"Max?" he'd whispered. "Max, you awake?"

"Go to bed, Newt," Max said from the bunk below, his voice so thick with sleep that his words ran together: *GotobedNewt.*

Newton had been shocked that Max and the others were able to sleep with those smells and awful noises beyond the door . . . maybe Max was just pretending to sleep to avoid talking about them. Maybe he'd thought sunlight was a cure-all.

Hours later, sunlight filtered through the sap-yellowed window, sparkling the dust motes that hung in the stagnant air. The boys rose and dressed silently, pulling on bulky sweaters and lacing their boots. Ephraim caught Max's eye, raised a quizzical eyebrow, and mouthed the words:

You okay?

Max shrugged, smiled wanly, finished double-knotting

his boots. Like the others, he'd caught a whiff of the rank sweetness drifting in from the main room, where the Scoutmaster slept. He'd heard the crunching sounds, too.

Max's grandfather was a farmer. The past few summers he'd paid Max and Ephraim seventeen dollars a day to dump chicken bones into "Jaws," a stainless steel industrial grinder in the barn. He purchased the bones from a poultry processing plant in Summerside, a dollar a sack. Legally it was called "animal byproduct," same as cowflops, hog shit, and hen feathers. Max and Ephraim would slit the woven-fiber sacks and dump the clattering bones into Jaws's hopper. It was gross, mildly disturbing work—*Island* work, wearying and melancholic, and there was an expectation that all boys should enjoy it.

At least they got to do it together. Max and Eef were best friends. They'd been so for years informally, but a few months ago they'd cemented it: they'd both notched a shallow cut in their thumbs with Ephraim's Swiss Army knife, pressed them together, and solemnly intoned: *Forever friends*. They were one better than BF's—they were *FF's*.

Once the bones were in the hopper, Max's grandfather would switch the machine on. The gears made quick work of them; when the collection receptacle popped open, inside was a drift of fine white powder.

Bone meal, Max's grandpa said. *It's magic, boys—nothing grows plants any better than bones.*

Hearing this, Max wondered why farmers didn't plant potato fields over cemeteries . . . the answer had dawned on him before long.

Last night, lying quietly in bed, Max wondered if Ephraim was awake, too. Was he hearing those crunching noises? If so, was he thinking what Max was thinking—that it sounded like tiny brittle bones pulverized between the steel teeth of Jaws?

After dressing, the boys followed Kent into the kitchen.

Tim greeted them in the main room with a wan smile. The strange man lay on the chesterfield, his body covered in blankets. All they could see were the contours of his face: the sunken cheeks and eyes, teeth winking through the blanched fillets of his lips.

Crumbs lay scattered round the easy chair. Newton spotted those same crumbs on Tim's lumberjack vest, though the Scoutmaster brushed most of them off. An econo-size box of soda crackers lay in the trash can, along with some wadded-up cellophane cracker sleeves.

Tim caught Newton's look. "Attack of the midnight munchies, boys. I had to keep an eye on this guy."

Newt scanned the kitchen. He couldn't help but notice the busted radio. A pinworm of dread threaded into his chest. *What if that storm rolled in? What would we do?* He eyed the cabin warily—the frame seemed sturdy enough, but the roof was old. He'd seen what those late autumn storms could do. A few years ago, one of them had ripped across the mainland and dragged a car across the street into a ditch. Newt had watched it happen through the window of Dan's Luncheonette on Phillips Street. The car was an ancient Dodge Dart—what the old-timers called "two tons of Detroit rolling iron." The driver was equally ancient: Elgin Tate, a long-retired music teacher. Newt had watched him white-knuckled and greasy-faced behind the wheel as the wind hammered the car amidships, rocking it up on two side wheels and letting it fall with an axle-grinding thump, then gusted again and bore it steadily across both lanes into the ditch. The Dart's tires had been pure *smoking* as Tate tried to muscle it back onto the road, but its hind end tipped over the edge of the ditch, its front wheels canted up and spinning uselessly. Once the storm had passed, Tate clambered out the window and staggered onto the road. His gray hair was stuck up in wild corkscrews and he was smiling like a man who'd cheated death. *Hellfire!* he'd shouted at nobody at all. *Hellfire and damnation!*

"What are we gonna do?" Newt asked.

"That's what I'm trying to figure out." Tim hooked his thumb at the stranger. "He's obviously sick. He also, as you can see, smashed our radio. Why, I don't know. Could be he's in trouble—maybe with the law. I certainly don't know who he is."

"What about his wallet?" Ephraim said.

"I checked." Tim's hands groomed each other, an unconscious gesture: one hand washing the other. "His pockets are empty."

"*He* looks empty," Shelley said softly.

The boys' eyes kept flicking to the man, then just as quickly away. Newt threw his entire head back as if the very sight repelled his gaze.

"He probably didn't look like *that* all his life," said Kent.

"Of course not," Tim snapped, annoyed at Kent's unalloyed disgust. "As a precaution, I've tied his arms and legs. Who knows what else he'd decide to bust up."

"Yeah, good idea," Shelley said. "I mean, he could go berserk. Kill us all with a butcher knife."

Tim glanced at the tall, slender boy with the blank gray eyes. His brow furrowed, then he said, "I have something to ask all of you. I want you to be honest. I promise you I won't be angry. Tell me: Did any of you bring a phone?"

Newt said: "You told us not to."

"I know what I said, Newton. But I happen to know that teenage boys don't always do as they're told." He looked at Ephraim. "What about it?"

Ephraim shook his head. "I thought about it, but . . ."

"*Shit*," Tim hissed, pushing the word through his teeth on a burst of pent-up air. He tasted a weird sweetness, a saccharine tang on his tongue. "Listen, boys, we're going to be fine. Really. This is unexpected, is all. My only concern is that this guy needs medical attention in short order. I don't have the proper equipment."

"You said he came by boat," said Kent.

Tim had already been down to the dock at sunup. The boat wouldn't start. The spark plugs were gone. Could this man have unscrewed them and . . . what? Thrown them into the ocean? Hidden them somewhere? Why do that?

"There's a boat, yes," Tim said for now. "Oliver McCanty's, by the look of it. You know how small it is. We can't all ride back in it."

"A few of us could," said Kent. "We could tell my dad what happened."

Kent's father was Lower Montague's chief of police, "Big" Jeff Jenks: a towering six feet seven inches and two hundred and fifty pounds of prime law enforcement beef. Most afternoons he could be spotted behind the wheel of his police cruiser (looking, Tim thought, like an orangutan stuffed into a kitchen cupboard), circuiting the town. If anything, his face reflected sadness—perhaps at the fact God had given him a body so big and strong that he considered it a cosmic injustice that he couldn't put it to use on deserving criminals. But he'd picked the wrong jurisdiction: the closest thing to a felonious mastermind in Montague County was Slick Rogers, the local moonshiner whose hillside stills occasionally exploded, burning down an acre of scrubland.

"You guys are going on your wilderness trek as scheduled. You were going to be trekking solo, anyway, as part of your merit requirement. So just fend for yourselves and navigate your way back. No help from me."

"That's crazy, Tim!" Kent stabbed one thick finger at the stranger. "We need to neutralize the threat"—one of his father's pet phrases—"or else . . . or else . . ."

Kent trailed off, the words locking up in his throat. Tim dropped a hand on Kent's shoulder. The boy's eyes narrowed—in that instant Tim was certain he'd brush his hand off. When that didn't happen, he said, "What we need is to remain calm and proceed with the established plan."

"But it's all different now. The plan is . . . it's *fucked*."

A shocked gasp from Newton. Nobody ought to speak that way in front of an adult—in front of their *Scoutmaster*. Tim's eyes took on a hard sheen. His hand tensed on Kent's shoulder, fingernails dimpling the fabric—close to but not quite a claw.

"Scout Law number seven, Kent. Repeat it."

Kent wormed in Tim's grip. His eyes held a bruised, hangdog cast.

"A Scout . . ." Tim said softly. "Go on, tell me. A Scout . . ."

Newt said, "A Scout obeys his—"

"Quiet, Newt," said Tim. "Kent knows this."

"A . . . Scout . . . obeys . . ." Kent said, each word wrenched painfully from his mouth.

"Who does he obey?"

"He obeys his Scoutmaster without . . ."

"Without *what*, Kent?"

". . . without question. Even if he gets an order he does not like, he must do as soldiers and policemen do; he must carry it out all the same because it is his duty."

"And after he has done it," Tim continued, "he can come and state any reasons against it. But he must carry out the order at once. That is discipline."

Tim forfeited his grip; Kent stepped back, rubbing his shoulder. Tim pointed to a pair of walkie-talkies on the table.

"You get into a jam, radio me. We've done plenty of

orienteering together, right? This won't be anything new. It's a nice morning, no foul weather in today's forecast."

No other boy spoke against the Scoutmaster's plan. Nobody wanted to be here, in this cabin, with . . . *that*. They were all too happy to invoke that particular license of boyhood, the one that stated: *Let the grown-ups handle it*. Events that seemed overwhelming and terrifying to their boyish brains were dispelled like so much smoke when the adults took over. Adults were Fixers; they were Solvers. The boys still trusted Tim, even Kent. So they would depart into the crisp autumn sunshine, their lungs filling with clean air; they would wrestle and run and laugh and enjoy their freedom from this strange responsibility, whatever it entailed. And when they returned, everything would be fine. They sincerely believed this because, up until that very point in their existence, it was a fact that had always held true.

It truly had been Tim's intention to go with them. But he needed time to figure out what the hell was the matter with this man. The fact the spark plugs were missing was an additional worry—and not only because it cut them off from the mainland. What kind of man would incapacitate his only method of escape? A criminal? A hunted man, perhaps. Or a man on an extinction vector.

Once the boys had left, he'd go down to the ocean, roll up his pants, and search for those damn plugs. Anyway, the boys were resourceful. The island was safe. There were more hazards on the mainland: pellet guns, dirt bikes, Slick Rogers. They'd hike a few hours, complete their trail-craft requirements, and be back in time for supper—by which time he'd have this mess sorted out. He, too, believed in the power of adults.

Tim didn't feel quite up to a hike today, anyway. He shot a quick look at the man on the chesterfield, hoping the boys didn't catch the quiver in his eyes. The spot where the man coughed on his skin burnt with an edgeless heat; he pictured it eating right through his skin, a gaping hole in his cheek—the glistening connective tissues of his jaw, iron fillings winking in his molars—and shook his head, dispelling the image.

Could be he was coming down with something. A fever?

Starve a cold, feed a fever, right?

Yes, *definitely* a fever.

He picked up one of the walkie-talkies. After a short deliberation, he gave it to Max, ignoring Kent's miffed look.

He gave the boys a curt salute. "You've got your marching orders, dogfaces."

From *Troop 52:*
Legacy of the Modified Hydatid

(AS PUBLISHED IN *GQ* MAGAZINE) BY CHRIS PACKER:

THE HUNGRY MAN. Patient Zero. Typhoid Tom.

Before he was known by these names, he was known by the one his mother christened him with: Thomas Henry Padgett.

Tom was born in St. Catharines, Ontario, 1,100 miles from Falstaff Island, where he would die thirty-five years later. Birth records from St. Catharines General show that Tommy was a healthy nine and a half pounds at birth.

"He was a chubby baby," says his mother, Claire Padgett. "Chubby kid, chubby teenager. I'd take him shopping in the Husky Boys section at the Hudson's Bay."

She sits in her kitchen, leafing through a photo album. Her boy lies frozen in time under the laminated pages. Sitting in the tub as an infant, his mom working baby shampoo into his hair. Halloween as a toddler, dressed as a giant pumpkin. Tom had an open smile and unruly red hair. In one photo, he is captured building a sandcastle at the beach, his stomach hanging over the band of his swim trunks.

"He was a good eater," Claire Padgett says. "As a kid, anyway. Then he got older and the shame set in. He didn't like being big. Kids, right? They find the easiest soft spot and pick at it."

Claire Padgett looks nothing like her son. It strikes this observer that she may subsist entirely upon Player's Light cigarettes—she chain-smokes them ruthlessly, lighting each fresh soldier off the ember of the dead one. But hers is a flinty, chapped-elbow leanness—a body built for a mean utility.

"Tough kid," she says of her son. "Some boys thought that because he was fat, Tom must be a marshmallow. But he could defend himself. After Tom busted a few boys' noses, the wisecracks about his weight stopped."

As cutting as those schoolboy taunts had been, her son has been treated far more cruelly in death. Consider his media-given nicknames. The Edible Man. Mr. Stringbean. Consider his legacy as the man who could have kick-started a toppling-domino contagion worse than the Black Plague. Consider the fact that Dr. David

Hatcher, head of the Centre for Contagious Disease, memorably labeled him "a runaway biological weapon."

Tom Padgett has been badmouthed by scientists and politicos worldwide for—for *what*?

For being a pawn? For aligning himself with Dr. Clive Edgerton, who earned his own nickname: Joseph Mengele 2.0? For being the kind of scratch-ass petty criminal who might actually *accept* Edgerton's offer?

No. Tom Padgett is hated in death because he *ran*. Because he failed to truly grasp the magnitude of what he was hosting and bolted. But mainly Tom is hated for the perception that he may have somehow thought he could *prevail* over the monster lurking inside of him.

Tom Padgett is hated for his ignorance of the fact that he was dead on his feet well before he reached Falstaff Island. His body just hadn't gotten the memo yet.

"I guess some people must find it funny that Tom was a fat kid." Claire Padgett smiles, but there's not a drop of humor in it. "Yeah, I guess a certain type of person would find that deliciously ironic, considering how things came out in the wash."

Chapter Eight

Maximilian Kirkwood and Ephraim Elliot had been friends since they were two years old—although Max wondered if that was precisely true.

They'd *been around* each other since they were two, anyway: Max's mom would drop him off at Mrs. Elliot's house every morning; she always paid her babysitting fee in cash, as the island's underground economy dictated. Mrs. Elliot said Max and Eef were the very best of friends—sharing their blocks, drinking out of the same sippy cup—but Max didn't remember that, same as he didn't remember being born or cutting his first tooth. When his memories kicked in, though—*click!* like a light switch—Ephraim was right there.

You'd never find a stranger pair. Ephraim was a creature of pure momentum, pure chaos: 140 pounds of fast-twitch muscle fiber packed into a long, quivering frame. The air closest to Eef's arms and shoulders seemed to shimmer, same way a hummingbird's wings exist in a blur of motion. Max was stouter—not fat, *solid*—and possessed a preternatural state of calm unusual for his age; it wasn't hard to picture him in the Lotus position on North Point beach, eyes serenely shut, totally Zen-ing out.

It shouldn't have worked—the differences in the boys'

personalities should've repulsed one from the other, like trying to touch magnets of matching polarities—but the opposite held true.

On summer nights, Max and Ephraim would hike to the bluffs behind Max's house, through the long, dry grass frosted white with the salt spray off the sea. They'd pitch a tent on the highest peak, the lights of Max's home only a pinprick in the dark. Lying on their backs under the endless vault of sky—so much wider than in a city, where buildings hemmed in that same sky, light pollution whiting out the stars. They knew some of the constellations—Scoutmaster Tim had taught them, though only Newton bothered to earn a merit badge in astronomy. They could recognize the stars in their simplest alignments: the Big Dipper, Ursa Major and Minor.

"It doesn't really look like a bear," Max said one night.

"Why should it?" Ephraim said, sounding angry. "That's humans trying to, like, organize the stars to our liking. You think the Big Guy, the Grand Creator, Buddha or the Flying Spaghetti Monster or whoever said: *Oh, guess I'd better make these flaming balls of gas look* exactly *like a bear or a fucking spoon so those stupid goons on rock 5,079 don't get confused*?" He lip-farted. "*Ohyeahriiiight*," stringing the words all together.

They talked about the stuff best friends ought to. Stupid stuff. Their favorite candy (Max: Swedish Fish, especially the rare purple ones; Eef: Cracker Jack, which Max claimed wasn't exactly *candy* but Eef said was sweet enough); who had bigger boobs, Sarah Matheson or Triny Dunlop (both agreed Triny's were technically bigger, although Ephraim held the opinion, sadly untested, that Sarah's were *softer*); whether God existed (both believed in a higher power, though Eef thought churches treated their parishioners like ATMs); and who'd win in a fight: a zombie or a shark?

"A zombie," Eef said. "*Of course*. It's already dead, right? It's not gonna be scared of . . . hey, what kind of shark? A sandy? A whitetip? *I* could win against a sandy!"

Max shook his head. "Great white. Biggest badass in the ocean."

"*Pffffft!*" Eef said. "Killer whales got it all *over* great whites. But anyway, I still say zombie. If it gets one bite in, it wins—the shark's a zombie!"

"Who says sharks turn into zombies?"

"*Everything* turns into a zombie, Max-a-million."

"Whatever. I say shark. You know how thick sharkskin is? I was down at the dock when a trawler came in with a dead mako. Ernie Pugg tried to cut it open on the dock—his fillet knife broke. Like trying to hack through a tire, man. Who says a zombie's rotted old teeth won't break, too? And anyway, what if the shark bites the zombie's head off? A zombie can't swim too well, its rotten-ass arms flopping around."

Eef considered this. "Well, if it bites the zombie's head off and swallows it, its head will be in the shark's belly—and it'll still be *alive*. Like, zombie-alive, which is really dead but whatever. So the zombie can bite the shark's guts out from the inside." Ephraim pumped his fist in victory. "Zombie wins! Zombie wins!"

"Ah, go to hell," Max said, conceding.

"I been to hell," Ephraim said, his voice pitched at a Clint Eastwood growl. "I ain't afraid to go back."

Sometimes their conversation meandered quite accidentally into topics of greater importance. One night both boys were in that gauzy-minded state preceding sleep when Ephraim said:

"I ever tell you that my pops busted my arm? I was like one year old, man. Can't even remember. Guess I was screaming in my crib and he comes in, all pissed, lifts me

53

up, and my arm gets stuck between the crib bars and he kept pulling and my arm just went kerflooey."

He rolled over and hiked up his sleeve, showing Max the pale scar below his elbow hinge.

"Bone came out right there. Anyway, he went to jail three months later. My arm was still in a cast. But here's the weirdest thing, Max. Two years ago, I went to visit him up in the Sleepy Hollow prison. Mom came with. We're sitting in the visitors' room, the chairs and tables bolted down, TV in a big mesh cage. Dad's not saying much—he never does, right?—but he looks at my arm and sees the scar and asks how I got it. Like, he thought I did it to myself." A stiff, barking laugh. "So Mom goes: *You did it, Fred. You broke his arm as a baby.* And my dad just gives her this shocked look. I'm telling you, Max, I *swear to God* he didn't remember. Like, there's this empty slot in his head where that memory should be. Maybe he even remembers my arm in a cast but he doesn't quite remember how it happened, right? For all I know his memory's full of holes like that, just Swiss-cheesed with 'em, which is why he's in jail. He can't remember any of the shitty stuff he does—his mind erases it, so he just goes and does it all over again."

In such ways are friendships built. In tiny moments, in secrets shared. The boys truly believed they would be best friends forever—in fact, as the boat had ferried them to Falstaff Island, Max had looked at the back of Ephraim's head and thought exactly that:

Forever friends, man. Until the very end of time.

The sky was scudded over with clouds by the time the boys shouldered their packs and made their way to the trailhead. They walked in the same order as always: Kent heading up the pack—recently Kent had even tried to break trail ahead of the Scoutmaster—then Ephraim,

Shelley, and Newt. Max pulled up the rear in his traditional sheepherding role.

Once they'd passed beyond sight of the cabin, Kent waved Max up.

"You better give me the walkie-talkie," he said, dead serious.

It wasn't worth fighting over—Kent might turn it into a fight. But Kent wouldn't throw punches. Wasn't his style. He'd put Max in a headlock and wrestle him down and simply take the walkie-talkie away. Or worse, make Max give it to him voluntarily, his head still smarting from the headlock.

Kent was old enough, fourteen years and a few months, to have lost the prominent tummy of childhood. You could see now that he might make a good linebacker, as far as width and bulkiness of shoulders went. The boys followed him for the simple reason that he was the biggest and strongest and harbored every expectation that he *should* be followed. It wasn't that he had the best ideas—those were often traceable to Newt. It wasn't that he was particularly charismatic, like Ephraim. It was that the boys were at an age where physical strength was the surest marker of leadership.

Kent had learned what little he knew of leadership from his father, who'd counseled: *It's all how you present yourself, son. Draw yourself up to your full height. Stick your chest out. If you look like you've got all the answers, people will naturally assume that you do.*

Kent's dad, "Big" Jeff Jenks, often bundled his son into the police cruiser and drove a circuit of town—a ride-along, he called it. Kent loved these: his father sitting erect and flinty-eyed in the driver's seat, sunlight flashing off his badge, the dashboard computer chittering with information of a highly sensitive nature—which his father was all too willing to share. *Got a call for officer assistance there a few weeks back,* he'd say, pointing to a well-tended Cape Cod belonging to Kent's math teacher, Mr. Conkwright. *Domestic disturbance. Trouble in paradise. The missus was stepping out—you know what I mean by that?* When Kent shook his head, his father said: *Breaking her marital vows. Enjoying the warm embrace of another fellow, uh? You get me? And that other fellow happened to be George Turley, your gym teacher.*

Kent pictured it: Gloria Conkwright, an enormously plump woman with bottled-platinum hair and heaving, pendulous breasts that stirred confused longing in Kent's chest, squashing her body on top of Mr. Turley, who always wore shiny short-shorts two sizes too small—*nuthuggers,* as his father called them—his oily chest hair tufting in the V of his shirt collars; he pictured Mr. Turley blowing on the pea whistle that was constantly strung round his neck, the air forced out in gleeful *whoof*s as Gloria's body smacked down onto his.

There's no fate worse than being a cuckold, his father said. *You can't let some woman go stomping on your balls—you just may acquire a taste for it.*

Those ride-alongs, his father enumerating the secrets and shames of their town, made Kent realize something: adults were *fucked.* Totally, utterly fucked. They did all the things they told kids not to do: cheated and stole and lied, nursed grudges and failed to turn the other cheek, fought like weasels, and worst of all they tried to worm out of their sins—they passed the buck, refused to take responsibility. It was always someone else's fault. *Blame the man on the grassy knoll,* as his dad said, although Kent didn't really know what that meant. Kent's respect had trickled away by degrees. Why *should* he respect adults—because they were older? Why, if that age hadn't come with wisdom?

Kent came to see that adults required the same stern hand

that his peers did. He was their equal—their *better*, in many ways. Physically this was already so: he was a full head taller than many of his teachers, and though he'd never tested this theory, he believed himself to be stronger, too. Morally it was certainly so. Like his father said: *Son, we are the sheepdogs. Our job is to circle the flock, nipping at their heels and keeping them in line. Nip at their heels until they're bloody, if needed, or even tear their hamstrings if they won't obey. At first the sheep will hate us—after all, we hem them in, stop them from pursuing their basest nature—but in time they'll come to respect us and soon enough they won't be able to imagine their lives without us.*

Suffused with this sense of righteousness his father had instilled, Kent held his hand out to Max. "Give me the walkie-talkie, man. You know that's the way it should be."

When Max handed it over, Kent clapped him on the back.

"Attaboy, Max." He swept his arm forward. "Tallyho!"

Stung, Max loafed back to his customary position. Newton tugged on his sleeve.

"You didn't have to give it to him, you know."

"I don't care. I don't need it."

"Yeah, but Scoutmaster Tim gave it to *you.*"

"Oh, shut up, Newt."

Max regretted speaking so harshly, but there was something so . . . *exasperating* about Newt. His hidebound determination to stick to "The Rules." Like this thing with the walkie-talkie. Who gave a shit? It didn't *matter* if Scoutmaster Tim had given it to Max—they were away from the adults now. Different rules applied. Boys' rules, which clearly stated: the big and strong take from the small and weak, period.

There was just something about Newt that made Max want to snap at him. A soft, obliging quality. A whiff of

57

piteousness wafted right out of Newt's pores. It was like catnip to the average boy.

Max felt a deeper, more inherent need to treat Newt shabbily this morning. It had something to do with the strange man on the chesterfield and the tight unease that had collected in Max's chest when he'd gazed at him. Something about the unnatural angularity of his face, as if his features had been etched with cruel mathematical precision using a ruler and compass.

Max's mind inflated the details, nursing the image into a freakish horror show: now the man's face was actually *melting*, skin running like warm wax down a candle's stem to soak into the chesterfield, disclosing the bleached bone of his skull. Max's brain probed the tiny details, fussing with them the same way his tongue might flick at a canker sore: the smashed radio (why had the man wrecked it?), the crumpled box of soda crackers in the trash (had the Scoutmaster eaten them?), and the itchy smile plastered to the Scoutmaster's face, as if fishhooks were teasing his mouth into a grin.

Max pushed these thoughts away. Scoutmaster Tim had made the right call by sending them off. It was easier out here: the dry rustle of leaves tenaciously clinging to the trees, the slap of waves on the rock face. He glanced at Newt—his wide ass hogging the trail, each cheek flexing inside tight dungarees. He reminded Max of a Weeble, those old kiddie toys.

Weebles wobble but they don't fall down . . .

Newt never *did* fall down. He withstood the boy's torments with stoic determination, which made it easier—Newt could take it, right? Picking on Newt uncoiled the tension in Max's chest. It was awfully selfish, yet awfully true.

Chapter Nine

"What would you rather," Ephraim said, "eat a steaming cowflop or let a hobo fart in your face?"

It was one of their favorite games, a great way to pass the time on long hikes. Had Scoutmaster Tim been leading, the game would've been far more vanilla—*What would you rather: get bit by a rabid dog or swallow a wasp in your Coke can?*—but now, no adults around, it took on a saltier tone.

"What kind of hobo?" Max asked. It was common to mull these choices from several angles in order to make an informed selection.

"How many types of hobos are there?" said Ephraim. "Your run-of-the-mill smelly old hobo, I guess, the ones who hang out at the train yard."

"How big a cowflop are we talking about?" Kent called back.

"Standard size," Ephraim said. The boys nodded as if that was all he'd needed to say—he'd perfectly set the size of this hypothetical cowflop in their minds.

"Is this hobo diseased or anything?" Max asked. "Like, his ass rotting out?"

"His morals are diseased," Ephraim said, after a pause to think. "But he's been given a clean bill of health."

"I'd eat the cowflop," said Newton.

"What a fucking surprise," Ephraim said.

Eventually they all agreed that, of both scenarios, scarfing a cowflop was marginally better than a strange, smelly man's hairy ass cheeks ripping a wet grunter in their faces.

"It'd singe your eyebrows off," Kent said to appreciative laughter. "It'd put a center part right down your hair!"

"What would you rather," Newton said, "give a speech in front of the whole school or get your bathing suit sucked down the filter at the public pool?"

Ephraim groaned. "Oh, for fuck's sake, Newt, that's so *laaaaaaame*."

"Yeah, but," Newton mumbled, "you'd be naked, right? Your bum hanging out."

"Your *bum*?" Ephraim scoffed. "Your *bum*, really? Your pink little tushie?"

Ephraim pulled a cigarette out of his pack, along with a brass Zippo. He fixed the smoke between his lips and lit it with an elaborate flourish: drawing the Zippo up his thigh, popping off the lid, then swiftly running it down again, sparking the flywheel on his trousers. He touched the flame to the tobacco, inhaled, and said:

"Nothing like a smoke when you're stuck out in nature."

Ephraim was the only boy in their grade who smoked. A recent affectation. He bought them in singles—four, five cigarettes at a time—from a high schooler named Ernie Smegg, whose doughy carbuncled face looked like a basket of complimentary dinner rolls.

"You smoke the wrong way," Kent said. "You're holding it all wrong."

"What?" Ephraim said. He pinched the cigarette between his thumb and pointer finger, the way you'd hold a pipe. "What's the matter?"

"My dad says only Frenchmen smoke like that," said Kent. "And *fags*."

Ephraim's jaw went stiff. "Shut your big fucking mouth, K."

"You shouldn't smoke," Newton said fussily. "My mom says it turns your lungs black as charcoal briquettes."

Ephraim's chin jutted. "Yeah? Your mother's so dumb she stares at an orange juice carton all day because it says: *concentrate*."

"Hey!" Kent barked, bristling. "Don't rag on his mom, man."

Ephraim snorted but eventually said, "Sorry, Newt. So what would you rather: jerk off a donkey or fingerbang Kathy Rhinebeck?"

Kathy Rhinebeck was a sweet girl who'd been branded the class slut due to the rumor—unsubstantiated by anyone aside from Dougie Fezz—that she'd masturbated Dougie Fezz "to climax" in the back row of the North Point Cinema. *Christ on a bike, she didn't know what the hell she was doing*, Fezz told a gaggle of pop-eyed boys in the school yard, his tone one of withering scorn. *What, was she yanking weeds out of a garden?*

"What's a fingerbang?" Newton asked, predictably.

"I'd jerk off the donkey," Shelley suddenly said. "Who wants sloppy seconds?"

This, the boys silently acknowledged, was precisely the sort of response you could expect from Shelley Longpre—he had this way of sucking the air out of the game; out of *any* game, really.

They hiked in silence around the eastern hub of the island. The trail deteriorated until it was nothing but a strip of loose shale edged by chickweed and stinging thistles. It led around a rocky outcropping facing out over the gunmetal sea.

"This the way?" Newton asked.

"Where else?" Kent said challengingly. "Tim didn't send us on a granny walk."

They worked their way up. The shale sat upon a base of solid granite holding the same pink hue of the outcropping. Loose stones kept pebbling away under their boots. The path—which had seemed quite solid at the outset—soon became a series of treacherous collapsing footfalls.

And it then narrowed at the midpoint of their ascent. They could barely crowd both their feet together on it. Below them lay a steep slope carpeted with the same soft shale. It was not so sheer that they risked free falling, but steep enough that they would slide painfully down, boots pumping and hands clawing for purchase. If they couldn't stop in time, they'd hit the cold, gray sea.

Ephraim said: "Whose smart idea was this again?" When nobody answered—they lacked the energy or inclination, focused entirely on their task, which had abruptly turned very grim—his gaze zeroed in on Kent, clumsily edging his bulk around the rock face.

You big dumbfuck, Ephraim thought. *You stupid shit, you.*

The boys turned their faces into the outcrop, edging along the rock face with hesitant stutter-steps. Newton cried out, his nose scraping on a pitted extrusion of granite, peeling off a layer of skin. Straggly weeds grew off the bare rock, the tips of their withered leaves frosted with sea salt. How could anything survive in such a place, tilted crazily over the water?

The boys' fingertips hummed over the rock like bugs, searching desperately for handholds. "Grab here," Ephraim told Shelley, pulling the boy's hand to the right spot. "That *seam* there. Feel it? *There.*"

Next Ephraim pivoted his hips and kicked one leg out, making an X with his body: one hand gripping the rock while the other was outflung in space; one leg safely moored, the other kicked out over the waves crashing a hundred feet below.

"Top o' the world, Ma!"

"Stop it!" Newton shrieked, sagging jelly-kneed against the rock face.

"Come on, Eef," said Max, his fingers hooked like talons into the stone.

Ephraim's eyes narrowed, a look indicative of future devilry, but he only swung himself back against the cliff. "Keep your skin on, Newt. Don't give yourself a heart attack."

Ephraim became aware of the sound of his breathing as it whistled madly against the stone. The waves crashed rhythmically into the cliffs below, the water sucking back out to sea with a foamy gurgle. His arms trembled. The long tendons running down the backs of his calves jumped.

We could die—this thought cleaved Ephraim's mind like a guillotine blade. *One of us could start to fall, and someone will try to help—Scout Law number two: A Scout is ever loyal to his fellows; he must stick to them through thick and thin—then another and another until everyone gets pulled down like a string of paper dolls.*

From his vantage at the head of the pack, Kent now realized this couldn't be the right route. But whose fault was that? *Tim's,* for sending them out alone. Dull metallic anger throbbed at Kent's temples. It was stupid Tim's fault that Kent's mind was now paralyzed by fear. Stupid stupid stupid . . .

The trail widened on the other side of a tricky ledgeway. Kent held out his hand to help Ephraim across, then Shelley, then Newt and Max. They walked silently along a shallow upswell, sweating and breathing heavily. The trail emptied onto a flat rocky expanse overlooking the ocean.

Ephraim set both hands into Kent's chest and pushed. The bigger boy staggered back.

"Great idea, brainiac."

"It wasn't— I didn't do it on purpose," Kent said, his neck bright red.

"Nobody better give you the keys to an airplane, man." Ephraim's chin was angled up, nearly butting into Kent's. "With your sense of direction, you'd fly everybody into the sun."

Ephraim's hands curled into fists. Kent knew Ephraim wasn't shy about throwing them. Eef had been in fights. Kent, not so much. Sure, he'd shoved other boys down and put them in headlocks—but he'd never squared off with another boy and thrown real punches. He'd never *had* to. Being bigger had acted as both threat and deterrent.

But here stood Ephraim, a creature of coiled muscle and quick rage, challenging him. Kent's hair was plastered to his forehead with clammy sweat. His blood beat a hi-hat tempo inside his skull. He pictured Ephraim's fist clocking him on the chin, saw himself falling with one leg twisted painfully beneath him. The image caused bitter saliva to squirt into his mouth.

Ephraim gave him a dismissive shove. "A fucking granny walk, eh? Bozo."

Kent hated the sudden shameful fear that rose in his throat, choking him—hated himself for feeling it. The sheepdog had behaved weakly—he himself had become a sheep.

Baaaah. His father's mocking voice kicked up inside his skull. *Baaaah, baaaah, Kenty-sheep, have you any wool? Yes sir, yes sir! Three bags full . . .*

Kent bit down on his tongue. His father's voice switched off like a radio as his mouth filled with the tinfoil-y taste of blood.

They stood on a stony promontory. The salt-heavy wind riffled and snapped at the boys' clothing. At their backs lay the darkness of the forest. Kent screwed his eyes against the shivering water. Perhaps a mile away the white surf crested on the rusted bones of a sunken freighter. The sky met the sea at the horizon. Kent found it impossible to separate one from the other: sea and sky welded together without a joint.

Sudden thunder arose. A helicopter breasted the lattice-work of trees. Black and muscular looking: not a traffic or sightseeing helicopter.

The boys' faces broke into delighted grins. They waved. The chopper climbed into the sky and rotated around with its nose tilted down, then dropped abruptly. The pulse of its blades burred painfully inside the boys' skulls. Kent could smell the frictionless grease the mechanics used to lubricate its rotors: a little like cherry Certs.

The helicopter lifted up with predatory grace, swung round, and fled into the open sea. Squinting, Kent could just make out a series of squat dark shapes strung across its flight path.

"Ships out there," Newton said. "Looks like they're anchored. The military does maneuvers out here sometimes . . . but I mean, that's an *awful* lot of ships."

"Maybe they're whaling ships," said Kent. "You better watch out, Newt—they're coming to harpoon your fat ass."

As the boys' riotous laughter washed over him, Newt's eyes returned to the water. Kent felt better; the equilibrium reestablished and he was in control again—Newt was always good for that—but still, a bitter alkaline taste slimed his tongue, as if he were sucking on an old battery.

Okay so Dr. Harley here it is. One page like
you asked. Who knew a psychologist would give
me homework!!!

So you wanted me to tell a story. Just a
story of why sometimes, out of nowhere, I
get real angry. Like really REALLY angry and
get in fights. Why I want to punch my fist
in a wall or in some stupid jerks face. At
first I got angry at you for asking WHY I
was angry. FUUUUUNY! But then I think, okay,
your just doing your job (sorry for my spelling
and all that). So here goes.

First, I KNOW I get angry. Mom says its my
dad in my blood. My dads a real bad guy ok?
Shes scared Im going to be like him. Which
makes me angry (shocker!). Anyway I TRY to stop
the anger. Like when I get real pissed Ill do
something to push it out of me. Cat walk my
bike off the seawall or climb up to the schools
roof. And ok those things are RISKY, I could
break my fool neck mom says . . . but the
anger goes away. Maybe the fear pushes it away?

I dont know why. Im not a scientist. Max calls me a dare devil but thats not it. To me its like a person taking a pill cuz hes got a headake, or that pink stuff cuz his tummy hurts. Medisin, right?

But thats just what I do when I GET angry. You asked WHY I get that way.

Remember the circus came? Maybe two years ago? Everyone at school was stoked. It NEVER comes. So we all buy tickets and go and its the saddest thing. The animals were all sick and skin-and-bones and stuff. Their hair was falling out in big chunks. The elefants were droopy, trunks in the dirt. Newton Thornton even started to CRY, can you believe? What a WUSS.

Remember how one of the animals got away? A tiger. Broke out of the cage and escaped into the fields. Everyone FREAKED. Kents dad was driving with a gun hanging out the policecar window. The cat was gone like 3 days? People started to figure it drowned in the sea or like that. But then one night Im pullin the trash can into the back yard and its there. The tiger in my yard.

It was so beautiful. Fatter and more hair like it was eating good things. MEAT. Its eyes were shiny like marbles, CAT EYES, that kind. It was hiding in the bush near the shed but it cant hide, its a TIGER. Looking at me too. I smelled its breath. Like raw liver, like mom left in the sink on liver night (also: I HATE liver).

Maybe it will kill me? Im thinking this. Rip me up. But Im happy too see it. Its wild and very special. More special than the birds or deers or coydogs around here. It doesnt BELONG here. It's a special kind of wild. And . . . ok, doc, this is where it gets weird, but you ASKED . . . I feel like that tiger must have felt. Like, LOST. Like I dont really fit this place . . . the earth? Maybe just North Point. And I love my mom & my friends. Max mostly. But I feel like the tiger some days. Not ALL days but some. And thats when I get mad.

The tiger looks at me in my eyes and SOUL and then it yawns like its sleepy and jumps over the fence like you step over a curb.

I hoped it would live, be happy, have tiger babys (HOW? No tigers on the island). I hoped for that . . . but Kents dad shot it and it died. Fucking Kents dad. I cried. I think that was ok too. Right?

Chapter Ten

"*Jesus . . . Jesus Christ . . . what is that?*"

These six words cracked over the walkie-talkie clipped to Kent's belt at four o'clock that afternoon.

"Tim?" Kent said. "Tim, what's wrong? Do you copy?"

The boys stood in a loose circle, waiting.

"*It's nothing, guys,*" came the reply. "*Just sat on this goddamn thing accidentally.*"

Kent glared, his eyes squeezing to slits. "What's the matter, Tim? Come *in*, Tim."

Tim's voice—ragged, frustrated: "*Why do you have the walkie-talkie, Kent? I gave it to Max. Anyway, how's it going? Fulfilling your merit obligations?*"

Ephraim snatched the walkie-talkie. "Kent almost walked us off a cliff."

Kent made a grab for the walkie-talkie; Ephraim stashed it behind his back, his chin assuming that challenging jut again.

Silence from Tim's end. Then: "*I hope you're joking. Where are you now?*"

Newton gave Tim the compass coordinates. Tim said: "*You're a bit off-track, but it'll be fine. Follow the path from here on out, okay?*"

The sun hung low in the western sky. Its reflective rays

69

turned the poplars and oaks into pillars of flame. The boys had rounded down from the cliffs around the northern hub of the island. Newton used his compass to keep them on track.

"None of this would've happened if Tim had come," Kent sulked. "It's his job, isn't it?"

"Oh, bullshit." Ephraim vented a harsh, barking laugh. "You wanted to play King Shit, Kent. Well, you played it. Now wear your crown of turds."

The muscles humped up Kent's shoulders—a defensive, kicked-dog posture. They walked in silence until Shelley said: "Kent's right, the Scoutmaster should've come."

Kent gave Shelley a look of pathetic gratitude. Next he was storming to the head of the line, which Ephraim was heading, elbowing the smaller boy aside to assume the lead. Shelley smiled fleetingly, nothing but a slight upturn of his lips—not that anybody noticed. Shelley had this way of hiding in a permanent pocket of shadow, that spot at the edge of your vision where your eyes never quite focused.

The boys came upon a large rock pile covered with spongy moss and decided to play King of the Mountain. It was a game they played often, but today it achieved a particular intensity—less a game and more of a fight. They played hard to dispel the jitteriness that had invaded their bones, a feeling whose root could be found back at the cabin. If they shoved and sweated and wrestled, it might just break the fear amassing inside of them, same way a good thunderstorm could break the intolerable heat of a summer afternoon.

Kent took command of the hill and repulsed their half-hearted attempts with hard shoves. He shoulder-blocked Max's anemic challenge and flexed his biceps, his budding linebacker's body set in a defensive stance. Dying sunlight petaled through the tree branches, glinting off his dental braces.

"Bring it on, Eef! I double-dog dare you!"

Ephraim stood at the base of the hill, arms crossed over his chest, hands cupping his elbows. A thin boy—*so skinny he could slip down the drain hole,* as his mom said—but his limbs were roped with powerful fast-twitch muscles, elbows and kneecaps hard as carbon. He thought about the mantra of his counselor, Dr. Harley: *Don't be a slave to your anger, Ephraim.*

It was so *hard.* It bubbled inside him like that stupid geyser at Yellowstone Park, Old Faithful—except the geyser was, like, *faithful:* at least you could time it. Ephraim's anger rose out of nowhere, this giddy charge zitzing through his bones and electrifying the marrow. His rage was a dark cloud passing over the sun where just moments before the sky had been clear blue.

"You chicken?" Kent flapped his arms. "Chicken-chicken brock-brock!"

Lips skinning from his teeth, a feral growl rising in his throat, Ephraim sprinted up the pile to tangle with Kent. He saw it in Kent's eyes: this desperate, crawling fear. Fear of losing partially, but also fear of how far Ephraim might take it. And Ephraim saw how easily it could happen. His fist coming up over Kent's clumsy arms, his fist hammering Kent in the mush, flattening his thick drool-flecked lips against the barbed braces, cutting the flesh open as the big boy toppled like a sack of laundry, Ephraim following him down, fists pumping like pistons to destroy the crude symmetry of Kent Jenks's fuck-o face . . .

Ephraim saw all this in the elastic instant they were perched atop the pile—a silly prize, really; a mossy heap of rocks—and the possibility of violence, his easy *capacity* for it, drained the strength from his limbs. Kent took advantage, flinging the smaller boy down. He copped a bodybuilding pose, the flexed double crab, face set in a caricature of a despotic monarch.

"I . . . *am* . . . invincible!"

Ephraim frowned and rubbed his elbow—the skin torn, blood weeping sluggishly to his wrist.

"Not cool, big K."

Ephraim found Newt scraping moss off a log. Newt was always wandering off to press stupid leaves into his stupid notebook, cataloging everything with a black Sharpie. *Eastern Sumac. Indian tobacco.* God, so dorky!

Ephraim wound up to give Newt a kick in the ass, feeling sort of guilty—Dr. Harley wouldn't approve; nor would his mother—so he delivered a lighter kick than usual.

"Where's the first aid kit, numbnuts?"

Newt rubbed the seat of his pants. "I got ears, Eef. Don't have to kick me."

"I figured your ears were in your ass, Newt. Looks like everything else is—I was just knocking the wax out of them. Aren't you gonna thank me?"

Sighing, Newt dug the kit out of his knapsack.

"Sit down, Eef."

This was Newt's role: the nurturer, the motherer. He had a natural affinity for it, and the boys sporadically accepted his ministrations—accepted them, then returned to making Newt the object of their torments. And Newt allowed it, because it had always been so.

He tore open a peroxide swab packet, pressed it to the wound on Ephraim's elbow. Ephraim hissed between clenched teeth.

"It's just fizzy," Newt said. "Shouldn't hurt."

Ephraim slapped Newt's hand away. "I'll do it."

Newton's eyes drifted to the sky. His nostrils dilated.

"What are you doing?"

"I think that storm's coming," Newt said. "You can smell it. Like, an alkaline smell, like when you rip open a bag of water-softener salt."

"We don't have a water softener, Richie Rich." Ephraim bared his teeth in a mock-snarl. "We like our water *haaaaard.*"

"You can spot it in the water, too. See?" Newt pointed to the sea. "The water always turns red before a storm. Not quite bloodred, but close. The electricity in the air as a storm brews, right, it causes plankton protozoans to lift up off the seabed; these tiny little creatures—like, the tiniest living things on earth—inflate with oxygen and turn deep red, covering the whole sea and making it red, too."

Ephraim slapped a butterfly bandage on his elbow.

"Holy shit, dude. Your brain's too big. Why doesn't it ooze out your ears?" His eyes went wide. "Actually . . . fuck me! I see it oozing out right now!"

Ephraim licked his finger and went to screw it into Newt's ear—a classic Wet Willy. His finger stopped just short, though, a runner of saliva clung to a whorl of his fingerprint. It seemed a heartless thing to do, considering.

He wiped the spit on his pants, bounded to his feet, and raced off to join the other boys.

"Saved your life, Newt! You owe me one!"

The trail descended to a pebbled shoreline lapped by the ocean. The boys doffed their boots and rolled up their pants, wading in the icy October sea. Their ankles turned pig-belly pink. They hunted for the smoothest stones and had a skipping contest, which Kent won with ten skips by his count.

"Hey, guys," Ephraim said. "Check this out."

He directed them to a deep cut within the shore rocks, fringed with sea moss. The boys gathered round. Flashes of shining skin made oily in the guttering light; unknown shapes humping over one another. Silky sibilant esses— *husssss, husssss.*

"It's a snake ball," Newton said.

How many snakes? Impossible to tell. Their bodies were entwined, a writhing network of tubes like an elastic-band ball. Their bodies were dark—sea serpents?—and wet like living, livid oil; that peculiar reptile smell met their noses: wet and fetid like a dewy field spread with dead crickets.

"What are they doing?" said Ephraim.

"They're . . ." Newt's face went pink. ". . . y'know . . ."

"Fucking?" Ephraim made a gagging noise. "That's how snakes fuck, all twisted up in a ball? Like . . . a snake orgy?"

Kent and Max laughed. Ephraim was so perverted. A snake orgy. Inevitably someone tried to push Newton into the snake ball, make him touch it—Shelley in this case. Newt squirmed free of Shelley's long simian arms, out of his smooth rubbery grip—almost like tentacles without the suction cups—and screamed at him to stop.

"Quit it, Shel! Lay off!"

The other boys watched idly. There was something off-putting—sickening, really—about the scene. A bit like watching a blind boa constrictor pursue a plump mouse around a cage: the chase might go on a while but the snake was dogged, plus it was a natural predator. Sooner or later it'd eat the fat little fucker.

"Stop it, Shel," Kent said in a bored tone. "You're gonna make him piss his pants again."

Shelley quit abruptly, turned, and wandered toward the shore. Newton smoothed his untucked shirt over his pendulant belly, turned to Kent all stiff-spined, and said:

"Thanks, Kent . . . but I only did it the one time, and I was six years old and we were on that bus trip to Moncton that went on forever and okay, I drank too much McDonald's orange drink but—"

"Shut up, tinkle-dink," Kent said. "Don't get too excited or you'll piss your pants, remember?"

While the boys horsed around, Shelley waded into a shallow tidal pool. He found a crayfish. It fit perfectly in his palm.

He studied it closely. It looked weird and funny. He tried to imagine the world as seen through the black poppy seeds of its eyes, sitting on spindly stalks. What a stupid creature. What were its days like—what was its *life*? Crawling around this dreary itsy-bitsy pool, choking on fish shit, eating garbage. It had no clue about the world outside its filthy puddle, did it? *Dumb is as dumb does,* as his mother would say—which had always struck Shelley as a dumb expression, something only a dumb person would say.

How would it feel to pull the crayfish apart? He didn't mean how would the *crayfish* feel—he didn't care about that, and anyway, with its piece-of-lint brain and elementary nerves, it may not feel *anything*. Distantly, Shelley considered that possibility: that this creature could watch itself be shredded like paper and feel nothing, caring not at all.

Oh, there goes my leg. Never mind. And there goes my other one. Ooops—now I can't see. My eyes must be gone.

Shelley was something of a sensualist. He relished touch—*pressure.* How *would* it feel, physically, to take this creature apart? Would its pincers snap at his fingers as he pulled? Would its stupid crustacean anatomy fight its own dismemberment—that wonderful tension as he pulled each limb off, the sucking *pip!* as this or that part detached from the whole? The crayfish could fight, yes—and dimly, Shelley sort of hoped it would—but it wouldn't matter: he wasn't scared of being bitten or clawed, plus he was so much bigger. As usual with Shelley, if he wanted to do something—and if nobody was watching—he simply did as he liked.

He pinched one of the crayfish's comical little eyes. It ruptured with a mildly satisfying *pop.* The texture was grainy—a tiny ball of honeycomb candy coming apart. The remnants were stuck on his finger like the shards of a very small and dark Christmas tree ornament. The crayfish spasmed in his palm, jackknifing open and closed. Shelley was transfixed. His eyes took on a hard sheen. Saliva collected in his mouth, a gossamer strand of spit rappelling over his quivering lower lip.

He burst the crayfish's other eye. He carefully pulled off one of its pincers, relishing that thrilling tension. *Pip!* The pinky-translucent claw continued to open and close even when separated from the body. He dropped it and watched it sink, opening and closing.

"Hey, Shel," Ephraim called over. "Newt's going to light the one-match fire. We need you as a windbreak."

Newton was in charge of the fire. The boys were content to let him take the lead. Besides, Newton was best at almost all the basic survival skills: firecraft and orienteering and berry identification.

Newton lit the pile of old man's beard and nursed the fledgling flickers. Fingers of flame crawled up the bleached wood. They crouched around the fire to soak in its heat. Sunlight painted a honey-gold inlay on the slack water between the waves.

"My grandma died of cancer," Ephraim said suddenly. "Liver cancer."

Max said: *"What?"*

Ephraim gave him a look: *Just listen to me.* "Her skin went yellow. All she could get down were those meal replacement things that old people drink. *Ensure.* Her hair came out because of the radiation chamber they stuck her in to kill the cancer." He exhaled heavily, blowing his dark locks off his forehead. "When I saw that guy this morning, the first thing I thought about was Grandma."

The man hadn't entered their thoughts directly, but he'd been hovering at the margins all day. His sick-looking face. His matchstick arms and legs. The sweet smell of the cabin.

Ephraim's streamlined and unconventionally handsome

face took on a rare pensive aspect. "What do you think's the matter with him?"

Kent grabbed a stone and hurled it into the water with a vicious sweep of his arm.

"Who knows, Eef? If it's cancer, then it's cancer—right? People get cancer." Kent stared at the others with savage solemnity. "Maybe he's got what-do-you-call-it . . . alpiners or whatever."

"Alzheimer's," Newton said.

"What-the-fuck *ever*, Newt. He's got that."

"He's too young," Newton said. "That's an old people's disease."

"You guys're being babies," Kent said, drawing the last word out: *baaaaay-bies*. "My dad says the most obvious conclusion is usually the right one. Ninety-nine-point-nine-nine percent of the time."

"So what's the most obvious conclusion?" Shelley asked, his vapid face oriented on Kent. "His skin looked like it was *melting*."

The boys fell silent.

"I just think the guy is sick, is all," Max said after a while. "And I've been thinking about it."

"So have I," said Ephraim.

"And me," Newt said.

Kent snorted. "Tim's a doctor, isn't he? That's his *job*, isn't it? By the time we get back, he'd better have everything sorted out."

He kicked the fire apart, scattering bits of flaming driftwood.

Before departing, Newton gathered the still-glowing sticks and doused them in the ocean. Scout's Law number four: *Honor and protect Nature in all her abundance.*

Dear Dr. Harley,

I'll compose this like a letter, because
I write a lot—I've got pen pals in Australia,
England, and Dubuque, Iowa. Who doesn't like
opening the mailbox and finding a letter from
a friend, even one you've never met in person?

So . . . a confession, huh? You think I
keep things bottled up, and confession's good
for the soul. Right? I'd talk more if people—
I mean the other kids at school—gave two
cruds what I have to say. Most times they'll
just laugh, call me a nerd, a geek, call me
fat, call me a nerdy fatty-fat geek (which
is overkill, right? Nerds and geeks are
pretty much the same . . .). So I don't
talk much, except to my teachers and my mom.
And now you.

The thing is, you can be a different person
in letters. On the Internet, too. Because
there, you're not YOU. Okay so yes, you are,
but not the physical you. So not fat (it's
glandular), sweaty (it's also glandular), weird

(for North Point, anyway. I don't like bow hunting or spearfishing or killing things, I'm too clumsy for stickball and I actually *LIKE Anne of Green Gables* . . . so yeah, weird!) and awkward and gawky and according to Ephraim Elliot sometimes I smell like rotten corn, like when you shuck an ear and it's all black inside? (By the way, I hear you're counseling Eef, too; you're doing a good job—he hasn't given me a Wet Willy, a Rooster Peck, or a Titty Twister in like a month.)

But online I'm not that person. I can be my very best self. According to Mom I'm a sensitive boy. Also, I'm a polymath, which means I know a little bit about everything (which, okay, IS nerdy). Online I can be my brain without my body.

So . . . the confession. Forgive me, Father . . . hah! Anyway, you won't tell anyone. Patient-doctor confidentiality. I read about it.

A year ago my cousin Sherwood died. He lived in Manitoba. He fell asleep in a field and a combine ran him over. He tried to run but those combines are like forty feet of whirring blades. At his funeral the coffin stayed closed.

I loved Sherwood. We hardly got to see each other—we don't have a lot of money (I don't even know how Mom affords you) and

Sherwood's parents are farmers. But every summer they came for a visit. I'd take Sher to the ocean. No ocean in Manitoba, right? We got along great. When I told him a little nugget of info, Sher was genuinely interested.

We stuck to the out-of-the-way places, the ones only I knew. I didn't want to run across any kids from school—they'd call me lardbucket or tub-a-guts. I was scared that if Sher saw that he wouldn't like me anymore. Which wasn't really fair to him. Sher would've helped me, because blood is thicker than water, right?

Sher was tall with wide shoulders and lots of muscle—farmboy muscles, he called them, laughing and telling me everyone had them back home, he wasn't so special. But Sher WAS special. Handsome (I can say that about another boy, it's not weird) and people just . . . they gravitated to him, is I think the word. Like a magnet drawing iron filings. Everyone wanted to be around Sher.

Then he died, a stupid unlucky accident, and everyone was so sad. The world had lost a great light—everyone said so. I wondered what they'd have said if it was me who died? I didn't really want to guess.

After the funeral I dug out my box of photos. My mom bought me a Polaroid for my birthday and it got a lot of use. Mainly they were of Sher—I was the one snapping the photos, plus I don't like how I look on camera.

I was going to put up a memorial wall. On Facebook, right? Something to remember Sher by. My idea, sincerely. But somewhere along the line it changed.

I scanned the photos, put them in a file on my computer. But instead of a memorial wall I . . . well, I created a person. I guess that's what I did, yeah.

Alex Markson. The boy's name. I don't know where I got it from, but it seemed a strong name—it fit well with the photos. Alex Markson had Sherwood's face and body. Alex Markson had my words, my interests. Alex was me and Sherwood, combined.

I put up the profile. I knew it was wrong. My heart hammered like a drum when Sher's face went POP! up on the screen. It was . . . sacrilegious? I almost deleted it. Almost.

I started posting stuff. Nothing much at first. Just things that interested me—the stuff kids around here pick on me for. My words pasted to Sher's body.

The super-weird thing is . . . Alex started to get friend requests. I mean, a LOT. People neither of us had met. Not weirdos either. Normal, cool people. Boys (and girls!) my age.

At first I was scared to accept them—I saw Sher up in Heaven, shaking his head—but after a while I did. People posted on my wall and I'd post on theirs, as Alex. Sher's face bloomed like a flower on strangers' Facebook pages.

But the thing is, Alex's interests were mine. And people thought he was smart and funny and, well, COOL. Isn't that weird? When I say those exact same things it's nerdy, because people think I'm a nerd. Like, a self-fulfilling prophecy.

So then—and this is really embarrassing—I sent some requests. To Max Kirkwood and Ephraim Elliot and Kent Jenks. I even sent one to Trudy Dennison, who sits in front of me in homeroom and is the most beautiful, funniest, and just all-around best girl in the whole entire world. Not that I've ever really talked to her, except for that time she borrowed a pencil in social studies . . . which she never gave back, come to think of it. Maybe she thinks "borrow" means "keep," same as Kent does . . . probably she just forgot.

Anyway, guess what? They accepted, even though they never met Alex. How could they, right? They just thought he was handsome, and loose, and cool.

I thought: This is how it COULD be. If I wasn't ME. If I existed in a different body, an acceptable body, a body everyone loved. If I didn't live in North Point, where I'm like this train on rails: I know where I'm going, hate it, but can't change course. This was who I could've been if the ball had bounced just a bit differently, you know?

My own Facebook page has ten friends. My mom, a few uncles and aunts, my grandmother—"I bought you a new pair of jeans from the Husky department at Simpson's Sears in Charlottetown, Newtie!"—and a few pen pals . . . my pal from Dubuque de-friended me.

Now here's the big confession, Dr. Harley, the solid gold bonanza, the secret that says just about everything, I guess:

Alex Markson isn't friends with Newton Thornton. Not on Facebook. Not anywhere on earth or in this life.

Sincerely,
Newton Thornton

Chapter Eleven

It was dark by the time they returned to the cabin. A fire flickered in a ring of rocks. Scoutmaster Tim was sitting on the far side. The tendons on his neck stood out in sharp relief: they looked like tiny trees all tenting inward.

"Don't go inside," he told them.

"My warm coat's in there," Kent said.

"The fire's warm. You'll be fine."

"I'd rather have my coat."

"I don't care what you'd rather have," Tim said in a dead voice. "The man inside is sick. Sick in a way I've never seen before, at least not that I can diagnose here."

The boys settled themselves around the fire. Newton said, "Sick how?"

"At first, I thought cancer. As a doctor, that's always the first thought. But cancer is almost always typified by loss of appetite and . . ."

Tim saw no good reason to tell the boys that the man had stirred that afternoon—lunged upward like a heart-staked vampire from its coffin. His eyes crawling with burst vessels . . . his tongue a knot of sinew as if something had sucked the saliva out of it . . .

The man had sunk his teeth into the chesterfield and torn at the fabric with savage bites.

The *mindlessness* of it had horrified Tim.

Tim managed to sedate him before he swallowed too much. There was a good chance he'd choke to death on the chesterfield's musty old foam. He'd cradled the man's neck as he laid him down. The man's head tilted back and his jaw hung open . . .

Tim had seen something. If anything, it resembled a white knuckle of bone—the bone of a greenstick fracture except curved and gleaming. Visible only for a harried instant. Lodged in his throat below the epiglottal bulb. Gently ribbed and somehow gill-like . . .

Next the man's rib cage bulged in a bone-splintering flex as something settled.

". . . and this man is very hungry," Tim finished.

"So what are you going to do about it?" said Kent.

Tim ignored the boy's cheeky defiance. "He may have some kind of internal sickness. By the time the boat picks us up, I believe he'll be dead."

Newton said: "Can you operate on him?"

Shelley said: "Cut him open?"

Tim said: "I haven't done a lot of surgery, but I know the basics. Max, has your dad ever had you help him out on the job?"

Max's father was the county coroner. Also its taxidermist: if anyone wanted his trophy bluefin mounted on a burled-oak backing, he was the one to call. An insistent voice in Tim's head told him not to involve the boys—keep them clear of this. But a new voice, a silky whisper, told him no worries—it'd be just fine.

You've got it all under control, Tim . . .

He didn't, though—he'd become hyperaware of this fact. This night would determine whether the man lived or died . . . maybe only a few hours of the night. This was why he would've bombed as a surgeon: Tim lacked the quick-cut instincts, that private triage room in his head. He was a thinker—an *over*thinker. Overthinking matters was just a harmless quirk in a GP but now, when swift action was needed, he could feel himself coming apart.

"I've helped taxidermy animals," Max said.

"Helped in what way?"

"Threading needles with catgut. Shining up the glass eyes and like that."

It's an internship, said the voice in Tim's head. *Consider it an early residency. Max's folks wouldn't mind, would they? A man's life is at risk, right? Max is smart, Max is careful—and you can protect him should anything happen.*

Tim pointed at the others. "You all stay here. No arguments. This guy . . . I don't know what's the matter. He may be viral."

Ephraim said: "Viral?"

"Like, he's catching," Kent said. "You know, *contagious*."

"You sure, Scoutmaster?" Newt said. "I mean, Max is just a . . ."

Boy was the word Newton swallowed. Just a boy and Tim was taking him into a cabin occupied by a man who was sick in some unknowable way.

Tim's left eye twitched, the nerve gone haywire. *Plikka-plikka-plikka* like the shutter on a camera. He squeezed his eyes shut, slowly counted to five in his head. A small, persistent, maddening voice deep within the runnels of his brain was now asking questions.

What are you doing, Tim? Are you really sure, Tim? The voice's cold, stentorian tone reminded him of HAL 9000, the computer in *2001: A Space Odyssey*. It wouldn't shut up, kept nattering on with icy certainty.

Just what do you think you're doing, Tim?

He was dimly terrified that this was the voice of common

sense—the logical voice that he'd listened to all his adult life—and that he was gradually abandoning it.

"You don't have to do this, Max," Ephraim said. His gaze fell upon the Scoutmaster. "He doesn't have to, does he?"

Tim swallowed. He'd begun to do so compulsively—it felt like a pebble had gotten lodged in his throat. "No . . . no. But I don't think I can do it alone. And we will take all precautions."

Max said: "It'll be safe?"

Tim swallowed, swallowed . . .

Are you sure, Tim? Is this really—

It will be FINE. You can HANDLE it.

A new voice rose over HAL 9000's prissy hectoring. A louder, more imposing voice, belonging to a man of action. It crowded out the other voice, which was just fine—Tim was tired of listening to it.

"It's safe," Tim said.

The new voice said, *It's safe enough, anyway.*

Tim hooked his thumb at Max. "Now *come on.*"

Chapter Twelve

The air inside the cabin was sickly sweet. Closing his eyes, Max could picture himself under a canopy of tropical fronds hung with fruits swollen with decay.

Tim splashed rubbing alcohol on a long strip of gauze. "Press this over your mouth and nose. No matter what happens, Max, don't take it off."

"Aren't you wearing one?"

"I don't know if that matters so much now."

Tim had been busy. He'd already set up a crude operating theater on the table: suture needles threaded with filament, scalpels, hypodermic needles and vials, a bottle of scotch, and a soldering iron.

"I scrounged that out of Oliver McCanty's boat," Tim said, pointing to the iron. "I might be able to cauterize the bigger blood vessels with it."

The cupboards hung open. Max saw empty hot dog wrappers and bun bags in the trash. A huge sack of oatmeal was torn open and most of it was gone. The trail mix . . . the beef jerky . . . their food for the entire weekend.

Tim rubbed his palm over his face, gave Max a sheepish smile, and pointed at an orange plastic cooler.

"The food in there I haven't touched. Take it outside, please. Right now."

Max did as he was told, the numbness growing inside. He overheard Newton saying "What would our folks say about it?" and saw the questioning looks on his fellow Scouts' faces; he put the cooler down and turned, ignoring them, heading back to Tim. A gust of wind pulled the cabin door shut behind him. He dug his feet into the floor—he didn't want to be anywhere near the stranger.

"Prop a chair under the doorknob," Tim said, pouring scotch into a jelly glass. "I don't want them coming in."

In the cabin's light, Max now saw how much the Scoutmaster had changed in the hours they'd been gone. His chest was sucked inward where his rib cage met. His shoulders arrowed down and his neck stuck between them like a bean plant threading up a bamboo pole. His fingers spider-crept over the bottle—they looked spiderish themselves.

Max remembered something his father had said about Tim: *Dr. Riggs has GP hands. Real meat hooks! He doesn't have surgeon's hands. A surgeon's hands are weirdly delicate. Like they've got extra joints. Nosferatu hands—the sort of pale and freaky things you could imagine reaching out of the shadows to grab you!*

Well, Scoutmaster Tim had surgeon's hands now.

Tim caught the question in Max's eyes. He said: "Yeah . . . I think so, buddy. He coughed something up on me last night. Rock slime, I figured, but since then I've lost . . . twenty pounds? In a *day*?" He spoke dreamily, with awestruck bafflement. "At least twenty. More every minute."

Max could tell his Scoutmaster was trying to stay calm—to look at this situation as a doctor—but his diminished body was trembling with insuppressible, jackrabbit fear. A single word looped through Max's head: *RunRunRunRunRun.*

He didn't, though. Perhaps it had something to do with their long history, the innate trust he placed in his

Scoutmaster. Maybe it was Pavlovian: when an adult asked for help, Max offered it. A man would have to be pretty desperate to ask a kid, wouldn't he?

Scoutmaster Tim upended the glass. Rivulets of scotch spilled down the sides of his mouth. He stared radish-eyed at the boy.

"This is not just for me, Max. It's for you and the others, too."

Max thought back to a night years ago when his father had gotten hurt on the softball diamond. His team was playing the police union's team, captained by Kent's father. Max's father was the catcher and, on the final play of the ninth inning, score tied at ten-all, "Big" Jeff Jenks steamed around third base, chugging hard for home. The cutoff man got the ball to Max's dad a good ten yards ahead of Jenks's arrival—league softball rules stated the catcher didn't need to apply a tag, so there was no earthly reason for a runner to plow into the catcher in hopes of popping the ball loose.

That hadn't stopped Jenks from smashing his 250 pounds into Max's dad—who weighed 160 soaking wet—pancaking him at home plate.

Max heard the high sweet *crack!* which lingered under the vapor-halogen spotlights. His father stood woozily, his arm hanging at a funny angle: bent back at the elbow, the lower half dangling like a cooked noodle. A shard of bone protruded from the joint, shining wetly under the lights.

The second baseman had driven his father's car to the ER. Max sat in the backseat, his father in front. He leaned over the seat rest, smiling gamely. *It's okay, Maximilian. It's just a flesh wound,* he said, repeating a line from one of their favorite movies. At the hospital, Max's dad sat on a bed encircled by a white curtain. Max wasn't allowed to sit with him because, as his dad said, *This is bound to be gross.* So he'd only heard the rattle of the bone-setter's tray and the crisp, blood-jangling *click!* as his father's broken bone was set back in place. When the curtain withdrew, there he was, his arm in a sling and a tired, doped-up smile on his face.

Jeff Jenks showed up to say he was sorry but not really— some men are incapable of offering a sincere apology, Max realized; something in their nature refuses it, so instead they frame it as an accident, a misunderstanding, or a *"sorry you're so upset"* sort of thing that placed subtle blame on the other person for making such a big deal. Kent was there, too, and told Max he was sorry about what'd happened— which wasn't an apology, either. Max would always remember that glint of pride in Kent's eye.

Afterward Max's father drove them home. *Can you drop the transmission into drive, son? I can't manage it.* They drove through streets wrapped in darkness, his father palm-guiding the wheel. *Getting old, kiddo.* His father smiled. *And I'm barely hanging on to the "getting" part.* A sudden fear had stolen over the crown of Max's skull—fear and sadness intermingled, so powerful he wanted to cry. Up until that night, he'd sincerely believed that his father was invincible. He was mammothly strong, capable of reshingling a house or chopping down trees with a sharp axe. But that night he'd looked frail, tired, and vaguely spooked. *Vulnerable—* something Max had never seen. All bodies fail, he realized. They fall to pieces *in* pieces, bit by torturous bit, and a man had to watch it fall apart around him.

Max now thought of this as he looked at the Scoutmaster, and shivered.

"I'll need your help, Max. I'll need it quite a lot in the next few minutes."

Max said: "Um, what do you want me to do?"

At fourteen, Max was a little smaller than average, but there was a wideness to his shoulders and a thickness to his chest. He moved with a litheness that was not at all common for boys his age—most of them were made of knees and elbows all held together with scabs. His face was Rockwellian: the bristle-brush red hair and star-spray of freckles over his cheeks. He looked like a more compact and muscular Opie.

What set Max apart from the other boys was his reservoir of remoteness and cool self-control. Tim didn't believe his father had inculcated this into him: Reggie Kirkwood was a good man but flighty as a hummingbird, prone to gossip and drink. Tim had seen the same cool quality in some of his classmates at med school who'd gone on to become the top "blades" at Johns Hopkins and Beth Israel. It wasn't exactly cockiness: more an absence of panic or hesitation. They trusted their instincts and they trusted their hands to carry those instincts into action.

Tim would try to not ask too much of the boy during the coming operation—but even asking him to be here at all was a terrible request. HAL 9000's maddeningly reasonable voice echoed this.

Tim, I think you're losing it. Tim could see HAL in his mind's eye: a reflective glass eye, very dark, a dot of redness expanding and contracting like a dilated pupil. *And now you're taking a child down the rabbit hole with you.*

Don't listen to that bullshit, the other, more comforting voice boomed. *This is your duty as a doctor—what other choice, just watch this man die? And you can't do this alone, can you?*

He couldn't. It was that simple. Tim switched on the soldering iron to let it heat. "I've doped him up."

It wasn't true anesthetic—two crushed Vicodin discovered in a forgotten pocket of his backpack; he'd been prescribed it years ago while recuperating from a calf infarction. It could very well be expired, but what the hell, better than nothing.

"He shouldn't wake up." Tim gripped the blankets gathered at the man's throat. "Ready?"

Max nodded. Tim pulled the blankets away.

Max couldn't keep the look of horror off his face. It was instinctive, what most would feel when faced with a member of humankind who no longer looked like he belonged to the species.

The stranger didn't wholly resemble a man anymore. More like something a dull-witted child might have drawn with a crayon. His body was lines. His arms were scribbles. His fingers were calligraphic spiders. The skin draped his rib cage with terrible intimacy, pinching around each rib to show the striation of muscle. His sternum was a knot, his pelvis a gruesome hinged wishbone. The skin of his face had the patina of old copper and was sucked so tight to his skull that Max could see the glaring rings of bone around his eye sockets. His ears protruded like jug handles, so thin that they curled inward, like charring paper.

"Unbelievable. My God. Even his cartilage is disintegrating," Tim said in horrified awe.

He looks like the oldest man who's ever lived, Max thought.

His stomach was the only robust thing about him. A tightly swollen bulge. It looked like he'd swallowed a volleyball.

"I'm going to do something called a gastrostomy," Tim said. "I'll make a small incision over the outer third of the left rectus muscle. So basically here." He drew his finger below the edge of the man's lowest rib. "It should be a short trip into his stomach. Very little visceral or abdominal fat to get through."

"Is there *any* fat?"

Tim said: "His body must have started eating its muscle a while ago. I have to worry about the liver . . . but I can pretty much see it right now." He pointed to a soft ridge along the man's side. "It has probably shut down its function. It's in a state of premortification and it's hardening fast."

"Can you save him?"

To Max, it seemed impossible. This man already belonged less to Max's world, the living one, than to his father's: the world of the motionless dead in the mortuary vaults.

"I can't say. It's some kind of voodoo that he's still alive. But we have to do something, Max." Tim stared searchingly at the boy, his eyelid going *plikka-plikka.* "Don't we?"

Max wasn't sure. Why was it their responsibility? Maybe this man had done it to himself—a result of bad luck or bad decisions.

Tim tried to smile but couldn't quite get his muscles to cooperate: more the leer of a crazed loon. His face kept shifting polarities, giddy to mortified, great forces working beneath its surface. Max wondered: Did the Scoutmaster really want to save the man, or only investigate for symptoms of his own condition? He contemplated the selfishness of that as the soldering gun sent up pin curls of smoke.

"What do you think it is?" Max asked softly.

Tim picked up the scalpel. He stared at his hand until it stopped trembling.

"I've stopped trying to guess, Max. I'll open him up a little. Just a little, okay?"

Tim thought back to med school, an operating theater where a doctor-instructor leaned over his patient and said: *This is the God moment, folks. You hold it all in your hands right now. So honor the body beneath your blade.*

Tim would do his best to honor this man's body . . . what was left of it.

"Ready, Max?"

The boy nodded.

"Just follow my instructions. Don't be scared if I yell or get demanding—it won't be your fault." He offered a strained and cheerless smile. "I'll try not to raise my voice."

Tim positioned the scalpel over the man's flesh, which was stretched so tight that he could see the individual pores: a million tiny mouths stretched into silent screams. He lacked the cool confidence of a true "blade"—you could wake one of those guys out of a dead sleep, shove him into the operating theater and stick a knife in his hand, and he'd say *I've got it from here* and get down to cutting.

That was a rare gift. Tim had been given a smaller gift, which was why he'd ended up as a small-town GP wielding tongue depressors and blood pressure cuffs. He'd always been okay with that, too—but as the scalpel hummed over the man's flesh, he dearly wished for the unerring self-belief of his med-school pals.

The man's skin opened up as if it had been aching to do that very thing. A V of split flesh followed the blade as it sliced below the ribs, widening out like the wake of a yacht. Everything inside existed in shades of white: the silver skin draping the man's ribs and the layers of muscle.

"Soldering iron, Max."

Tim cauterized the severed veins. Medical instruments were often just precision variations of the same tools handymen used.

"Gauze," he said.

Tim dabbed the blood out of the half-inch-deep slit in the man's torso—then absentmindedly dabbed the sweat off his forehead. The stranger's breathing was unaltered. Tim wasn't surprised. A single baby aspirin would be enough to knock him on his ass. He already may have slipped into a starvation coma.

HAL 9000 spoke up: *Timothy Ogden Riggs, are you sure you're making the right decision? I think you should stop.*

The new, conflicting voice—the Undervoice, as Tim now thought of it—boomed back: *How could you stop now, even if you wanted to? Don't you want to know, Tim? Don't you NEED to know?*

The blade slit through bands of taut sinew to reveal the stomach lining. Milky-pale and fingered with blue veins. Tim was reminded of childhood trips to his Scottish grand-mother's home and the boiled sheep's stomachs she'd laid out on the kitchen counter, waiting to be made into haggis: they had looked like deflated, overthick birthday balloons.

Jesus . . . Jesus Christ.

Tim wished so dearly that he were in a hospital right now, a sterilized surgical suite with nurses and orderlies buzzing about like helpful bees. Most desperately of all, he wished the blade weren't in his hand.

It doesn't have to be, Tim, HAL 9000 said softly. *Just put the blade down. Take Max's hand—or maybe you shouldn't touch him, just in case. Stitch this poor man up and leave the cabin. Both of you. Just go.*

The Undervoice, nasty and baiting: *You fucking coward. Grow a set of balls, man! In for a penny, in for a pound—and you're neck-deep now, sonny boy!*

Tim drew the blade along the stomach lining. A gout of gray ichor oozed around the lips of the incision like conges-tive mucus. Then . . . more white. Another layer of tightened white flesh.

". . . gauze," Tim said tentatively.

Max put a square in his hand. Tim dabbed away the warm ichor. The smell was horrible, like rancid grease. This made no sense. He'd cut into the stomach, hadn't he? He hadn't expected to find a dark vault, but he had expected a cavity, an expulsion of pressurized stomach gas . . . *something.*

It seemed as if he'd simply sliced into a secondary

layer of stomach lining—which was impossible. Was this man's stomach the equivalent of a Russian doll, stomach inside stomach inside stomach?

Something very disturbing is happening here, Tim. HAL 9000's voice, indistinct and watery. *Something is horribly, drastically wrong . . .*

Tim felt a species of fear enter his heart that he hadn't felt since his stint as a foreign aid doctor in Afghanistan. Although he'd been scared most of his time there, it had at least been a coherent fear: fear that a bomb might come whistling out of the chalky desert sky and through the canvas roof of his jury-rigged triage ward, or fear that some human grenade might dash inside their compound and pull the pin on himself.

But the fear he felt now was childlike, dreamy. There was no reference point to it. The man was just sick—that was all. He didn't have multiple stomachs. There had to be a rational cause for all of this. It was a serious occlusion, of course . . . but there was no reason, really *no reason*, for his eyes to be drawn to that ribbed whiteness within the duller whiteness of the stomach's lining and for his mind to fuse shut at the possibilities . . .

. . . Jesus, he was *hungry*.

Why had he given the boys all that food? They would be fine until the boat came. But he *needed* it. Now. He'd packed it and paid for it. By rights it was *his*.

Tim stared at his patient. The man's lips were so thin that they'd twisted into a permanent grin. He seemed to be laughing at Tim. Mocking his hunger.

Hey, buddy, the Undervoice piped up. *What would* you *do for a Klondike bar?*

"Shut up," Tim croaked.

Whoa! No need to get testy. The voice had gone vile and poisonous. *You deserve a break today, pal. Two all-beef patties special sauce lettuce cheese pickles onions on a sesame seed bun . . .*

"Scoutmaster Tim . . ."

Tim couldn't take his eyes off the man's face. Lying there like a ghoul. *Smiling.*

"Tim? Tim! *Tim!*"

Tim turned dazedly toward Max. The boy's eyes were bulging out of the whitened mask of his face. His nostrils were dilated like a bull's before it charged at a red cape.

"Wha . . . ?"

Which was when Tim felt something touch his hand. Which was when he looked down.

Which was when he saw it.

Which was when he screamed.

Chapter Thirteen

Max saw it first. A white stub protruding where Scout-master Tim had made the incision.

It looked silly. Like a balloon, maybe: one of those long, skinny ones that the clowns made balloon animals with at the Cavendish County Fair. Max had gotten one last year—a giraffe. The clown who'd made it had approached Max near the Shetland pony pen. He'd been short and dumpy, in slappy red shoes with the toes all squashed like they'd been stamped on by an elephant. The greasepaint on the clown's face had been badly applied over his stubbled cheeks; the red circles around his eyes were melting down his face in the heat, making him look like a sick beagle. His clown suit was dingy, with yellow patches under the armpits. When he smiled, Max saw brown grime slotted between his teeth. When he blew up the balloon, Max got a good whiff of him: rank sweat and something odder, scarier—a hint of shaved iron. The clown gave the balloon cruel twists with his nublike fingers; the balloon squealed as if in pain. The giraffe was all neck: a bulb of a head, thumblike legs. Max pictured the poor thing dragging its neck through the dirt across the Serengeti . . .

What now came out of the man's stomach reminded Max of that.

A balloon. Or as though the man's belly had blown a funny little bubble. Except this bubble was solid—Max could tell that immediately—solid and weirdly muscular.

Whatever it was, it relaxed back inside the man. The balloon or cord or tube—which was maybe the closest corollary: a thick shiny tube, like an inner tube but white instead of black, filled not with air but with some kind of thick pulsing fluid—the tube flattened back into the incision. Tim and Max watched, transfixed in the perfectly still eye of horror. The tube curved around in the man's stomach; it seemed to be made of different parts, different elements—it reminded Max of the snake ball Eef had found that afternoon. A few dozen snakes twisted into a ball, having sex.

Copulating, as his health teacher, Mrs. Fitzhue, would say, stringing the word out—*coppp-hugggh-late-ting.*

The thing flexed, constricting; the man's spine curled up as if parts of the thing were twined all through him—when the tube constricted, his body did, too. The idea that this *tube* could be spread out into every part of the man was terrifying.

"Scoutmaster Tim . . ." Max's words came out in a papery whisper, his mind tightening shut in baffled horror. "What . . . ?"

Tim didn't answer. The only sound was the creak of the floorboards beneath the man. A few of the cauterized veins split open; dark arterial blood wept down the man's pale skin.

The tube swelled monstrously, pushing itself out of the rubbery slit in a sudden surge. It emerged incredibly fast, its whiteness stretching to a milky translucence. Tim and Max shielded their faces instinctively, petrified it would explode, splattering them with the contents of its alien body—what could possibly be *inside* such a thing? Its guts were visible through that sheer web: crazed threshings and phantom pulsations—Max felt as if he were staring through a lard-streaked window into . . . God, into *what*? His fear was whetted to such a fine edge that he could actually feel it now: a disembodied ball of baby fingers inside his stomach, tickling him from the inside. That's what mortal terror felt like, he realized. Tiny fingers tickling you from the inside.

The tube deflated back inside the man's stomach for an instant, inflated even more so, and deflated again: its movement echoed a huge lung inhaling and exhaling. Only a few seconds had ticked off the clock, but Max felt as if a minor eternity had passed. Everything moved in slow motion . . .

Then, with a brutal whiplash, the world sped up.

The tube propelled itself out of the man's side in a series of fierce pulsations, or what Max's science teacher, Mr. Lowery, would have called *peristaltic flexes*. It came with a sly squishing noise, like very wet clay squeezed in a tightened fist.

The balloon or tube or whatever it was became something else. It twisted and split and became a thick white loop: it looked a little like the U-magnets Max used to push around iron filings in Mr. Lowery's class.

Could it be a hernia? Max's uncle Frank had one of those. He'd taken off his truss at a family picnic and showed it to him. It had looked like a fist pushing against the flatness of his stomach. *I tried to pick up two sacks of cement, Maximilian,* Uncle Frank had told him. *One sack too many. The pressure forced a little-bitty bit of my innards to squeeze right through the muscle.* Uncle Frank had then made a rude farting noise. *Out she come, slick as goose poop! It's peeking through like a clown nose, huh? See it there? Peek-a-boo, Maxxy, I see you!* Uncle Frank had given the herniated intestine a little squeeze. *Honk, honk! Oh! I feel my lunch moving through . . . yup, there goes the corn bread.* Uncle Frank had not been invited to the following year's picnic.

But this wasn't a hernia. Logic told Max so. A hernia was just what his mind had feverishly cobbled together to excuse what he was seeing. A hernia didn't move. A hernia didn't pulsate like that.

This thing . . .

This *thing* . . .

The loop became a pale ribbed tube roughly seven inches long. Thicker than a garden hose. Tapered slightly at its tip. It seemed to be made of millimeter-thick rings stacked atop one another. Each ring was gently rounded at its edge. Pearlescent beads squeezed from its surface, clinging to the tube like grains of sand to wet skin.

"Get back," Tim breathed. "Max, you get the hell *back*—"

The tube paused. Max got the weirdest sense that it was *presenting* itself. The gaudiest belle at the debutantes' ball. Appendages began to unglue themselves from its trunk. It reminded Max of the time he'd come upon a half-hatched bird struggling out of its egg, its wings pulling free of its body all stuck with webby strands of mucus . . . this looked much the same—or like a Swiss Army knife unfolding its many blades and attachments. These smaller appendages unkinked with the slow, showy grace of a contortionist; they unfurled tortuously in the cabin's dim light, making gluey lip-smack noises. They looked like the fleshy leaves of desert plants—*succulents*, those plants were called. Max learned that in science class, too. The very tips of these appendages split in half, lolling open. Max saw tiny fishbone teeth studding each mouth—it was sickeningly beautiful.

Peek-a-boo, Maxxy, I see you.

There is an emotion that operates on a register above sheer terror. It lives on a mindless dog-whistle frequency. Its existence is in itself a horrifying discovery: like scanning a shortwave radio in the dead of night and tuning in to an alien wavelength—a heavy whisper barely climbing above the static, voices muttering in a brutal language that human tongues could never speak.

Watching that lithe tube now hunt toward his Scoutmaster like a blind snake, Max hit that register.

"Tim Tim TIM!"

As a doctor, Tim had seen plenty of things in human stomachs. Rubber bath plugs and toy cars and Baltic coins and wedding rings. Most of these could be purged using simple regurgitative or saline laxative procedures. The human form held few surprises for him anymore.

But when that white tube threaded out of the incision and tip-tip-tipped toward him as if it were ascending an imaginary staircase, Tim squealed: a shocked piglike sound. He couldn't get a grip on his sudden fear: it slipped through the safety bars of his mind and threaded—*wormed*—into the shadowy pockets where nightmares grew.

His scalpel slashed wildly, severing the leading inch of the flickering white tube. The amputated nub fell between Tim's feet. It writhed and leaked brown fluid. Its plantlike appendages studded with tiny mouths gawped open and shut.

Tim's arms pinwheeled madly as he tipped backward, landing awkwardly on his ass. The remainder of the tube sucked itself back into the incision like a strand of spaghetti going into a greedy child's mouth, whipping and snapping and spraying stinking brown gouts.

"Cover your mouth!" Tim screamed. *"Don't let any of it touch you!"*

Fists battering the door so hard that dust sifted down from the rafters. The boys' massing voices, dominated by Kent's.

"Tim! *Max!* What's going on? Open the door!"

The stranger's body rocked side to side. His feet slipped off the chesterfield and hit the floor with a brittle rattle.

The tube now shot straight up out of the wound, rising in a monstrous ripple. A foot. Two feet. Three feet of oily tube weaved out of the man—*the dead man,* Tim prayed, *the dead man who please God feels none of this*—like a headless albino cobra out of an Indian fakir's basket. It threshed like some obscene bullwhip, leaking brownish fluid. It stood quivering for a long instant, flicking back and forth: it looked as if it was tasting the air, or hunting for smaller and weaker creatures within striking distance.

Which was when the stranger woke up.

His eyelids fluttered, then his eyes went wide—wider than ever should be possible. It was as if the man had awoken from a terrible dream only to find that those terrors were dwarfed by those in the waking world. He loosed a volley of piercing screams—they almost sounded like the snarls of a terrified dog.

"Stay away, Max!" Tim yelled. "Stay back!"

The stranger reached instinctively for the thing coming out of him—his hand died before reaching it, his fingers softening into a caress. His eyes were miserably bright and aware, bulging with pure shock and horror: the eyes of a little boy who'd come face-to-face with the nameless horror lurking under his bed.

"Ug . . ." was the single syllable that came out of his mouth. A caveman's grunt of disgust. "Uhg . . . ug . . ."

"*Tim!*" Kent screamed. "Open this freakin' *door* right *now!*"

The tips of a boy's head bobbed at the cabin's lone high window, a pair of hands hooked on the sill—Ephraim's hands; they had to be Eef's—set to boost their owner up for a look inside.

Tim realized he was watching a man die.

He'd seen it before, of course—but Max hadn't. Here was a man neither of them knew the first thing about. And now, in a way that was somehow obscene, Max would witness this man during the most private moment any human being would ever have: the moment of his death.

The man's eyes rolled back. He exhaled. Mercifully, his eyes closed.

The tube dropped onto the man's chest like a length of rope. It lay in a loose coil for a moment before twitching and crawling under the man's shirt. Tim imagined it working up the man's neck and into his mouth. Thrashing its way down his throat and back into his stomach to link up with the rest of itself. Eating its own tail—or its own head?

Out of his peripheral vision, he saw Max reaching for the soldering iron—

"Don't!" Tim said. "Don't you fucking dare, Max."

The tube wrapped around the man's bird-thin neck, encircling it in a greasy ringlet. It elongated slightly, the many rings that constituted its body thinning with cruel, purposeful tension.

Jesus Christ, it's constricting, Tim's mind yammered. *It's choking him.*

Tim tried to stand, but his legs were cramped with the sudden dump of lactic acid. He pulled himself forward. His hand slipped on the severed link of tube, which pulped under his palm like a rotten banana.

The man's face had turned the blue of a sun-bleached parking ticket. Tim was shocked that this thing—

It's a worm, the Undervoice said. *A fucking WORM that's what the fuck it is and you better wrap your head around that buddy, oh pal-o-mine*

—had the strength to do what it was doing.

He dragged himself forward, scrabbling for the scalpel that had skittered under the chesterfield's skirt. He hunted amid the dust bunnies and insect corpses while a thick, hopeless whimper built in his throat . . .

Kent's fists pounded on the door but that sound was far away now—a dream-noise not attached to the waking world. The tube flexed. The man's neck bent at a sudden unnatural angle. His body stiffened before going limp.

Oh no, Tim thought. His next thought was: *Oh thank God.*

The tube released from the man's throat, retreating once again into the incision. Tim grabbed at it through the man's shirt. The thought of touching it directly brought on a mind-numbing revulsion. He pictured it feeling like a lubed length of nautical rope burning through his fingers. But when his hand closed around it, the tube was warm and pulsating and horribly smooth. Its flagellate body was already going limp as if it had a pinhole leak. He slashed the scalpel through the man's shirt and through the thing's body. It was like cutting through ripe stinking cheese. It took no effort at all.

He saw inside the severed portion. There was no identifiable anatomy to the thing. No vertebrae or organs. It was full of loose brownish goo. Some massive carnivorous leech. The unsevered portion slid sluggishly back inside the wound. Its skin continued to weep those pearly pustules.

The man's stomach deflated. Brown filth bubbled out of the wound. Half-digested bits of chesterfield foam bobbed on its surface.

Squinting, Max thought he saw something deeper inside. Two objects? Long and glinting, their angles man-made.

Tim and Max stood breathing heavily in the dim light of the cabin. The hacked-off portion of the tube slid out of the vent in the man's shirt, hitting the floor and wadding up like a huge tube sock. The brown goo had run over Tim's fingers and down his knuckles like watery molasses. Overcome by instinctive revulsion, Tim wiped his fingers on his pants—and when even that closeness was too much, he unbuttoned them, yanked them down and off, wiped his hands on the fabric, and hurled the pants into the corner. He stood shivering in his underwear. His thighs were unbearably thin: knobbed sticks on a forest floor.

"Jesus," he said softly, then gave Max a sharp look. "Did you swallow any of that stuff? Get any in your mouth or eyes?"

"I don't think so."

"That's not good enough."

"No," Max said. "I didn't get anything in me."

"You kept the gauze over your mouth the whole time?"

"Yes."

"Okay . . . okay, good."

Tim staggered to the table and drank scotch right out of the bottle.

"If you drink whiskey, you'll never get worms, Max."

Kent pounded on the door unrelentingly. "Tim! *Tiiiiim!*"

The Scoutmaster stumbled to the sink and washed his hands. He did this for some time; the hard island water made it difficult to get a good lather going. His legs trembled like a newborn foal's. When he was finished, his hands were a raw, nail-scraped red. Did it matter anymore? He shuffled into the bedroom, not speaking to Max, coming out with pants on.

He kicked the chair away from the door—he had to kick three times; he seemed to lack the energy to do it properly—and flung the door open to catch Kent red-faced and fuming, his hand raised in mid-knock.

"Get away from the fucking door, Kent." Tim's voice belonged to something recently dug from its grave. "Get your ass far, far away."

Chapter Fourteen

 Tim sat at the fire and explained what he could. Most of it failed to make sense to him at all.

"A *worm*?"

"Yeah, Newton: a worm. Not a night crawler or something you'd dig out of your mom's garden. A tapeworm."

Tim had experience with tapeworms. Any GP would. They were a common enough affliction. A person could pick them up anywhere.

As easy as petting your dog. Providing your dog had rolled in a pile of shit earlier that day—as dogs tend to do—you could get microscopic particles of said shit on your fingers without even knowing. A thousand eggs stuck between the whorls of your fingertips. And after petting ole Spot, let's say you ate a handful of popcorn and licked the salt off your fingers. Bingo-bango-bongo. You've got worms.

At least once a month, he'd see a kid in the waiting room scratching his keister through the seat of his pants and say to himself: *worms.* One time a kid's mother handed him an ice cream tub with one of her child's chalky turds inside. "I thought you'd want a sample," she'd told him solemnly. "For proof."

Tim would prescribe an oral remedy that demolished the tapeworm colony over a few days. Tapeworms were, at most, a nuisance.

"He's dead," Tim said simply.

Ephraim said: "From *worms*?"

"No, Eef—from *a* worm."

Kent said: "How the hell can a tapeworm kill someone? I had worms when I was eight. I crapped the little buggers out."

"I know," Tim said. "I gave your mother the medicine to do it."

This one wasn't the size of any regular worm, Tim thought. He'd heard that beef tapeworms—the ones you can get from eating tainted meat—could get pretty big. Twenty, thirty feet. He recalled a case study where a doctor pulled one out of a cattle rancher's leg. It had balled up between the layers of muscle. A lump the size of a baseball. The doctor made a slit into the muscle and pulled it out of the rancher's leg like teasing out a piece of thread. The worm was incredibly skinny, like a strand of angel hair pasta. It snapped. The rest of the worm died inside the muscle and started to rot. The rancher almost lost his leg. But even so, the longest worms weren't really that *thick.*

Ephraim said: "What did it do to him?"

What could Tim tell them? The *truth*? The truth—which even he wanted to avoid—was that the tapeworm had done what tapeworms do: eaten everything the man was supposed to eat. Like having a furnace turned up to full blast inside of you: everything you throw into it, it burns up. No fuel left for you. Tim thought about the blood-leeched whiteness of the man's flesh and realized the worm may've consumed other things, too. His blood and enzymes. That would have shut down his kidneys and liver and other organs . . . some kind of vampire.

But he couldn't say this. It would terrify the boys. And yet he'd nearly told them anyway—sharing the terror seemed like the only way to defuse it, even minimally. But they were just kids. Even now, with the mainland and hospitals and *help* seeming so far away, Tim understood his obligation to these boys and to their parents. He must keep them safe. Scout's honor.

"Are you okay?" Newton asked. "You and Max? Did anything . . . y'know, *touch* you?"

The boys stared at Tim, all probably wondering the same thing. Now, in the aftermath, Tim wondered why he'd done it. Not the operation itself, but involving Max. He'd told himself that he needed help—no surgeon operates alone. But now he was less sure.

"Tim?" Kent said, his eyes holding a rook's sheen. "Did . . . anything . . . *touch* . . . you?"

Fuck off, you pushy bastard, the Undervoice spat.

"I don't think so," Tim said. "It happened very fast."

Kent turned to Max. "You okay, man?"

Max nodded, eyes not leaving the ground. When Tim saw this, a cold, hard stone lodged somewhere in his diaphragm.

You made a mistake, Tim, HAL 9000 said. *Don't go compounding it.*

"What happened?" Ephraim said. "Tell us."

Tim nibbled his lip compulsively, as if his unconscious desire was to consume his own flesh. He caught himself, smiled queasily—his eyes shone in the firelight, hubbed by skin drawn tight over his sockets—and said: "I cut into the man's stomach. The worm was in there. Nesting. It came out through the incision. It crawled up the man's chest and wrapped around his neck. It . . ." He couldn't stop swallowing. "Killed him."

"You cut him up?" Kent asked, incredulous.

"I told you, it happened so fast." Tim's mouth was a dry wick, his spit all dried up. "It was like something out of a dream."

"Amazing," said Kent. The sneering derision was unmistakable. He sounded very much like his policeman father.

"I was scared," Tim said. It came out as a whisper. He observed the boys' faces clustered round the fire—all wearing matching looks of diminished respect—and wished he could take those honest words back.

"Yeah, well, this is no time to be scared, Tim," Kent said.

Tim wanted to slap the mouthy little prick across the face, but his strength had utterly deserted him.

Mosquitoes jigged around their heads. *Why aren't they landing on me?* Tim wondered. His hands were clean, yet they still felt sticky with goo; he felt it in the creases of his fingers, in his nail beds—an antic, wriggling itch. He closed his eyes and envisioned that goo drooling out of the worm's cleaved body. The firelight glowed against his eyelids, lighting up the capillaries that braided under his skin.

"So it's dead?" Newton said.

Max nodded. "Scoutmaster Tim cut it in half."

"It was effectively dead before that," Tim said. "Once the host is dead, the parasite dies, too."

"Why would it do that?" Newton asked. "Wrap around the man's neck and kill him? That's like a baby strangling its mom or something."

Tim gave a helpless shrug. "Worms don't have any brains to speak of. Worms shouldn't grow to that size. But that's what happened. We saw it. You've got to trust the evidence of your eyes."

Newton said: "Do we even know the guy's name?"

His words fell like an anvil. Suddenly the man's name seemed critical. The idea of a man dying as a stranger surrounded by other strangers struck the boys as staggeringly tragic.

"I want to go home," Shelley said softly. "Take us *home*, Scoutmaster. *Please*."

In the firelight, Shelley's face molded into a beseeching expression—*mock-beseeching?* The expression rang hollow, inorganic and somehow clumsy, like an animal trying to replicate human endeavor: a bear riding a bicycle or a monkey playing a milk-carton ukulele. In Tim's fevered mind, it seemed like the boy was purposefully stirring fear within the group by asking for something beyond Tim's capacity to deliver.

"Tomorrow, Shelley. We can leave—"

"Why not tonight, Tim?" Shelley said, adopting Kent's derisive tone. "Why can't you get us home tonight?"

Because I'm too fucking tired, you awful little shit. Tired and hungry as hell.

"Tomorrow. I promise."

Shelley stared at Tim—there was something insectile about his gaze. The wind gusted, blowing the flames slant-ways, and in that instant, Tim watched Shelley's face liquefy like hot wax, the skin running, bones shifting and grinding like tectonic plates to arrange themselves into something infinitely more horrifying.

Kent said: "I want to see it."

Tim said: "It?"

"The worm, Tim. I want to see the worm."

"No."

Kent gave his Scoutmaster a sidelong look, eyeing him down his hawklike nose the way a sniper stares down a rifle's sights.

Without another word, Kent stood and strode off toward the cabin. Tim was dismayed to find he lacked the voice to stop him.

Test subject 4. Beta series.
GUINEA PIG (Zoologix, Inc; breeding batch
EE-76-2)
Subject's pre-test weight: 1350 grams

/Date: 07.19/

07:00	Introduced modified hydatid (Genetic Recombination M3-11) via injection. Between 100 and 250 post-embryonic-stage eggs delivered via liposome vehicle. Subject is alert and energetic. Eyes are clear. Evidencing no overt signs of distress or pain.
08:00	Subject unchanged.
09:00	Subject unchanged.
10:00	Subject unchanged.
10:13	Subject emits series of squeals.
10:47	Subject appears disoriented. Bumping into bars of its enclosure. Emitting distressed squeals at a significantly

higher pitch and with increased frequency.

11:07   Subject is observed chewing bars of its enclosure.

11:09   Subject is observed consuming cedar shavings lining its enclosure.

11:15   Subject is observed consuming own fecal matter.

11:22   Sizable evacuation of larval-stage hydatid via excretory tract.

11:41   Subject emits squeals reaching a prolonged high pitch before ceasing. [post-test note: subject vocalizations cease at this point]

11:56   Subject is observed consuming portion of left front paw. Eyes glazed. Breathing rapid. Overall bodily torpor. Subject appears either unaware of its actions or beyond pain. Bleeding is minimal.

12:03   First gastrointestinal rupture observed. Occurs along transmedial cleft. Fissure observed to be 1/8in. Quantity of adolescent-stage hydatid worms observed exiting the subject's body.

12:08   Subject exhibiting signs of late-stage morbidity. Noticeable stiffening of joints, labored breathing, milky film developing on eyes. Subject's mouth

opening and closing repeatedly. Appears
to be chewing on the air.

12:16   Second   gastrointestinal   rupture
        observed. 1/2in below original fissure.
        Large   quantity   of   adolescent-stage
        hydatid worms observed extruding from
        subject's stomach cavity.

12:19   Subject/host deceased.

12:22   Remaining hydatids deceased. Test
        concludes.

Test duration: 5 hours 22 minutes
Subject's post-test weight: 490 grams
Total weight loss: 860 grams

_____

Chapter Fifteen

Fifteen minutes later, Scoutmaster Tim would be locked and shivering inside the cabin's utility closet.

It would be Kent's idea. He would suggest that the boys lock their Scoutmaster up for a rational reason—but ultimately he would do it simply because he *could*. There was something thrilling about leading the others in such an enormous act of rebellion.

Kent set off from the fire at a determined clip. He figured Tim may try to stop him, but more and more it seemed he lacked the resolve. Tim was scared. He'd said so, practically blubbering his guts out around the fire.

Kent wasn't scared, though. Hell, no. It wasn't any part of his character. They needed a proper leader right now, not a big ole 'fraidy-cat.

The other boys would follow. Kent was positive. All it required was for him to take that first step. Who the hell was Tim, anyway? In the view of Kent's father, Mr. Timothy Riggs was a lonely middle-aged fairy. Not a pedo—Jeff Jenks would cut his own balls off before he'd leave his kid in the woods with one of *those*. No, according to "Big" Jeff, Tim Riggs was probably just a willowy, sorrowful queer who lived alone in his big house on the bluffs.

You've got every right to see what's inside that cabin, son— every legal right! Kent heard his father saying. *Don't let this noodle-wristed flamer make that decision for you. Not now, with the stakes this high. Don't you see what he's done? The quack's cut open a complete stranger*—gutted *him, field-dressed the poor bastard like a five-point buck; he's admitted as much—and now he wants to cover up his act. A man is* dead, *son! It's up to you to get this under control. What, Tim's going to stop you?*

"Listen, Kent, it's a total mess in there," Max said from behind. "I mean, a *dead* guy. No joke. Why the hell do you want to see it so bad?"

"I wanna see it, too," came Shelley's voice from someplace in the dark.

Kent laid his hands on Max's shoulders the same way his father did when one of his deputies got a case of the jitters.

"Max, *I* need to see. Okay? If I don't see what the problem is, how can you expect me to deal with it?"

Max's brow furrowed. "Yeah, but—"

"But nothing. We have every right."

"Okay, but you better put gauze over your mouth and eyes."

"Why?"

"Infection."

Kent nodded somberly. "Yeah. Good thinking."

Tim had nearly caught up. Kent heard his labored breathing like a sick Pekingese. "Kent Jenks! If you set one foot inside that—"

Kent shouldered his way through the door. The smell hit him like a ball-peen hammer. Sweetly fruity top notes, rancid decay lurking underneath.

The man lay on the chesterfield with his wrists and ankles bound. His shirt was slashed open, his white flesh glazed with sludge. He would look almost peaceful if not for those skinned-back lips setting his mouth in a horrible leer. He looked like a man holding a carnal secret.

A segment of the worm lay on the floor. To Kent, it looked like a much bigger version of the condom he and Charlie Swanson had once found under the football bleachers at Montague High. Charlie had poked the condom with a stick. Sluggish late-summer flies took flight, their drone thick in Kent's ears. *What is it?* he'd said. Charlie said: *You've never seen a 'domer? You pull it over your wick before you screw a chick so you don't get her preggers.*

Charlie had two older brothers. He *knew* things. Kent remembered feeling vaguely ashamed of his innocence. Also, a little sick.

But the sight of the man stunned him now. He was *dead*. Maybe Kent had expected it to be like his grandmother's funeral: Grandma lying restfully in a mahogany coffin in the beige parlor while a pianist played "Nearer My God to Thee." Serene with her eyes closed and her cheeks gently rouged.

This man was graceless in death. A ring of purple bruises encircling his neck. A brown shitlike mess leaking out of his side. One eye wide open, the other at half-mast like he was tipping a dirty wink. Fruit flies shimmering over his wound to drink the sweet filth. The man had died unloved and without dignity.

Kent wished he could act as his father would have right now. He'd cordon off the area and call for a forensic appraisal. He'd grab a bullhorn and calmly say: *Disperse, people. Nothing to see here.*

But that wasn't true, was it? Jesus, there was *everything* to see here.

Fear stole into Kent's heart like a safecracker. It embarrassed him—he'd pushed for this outcome, hadn't he?—but right then he wanted to take it all back. He wished he were on the mainland, safe in his bed with his Labrador retriever,

Argo, sleeping soundly beside him. He wished for that with every atom of his body.

Tim plowed through the throng of boys, splashing rubbing alcohol on the fronts of their shirts.

"Pull them over your mouth and nose! Hey—do it! *Now!*"

The boys obeyed. Their gazes were fogged with shock above their pulled-up collars—all except Shelley's, whose eyes held an excitable glittery quality.

Tim shoved Kent. Both hands planted in the boy's chest. Kent went down so hard his ass bounced off the floor.

"I told you to goddamn well stay out of here, didn't I, Kent?"

Tim hunched over the fallen boy. He grabbed his shoulder roughly and shook him. Kent's body rag-dolled in his grip.

"This is the site of a *disease*! Now you all run the risk of infection!"

Tim ran his hands through his hair, which stood up in smoke- and sweat-hardened spikes. His mouth hung open like a panting dog's, the flesh drawn tight over his cheekbones.

You're acting irrational, Tim, HAL 9000 said coolly. *You've harmed a child now—and is it really the first time you've harmed a child tonight?*

"Worms spread by *contact*," he said, ignoring that voice. "Do you understand? If you eat something full of worms or worm eggs, then you *get* worms. There's nothing for you to *do*, Kent. There's nothing to be fucking *fixed*. If your dad, the mighty Jeff Jenks, tried his dick-swinging act here, he'd end up just like that guy over there. Okay?"

Tim pictured Jenks the senior: his blue uniform stretched over his gut, buttons taxed to their tensile limit, hairy-knuckled hands hooked through his belt loops as he surveyed the scene with a caustic eye. *Wellsy wellsy wellsy, Doc, what's the rhubarb here?*

"Don't you talk about my dad like that," Kent said weakly.

"*Shut up!*" Tim slumped heavily at the kitchen table. "Just *shut . . . up!* I mean it, Kent. If you pull any more shit, I will truss you up like a Christmas turkey. Do you know one goddamn *thing* about contagion—any of you? We don't know what we're dealing with here. Could be orally borne. Could be waterborne. Jesus, it could be airborne."

"Then why cut him open?" Shelley said, covering his mouth so his words were muffled by his fingers. "Why drag Max into it? Or us?"

Tim looked from boy to boy to boy, seeing nothing he could recognize anymore: only disdain and suspicion and slowly kindling rage. That trust he'd worked so hard to build up, an undertaking of many years, had worn down to a brittle strand. The possibility that it could snap at any moment left him paralyzed with fear.

He pointed to the cleaved segment of worm on the floor. "That is like nothing in nature, boys. Do you understand me? These things should not *exist*. It's nothing God ever made. So we have to be incredibly careful. We have to step very lightly."

"We should burn down the cabin," Shelley mumbled.

Tim shook his head. "That could just put the contagion into the air. What we are going to do is this: Go outside. Sit by the fire." Tim worried the ragged edge off one fingernail with his incisors and swallowed it convulsively. "We'll wait for the boat to come the day after tomorrow. That's all we *can* do."

The fixed drone of a helicopter worked its way across the open water. It seemed to hover directly above them. Coin-bright wedges of light—the glow of a searchlight—shafted through apertures in the roof. The helicopter's wings sent gusts of sea-scented air through gaps in the cabin's log walls. The light dimmed abruptly as the helicopter continued out to sea.

"Will the boat even come, Scoutmaster Tim?" Newton asked.

"Of course. We'll all go home. Your parents will be thrilled to see you. They'll send a research team out. Now come on. Let's . . . let's . . . go on out . . . outsi—"

A wave of dizziness rocked the Scoutmaster. Gnatlike specks crowded his vision. His sinuses burnt with ozone: the same eye-watering sensation as if he'd jumped off the dock into the bay and salt water rocketed up his nose.

He licked his threadlike lips. "We have to . . ."

Kent hauled himself up. His eyes reflected a horrible awareness.

"You're *sick*," he said in a trembling voice. "You're infected. You've got the *worms*."

"I don't—" A childlike sick feeling hived in Tim's stomach: as if he'd eaten too much cotton candy at the Abbotsford carnival and gone on the Tilt-A-Whirl. "It's so important that we . . ."

"We have to quarantine him," Kent said to the others. "He could make us all sick. Like him."

Kent advanced with a determined gait. Tim held his arms out. Jesus! A pair of fleshy javelins. He pushed the boy. His hands sunk harmlessly into the boy's chest as Kent's shoulders sagged to dampen the impact.

Tim stumbled away on legs that felt like wooden stilts screwed into his hips. "Please," he said. He pushed again, kittenishly. Kent was smiling now. It was not a kind look.

This transgression had been building in Kent—it enfolded him with a cold sense of assurance. He was *right* to act against his elder. If you exerted your will and held fast to that course of action, things inevitably worked out. All the

121

gifts that came to you—gifts befitting your inflexible strength of character—would be rightfully earned.

He pushed his Scoutmaster. Tim fell comically: arms outstretched and mouth open like a fish in its dying gasp. He hit the floor with a spine-jangling thud. His intestines jogged in the loosening vault of his gut. He did a very natural but terribly unfortunate thing.

Tim passed gas. A reedy trumpeting note that daggered through the shocked silence. A ripe reek wafted through the room.

"I'm sorry," Tim said. "I don't—"

Shelley snickered. "You *stink*."

Kent pinned Tim with that rifle-sights look. "Lock him in the closet."

"No," Tim said, the word escaping his mouth as a sob.

The boys were held in a dimple of tension. Many possibilities tiptoed along the edge of that moment.

Next they were upon him. Shelley went first. Kent followed. They surged down upon their Scoutmaster, leapt on him, screaming and grabbing. Ephraim next. Then Max, with a low, agonized moan. They were filled with a giddy exuberance. All of them felt it—even Newton, who came last, regretfully, mumbling "No, no, no," even as he fell into the fray, unable to fight the queasy momentum. They were carried away on a wave of thick, urgent, blind desire.

It happened so swiftly. The pressure that'd been building since last night, collecting in drips and drabs: in the *crunch* of the radio shattering in a squeal of feedback; in the black helicopter hovering high above them; in the snake ball squirming in the wet rocks; in the sounds emanating from the cabin as Tim and Max operated on the man; and most of all in the horrifying decline of their Scoutmaster, a man they'd known nearly all their lives reduced to a human anatomy chart, a herky-jerky skeleton. It brewed within them, a throbbing tension in their chests that required release—somehow, by any means necessary—and now, like a dark cloud splitting with rain, it vented. The boys couldn't fight it; they weren't properly themselves. They were a mob, and the mob ruled.

It's just a game, a few of the boys thought. It was a game as long as they could ignore the look of sick terror in their Scoutmaster's eyes. The helpless fear of an adult—which ultimately looked not much different than the helpless fear of an infant. It was a game as long as they could ignore the dead man on the chesterfield leaking brown muck.

A game, a game, a game . . .

They dragged Tim to the closet. He unleashed a series of shrill yipping shrieks. He was terrified of forfeiting control—of how *fast* it had happened. Terrified of that closet. But mostly he was terrified of whatever might very well be inside of him.

"Please, boys," he whimpered. "Please no—I need *help*—"

They would not listen. The wave reached its mad crest. They pulled the Scoutmaster with ease. With his weight distributed among the five boys, he weighed no more than a child. Ephraim's hands slipped under Tim's shirt. He felt the abrupt cliff where the flesh fell off his lowest rib. His body was divoted and warped. Ephraim's hands fell upon Tim's stomach . . . he reared back, shocked by the fretful lashings that met his fingers.

Shelley's lips skinned back from his teeth. He looked like a hyena prowling among the corpses on a battlefield. Kent flung the closet door open. It was empty save a few jangling coat hangers. They barrel-rolled Tim inside. The Scoutmaster's quivering fingers stuck out through the doorjamb. Ephraim gently folded them into the darkness of the closet.

They set their weight against the door. Their breath came out in jagged gusts. Kent dashed into the bedroom, returning

123

with a combination lock. He fastened it through the lock hasp and clipped it shut.

The boys came back to themselves with a jolt. Max and Ephraim passed nervous unsmiling looks. Their Scoutmaster's whimpers carried under the door.

"When do we let him out?" Newton said.

"When the boat gets here," Kent said coldly. "No sooner."

"What if it doesn't show up?"

Kent said: "Shut up, Newt."

Nobody bothered asking for the combination; they knew Kent wouldn't tell them. The bottle of scotch stood uncapped on the table. A man's drink. *General George Patton drank a shot of cheap scotch before battle,* Kent's dad always said, *and a glass of good scotch after a victory.*

What was this if not a victory? When the boat arrived tomorrow, his quick thinking would be hailed.

"Go on, Kent," Shelley told him. "Have a drink."

Max said, "No—*don't*—"

But Kent had already raised the bottle to his lips. It went down like molten iron. He sawed his arm across his mouth. His grimace became a broad grin.

"Everything's going to be okay, guys."

From the sworn testimony of Nathan Erikson, given before the Federal Investigatory Board in connection with the events occurring on Falstaff Island, Prince Edward Island:

Q: Mr. Erikson, state how you came to be associated with Dr. Clive Edgerton.

A: I was just out of school. A few guys who graduated with me caught on as associate profs, but they were the creme de la creme. I was more like the flotsam.

Q: At loose ends?

A: You could say so. Not a lot of companies have much use for a theoretical molecular biologist whose doctoral dissertation was "The Human Aging Process as Relating to the *C. elegans* worm."

Q: *C. elegans* worm?

A: It's a roundworm. About a millimeter long. *Caenorhabditis elegans,* but everyone just calls it *C. elegans*. During its lifetime it exhibits many familiar signs of human aging: reduced movement, wrinkling, tissue degradation, decreased ability to fight infection. I was trying to locate genes that might slow down the human aging process.

Q: A noble ambition.

A: Yeah, well. I was blinded by science.

Q: How did Edgerton know of you?

A: A lot of researchers sniffed around the program, right? They figured they could poach a recent grad—someone willing to do the scut work.

Q: So Edgerton sought you out?

A: It was more a situation of mutual desperation.

Q: What drew him to you?

A: Like I said, the fact that I came cheap and didn't have any other options. But I had done work with the *C. elegans* worm—which bears about the same similarity to the hydatid as a minnow does to a great white shark. And neither creature is anything like what Edgerton bred.

Q: *He* bred? Didn't you both work on the mutated specimen?

A: Listen . . . I'll always carry the guilt. I could tell you that the outcome was unknown—that I was pursuing science—and if I'd had an inkling of what was to come I'd've burned that lab to cinders. After all this is over you'll send me to prison. I deserve that. Deserve *more*, but for some crimes there exists no fit punishment. I was part of it, but I was the lesser part. On every level.

Q: How so?

A: Clive Edgerton is a genius. He's also ratshit crazy, pardon my French, possibly a sociopath, but undoubtedly a genius. Even though my IQ is likely higher than most people's in this room, I was no more than Clive's lab monkey. I can't *see* biological processes the way he does. Can't see the chains in order to break and reorder them. So I knew what we were doing, yes—theoretically, anyway—but I didn't create any of it. I can't.

Q: But you knew?

A: Yes.

Q: And you told nobody?

A: That's right.

Q: Why?

A: Trade secrets. We were working on something that, if successful, would have been a billion-dollar enterprise. Edgerton was working under a grant from a biopharmaceutical company. Secrecy was crucial.

Q: So crucial that you'd risk lives?

A: We didn't *know* lives were at . . . We're talking about one of the three holy grails of modern medicine: a cure for male pattern baldness, a method to reverse the aging process, and a means to lose weight without effort. If anyone invents a pill that you can pop at night and wake up with a fuller head of hair or the crow's-feet diminished around your eyes or five pounds lighter? There's no saying how much that could be worth. Clive used to cite that old motto: *You can never be too rich or too thin.* He'd say, "If I can make the rich thin, they'll make *me* rich."

Chapter Sixteen

Toward midnight, Max stood down by the shore. The sky was salted with remote stars. The beach was a bonelike strip unfurling to the shoreline. The sea advanced up the shore with a series of minute sucking inhales. It sounded like a huge toothless creature swallowing the island.

Newton joined him. His hand thrummed against Max's bare arm. His fear leapt the threshold between their bodies— Max felt it now, too.

"We shouldn't have done that to the Scoutmaster."

"He's sick, Newt."

"I saw that. But not a closet. Am I wrong? Not that way."

"You did it, too," Max said tiredly.

Newton swallowed and nodded. "I did. It could have been what my mom calls a coping mechanism. You know, when things get rough, we do things to make it better. Or just to distract ourselves. Do you think that's what it was, Max?"

"We got carried away, Newt. That's all."

Last summer, Max had shared his house with a family of shearwaters—a much fleeter version of a puffin. They colonized the cliffs overlooking the Atlantic, nesting in the rocks. But due to a population explosion, shearwaters had begun to nest in the houses of North Point. They'd chip away the Gyprock exterior, tugging loose Styrofoam and pink insulation to make room for their nests.

A family of shearwaters made one above Max's bedroom window. In the morning he'd crane his neck and see the daddy shearwater poke his head out of the hole he'd chipped in the house's facade, darting it in both directions before arrowing out over the water to hunt.

Max's father, however, wasn't impressed. The lawn was covered in Styrofoam and pink rags of insulation. The birds would wreck the home's resale value, he griped—despite the fact that he'd lived in North Point his whole life and would likely die in this house. He drove to the Home Hardware, returning with a bottle of insulating foam sealant. He clambered up a ladder to the nest, shooed the birds away, stuck the nozzle into the hole, and pumped in sealant until it billowed out and hardened to a puffy crust. He climbed back down with a self-satisfied smile.

But the shearwaters were back the next day. They'd torn away at the sealant, ripping it off in chunks with their sickle-shaped beaks. Now the lawn was covered in Styrofoam, insulation, *and* sealant. Max's father repeated the procedure, believing the birds would relent. But shearwaters are cousins to homing pigeons—they always come back. *I should shoot them*, Max's father groused, though he could never do such a thing.

Still, he was angry—that particular anger of humans defied by the persistence of nature. He drove back to Home Hardware, returning with another can of sealant and a few feet of heavy-duty chicken wire. Using tin snips, he cut the wire into circles roughly the size of the hole. Clambering up the ladder, he made a layer cake of sorts: a layer of sealant, then chicken wire, sealant, wire, sealant, wire. *Okay, birds*, he'd said. *Figure that out.*

Max returned from school the next day to find a dead

shearwater in the bushes. The daddy—he could tell by its dark tail feathers. It lay with its neck twisted at a horrible angle. Its beak was broken—half of it was snapped off. Its eyes were filmy-gray, like pewter. It'd made a mess: shreds of sealant dotted the lawn. But his father's handiwork held strong. The daddy bird must've broken its neck—had it become so frustrated, so crazy, that it'd flown into the barrier until its neck snapped?

When Max's father saw the dead bird, his jaw tightened, he blinked a few times very fast, then quietly he said: *I just wanted them to find someplace else to live.*

In the middle of the night Max had been woken by peeping. The sound was coming from the walls. Max padded into his parents' room. His father rubbed sleep-crust from his eyes and followed Max back to his bedroom. When he heard those noises, his face did a strange thing.

At three o'clock in the morning, Max's dad climbed the ladder. His housecoat flapped in the salt breeze. Using a screwdriver and vise grips, he tore out the sealant and chicken wire, working so manically that he nearly fell. By the time he'd ripped it away the peeps had stopped. He reached deep inside the hole, into a small depression he'd not realized was there. He placed whatever he'd found in the pockets of his housecoat with great reverence.

In the kitchen, his face white with shock, he laid them on the table: the mama bird and two baby birds. The mama bird's wing was broken. The babies were small and gray-blue, still slick with the gummy liquid inside their eggs. All three were still.

I didn't know, was all Max's dad could say. *If I'd known I'd've never . . . I got carried away.*

Max thought of this now, in relation to what they'd done to Scoutmaster Tim.

They'd gotten carried away, was all. It happened to

adults, too. When you got angry and frustrated and scared enough, it was so, *so* easy to get carried away.

"I never seen a dead person before," said Newton. "My hamster died. Yoda. He got out of his cage and got his neck broke by getting caught in a sliding closet door. He was just a hamster but man, he died in my hands. His neck hung all funny. I couldn't stop crying." Newton swabbed his wrist across his eyes and fetched a deep sigh. "We buried him in a shoe box in the backyard. I made a cross out of Popsicle sticks. That's kinda dumb. Jeez. Don't tell the other guys, huh? They'll rag me a new one."

Max's father had buried the birds in a shoe box, too, lining it with lush coffin velvet. "It's not dumb, Newt. It was the right thing to do, I think."

"Yeah?" Newt smiled, but his expression darkened by degrees. "Do you think we could let the Scoutmaster out?"

"Kent's the only one who knows the lock combination."

The boys squinted at the pinpricks of light on the mainland. There appeared to be more than usual. Smaller lights zipped back and forth beneath its awning like phosphorescent ants pouring out of a neon anthill. A remote sense of calm settled over Max. A sense of Zen forbearance, even, as his body marshaled its remaining strength—as if it knew, in advance of his mind, that he'd need every ounce of it over the coming hours and days. Distantly, Max wondered if this was how men felt in a war. Even more distantly he wondered about his parents: in bed, probably, sleeping soundly with no earthly idea what was happening.

"Do you really think the boat will show up?"

"Shut up, Newt. Please."

Part Two

INFESTATION

Lead news item from CNN.com, October 22:

FALSTAFF ISLAND QUARANTINED DUE TO BIOLOGICAL INCIDENT OF UNKNOWN ORIGIN

As of 7:15 a.m. the tiny (18-square-kilometer) island of Falstaff, 3 miles off the northern coast of Prince Edward Island, has been officially quarantined.

A memo released by the Military Attaché office cites the cause as "a biological incident of unknown origin." This could mean an outbreak of contagious disease, fungal infection, parasite, or a water- or airborne contaminant that poses a significant risk to human and animal populations.

The military continues to mass in the small town of North Point. Sources indicate the military is working jointly with the Public Health Agency— specifically the Centre for Contagious Disease.

As yet no information has surfaced regarding either the specific cause behind the quarantine or the nature of the biological threat.

According to the military, the island is currently unoccupied.

Chapter Seventeen

They had locked him in the closet. Their Scoutmaster. The town's only doctor. Almost unbelievably, this had happened. They'd ganged up. Kent and Ephraim, and Shelley with his ball-bearing eyes. Even Newton and Max had joined in.

You deserved it, Tim, HAL 9000 chastised. *You put the boys in danger. Knowingly or not, but they were your responsibility. Remember the Scout Code.*

How was it my fault? Tim asked himself. Had he invited the sick man onto the island? Had he purposefully, maliciously set events on an extinction vector? No, *no.* He'd acted out of kindness. He'd done what any caring person would do. He'd tried so hard, under such desperate circumstances, to make the right choices—how was he to know it would turn out so horribly wrong?

It ended in this: Tim locked in a closet, alone with his thoughts. And his hunger. And the sick sweet stink of his body.

He was resigned to the fact he'd forever be known as the Scoutmaster who'd been mutinied by his own Scouts. That ought to make "Big" Jeff Jenks bust a gut.

Tim sat with his spine flush to the closet wall and his knees drawn tight to his chest. He tested each joint for weak spots. No luck. Solid wood nailed at inflexible angles.

A thin bar of sunlight wept under the door. Tim ran his fingers along the dissolving edge of light. Hugely comforting. A link to the world outside the closet. To the mainland and the sureties it held. To his cold cellar and its shelves stocked with preserves. To the glass canister of tongue depressors in his examination room.

He breathed heavily and focused. He could untwist a coat hanger and thread it under the door and . . . what? Jab someone in the ankle? Trip one of the boys? Why bother? Maybe he deserved to be here.

There's no maybe about it, Tim, said HAL 9000.

He was trapped. Impossibly, inescapably. Maybe it was for the best. Fact: he *was* ill. The boys may have been right to lock him up. It hurt tremendously that they'd done it—a sudden feral act that made a mockery of all those years they'd been together, a close-knit group under his command. And now, cooped up in here, he couldn't help them anymore—and that scared him profoundly.

Were you helping them, Tim? Really?

"Shut up, HAL," he croaked, sounding like a drainpipe clogged with sludge. "You're not my pal, *HAL*."

You're becoming irrational, Tim. This conversation can serve no purpose anymore. Good-bye.

"Good. Scram. Get lost."

Tim's thoughts returned to his Scouts. They were running wild, a quintet of lost boys. Did they have any inkling of the peril they were in? How could they, really? Boys didn't process fear the same way as adults, especially when it came to sickness. Their scabs healed like magic, their coughs dried up overnight. But Tim knew the frailty of human bodies; he'd seen how even the stoutest ones could collapse into a sucking pit of disease and death.

Not to mention the fact that they'd also laid their hands all over him while doing the deed. They had breathed in the air he'd exhaled in fear-sick gusts. He may have even spit at them. Dear God, had he actually *spat* on the boys?

Part of him—a shockingly large part—was okay being in here. Perhaps he was unfit for command. Fact: he was paralyzed with hunger. He kept catching whiffs of cotton candy from someplace. His eyes blinked uncontrollably. He kept hearing his mother, dead six years now, calling him home for supper. *Timmy, chowder's ready!*

Eat, said this funny little voice. It wasn't HAL or the Undervoice. This one was different—sly and insistent, like baby rats clawing the insides of his head.

But there's nothing to eat in here, he told the voice.

Sure there is. There's always things to eat, silly.

The rats kept clawing, clawing; before long they'd claw through the soft meat of his brains and scratch through the bone of his skull. Tim pictured it: his skull bulging, his scalp and hair stirring with antic life, the skin splitting with the sound of rotten upholstery as a tide of hairless pink ratlings spilled from the slit, slick with blood and grayish brain-curds, squealing shrilly as they sheeted clumsily down his face, past his unblinking eyes, bumping and squalling over his lips spread in a vacant smile.

Okay, he answered that funny niggling voice. *But what should I eat?*

Oh, eat anything, it said with cold reasonableness. *Any old thing you can find*.

The closet was wallpapered. Who the hell wallpapered a closet? The paper was torn in flimsy tatters. He tweezed a curl between his fingers. It ripped down the wall with a lovely zippering sound.

He placed the strip of wallpaper on his tongue. The ancient paste was vaguely sweet. He swallowed hungrily.

Lovely, the voice said. *Just lovely. Now eat more*.

Tim did as the voice asked.

Peeling and eating and peeling and eating.

The funny little voice was easy to obey. It didn't ask for much and what it did request was simple to accomplish.

Just *eat*.

And eat.

And eat.

A body settled against the other side of the door. Tim licked his paper-cut lips; his tongue had gone thick and gluey with paste. He whispered:

"Max? Is that you?"

Silence.

"Newt? Ephraim?"

A song—sung in a low mocking warble:

> *Nobody loves me*
> *Everybody hates me*
> *I'm going to the garden to eat worms, to eat worms*
> *Big fat juicy ones, long thin slimy ones*
> *Itsy-bitsy crawly-wawly woooorms.*

The singer was plugging up the space between the door and the floor.

Shelley?

Tim's precious bar of light vanished in heart-stopping chunks.

"No," he moaned. "What are you doing? No, please, no, please don't . . ."

He pushed his fingers under the door to dislodge the barrier but his fingertips met with resistance. Next came the *whooonk*ing sound of duct tape stripped off a roll. The last meager particles of light filching under the door disappeared entirely. Tim sat in total darkness.

He opened his mouth to beg for his light back. It was all he *had*, for God's sake. The childlike plea died on his lips.

Somewhere down inside of him—not too far down, either—
he could feel that relentless squirming. His teeth snapped
shut.

EAT.

The voice wasn't so small or funny anymore.

Tim did as it said. He wept softly without realizing.

Chapter Eighteen

Shelley placed the tape back in the kitchen drawer. His heart was beating a little heavier than normal. His eyes were hot and watery with dull excitement. The Scoutmaster was making faint pleading noises from inside the closet.

Shelley tried very hard not to laugh. He did not think the Scoutmaster's noises were very funny—Shelley didn't find anything funny, really. Not ever.

He inhaled through the alcohol-soaked gauze over his mouth and nose. He understood the danger—he could practically *see* the microscopic eggs ringing the scotch bottle's rim, the one Kent had drunk from last night. He saw the eggs hovering in the cool air above the dead man's chest. This didn't scare him. If anything, it excited him.

He glanced at his handiwork on the closet door. He'd wedged two dish towels underneath and taped them in place. Now the Scoutmaster had no light at all. If the other boys asked why he did it, he already had an excuse: Shelley had heard the Scoutmaster's consumptive hacking and sealed him in so they wouldn't all get what Tim clearly had.

Shelley opened the cabin door and slipped quietly outside. A fine band of golden light striped across the horizon. The others still slept round the fire.

He went round the side of the cabin and found a

142

spiderweb suspended between the east-facing wall and the overhang: an intricate hexagonal threadwork hung with beads of morning dew.

Shelley plucked a strand of gossamer near the web's center as if he were strumming the world's most fragile guitar. A spider crawled out of a knothole in the log. Its legs pushed out of the hole as one solid thing, all bundled tight like the ribs of a shut umbrella. To Shelley, it looked like an alien flower coming into bloom.

This one was big. Its bell-shaped body was the size of a Tic Tac. Its color reminded Shelley of the boiled organ meat his mother fed their dog, Shogun. The spider picked its way nimbly across its web. It had mistaken Shelley's gentle plucking for a trapped insect.

Shelley pulled a slender barbecue lighter from his pocket. He always carried one. Once, his teacher Mr. Finnerty had caught him burning ants near the bike racks after school. The fat carpenter ants had made weird *pop!* sounds as they exploded: like Shelley's morning bowl of Rice Krispies.

Mr. Finnerty confiscated his lighter. He'd given Shelley a frosty, revolted look as if he'd just accidentally stepped on a caterpillar in his slipper. Shelley smiled back complacently.

He'd simply bought another lighter. He bought one every few weeks from different stores around town. He also bought mousetraps and ant traps. One time, a shopkeep had remarked: *You must live with the Pied Piper, son, all these mousetraps you buy.* That had concerned Shelley a little, and he'd made sure to steer clear of that store. It wasn't wise to establish a pattern.

He flicked the ignitor. A wavering orange finger spurted from the metallic tip. Shelley worked carefully. It wasn't a matter of savoring it—he'd done this so many times that his heartbeat barely fluctuated. He was simply methodical by nature.

He touched flame to the web's topmost edges. The

gossamer burnt incredibly fast—like fuses zipping toward a powder keg—trailing orange filaments that left a smoky vapor in the air. The web folded over upon itself like the finest lace. The spider tried to scurry up its collapsing web, but it was like trying to climb a ladder that was simultaneously ablaze and falling into a sinkhole.

Shelley idly wondered if the spider felt any confusion or terror—did insects even feel emotions? He sort of hoped so, but there was no way to be sure.

He set fire to the web's remaining moorings. The web fell like a silken parachute with the spider trapped inside. Shelley harassed the spider through the grass, nipping it with the flame. He liked it best when he could sizzle a few legs off or melt their exoskeletons so some of their insides leaked out. He tried not to kill them. He preferred to alter them. It was more interesting. The game lasted longer.

He harried the spider until it scuttled under the cabin. He exhaled deeply and blinked his heavy-lidded eyes. Soon the spider would crawl back to its hole and build another web. Spiders were very predictable. When it did, Shelley might return and do it all over again.

Shelley scuffed his feet over the charred grass. It was best to leave no evidence. *Take only photos, leave only footprints.* He worked carefully, reflecting on the fact that this—what he'd just started with the Scoutmaster—was something new entirely. Something terribly exciting.

Spiders couldn't tattle on you; mice couldn't squeal— well, they *could* . . . but now Tim, he might just tell the boys what Shelley had done. But Shelley had an innate sense of leverage, a sixth sense he must've been born with; he understood that people in compromised positions were less believable. And even if the boys *did* believe Tim, or only a few of them—Max might; Newt *definitely* would—well, Shelley wasn't sure that mattered now. He felt the pull of the island in his bones, a strong current anchoring him to it. The sun crawled over the water, and Shelley felt this day, which had only begun, might go on forever.

The boys had not yet stirred. When they did, talk would turn to tiresome matters: when the boat would show up, how badly their folks would flip out, the identity of the dead man in the cabin. Most of all, they'd talk about how they'd be safe, real soon.

But Shelley was positive the boat wasn't coming.

Shelley wasn't particularly intelligent, at least according to the methods society had developed to measure that. He'd scored low on his IQ test. In school, he earned Cs and the odd D. His teachers gazed upon his pockmarked cheeks and slug-gray eyes and pictured Shelley fifteen years later in a pair of grease-spotted overalls, his slack and pallid moon-face staring up from the oil-change pit at a Mr. Lube.

Shelley was aware of their opinions, but it didn't trouble him. Shelley was actually happy with this perception. It made it easier to engage in the behaviors that gave him pleasure—though he failed to experience pleasure in the ways others did.

Shelley was far more perceptive than most gave him credit for. His impassive face was the perfect disguise. His expression hadn't changed when he'd seen the dead man on the chesterfield, but his practical mind had immediately aligned it with the black helicopter that had hovered overhead during the hike.

He had also aligned the thick white rope that had come out of the dead man with the thin white rope that had come out of his dog's bum a few years ago.

Shogun, the family sheltie, had gotten into some spoiled chuck in a neighbor's trash can. He passed a seven-foot worm weeks later. Shelley was home alone when it happened. He heard Shogun yowling in the backyard. He found the dog squatted in the zinnias. A white tube was spooling out

145

of his butt, some of it already coiled up in the cocoa shells his father had spread over the flower beds.

Shelley crouched down, completely fascinated. He flicked at the white tube, mesmerized. The thing wriggled at his touch. Shelley giggled. He flicked it again. Shogun reared and snapped at him. Shelley waited, then touched the tube again. Flicking and flicking it gently with one finger. It was slick with the dog's digestive juices. Shogun mewled pitifully and craned his skull over his haunches to stare at Shelley with wounded, rheumy eyes.

After shitting it out, Shogun tried to bury the worm. Shelley shooed the dog inside. He wanted to study it. It was dying very fast. Its head was a flat spoon shape. Many smaller spoon shapes branched off the biggest spoon: it looked like a Venus flytrap—the only plant Shelley found even remotely interesting. Each of the spoons had a slit down the middle studded with tiny translucent spikes. That must've been how it had moored to the dog's intestines . . . fascinating.

Shelley thought back to that sunny afternoon in the garden, Shogun's plaintive yipping as that greedy tube spooled out of its bottom. He was filled with a certainty as keen as he'd ever experienced.

The boat wouldn't come. Not today. Not for a while. Maybe not ever.

And that was just fine with him. That meant he could play his games.

And if he played them patiently enough, carefully enough, he might be the only one left to greet a boat when—*if?*—it did show up.

He turned his vaporous test-pattern face up to the new sun. It was warm and not unpleasant. It would be an unseasonably hot day. New life could grow in this kind of heat. He walked back to the fire to rejoin the others.

Chapter Nineteen

When the boys awoke, the cooler was gone.

It contained all the food Scoutmaster Tim set aside. Wieners and buns. A six-pack of Gatorade. A bag of trail mix. Hershey's Kisses. All they had left until the boat arrived. Max had placed it next to the fire the previous night. When they woke up, it was gone.

"Where the hell is it?" Ephraim said. He stamped around the campsite, knuckling sleep-crust out of his eyes. "I'm hungry, man."

The others roused themselves slowly. Their sleep had been fitful, thanks to the ominous howls and sly scuttlings of the wild creatures lurking beyond the fire's glow.

Newt said: "The cooler's missing."

"No shit, Captain Obvious," Ephraim said. "Which one of you guys took it? Was it you, Newt, you lardo?"

Newton beheld Ephraim with bruised eyes. "Eef, why would I . . . ?"

"Because you're a big fat fat-ass," Ephraim stated simply.

"Newt slept next to me the whole night," Max said; he knew it was wise to calm his best friend down before he "lost it," as Eef's mom would say. "If he'd tried to take the cooler, I'd have heard him."

Shelley came round the side of the cabin.

"Where the hell were you?" Ephraim said, the challenge clear.

"Hadda take a piss."

"What happened to the cooler?"

Shelley set his flat-hanging face upon Ephraim's. "Dunno, boss."

Ephraim balled his fists. He wanted to plant one between Shelley's cowish eyes. But he was distantly fearful that his fist would sink right into the placid emptiness of Shelley's face. It would be like sinking into a bowl of warm dough studded with busted lightbulbs. Worst of all he got the queasy feeling that Shelley wouldn't exactly mind it—and that his face would *eat* his fist. Dissolve it somehow, like acid.

Ephraim inhaled deeply, willing himself to stay calm. His mother said he had a temper just like his father's. The father who'd headed out to catch the afternoon stakes at Charlottetown downs and never came home. The shithead who'd busted his own son's arm and didn't even remember. The father who was currently a guest of the province at the Sleepy Hollow correctional center following a string of convenience store thefts—one of which netted the princely sum of $5.02.

He was also the man whose footsteps many figured that Ephraim would inevitably follow. *The apple never falls far from the tree*, went the whispers around town. It didn't help that Ephraim looked almost exactly like his father: the same antifreeze-green eyes and open-pored olive complexion.

And, Ephraim knew, the same temper.

One afternoon he and his mother had come across a construction site. An open sewer with a nest of hoses running down into it. Workmen had set up a large reflective warning sign. The top left side of the sign was crimped so that it read:

ANGER
KEEP
CLEAR

You should heed that warning, his mother had said.

And Ephraim *tried* to. But people were always pushing his buttons—which he had to admit were more like huge hair-trigger plungers. Whenever his emotions threatened to spill over, he'd follow his mother's suggestion to breathe deeply and count slowly backward from ten.

10 . . . 9 . . . 8 . . . 7 . . . 6 . . . 5 . . . 4 . . . 3—

"Wild animals must have dragged it off while we were sleeping," Kent said. "We should have hung it in a tree or something."

Kent looked nothing like last night's world beater. A dirty ring of sweat darkened his T-shirt collar; the same dark patches bloomed under his armpits. His eyes sat deep in his skull, the flesh around them netted in fine wrinkles: it looked a little like the wattle on an old biddy's neck.

"Bull*shit*," said Ephraim. "How would we not have heard animals making off with it?"

"I was pretty zonked," Max said.

Ephraim pointed at Newt. "You figure the Masked Skunk made off with it, too?"

Newton winced. "I was wiped last night, too. I mean, it *could* have—"

"Fuck, man—if one of you took it, just *admit it*," Ephraim said, his voice taking flight to an upper octave. "What do you think I'm going to do—go crazy? Start laying you guys out?" He raised his hands, all innocence. "You couldn't have eaten it *all*, right? So we'll just say you've had your fill and leave it at that."

"Animals," Kent croaked.

White-hot rage pounded at Ephraim's temples. His

molars ground together so hard that he could hear them in his skull: thick plates of shale scraping against one another.

He stalked away from the campfire in the direction of the cabin . . . but he took a wide berth around it, continuing on into the sparse woods behind.

He pulled a battered old Sucrets cough drop tin from his pocket. Three lonely cigarettes jostled inside. He'd hoped to duck away with Max, sharing a smoke down by the shore while they stared at the stars. Max didn't smoke, but Eef planned to convince him to be his smokin' buddy. Otherwise it was just him, alone, launching off lung rockets. Snacking on cancer sticks. Which painted a pretty lame picture, actually.

He poked a cigarette into his mouth, flicked his brass Zippo, and touched the flame to tobacco. He inhaled, coughing as the gray vapor rasped his throat—at first it'd felt like swallowing fiberglass insulation, the pink kind stacked in bricks at the hardware store—hissing the smoke between his teeth. He tried to blow smoke rings, puffing out his cheeks, but the wind rose out of the west and tore them apart.

Birds called in a metallic *rhree-rhree-rhree:* a sound like a rusty axe drawn across a cinder block. The nicotine hit his system, nerve endings a-tingle.

Settle down, he chastised himself. *So what if one of those assholes ate the food. You'll be at your own kitchen table with a big plate of spaghetti in, like, what, two hours, right? Away from this island. Away from . . .*

From the dead man. Which, truth be told, had freaked Ephraim out more than anything in his life. Seeing the man laid out stiff with his limbs jutting at weirdo angles and his chest slicked in brown gunk—that had been the worst part: that he'd died streaked in filth—Ephraim had barely managed to tamp down the high-pitched wail that had threatened to spill over his lips.

He'd never seen a dead person before. The closest he'd

ever come to anything remotely like it was the time he'd been walking home from school and saw a hydro worker get blown off a power pole by a jolt of electricity. The guy had been thirty feet up in a cherry picker. A current surge must've ripped through the transformer. Ephraim remembered the guy's face and body lighting up like a Fourth of July sparkler. The flash was so bright that it printed everything on Ephraim's eyes in negative for a minute afterward.

The man rocketed out of the cherry picker as if there were dynamite in his boots. He hit a sapling on his way down; the limber little tree bent with his weight before snapping with a crisp green sound. By the time Ephraim ran over, the workman was up and walking a dazed circle. The electricity had melted the treads of his boots: the rubber pooled around the soles as if he'd stepped in black jelly. Ephraim found it painful to breathe: the dissipating electricity left a lingering acidic note. Smoke spindled out of the man's overalls, right through the coarse orange weave of the fabric, rising off his shoulders in vaporous wings.

"Ah God ah God," the guy was saying over and over. Mincing around in stiff stutter-steps like a man walking barefoot over hot coals. "Ah God ah God ah God ah God . . ."

The flesh over his skull had melted down his forehead. The electricity had somehow loosened his skin without actually splitting it. Gravity had carried the melted skin downward: it wadded up along the ridge of his brow like the folds of a crushed-velvet curtain, or the skin on top of unstirred gravy pushed to one side of the pot. His hair had come down with it. His hairline now began in the middle of his forehead. The man didn't seem to realize this. He kept hopping around saying "Ah God ah God . . ."

In the calm eye of horror, Ephraim became aware of the tiniest details. Like how the hairs on the man's head were melted and charred, like the bristles of a hairbrush that had drawn too near an open flame. Or how the skin on the man's head—sheerer and hairless and now stretched with horrifying tension over the dome of his skull—was threaded with flimsy blue veins like the veins on a newborn baby's skull.

Ephraim had run to the truck and babbled into the CB radio. He was still babbling for help when the paramedics showed up.

That was the closest Ephraim had ever come to death until last night. And the dead man here (*who the hell* was *he, anyway?*) had been so much worse because he had been so much more *final*. The dead man couldn't get skin grafts and a hair weave like the workman could. All that lay in wait for the dead man was a lonely hole in the dirt.

And now Scoutmaster Tim was pretty sick, too. Maybe the same way the dead man had been?

They'd locked him in that stupid closet; Ephraim hadn't quite felt right about it—he got carried away, was all. And now Kent looked like he'd been attacked by vampire bats in the night; they'd sucked a gallon of blood out of him and soon—

He inhaled deeply. Held it. Let it go.

10 . . . 9 . . . 8 . . . 7 . . . 6 . . . 5 . . . 4 . . . 3 . . . 2 . . . 1

Are you angry, Eef? came his mother's voice. *Or are you scared?*

Ephraim realized that those emotions existed on two sides of a razor-thin line. One bled into the other so easily.

Anger. Keep Out.

Fear . . . Keep Out?

It's always good to have a little fear, son, especially at your age, he heard his mom say. *Fear keeps you honest. Fear keeps you safe.*

Ephraim stubbed the cigarette, dug a small hole in the earth—*a little grave for my coffin nail,* he thought cheerlessly—and buried the butt. He headed back to the campfire, confused in his thoughts.

From the sworn testimony of Nathan Erikson, given before the Federal Investigatory Board in connection with the events occurring on Falstaff Island, Prince Edward Island:

Q: Dr. Erikson, please describe the discussion between Dr. Edgerton and yourself regarding the selection of a human test subject.

A: I wouldn't really term it a discussion at all. Edgerton said he was doing it and I could come along for the ride if I wanted.

Q: And you agreed?

A: In for a penny? But I also thought . . . maybe I could help things somehow. Keep it under control.

Q: You could have kept it under control by informing the police.

A: I could have.

Q: But you didn't. Why not?

A: It's a tough thing to describe. Now that I'm away from it, the answers are so simple. Men like Edgerton are obsessives. Notions of right or wrong have this awful way of draining away to irrelevance with men like that. The only things that matter to them are *answers*. *Progress*. Unlocking doors. And if you can't unlock them, you just kick at them until they give. I guess I was sucked up in it, too.

Q: Tell me how Dr. Edgerton went about finding Tom Padgett, the first human test subject.

A: It wasn't so hard as you might think. It's amazing how many people are so down on their luck they'll take just about any offer that's flung at them. Edgerton went to bars. Not the campus bars where the fresh-faced, rosy-futured kids drank. The scumpits on the edge of town. He . . . *trolled,* is I guess the word. Threw his bait in the water and waited for a bite.

Q: He told Padgett his plan?

A: Not right off the bat. He did it in stages. I don't know the exact run of their conversation. You'd have to ask Edgerton.

Q: Dr. Edgerton is not an easy man to get a straight answer out of.

A: Edgerton just brought Padgett back one night. Guy smelled like he'd been marinating in a tub of Old Grouse. Edgerton explained it all calmly and evenly. He'd take the injection and sit in the room. We'd monitor him. If things got out of hand, we'd call a doctor—never mind the fact that no doctor on earth had a cure for what Edgerton would stick him with. Edgerton handed him a nice fat envelope. I don't know how much cash was in there. I guess it was enough.

Chapter Twenty

The cooler was discovered two hundred yards down toward the shore. There was no physical evidence to indicate it had been dragged: no zigzag lines through the soft dirt or trampled weeds. This suggested it had been picked up and carried to its present spot. It lay overturned in a patch of purple-pink shrubs.

But the crude way that the food had been shredded *did* suggest an animal. The hot dog packages had been torn open. Raw rags of the granular pink meat lay scattered about the cooler, alit upon by listless late-October flies. M&Ms were strewn around like multicolored jewels.

Ephraim kicked dirt over a half-chewed hot dog. His jaw was set at a sideways angle, his eyes hooded.

"Fuck it. Boat'll be here soon."

The boys walked down to the shore. They hadn't packed their bags—none of them wanted to go inside the cabin, though none of them spoke those words. The air was crisp, with a soft undernote of peppermint. The face of Newt's Timex Ironman read 8:23. The boat was scheduled to arrive at 8:30.

Kent slumped on a boulder carpeted with moss that resembled the fuzz on a tennis ball. When he was sure nobody was watching, he pinched some moss and stuffed it into his mouth.

He didn't know why he'd do such a thing. It shamed and disgusted him.

He was just so damned hungry.

Newton sidled up. Cautiously he said: "You okay, K?"

"I'm fine."

"You look a little green." Newton gave him a chummy smile and pointed to the water. "Like me when I get seasick. The rest of my family have great sea legs, but not me. When the boat gets swaying, I just toss my cookies. Lose my lunch every time."

"Newt, screw off." Kent gave Newton a look more pleading than threatening. "Okay? Please?"

He turned away and caught Shelley gawping at him. That same vapid look as always—was it, though?

Kent had been sure the others were asleep when he'd woken last night. The growl of his stomach had drawn him out of a deep slumber: an aching burr like a chain saw revving endlessly. He'd sat up with his hands reflexively clawing his belly.

His eyes had darted to the cooler. Next he'd glanced at the other boys, scrutinizing them carefully. They were asleep, Newton snoring loud as a leaf blower.

His gaze had been drawn helplessly to the cooler. The hunger was like nothing he'd ever known. Beyond an ache. More like an insistence. A *summoning*. There was a big, dark pit inside of him—something that had started out as a pinprick hole but had rapidly grown into a vortex, the equivalent of a violent tornado, but instead of the random objects that a twister pulls into its funnel—trees and mailboxes and lawn mowers—the one inside of him was sucking at his own insides, his liver and kidneys and lungs and stomach, with the incredible pressure of industrial machinery.

Kent had been terrified that if he let it go on much longer, the hole would suck clean through him—*out* of him.

He'd stood silently and crept to the cooler. His heart beat a staccato hi-hat behind his rib cage. His bladder was so tight he thought he might piss himself. Kent had forced himself to exhale softly—otherwise his breath would escape in shrill peeps like a baby bird calling for food. And what did baby birds eat? Worms. Their mothers chewed them up in their flinty beaks and regurgitated them. Worms just like the one that still lay on the cabin floor next to the dead man. Except not that big. And not so maggot-white. It would take a million birds to eat a worm that huge.

Kent's hands had crawled over the cooler's lid. The pebbled plastic reminded him of summer picnics. An ice-carpeted cooler with the brown necks of Coke bottles poking up. Watermelon sliced two inches thick. He'd bite through its pink flesh and spit the black seeds . . . seeds that looked a little like blood-swollen ticks, now that he thought about it.

His hands flirted over wieners and buns and teardrops of chocolate wrapped in silver foil. Surely one couldn't hurt? It was *his* anyway. One-fifth of this food was earmarked for him. So what if Kent wanted to eat his share in the middle of the night?

He'd plucked a Hershey's Kiss from the bag with trembling fingers. A runner of drool stretched into a glimmering ribbon in the firelight. He'd unwrapped the chocolate quickly and popped it into his mouth. Chewing and swallowing . . .

Before his mind could catch up to the mechanical movements of his fingers, the bag was empty. He'd lost track of things. His fingers and lips were streaked with brown chocolate. *Brown*—Kent's gorge rose with quick revulsion—brown like the muck pooling out of the dead man's stomach.

With swift, silent movements, he carried the cooler down near the shore. Things went hazy from there. Kent could only recall brief glints and flashes. Tearing and rending. Shoveling and swallowing. He may have wept while doing it.

At some point he'd glanced up and saw Shelley watching. Shelley, who should have been sleeping. Shelley, whose face had gone wolfish in the moonlight.

Go on, he'd mouthed to Kent. *Keep eating. Enjoy it.*

When Kent came back to himself, the cooler was empty. The persistent internal suck had ebbed to a muffled quaver in his gut. It was more than he'd eaten in his entire life. Guilt settled into his bones like lead. He pictured his father hovering over the scene with an accusatory eye.

You don't get it, Daddy, he'd wanted to say. *You don't understand what I'm going through.*

I understand weakness, son. Prisons are full of weak-willed men.

Afterward, Kent had stepped into the ocean to clean his hands and face. The cold water pinkened his fingers. Even at that hour, the mainland was a flurry of light and motion. He cupped water in his hands and walked back to the cooler, wiping his chocolaty fingerprints off the handles.

On the way back to the fire, he'd found Shelley lingering beneath the leaves of a weeping willow. Kent curled a fist and settled it under Shelley's chin.

"Say anything and I'll kick the shit out of you," he whispered.

"If you say so."

Kent took a step back. Something in Shelley's placid expression nearly made his knees buckle.

"You know what, Kent?" Shelley said. "Your breath stinks like shit. Like cotton candy that someone took a big piss on. Can't you smell it?"

Kent *could* smell it. The treacly-sweet stink with its ammoniac undertone nearly made him gag.

"I mean it, Shel. Keep your lip zipped."

Kent plodded back to the fire and struggled into his sleeping bag. But by morning, despite his devouring the cooler's entire contents, the hunger pangs had already returned.

Newton glanced at his Timex again: 9:02.

Stanley Watters's skiff should have puttered up to the wharf a half hour ago. It was not like Mr. Watters to be late. Before his retirement, he'd been the logistics coordinator at the local FedEx depot; the time of day was practically imprinted in his blood. Watters's favorite parlor trick was to look at his bare wrist when you asked what time it was—Watters never wore a watch—and give it to you to the very minute. Freaky. He might be a minute or two off nowadays but still, for him to be a half hour late? That was a rare occurrence indeed.

"You think something happened?" Newton said. "Mr. Watters is what, seventy?"

"Do you think we could swim back?" Ephraim said.

Newton scoffed. "Are you nuts? With these currents? They run the Atlantic Ironman Triathlon off Baker Beach." He pointed in the general direction of North Point. "I went with my mom once to watch it. Guys were staggering out of the ocean. Their teeth were bashing together so hard I could hear it. Most of them puked, they were so exhausted. And those were *athletes*. Grown-ups. And it was only a thousand meters. From here to shore is three miles."

"There are sharks, too," said Shelley.

Their heads swiveled. Shelley's vulpine face was pointed toward the slate-gray water, his expression unreadable.

"Oh, bullshit," said Ephraim.

Shelley's scarecrow shoulders joggled up and down. "Whatever. My uncle's seen plenty of sharks. He said one time a couple of oystermen caught a great white down around Campbellton. It swum into Cascumpec Bay after a storm. He says when the oystermen slit its belly open, two full wine bottles slid out onto the dock."

Shelley's uncle was a lobsterman, so it could be true.

Ephraim made a fist and slugged his thigh. "Could we make a raft or something?" He pointed at Oliver McCanty's boat. "Or try to get the motor working on that? What do you think, Max?"

"Why wouldn't we just chill out?" Max said. "He's only a half hour late—"

"Almost forty-five minutes, now," Newton said.

"It's probably nothing," said Max. "Maybe he's constipated."

This earned a laugh from the others. Ephraim said: "Old man Watters *is* a total tight-ass."

Thunderheads advanced. The boys watched the sky, enrapt. Thunder rolled across the water and echoed back on itself: a sound that was somehow feathery and alive. The clouds shaded purple to jet-black and then whitely incandescent, creased with lightning, billowing up like huge lungs inflating themselves. They spread across the water like a determined battalion. Rain washed down from the leaden clouds to tint the air beneath them a misty gray.

"Maybe old man Watters knew a storm was coming," said Max. "Maybe that's why he hasn't shown up."

Newton said: "Why not just come early then? He knew what time to come. Why leave us out here with a big storm coming through?"

"We don't know it's a big storm . . ." Max said uncertainly.

Soon they spotted the silvery shroud rolling across the water—which itself had taken on a brooding hue. It stretched over the ocean in a menacing canopy, pushing back the blue sky and blotting out the sun. The water bloomed deep red.

"Shit, it's bad," Kent said thickly. "We have to take cover."

They picked their way up the beach toward the cabin. Newton cast a panicky glance over his shoulder. The silvery pall was advancing at a terrific pace. Its contours had settled into a definite shape. A diaphanous funnel connected the water's surface to the corpulent black thunderclouds above; it rocked side to side like a hula dancer's hips.

A cyclone.

Newton recalled that one of those had touched down in Abbotsford a few years ago. It tore through the saltbox shacks lining the shorefront cliffs, smashing them to matchsticks. It picked up million-dollar yachts owned by rich American cottagers and flung them about like a child tossing his toys during a playroom tantrum.

"We've got to get inside!" he shouted over the banshee wind. "Or underground. *Fast!*"

By the time they reached the cabin, the shaker shingles were slapping against the roof—a brittle *racck! racck!* like the clatter of dry bones.

As one, they hesitated at the door. The dead man was in there. Scoutmaster Tim was locked in the closet. It was like revisiting the scene of a murder—one they'd all sworn in a pact to never talk about.

Lightning daggered through a bank of roiling purple clouds and forked sharply into the ocean. The water lit with a mushrooming sheen as if a tiny atom bomb had gone off below the surface.

Newton said: "We *have* to get inside. It's going to hit us any minute."

"We need to take cover, but not in there," said Kent. His face was bleach-white except for the jaundiced flushes painting his cheekbones. "I don't want to see that man again."

Ephraim jeered: "You wanted to see him bad enough last night, didn't you?"

161

"Scoutmaster's in there, too," said Newton.

Kent set his body in front of the door. A trivial gesture, like having a scarecrow guard a bank vault. The wind rose to a breathless whistle that ripped around the hard angles of the cabin, making an ululating note like a bowstring drawn across a musical saw.

"They're sick," Kent said simply.

"Sick?" said Newton. "Kent, one of them is *dead*."

"Him, then. Tim. *He's* sick. The whole place is sick."

"How about this, Kent? How about *you're* sick."

It was Shelley who spoke. The boys almost missed it: the wind tore the words out of his mouth and carried them away over the whipsawing treetops.

Newton said: "What? Who's sick?"

"Isn't it obvious?" Shelley said, louder now. "*Kent.* He's sick as a dog. Last night I saw him—"

"Shut up!" Kent almost sobbed. "You shut your dirty mouth, Shel!"

"Last *night*," Shelley said, enunciating each word with utmost care, "I caught Kent eating the food. He stole the cooler and took it down to the water. By the time I got there, he'd eaten it. He—"

Shelley was opening his mouth to say something more when Kent strode forward and dealt him an openhanded slap to the face.

"You shut your lying fucking mouth. I'll *kill* you, you crazy little fuck."

Shelley just stood there. A trickle of blood ran from his split lip like heavy sap from a tapped maple tree. Did he even notice, or care? The empty vaults of his eyes filled with vaporous white, reflecting the lightning that flashed over the bluffs. They became the glass eyes of a toy clown.

"He did it," Shelley said softly. He didn't have to speak very loud anymore: the boys were attuned to his every word. "Yes, he did. Ate all our food. He couldn't help himself—could you, Kent? That's why I didn't say anything at first—I felt *sorry* for you, Kent. You're sick. You've got the worms."

Kent sagged against the door. The effort it had taken to slap Shelley seemed to drain his meager power reserves.

"We're not going . . . in," he said haltingly.

"Listen, Kent." Ephraim spoke with cold menace. A brick-hued flush was draining down his cheeks to pinken his neck. "You ate our food. Fine, whatever, it's been done. But I'm not standing out here waiting to get crisped by lightning. So I'll tell you what—take a quick count of the teeth in your mouth. Then get ready to kiss about half of them good-bye, because if you don't get out of my way in about two seconds, you're going to be picking your pearly whites off the ground."

Without waiting for an answer, Ephraim laid his shoulder into Kent's chest. Kent folded like a lawn chair. Ephraim barreled through into the cabin. The sickening sweetness hammered him in the face—the air inside a decayed beehive could smell much the same.

Wind screamed through the gaps in the walls—the sound of a thousand teakettles hitting the boiling point. A swath of shingles tore off the roof to reveal the angry sky above: bruised darkness lit with shutter flashes of lightning. The wind curled in through the new aperture to swirl scraps of bloody gauze around the cabin like gruesome snowflakes.

"We have to get to the cellar!" Newton said.

"What about Scoutmaster?" Max shouted back.

They all turned to Kent, who had just dragged himself up off the floor. Lightning lit the sky and seethed through every crack and slit in the cabin.

"He's sick," Kent said.

Ephraim said: "You're sick, too!"

163

"I'm not!" Kent held out his hands—they did not make for compelling evidence of his claim. "I'm not fucking *sick*!"

"Max," Ephraim said. "Is Kent sick or not?"

"I think maybe so," said Max—not because he wanted it to be so, but because there was no other answer for what he was seeing. "I'm sorry, Kent."

"What a fucking shock!" Kent snarled. "The Bobbsey Twins agree!"

The wind hit a momentary lull. In that dead calm, the boys heard Tim's voice calling them from the closet.

"I *am* sick."

Kent pointed at the door. An expression of smug elation was plastered on the strained canvas of his face. "You see? You *see now*?"

Max knelt at the closet and tore the strip of duct tape off. Who the hell had put it there? He started yanking the tea towels stoppered under the door—then stopped abruptly. What if something squiggled out from under the door? The Scoutmaster's fingers, even, gone thin and witchy like long pointed wires?

"There's a big storm coming," he said to the door, to the Scoutmaster. "It's already here."

"I can hear it." Tim's voice was weird. "What you should do is get some candles and blankets and head down to the cellar."

"What about you?"

"I think . . . I'll stay right here, Max."

The hopelessness in his voice sent a volley of cold nails into Max's chest.

"Why?"

"You know why, Max. Are any of the other boys looking bad?"

"Yeah, I think Kent is."

"I'm not *sick*!" Kent screeched pitifully.

"You shut your mouth or I'll shut it for you," Ephraim said with calm contempt.

The wind dropped to a brief lull. Tim's voice could be heard clearly.

"You have to be careful," he said, sounding immensely tired. "Whatever this is, it's catching. I don't know how. But it can be passed around . . . round and round . . . I'm so hungry, Max."

Thunder crashed overhead like massive two-by-fours being *thwack*ed together. The hair at the nape of the boys' necks stood at attention. A string of blood trailed under the closet door. The ventricles of Max's heart ran with ice at the sight.

"You're bleeding," he whispered.

"Am I?" Tim did not sound surprised or alarmed. "I don't know where it could be coming from. I don't feel it at all. Now go on, Max. Get down to the cellar. Go, hurry."

Test subject 13. Alpha series.
CHIMPANZEE (Marshall BioServices; breeding
batch RD-489)
Age: 3 Years, 7 months. Female.
Subject's pre-test weight: 105lbs

/Date: 09.22/
OBSERVING RESEARCHER: DR. CLIVE EDGERTON
09:00   I introduced the modified hydatid
        [Genetic Recombination Y8.9-0] via
        injection. Subject is alert and ener-
        getic. Enjoying the use of its large
        enclosure with swing bar, reflective
        steel mirror, and splash pool. Subject
        is evidencing no overt signs of
        distress or pain.
10:00   Subject state is unchanged.
11:00   Subject state is unchanged.
12:00   Subject state is unchanged.
01:00   Subject state is unchanged.
01:54   Subject displaying signs of agitation.

Pacing its enclosure. It issues a
series of vocalizations . . . shrill
doglike yips.

02:13   Pacing continues. Vocalizations climb
to a high and possibly pain-stricken
pitch before softening. Subject is
scratching its posterior aggressively. Blood observed in small
quantities.

03:09   Subject has consumed all foodstuffs
placed in its enclosure. Approximately
5lbs peeled and diced fruit, 1lb dried
mealworms, 5lbs root vegetables.
Equivalent to 10% of subject's total
body mass consumed in less than forty
minutes [02:29 03:07]. Subject failed
to masticate food fully. Subject choked
on fibrous tubers. Subject regurgitated
said tubers. Shortly thereafter subject
consumed them again.

04:00   Subject continues to scratch its posterior aggressively. More blood. Half
a pint lost? Possible risk of anal
fissure.

05:00   Scratching has largely stopped.
Prominent indentations under the ribs
indicate rapid weight loss, although
at perhaps a slightly slower rate than
that registered in both rodent and
feline test subjects. Weight loss still

far too rapid to have any practical applications.

05:23 Visible folds of skin now gird the subject's pelvic brim. Eyes sunken into skull. Tissue degradation evident. Subject's demeanor placid and seemingly unconcerned. Hydatid has narcotizing effect? [post-edit note: see *H. diminuta* transfection case study]

05:45 A large hydatid has extruded from the subject's anus. Approx seven inches long. Significant tissue damage, swelling, and redness evidenced at extrusion site. Possible anal prolapse. Subject appears to be in no evident physical pain. Hydatid now approx one foot long as of recording . . . two . . . now two and a half feet.

05:50 Subject paces enclosure. Movements sluggish and hesitant. The extruded worm—now five feet long—is trailing from subject's anus. Hydatid is thicker toward midbody: diameter of a medium-gauge electrical cord.

05:52 Hydatid has fully extruded from subject. Approx ten feet in length. It lies in a cochlear coil on the bare cement. Subject seemingly unaware it has passed the worm. Eyes vacant and glazed. Bumping into walls. Visibly disoriented.

06:12 A bloody froth emits from subject's mouth. Thick, creamy lather resembling milk foam. Subject evacuated froth with surprising force—hard enough that a copious quantity of blood simultaneously ejected from subject's nose. [post-test update: investigation of froth showed it to be teeming with dwarf hydatids] Subject is seemingly unaware of trauma.

06:30 Definite prolapse of anus. Severely hemorrhaged fistlike section of lower colon plainly visible. Dark purple in color. Subject exhibiting no evident signs of distress.

07:00 Subject lies down heavily on nest of hay and sleeps.

08:00 Subject continues to sleep. Rapid aspiration of lungs.

09:00 Subject continues to sleep. [post-test update: upon consulting microphone rigged to pick up ambient sound inside the enclosure, a definite squirming sound could be heard between 09:13 and 09:16. Hypothesis: sounds emanating from *within* subject?]

10:10 Subject wakes suddenly. Eyes quite wide. The visible white portions are networked with burst blood vessels. Subject is in deeply agitated state. Clawing at face and body. Subject is gibbering uncontrollably.

10:12   Subject calm again. Hangs listlessly from play-swing.

10:14   Subject sits in play pool. Splashes water upon self apathetically. Water tinted red with blood from bodily wounds. Subject appears to be developing skin-surface lesions. Swellings noted on chest and arms and legs.

10:16   Subject pulling off hanks of fur. Subject staring at said hanks in a stunned and remote manner.

10:17   Subject is ingesting own fur. Subject is tearing off fur from arms and stomach and neck. Subject is ingesting more fur. There is blood . . . quite a lot of blood.

10:42   Subject steps out of pool. Moving with great difficulty. Ribs very prominent now. Outline of subject's skull visible beneath thin skin. Much fur has been forcefully removed from body and face.

10:43   Subject staring into steel mirror. Subject appears to be examining itself. Subject is pawing the mirror gently.

10:45   Subject attacks mirror. Pounding it

with great force. Subject leaves bloody prints on the steel. The subject is screeching and screeching and smashing fists into the mirror as if wishing to shatter it, shatter the reflection.

10:46   Subject moves away from mirror. Subject lies on concrete of enclosure. Subject emits low groaning sounds. Also hissing sounds.

11:00   [Dr. Edgerton exits observation booth. Dr. Nathan Erikson undertakes observational role]

11:15   Subject . . . suh-suh-subject is . . . Jesus. Jesus Christ . . . subject . . . subject is . . . subject is *not* a subject anymore. I mean, holy God, *is* she? How could she be? Subject is more bone than anything. Subject . . . Jesus, you poor thing. You poor fucking thing, you . . . I just . . . Clive, you bastard . . . this is . . . oh, Jesus. She's trying to move. Subject—she is—she is trying to crawl over to something. I don't know what . . . what the *hell* is that? Subject is—oh, Christ. Oh this can't . . . subject clearly has a prolapsed anus. This is where the worm—I can now identify the coiled shape on the floor as a worm—where the worm must have exited her body. The subject is making her way toward the worm. The worm is long and white and greasy. The subject's body and face are covered in lesions. They look like very large and terrible bee stings. Some are the size of golf balls. The subject's mouth is opening and closing on nothing. *Nothing.* She's bitten through her tongue. The subject is *hissing*—I do not believe she is making this noise herself. I believe the worms are making this noise somehow. The subject has made her way to the evacuated worm. The subject is toying with the worm . . . flicking at it with a finger . . . the subject . . . oh dear God, dear God don't *do that* . . . oh . . . oh . . . the subject is—the subject is eating the worm. The subject is shoving the worm into her mouth. Force-feeding herself the worm. She's eaten the worm. She's eaten it all. It's gone. The subject is mewling. Drowning-kitten sounds. She is mewling and lying still. Her lesions are pulsating . . . I think I can see . . . fuck no . . . Jesus. Jesus Christ—*CLIVE!*

11:23   [Dr. Erikson exits examination booth. Dr. Edgerton reenters]

11:24   Lesions appear to be breaking open all over subject's body. Hydatids must have escaped the intestinal walls. They entered seams between pockets of subject's muscle strata. They are presently exiting from fissures eaten through the subject's swollen skin. They are smaller than the worm that exited the subject's anus. Threadlike specimens.

11:28   Several large-ish specimens are breaking through the flesh of subject's cheeks.

11:32   Subject drags itself to a standing position. Subject is reeling around clawing at self. Subject is tearing off swathes of infected flesh. Stark bone visible at subject's left elbow. Subject seems largely unaware of bodily devastation.

11:36   Subject is tearing a long strip of flesh off forehead. Eyes nearly white. Cataracts? Ocular occlusion? Blood running freely. Subject making no sounds to indicate pain or suffering. Methodically peeling flesh. Several white threads can be seen wriggling in mangled tissue of forehead.

11:40   Two large hydatids break through the lens sacs of subject's eyes. Worms infested the corneal vaults. Three-inch hydatids, quite thick, protrude from subject's eye sockets, wriggling rather animatedly.

11:42 Subject blindly consuming own stripped flesh.

11:47 Subject immobile. Worms braiding into each other on exterior of subject's body. Engaging in procreation?

11:50 Subject exhales heavily. Chest does not rise again.

11:55 Subject assumed deceased. Worms continue to exhibit movement, although not so energetic.

12:15 Exterior worm movement has ceased. Subject's lower abdomen continues to pulse faintly.

12:33 Large quantity of worms evacuated from subject via anus and mouth.

12:40 All organisms deceased. Bio-decontamination and disposal processes initiated. Test concludes.

Test duration: 15 hours 40 minutes
Subject's post-test weight: 44.3lbs
Total weight loss: 60.7lbs

Chapter Twenty-One

Before the boys entered the cellar, a fight broke out.

Ephraim ransacked the cabin cupboards for candles and a pack of matches. He picked nimbly around the dead man, whose limbs had stiffened at tragic angles and whose body now shimmered with fruit flies.

Newton dashed down to the fire pit and grabbed their sleeping bags. He cast a fearful glance at the ocean. The water was in complete turmoil. With the wind whipping about, Newton's feet didn't feel entirely moored to the earth anymore.

He raced around the side of the cabin to meet the others. Ephraim had thrown the cellar doors open, the plywood trembling in the wind. Snapped spiderwebs blew like the flimsiest lace over the yawning entryway. The fermented smell of the earth rose up. The sky had gone the color of a blood blister—only a weak sickle of light shone into the cellar. The first few dusty wooden steps were visible, but the remainder of the staircase was overtaken in pooling shadows.

Ephraim pointed at Kent. "Sorry, man. You aren't coming down with us."

Kent's face somersaulted from shock to rage to speechless terror at the prospect of being left alone outside.

"You can't . . ." He offered his hands in a wordless plea. "You can't just—"

Ephraim crossed his arms. "You did it to the Scoutmaster."

Max saw the strange electricity running behind Ephraim's face: cruel voltages quivered his skin.

"That was different," Kent said feebly.

"I don't think so. I think it was smart." Ephraim's hands spanked together in a polite golf-clap. "Very *smart*."

"We can't just leave him out here, Eef."

Ephraim wheeled on Newton. "You want to get sick next? Want to be sneaking off in the middle of the night to eat everyone's food?"

"I'm sorry," Kent whispered.

Ephraim cupped a hand to his ear. "What's that? Can't hear you."

"I'm *sorry*." Tears brimmed in the cups of Kent's eyelids. "Just let me come down with you. *Please*. Don't leave me out here."

"No can do," Ephraim said coldly.

"What are we going to do, Eef?" Max said, gesturing to the storm set to make landfall. "Just leave him?"

"He can go back inside the cabin," said Eef. "It doesn't matter n—"

Which was when Kent tried to bull past Ephraim into the cellar. Yesterday that confrontation would have been a coin flip. Now it was pitifully one-sided.

Ephraim pushed Kent—an instinctual move. His face wrenched with quick revulsion as he shoved Kent aside as one might a squirming sack of beetles. Kent went sprawling.

Newton said: "Eef, come on . . ."

Ephraim's lips curled back. "Stay out of this, you fat shit."

176

Kent crawled up and came again. For an instant, it looked as though Ephraim would step aside—this tormented expression came over him, stuck between confrontation and flight—but his rage took over. He punched Kent in the belly. His fist sunk into Kent's gut in some terrifying way: it was as if Kent's body shaped itself around Ephraim's fist, welcoming it. Kent's breath came out in a gust.

"Stay down," Ephraim told him.

Instead Kent dragged himself up. He looked like some bloodless creature risen from his grave. His face had the pallid sheen of a dengue fever victim. The other boys ranged into a silent ring around Ephraim and Kent, the same ring that seems to form organically in school yards whenever a fight's brewing. Rain now pelted down to soak them through to their skivvies.

Ephraim struck out impulsively at Kent. If his mother had seen him, she'd have noticed the quick, reckless anger in his eyes—so much like his father.

Eef's fists zipped out and back rapidly, as if repelled by Kent's yellowed flesh. In short order, he'd raised a goose-egg on Kent's forehead and bloodied his nose and smacked him squarely in the left eye—a wound that would blacken nicely before long. Kent held his arms out, fingers squeezing and opening convulsively. His skin tore like crepe paper, stretched too tight over the flinty outcroppings of his face. Blood leaked out of his wounds only to be rinsed away by the heavy rain.

Kent kept trying to speak as Ephraim's fists peppered him. "I'm sorry," he said penitently, his voice unheard amid the peals of thunder. "I'm sorry, sorry, sorry . . ."

Ephraim's fist sheared off Kent's jaw. Blood leapt through the electrified air. Ephraim's knuckles had split open. It went on forever, and then it stopped. Ephraim's eyes remained wild, his nostrils dilated.

"You can stay out here with him," he told Newton. "Your choice. But he's *not* coming down."

The hardest-hearted part of the boys realized that Kent had earned this. If you call the tune, you also have to pay the piper when he begs his due.

"We can't just leave him, Eef."

Ephraim rounded on Newton. "We can, and we're gonna. Or I'm gonna—and Max, too. And Shelley, I guess."

Shelley was already halfway down the cellar stairs. The other boys remained in the pelting rain, lightning spearing over the trees. Ephraim turned to Max.

"Come on, man. Let's go."

Max fell in behind Ephraim . . . then he checked up. Dark clouds massed overhead, throwing them into a sudden night. Lightning lit the twitching contours of their faces.

"Eef, man," Max said. "Can't we at least find someplace safer for him?"

The two boys stood face-to-face, shirts rain-stuck to their chests, heartbeats shivering their skin. Something passed between them—a subtle split, an inelegant falling away. Maybe it was necessary, maybe not, but it happened. Both boys felt it.

Eef said: "Do you have any idea how stupid you are, Max?"

"Don't lock the door," Max said, holding Ephraim's gaze. "We're coming back. Come on, Kent."

Three boys skirted the cabin's edge. The wind blew with such gale force that it elicited shrieks from everything it touched. The logs shrieked as it lashed at their unflexing angles; the trees shrieked as gusts threatened to uproot them from the ground; even the grass shrieked—a thin and razor-fine whistle—as the wind danced between every blade. Rain needled down so hard that they felt as though their faces and arms would be sliced open: like walking through a storm of paper cuts.

Kent stumbled, arms outflung. Max reached impulsively— Newton's hand manacled his wrist. Newton shook his head and mouthed: *You can't touch him.*

Kent dragged himself out of the muddy stew, his boots slipping—they looked too big all of a sudden, his feet swimming in them—and followed Newton to the woodpile. It was rung by stacked cinder blocks and edged by trees; the wind wasn't quite so bad.

"Stay here!" Newton had to holler to make himself heard.

Kent knelt, too tired to argue. The boys folded the woodpile tarp and settled it over Kent's shivering shoulders. Earwigs and millipedes and wood lice and deer ticks squirmed from the dead logs, startled by the storm. Crawling and twitching through the mud, they skittered up the tarp. Max reached out to brush them away, revolted at the thought of touching them but even more revolted at the possibility they'd alight on Kent's skin and hair. Newt grabbed his hand again.

Kent didn't seem to mind. His eyes darted, charting the course of those milling bugs.

Newton said: "We'll come get you soon!"

Kent's head swiveled. A mechanical motion, like a toy abandoned in the rain. Lightning creased the sky and seemed to penetrate his flesh, igniting his bones in skeletal relief. His lips split in a grin that sent gooseflesh up the nape of Max's neck.

An earwig squirmed round the cup of Kent's ear, tracked across his face, and hung like a squirming fat raindrop from the boy's lower lip.

"Kent," Max breathed, horror twining up his spine like a weed. "There's a . . ."

Kent's tongue snaked between his teeth, curled lovingly around the earwig, and drew it into his mouth. His eyes never left theirs.

Chapter Twenty-Two

When Ephraim was eight, his mother took him to visit the mausoleum where his grandmother was kept. He remembered feeling slightly curious beforehand. Back then, Ephraim still held a healthy curiosity about death.

He remembered the thin acrid smell that had attended their entrance into the granite rostrum. The sterilized smell of death. It wasn't the flyblown battlefield reek with its sweetness that was kissing cousin to a truly good smell—barbecued pork, maybe—a sensual similarity that made it all the more sickening. This was sanitized and tolerable. An ammoniac mothball smell overlying subtle decay.

Ephraim caught that same pungent smell as he'd crept down the cabin's cellar steps. His heart made a giddy leap—what had died down here?

Ephraim had watched as Max and Newton guided Kent behind the cabin, wind snapping their clothes against their frames like flags flapping on a pole. A thin needle of regret had lanced through his heart. He'd argued with Max about abandoning Kent—and they *never* argued. Rage had pounded at Ephraim's temples as his neck flushed with heat. No fists had been swung, but it'd been a fight all the same.

That bothered and confused him. Ephraim possessed a

keen sense of fairness. He'd inherited that from his father; the only phrase he could ever recall him saying was: *You pay what you owe.* And his dad was paying now, in prison. Kent had earned his ills, hadn't he? He needed to pay what he owed.

But where did that leave Ephraim now? In a cellar with Shelley Longpre—the last alignment he'd ever seek.

He pulled the doors shut, latching them from the inside. The wind and rain roared and bashed the cabin above. The swaybacked steps groaned under his feet. Long, straggly tendrils trailed lightly across Ephraim's face: they felt like the dangling, unnaturally long limbs of a daddy longlegs spider.

He lit one of the candles he'd scavenged. It illuminated Shelley's face—his skin seemed to radiate a light all its own, a greasy luminescence as if glowworms were stitched under it. Shadows, made misshapen and monstrous by the wavering candlelight, scurried along the cellar walls. The root systems of trees and plants dangled down from the roof.

Ephraim walked the perimeter. Empty, barren. A musty boat tarp was heaped in one corner. The heap seemed to expand and contract in the fitful light.

"Sit down, Eef."

Shelley sat cross-legged on the dirt. With his long limbs folded, knees and elbows kinked, he looked vaguely insectile, like a potato bug curled into a protective ball, only its gray exoskeleton showing . . . or one of those cockroaches that would scuttle up the drains during island storms—the ones that hissed when you squashed them.

"Nah, I'm good."

"You were right," Shelley said. "About Kent. He deserved it. He brought it down on himself."

Something unshackled in Ephraim's chest. He didn't hate

Kent—it was a question of fairness, was all. *You pay what you owe.*

"Max will understand," Shelley said softly. "Even Newton. Before long they'll see how right you were."

There was something oddly narcotic about Shelley's monotone drawl. Ephraim felt sluggish and just a bit queasy—that happy-sick feeling he got in his belly after riding the Tilt-A-Whirl at the Montague Fair.

"Come," Shelley patted the dirt. *"Sit."*

It seemed less a request, more a subtle directive. Ephraim sat. Shelley's body kicked off ambient warmth, moist and weirdly salty like the air wafting from the mouth of a volcanic sea cave. He slid one pale, whiplike arm over Ephraim's shoulder—an oily, frictionless, hairless appendage slipping across, smooth and dense like a heavy rubber hose. His fingers thrummed on Ephraim's bare flesh; Ephraim wanted to brush them away, their tacky warmth making him mildly revolted, but that narcotic sluggishness prevented him from doing so. Shelley's arm constricted just a little—he was stronger than he looked—pulling Ephraim close.

"You're in charge now, Eef. Isn't that just awesome? That's how it should've been all along, isn't it?"

"I don't . . . don't really care about that."

Shelley smiled—a knowing expression. "Sure you don't."

"I don't. Sincerely." Rage crept up Ephraim's throat, burning like bile. "Shut your fucking mouth, Shel."

Shelley's smile persisted. The edgeless grin of a moron. His teeth were tiny—Ephraim had never noticed before. Like niblet corn. Bands of yellow crust rimmed each tooth. Did Shelley ever brush his teeth? Did something like Shelley even think about stuff like that?

*Some*thing *like Shelley?* Ephraim thought. *Someone, I mean. Some*one.

"Relax, Eef. I'm on your side."

183

Where the hell were Max and Newt? Ephraim wished like hell they were here now; anything was better than being cooped up

(*trapped?*)

in this dank cellar with Shelley. Lightning flashed, igniting the slit where the cellar doors met in camera-flash incandescence. Thunder boomed with such force that it seemed to bulge the planks overhead, rattling Ephraim's heart in its fragile cage of bone.

"Jesus, Eef . . ."

Shelley was staring at Ephraim—at his hands.

"What?"

Shelley's arm slid off Ephraim's shoulder. He leaned away, swallowing hard, his eyes riveted on Ephraim's hands. His torn, bloody hands.

"What the hell are you looking at, Shel?"

"Nothing. It's . . . no, it's nothing."

Ephraim's arm shot out, snatching Shelley's collar. Shelley issued a mewling noise of disgust, heels digging into the dirt as he propelled himself away. He knocked the candle over, snuffing it.

"Your fingernails!" he said—a blubbery, spittle-flecked shriek. "I think I saw something moving under your fingernails, Eef."

Ephraim's hand fell away from Shelley's collar, his fingers knitting into a ball under his trembling chin. The darkness closed in, strangling, suffocating, squeezing the air from his lungs. The skin under his fingernails—skin he'd never even considered as a discrete part of his body—buzzed at a hellish new frequency.

"Wh-what did you see?"

"Something," was all Shelley would say. ". . . *something*."

Next fists were pounding on the cellar doors. "Eef! Open up, man!"

Ephraim tried to stand. He couldn't. The strength had fled his body. He curled into a ball, knees drawn tight to his stomach.

"*Eef!*"

Shelley hesitated for a long moment before mounting the cellar stairs. Newt and Max came down, windblown and dripping wet. Ephraim's heart swelled at the sight.

"You okay?" Max said.

Yes, Ephraim thought, shivering with cold anger. *It's nothing. Not a goddamn thing at all. Fuckin' Shel. I'll kill him.*

"It was nothing, Eef," Shel said, grinning greasily in the dark. "I was wrong, probably."

Newt said, "Wrong about what?"

"Nothing!" Eef shouted—and in the next instant there came a ripping and rending crash as the big oak cracked almost directly above them. The splintering mash of wood as the tree crashed through the cabin roof. *BOOM!* The air inside the cellar seemed to condense and turn to cold lead in the boys' lungs. The tree struck the floor with a terrible impact and bounced once. The cellar roof splintered—shafts of cold light streamed through the shattered slats. Next it bulged down threateningly.

"Oh God," Max said. "The Scoutmaster . . ."

Uncertainty flickered on the boys' faces. As the rain and wind hit a momentary lull, they could hear Kent outside at the cellar doors.

"Please—*please!*" he begged, the words coming out in hysterical yelps. He scratched on the doors like a dog pleading to come inside on a cold night.

Ephraim caught Max's eye, holding it. No words were spoken. Finally Ephraim bowed his head, blew at the hanging fringe of his hair, and tromped determinedly up the steps. The fear in his heart morphed into something else, at least temporarily—a breed of unflexing resolve. It seemed the best, perhaps only way to keep a lid on his terror.

He unlatched the door and threw it open. Rain arrowed through the entryway. Lightning lit the planes of Kent's twitching, horrible face.

"Get in," Ephraim said. "But you have to sit away from us. I'm sorry."

Kent nodded pathetically and dragged himself to the corner with the boat tarp, pulling it over him. Max caught Ephraim looking at Kent's wounds, then at his own split knuckles. It wasn't hard to guess what he was thinking.

From the sworn testimony of Nathan Erikson, given before the Federal Investigatory Board in connection with the events occurring on Falstaff Island, Prince Edward Island:

Q: Let's clarify for the record just what we're talking about. You were working on a diet supplement?

A: It was to be a pill. That's the grail, right? A pill you can pop before bed. A little white pill. That was the idea.

Q: And this pill would be made of . . . ?

A: Compressed dextrose. You know those candy hearts you get on Valentine's Day? Same stuff. Basically it's sugar pressed into a mold using pneumatic pressure.

Q: You mean a placebo?

A: Sugar pills are the classic test of the placebo effect—but no, these were fully loaded.

Q: Why a sugar pill, then?

A: Any delivery system would work—why not go with something sweet? Fact is, the mutagenic strain of the hydatid worm developed by Dr. Edgerton was incredibly hardy. They could have been packed into a dextrose pill and shot into space. If a creature with a human-like digestive system were to find those pills floating out in space a thousand years later and swallow them, those worms would hatch and thrive. Nothing beats a worm in terms of survivability.

Q: So these worms were packed into a candy pill—

A: The eggs were. Freeze-dried, like the Sea Monkeys kids used to buy in the back pages of old G.I. Joe comics. The dormant-state eggs would become larvae and later full-stage hydatids.

Q: And the expectation was that people would be desperate enough to consume these pills to lose weight? That was what Dr. Edgerton and his silent partner–slash–bankroller pharmacy concern expected?

A: People are *already* desperate enough. You've never heard of the tapeworm diet? You've got people eating tainted beef to *give themselves* worms. It's not nearly as uncommon as you'd think—it's illegal in North America, sure, but Mexican diet clinics are doing a brisk business.

Q: What made your method a better option?

A: A beef tapeworm is a great diet aid . . . *if* it stays in your gut. Problem is, tapeworms are wanderers. They go on walkabout inside your body. They'll swim out of your intestines—or needle through your intestinal wall—and encyst in your liver or brain or eyes or spinal cord. An encysted worm in your brain shows up the same as a tumor on a CAT scan. It can do the same level of damage, too. But the modified hydatid we were working on would be corralled in the host's intestines. Like those electric fences cattle ranchers use to keep their cows in their fields. Dr. Edgerton was working on reconstructing the worm's basic DNA sequence so that it would die as soon as it perforated the intestinal wall. It was a matter of weakening its natural immunities, making it more susceptible to white blood cell attack. White blood plasma would eat through Dr. Edgerton's worms like acid. Anyway, that was the idea.

Q: And when a person reaches his target weight?

A: An oral antibiotic flushes out the worm colony in a matter of days. The two-pill solution, we'd bill it. One pill to give you worms, the other to flush them out.

Q: And in between?

A: You'd lose those troublesome pounds.

Q: But the worm you helped Dr. Edgerton develop didn't act according to plan, did it?

A: I'd say that is somewhat of an understatement.

Chapter Twenty-Three

In time, the wind died down. The storm blew out to the northern sea. Water dripped all around them; it seemed terribly loud, each drop producing a watery echo. The boys huddled, shivering and soaked, in the cellar—all except Kent, who sat in isolation under the tarp.

"We ought to check on the Scoutmaster," Newton said.

Ephraim nodded. "Kent, you stay here."

Kent's face was wan and ghoulish above the burlap. It looked like the wooden face of Zoltar, that mechanical side-show oracle at the Cavendish County Fair: *25 cents to know your future!* Things were stuck in his braces, too . . . insect parts? Yes. Thoraxes and legs and antennae bristled from his mouth-metal. He was gnawing on the moldy tarp. Working the frayed edge like an old man gumming a carrot. A faraway look in his eyes—he could have been contemplating a lovely sunset.

"Okay," he said. "I kinda like it down here, anyway."

"You okay, K?" Newton asked, repulsion lying heavy in his gorge.

"Sure." A death's-head grin. "Never better."

A collective unease enveloped the boys—even Shelley. How long had it been? Less than twelve hours. Half a day ago, Kent Jenks had been one of them. The biggest and strongest of them all. The boy everyone in North Point forecasted great things for. Now here he was, curled in a cellar, insects gummed in his teeth, gnawing mindlessly on a tarp. Reduced and squandered in some nasty, terrifying, unquantifiable way. Whatever was wrong with him, this sickness, it was *rampaging*. Barnstorming through his body, devouring him. Newton sensed this: that Kent was being eaten from the inside out, his flesh loosening by degrees, the meat flensed from his bones as his body shrunk inside his skin until . . . until *what*? This sickness cared nothing for Kent—for the man he could've become, for the bright future that seemed so assured. It was coring him out, ruining him in unfixable ways.

They left him down there. Ephraim shut the doors and jammed a stick between the handles so Kent couldn't escape.

The Island was still in the passing of the storm.

As they'd heard from the cellar, the huge oak—one of only five or six truly big trees on Falstaff Island—had snapped, falling upon the cabin's interlaced log walls. The spot where it had broken looked like the butt of a trick cigar: splinters of wood stuck out of the trunk at crazy angles, perfuming the air with sap.

They inhaled the peculiar scent of the earth after a storm while surveying the cabin. The roof was cleaved in half, sagging inward like a huge toothless mouth. The door hung off its shattered hinges. Ephraim hauled it open. His gaze fell to scrutinize his fingernails. He shot a look at Shelley— who caught his eyes and held them evenly.

"Careful as we go inside," Ephraim said, sounding very much like Kent. "Cover your mouths like before."

The roof had collapsed in a solid flap that resembled a wave set to break. The boys walked through a corridor of shadow created by the fallen roof and found Scoutmaster

Tim in the splintered remains of the closet. The tree had snapped the two-by-fours and pancaked the closet's plywood walls. The trunk had landed on his head and shoulders.

"Tim?" Newton said in a small, disbelieving voice. "Are you . . . ?"

The final word—*okay?*—died on his lips. Scoutmaster Tim was definitely not okay.

The finality of the situation assaulted Newton. It was in the way the tree trunk sat flush with the floor. It was in the crushed eggshell of the Scoutmaster's skull, which was visible—barely but hideously visible—beneath the bark. It was in the jagged purple lines that raced all over his flesh: the pressure had bulged and ruptured his vesicles. His skin looked like some gruesome jigsaw puzzle. It was in the sweet smell that rose off his body and the darker undernote of death: a somehow *rusty* smell, Newton thought, like the smell that came off a seized engine block at the dump. It was in the boot that had fallen off his foot—more like *ejected* off when the tree came crashing down, causing his legs to spike upward in one spastic motion, flinging his boot away. It was in the pale knob of his toe poking through the woolen sock. It was in the cricket that rested in the split V of his open shirt collar, which just then began to rub its legs together to produce a high humming song.

"He looks like the witch in *The Wizard of Oz*," Shelley said. "The one the house landed on, not the one that melted."

"Shut the fuck up, Shel," Ephraim said hoarsely.

Newton's heart was a wounded bird flapping inside his chest. He wanted to scream, but the sound was locked up under his lungs.

"What should we do?" he said. "Is he really . . . ?"

He found it impossible to say. *Dead.* The word itself was somehow unapproachable. He knelt and touched

Scoutmaster Tim's hand. The flesh was cold and dank like a rock in a fast-running river.

"It's okay, Newt," Ephraim said. "It must have been fast, you know? I don't think he even felt it."

Newton spoke with his head down. "You think so?"

Max sincerely hoped it was so. He felt sick. His Scoutmaster—the adult he'd known longer than anyone besides his own parents—had died in a closet. The one person with the best ideas for getting them off this island was gone, and he'd left five dumb, piss-scared kids behind.

"Should we bury him?" Ephraim said.

Before any of them had a chance to respond, Scoutmaster Tim's stomach began to move.

At first it was barely visible; it seemed as if weak fingers were pawing at it from the inside. Max watched, his mouth unhinged. It was sickeningly mesmerizing.

"What . . ." Ephraim breathed, ". . . *is* that?"

A fragile white tube broke the surface of the skin an inch above the Scoutmaster's navel. It pushed through insistently, twisting around as if tasting the air. It was followed quickly by another and another. Soon there were seven or eight: it looked like the legs of an albino spider struggling to escape its spider hole.

Each tube was slightly pebbled—they seemed to be studded with something. Max squinted closer. They were . . . oh God, they were *mouths*. Little mouths like the ones on a sucker fish.

The Scoutmaster's stomach split soundlessly, like Saran Wrap, groin to rib cage. Hundreds of worms came boiling out, all much smaller versions of the single massive abomination that had come out of the other man—the stranger. Some were the thickness of butcher's twine, but most were frail and wispy, as insubstantial as the clipped threads of a spiderweb. They twisted and roiled and spilled down the

193

Scoutmaster's papery flesh: his skin empty of blood and nutrients, just a soft white covering like dry fatback.

Max noticed that the worms didn't appear to be singular entities. Rather they were twisted together—a pulpy white ball radiating dozens or hundreds. It was as if something had gathered them up and tied them all into a bulging knot, like that ball they saw yesterday in the rocks—a knot of fucking snakes. These spiky worm-balls tumbled over one another, squirming and shucking. A horrible low hissing noise emanated from the Scoutmaster's chest cavity.

"No," Newt said, his head snapping side to side. "No no no no . . ."

The hissing noise stopped. Slowly, achingly, the worms stretched as a single unit—a cooperative hive-mind—toward the sound of Newton's voice.

"Jesus," said Ephraim.

Then the worms swung in his direction.

Some of them swelled menacingly, a small bead crowning at their tips. There came a series of dim, pop-gun percussions. Delicate strands wafted through the air, sunlight falling along their ghostly wavering contours.

Ephraim stepped back. He swatted at the strands with a helpless look on his face. He stared at his knuckles, which were broken open and still weeping slug-trails of blood from his fight with Kent.

Max knew Ephraim so well that he could almost see the crazed thought forming in the other boy's head.

They can get inside of me through there. These wounds are basically wide-open doors in my body . . .

Through an aperture in the cleaved roof, Max spotted a slit of perfectly blue sky—that scintillating blue that comes on the heels of a bad storm—and below, a scrim of gray marking the mainland. His parents would be there. Why hadn't they come yet? His folks, and Newt's and Eef's and Kent's and Shelley's, too? Fuck old man Watters—if he couldn't get his ancient ass in gear, why wouldn't their folks show up? Kent's dad could use the police patrol boat—special dispensation, right? An emergency. But no, they'd left their kids alone on this killing floor of an island. Two men were dead already, and Kent was bad off. *Death warmed over*, as Max's mom would say. Except for Kent, death might come as a relief. A shudder fled down Max's spine—the very thought of Kent, dead, his body invaded by these things . . .

"DEVOURER VERSUS CONQUEROR WORMS:
THE DUAL NATURE OF THE MODIFIED HYDATID"

Excerpt from a paper given by Dr. Cynthia Preston, MD,
Microbiology and Immunology, at the 27th International
Papillomavirus Conference and Clinical Workshop at the
University of Boston, Massachusetts.

The evidence found in Dr. Edgerton's laboratory is breathtaking
both in the groundbreaking nature of what he was able to
accomplish and in the savage expediency of his methods.

Edgerton was viewed by his contemporaries as pathologically secretive. Conversations with him, according to the few
who spent time in his presence, were narrowly focused on
his work or the work of his rivals.

Edgerton was an only child. His parents passed away in an
automobile accident while he was attending graduate school.
By all outward signs he lived for his work.

His fellow researchers remember him as a hardliner
known to play fast and loose with scientific ethics. One oft-
reported incident—especially telling in light of the events at
Falstaff Island—recounts an evening when Edgerton was
discovered by campus police at his alma mater. He'd snuck
into a lab using a stolen passkey and was discovered in the
process of destroying the work of his closest rival, a senior
by the name of Edward Trusskins. Trusskins had been working
on a skin graft technique involving lab mice. Edgerton was
caught red-handed, as they say, with a syringe of
strychnine.

Despite this infraction and the chilling mind-set it signaled,
he was soon pursuing his work at another institute. He was
simply too talented. He also could be convincingly sincere
when circumstances compelled it.

There are those who say the best scientists occupy that dangerous headspace teetering at the edge of madness. By this definition Dr. Edgerton was most certainly a world-class scientist.

Edgerton's work with the hydatid worm rivaled what Dr. Jonas Salk did for immunology in the 1950s—not in terms of its immediate social benefit (all Edgerton *actually* created was the most adaptable and survivable parasite known to mankind), but in his successful genetic manipulation of this planet's simplest life-form.

He took a simple planarian worm and unlocked its genetic code. In doing so he allowed it to modify its basic anatomic and gastric substructure in ways heretofore thought impossible for *any* life-form. He enabled the hydatid worm to adapt to its environment on the fly. His *stated* aim was to rob the worm of its natural defenses in the interests of quarantining it within its host . . . what he accomplished was the exact opposite.

He opened a genetic Pandora's box.

When his hydatid was confronted with a cliff, it grew wings. Confronted with an unbridgeable sea, it grew gills. Its adaptability enabled it to mutate in a dizzying variety of ways. Just like snowflakes, no two of Dr. Edgerton's hydatids were exactly alike.

His worms broke down into two broad categories. In the interests of distinction let's call them "devourer worms" and "conqueror worms."

Some species of tapeworm will enter into a parasitic symbiosis with their hosts; they can live in the host for years, eating only enough to survive. But even unmutated hydatids do not behave this way: their genetic imperative is to populate and eventually overrun their hosts, overtaxing their immunodeficiency systems and essentially starving them to death.

This rarely happens; even the worst hydatid infestation can be flushed out with proper medication. But the video footage recovered from the Edgerton lab indicates that the modified hydatid is both extremely hardy and extremely aggressive: it spawns far faster, devours far more, and grows far larger.

As such, it is the equivalent of a Kamikaze pilot: its appetite quickens its own extinction cycle.

The mutated "devourer" hydatid does two things: eats and reproduces. After the infestation reaches critical mass it begins to consume the living tissues of its host—this behavior distinguishes it from the common hydatid, which is incapable of digesting anything beyond waste matter. A devourer will consume protein, fat, muscle tissue, even bone marrow and the vitreous jelly of a host's eyes. This accounts for much of the "wasting" effect on its host: they come to look like long-time starvation victims in a matter of hours.

The devastation is intensified by the fact that every molecule of nourishment a devourer consumes serves a singular purpose: to make more of itself. A devourer eats and lays eggs. It is not uncommon for a devourer colony to reach a critical state after an incubation period of only a few hours.

It is simply impossible for a host to take in enough nourishment to satisfy a devourer colony—whatever the host eats produces more creatures seeking more nourishment . . .

Chapter Twenty-Four

Kent was dreaming.

He was on the ocean with his father. Night was coming on. The eerie smoothness of the water, not a wave or ripple, was what made Kent realize that he was dreaming.

Kent was thinking about a girl in his class. Anna Uniak. Anna was pretty and trim and he was sure his father would approve. He often looked at Anna out of the corner of his eye—she sat one seat ahead and to the left of him at school. The light would fall through the classroom window and pick up the fine downy hairs on her cheeks. It looked like peach fuzz, Kent thought. He could eat Anna's skin just like that—just like a peach . . .

The sky was strung with strange clouds. A dull crimson and hanging very low, bleeding into the setting sun. Kent thought he could see shapes in them—sinuous squirmings as if the clouds were coming apart in the face of the ocean wind, or giving birth to multiples, or something else he could put no name to.

His father wore his police uniform. His badge winked in the guttering embers of the day's light. His father's wrists, projecting from his sleeves, were wasted looking and his fingers too skeletal.

"It'll be a long night," he said. "And goddamn, I'm hungry."

A flock of birds—not the ever-present gulls but jet-black, arrow-eyed ravens—flew overhead, shadowing their boat. Kent could hear their tortured cries and see their rotted beaks. Some kind of white, cindery dust was drifting down from beneath their wings. It fell through the air in little white ribbons, just like in a ticker-tape parade.

Fear stole into Kent's heart. He wished he wasn't so scared—his father had taught him that fear was a useless emotion. *Fear is just weakness exiting the body*, he'd said to Kent on many occasions.

But there was something wrong with the whole scene: the menacing shapes lurking within the clouds, the white things drifting down . . . and his father. *His father—*

The police uniform hung off his body. He lurched toward Kent with his arms outstretched—stick arms that wouldn't have looked out of place on a concentration camp prisoner—his fingers just clattering bone. His face was all cheekbones and bulging brow and parchment-thin skin stretched to the point of tearing.

"A long night!" this starved apparition screamed at him. *"A looong and hungry night! Yummy yum yum!"*

His father reached for Kent, bony hands clawing round his shoulders, digging in, piercing the skin. Jeff Jenks leaned in and his skin now came apart: rifts appeared in the fabric of his face, fine lines like cracks in bone china, and then those rifts all met and began to wriggle and suddenly Kent was staring into a face made up of hundreds of white pulsating tubes.

"Nobody loves me," his worm-father sang sadly. Writhing alabaster worms dripped off his lips and into his mouth, thrashing contentedly on the Swiss-cheesed root of his tongue. "Everybody hates me; I'm going to the garden to eat *you*."

Kent toppled into the bottom of the boat with his father atop him. His father's face fell apart in sections. The abominations detached and squirmed down his collar, pattering onto Kent's upturned face like warm raindrops. They found his mouth and nose and ears and eyes, infiltrating them with greedy abandon.

"This is only fear entering the body," his father said.

Newton was the one who suggested they make a list.

His own survival instincts told him this was the wisest plan. When the world was crumbling around your ears, your best bet was to set yourself a few simple tasks to focus your attention on. While you were working on those tasks, your mind had a chance to cope with the situation. If you could just get past the initial shock—the shock of death and of sudden isolation—then maybe a better plan would come to you later.

They stood down at the shore now: Ephraim, Max, Shelley, and Newton.

"Three things," Newt said. "First, find some food. Second, medicine for Kent."

"Why?" Shelley said. "He's just going to end up like Tim."

Newton glanced up sharply. *Shut up, Shel. Shut up and go away. Walk into the ocean and just sink.* "We don't know that. We don't know that at all."

Shelley only smiled—sadly, poisonously, impossible to tell—and wandered down to the shoreline. *That's right,* Newton thought. *Just keep walking, jerkoid.*

"Third," Newton went on, "we either make a raft or oars for the boat we already have."

Ephraim doubled over, clutching his knees, and vomited on the rocks. His body vibrated like a hard-struck tuning fork. He stayed that way for a while, breathing heavily, before straightening up and wiping his lips.

201

"I don't know." He stared at the other boys. "I don't know what to do now."

His gaze fell to his knuckles. He rubbed them with his fingers and spread blood down to his wrist. There was something obsessive about the way he did it.

Newton said: "It's okay—"

"It's *not* okay," said Ephraim. "The Scoutmaster's *dead.* He . . . oh my God, his belly split open and a bunch of worms fell out. *Worms.* How the hell did they *get* there?"

Max said, "We have to stay away from the cabin. Do what Newt said. Get some food. Make a raft or something. Find a way back home."

Shelley called from the beachhead: "You sure we'll be able to get back home?"

He was crouched by the shore, stirring the water with a stick. He pushed the tip of it against the fat body of a sea slug. He exerted slow pressure until the slug's body burst like a snot-filled bath bead.

The boys hadn't seen what he'd done. Did it matter, anyway? Part of him—a growing part—wanted to shed the mask that shielded his under-face. This possibility put a warm lump in his belly.

"What are you talking about, Shel?" Ephraim said.

He pointed across the water at the squat shapes on the horizon. "Those aren't trawlers. They aren't fishing boats. Those are *ships*—like, military stuff."

"So?"

"So think about it, Eef," he said. "That guy who showed up the other night. What was that *thing* that came out of him? And then Scoutmaster, then Kent. Whatever it is, it's spreading—right? That means it's a disease. Something that hops from person to person." He cocked his head at Ephraim, who kept rubbing his knuckles against the coarse

202

weave of his pants. "It gets inside of you somehow and starts . . . doing what it does, I guess."

Ephraim's hands clenched into fists. Blood was streaked down his pants.

"What are you saying, Shel?"

"I'm saying maybe they won't *let us* leave. Even if we build a raft. They'll keep us right here because we're contagious. We're *contaminated*."

"Shut up," Max said. "That's stupid bullshit. Nobody's going to keep a bunch of kids on an island, Shel. Our folks wouldn't let it happen. They're *adults*. Adults don't do stuff like that."

As his words echoed into silence, Max realized that he'd held the exact opposite viewpoint only minutes ago, inside the cabin. His mind wasn't centered anymore—it spun on confused, worrisome tangents.

"Can you explain those ships?" Ephraim asked Max hopefully.

"They *could be* army ships. All I'm saying is they're not going to stop us from going home."

"Then why aren't they coming to get us?" Shelley said.

Max had no answer for that. Newton said: "They could have a million reasons for staying away. *If* it's something contagious, maybe they have a cure. Then they'll be here quick as quick. But Max is right—they're adults. If they're making us wait, I'm sure there's a good reason. Until then we have to make do. That shouldn't be so hard, should it? We're Scouts, aren't we?"

"So what are we going to eat?" Max said.

Newton said: "There's berries and fungi. We should be able to catch something, don't you think? Scoutmaster showed us how to string a foot-trap, and there's rope in the cabin."

"Are you gonna get that rope?" Shelley asked.

"If I have to," Newton told him evenly.

Ephraim said: "What about Kent? If he's sick—"

"If? He *is* sick," Shelley said.

"If you don't shut up, I'm going to put your head through a tree," Ephraim said.

"Save your energy, Eef," Shelley said in a voice gone silky soft.

"Kent needs to throw it all up," Newton said. "That's the best way to get what's inside of him out. There are plants that can do that pretty safely. It's in my field book, which is still in the cabin. So I'd better—"

A boat motor kicked up beyond the spit of headland that projected from the southern tip of the island. The boys could just barely make out a boat streaking toward them.

"Hey, check it out—that's Mr. Walmack's cigarette boat," Ephraim said.

Calvin Walmack was one of the town's few summer people. He showed up every June with a mahogany tan, bleached white teeth, and his shrill wife, Tippy. Mr. Walmack owned a vintage cigarette boat that was moored down at the jetty. The Ferrari of boats, Max's father called it: pretty much just a huge motor strapped to strips of polished teak.

Mr. Walmack's boat hammered over the water, hitting the waves and skipping dangerously. It looked to be on the verge of hydroplaning. Two other boats were in pursuit: stockier and painted a dusty black. Gun turrets were mounted on their bows.

The cigarette boat skiffed off a big wave and came down with a *smack*. The engine cut out. A thin ribbon of smoke coiled up to smudge the sky. Newton could see two men in the boat, but they were too far off for him to make out faces. They were waving their arms.

The pursuing vessels cut around the cigarette boat in a scissoring move. Men moved swiftly about on deck. Ephraim thought he saw the sun glinting down their arms—glinting off the weapons they were carrying.

The boats bobbed on the surf. The boys watched with their hands canopying their eyes. The black boats returned the way they had come. The cigarette boat remained afloat but looked empty.

When the black boats were well clear, a small explosion rocked Mr. Walmack's boat. A gout of flame shot up from the engine. A sound like a shotgun blast trailed across the sea.

"What the hell?" Ephraim's face settled into an expression between bafflement and fear. "What just happened right now?"

Nobody had an answer—not for what happened to Mr. Walmack or his boat, or for *anything* that'd happened since that strange man staggered out of the sea two nights ago.

Nothing made sense anymore. Everything existed beyond logic.

The cigarette boat sank and was gone in a matter of seconds.

Chapter Twenty-Five

Before they entered the woods, Newton stepped inside the cabin. He needed his field book and the rope. His heart was beating like a tom-tom. Fat beads of sweat popped along his brow before he even walked through the shattered doorframe.

Don't do this, his mother's voice chimed in his head. *Please. This is so very dangerous, Newt.*

Newton's mom had always been protective of her only son. Elizabeth Thornton was crowned Miss Prince Edward Island the day after she'd fallen pregnant with Newton. "Fallen pregnant" was a common phrase on the island: as if local women were constantly toppling off things—stools, ladders, cliffs—and getting knocked up on the way down. The man who'd done it was a "contest stylist": a fey grifter who mentored unwitting contestants. For a fee, he'd teach them to Vaseline their teeth to a pearly shine or strap packing tape around their breasts to give the proper "uplift." Such men trailed along the pageant circuit like gulls following in the wake of a crab trawler, picking up scraps.

This particular stylist put a bun in Elizabeth's oven the night before the Charlottetown Spud Fest. He was gone the next day, no different from the itinerant potato pickers who descended on the island like locusts in the fall only to blow back to the mainland on the first winter wind. Newton never asked after his father. He and his mother made a tiny perfect circle, and he was happy within its circumference—and as for those skills a father might've taught, well, there was Scoutmaster Tim, who struck Newt as a far better (surrogate) dad than a contest stylist could ever be.

Complications during the delivery led to severe scarring of her uterine walls. Newton would be the only child Elizabeth would ever have.

Some people around here have lots of kids, she'd tell her son. *It's like they're trying to get it* juuuust *right—the perfect child. Well, I got that right off the bat! I guess this was God's subtle way of telling me I didn't have to try anymore. I can always find another man, but I'll never be able to find another son.*

Oh hell, and *could* Elizabeth find another man. All she'd have to do is step outside and whistle: they'd come running from all directions with flowers and heart-shaped boxes of chocolate clasped in their callused hands. Elizabeth Thornton was a pure stunner. Another common phrase—"Island women are like Christmas trees: nobody wants them after the twenty-fifth"—didn't apply to her: her face had taken on a luminous haunted quality as she'd aged. It only intensified her beauty. She had no shortage of suitors despite being saddled with a teenager—even one as oddball as Newton.

But she resisted all advances and lived alone with her son in a small house on the edge of town. She was happy. Her son was happy. But Elizabeth was a perpetual worrywart. Much to Newt's chagrin, she wanted to drape him in bubble wrap before sending him out into the world. She didn't even approve of him being in Scouts. But it was the only social outlet he had—the kids at school could be so cruel; the sons of lobstermen and potato farmers didn't understand her sensitive boy. At least Scouts was better than

Newt spending his afternoons in the woods alone, cataloging ferns and tubers.

"You be careful," she'd told Newton at the boat launch before he'd left for Falstaff. She kissed his forehead and mussed up his hair. "Don't eat any funny mushrooms or chase after things that might bite you."

"Mom, *please*," Newton had said, mortified.

Her voice was in his ear even now, ever present, as he made his way through the storm-splintered cabin.

Newt—oh Newt my baby boy, this is not a good idea.

What choice did he have? His books were in here. The rope, too. Without them they might starve. And Kent might die just like the Scoutmaster had.

For a fleeting instant, Newton had a very un-Newtlike fantasy: he pictured himself stepping into a throng of well-wishers, his fellow Scouts sitting gratefully in Oliver McCanty's boat, which Newt had fixed and piloted back to the mainland. Next the mayor would pin a badge on Newt's chest in a ceremony at town hall, Scoutmaster Tim's portrait in a gilt-edged frame, his mom waving from the crowd, Max and Ephraim safe and thankful—his *friends* now—Newt demurring when the mayor called him a true hero, saying only: "It was all due to my Scouts training, sir." This silly self-obsessed fantasy left him feeling a little embarrassed.

The cabin roof bowed in a rotted arc to touch the floor—or *nearly* so. There was still a portion where it failed to reach: a jagged lip where the fungal-encrusted shingles didn't quite touch the floorboards. Newton knew that on the other side of that lip—maybe only a foot away—lay Scoutmaster Tim's body. And the last time he'd seen Tim, he'd been writhing with . . . Newton didn't want to think about it. But the first real threads of terror had now begun to squirm into his belly. An awful silence sat heavy within his chest—it was mirrored by the same awful silence on the other side of the roof where the Scoutmaster lay.

Or was it entirely? Newton was almost positive he could hear *something*.

Newton, oh my baby get out of there get out of there this instant!

He thought of Sherwood, his cousin. Tall, stout-shouldered Sher, all roped in farm-boy muscle. Which made him think about Alex Markson, the boy he'd made up on Facebook—a fusion between Sherwood and himself.

What would Alex Markson do? Newton wondered. He turned it into an acronym: *WWAMD?*

So . . . WWAMD in this situation? Alex wouldn't be afraid—no, Alex *would* be afraid, because Alex was most certainly a sane person with the correct instincts for self-preservation. But Alex would do whatever was needed. He'd do the right thing.

How could the worms still be alive if their host was dead? Shouldn't be possible, right? Newton stared at the lip between the shingles and the floor. A fleeting band of light traced along its edge . . .

Yes, *there*, he swore he saw movement. Tiny wavering shadows flitted through the light.

Then he heard the noises like cockroaches scuttling and shucking in a bowl of not-quite-solidified Jell-O. Saliva squirted into his mouth, bitter and tangy as the chlorophyll in a waxy leaf. He felt faint with fear. His stomach flooded with cold lead as his testicles drew up into his abdomen.

Get out of here right NOW!

It wasn't his mother anymore—this was the lizard brain speaking, the cold voice of survival. He went jelly-legged: the bones felt as if they had been reduced to marrow soup. Pure fear invaded his mind, creating a carnival of terrifying images. Visions of clean-picked skulls and empty sockets, huge white worms barreling out of inflamed tunnels like hellish bullet trains, long, tubelike hands slipping from the shadows reaching for . . . for . . .

A shuddering groan escaped Newton. He put his hand over his face and stumbled back. His ass hit the cabin wall and he yelped in surprise.

"Newton?" Max called out anxiously. "You okay?"

Newton swallowed with difficulty. It was so good to hear Max's voice—to remember that the world was bigger than this cabin with its collapsing angles and alien sounds that made Newton's skin scream.

"I'm okay. Just stay outside. Be out in a sec."

Newton realized that he *could* just get the hell out—it was one of the perks of being a kid, wasn't it? Kids could abandon anything at any time with no real repercussions.

Except there were no adults around anymore. And he had work to do.

He edged down the wall into the bedroom. There, his books were on the far side. A sleeping bag lay five feet beyond his right foot. He hunkered down and crab-crawled toward it. He heard those distant popgun pops—*Pfft! Pfft! Pfft!*—and imagined those weightless ribbons surging through the air toward him. He crawled faster, a desperate moan swelling in his chest.

He reached the sleeping bag and pulled it over him. Just before he did, he saw the air above him shimmering with luminous squiggles. He lay under the bag, inhaling the scent of its owner: stale sweat and pine sap and illicitly smoked cigarettes, so it must've been Eef's.

Newton rose with the bag tucked over his head. *Pfft! Pfft! Pfft!* He oriented himself, swallowed his fear—a plum stone lodged in his throat—and shuffled toward the closet with the bag held up like a shield. The squirming was very loud now, even through the cloth of the bag; it sounded eager and agitated at once.

Even though his heart was beating hard enough to shudder every bone in his body and adrenaline-rich sweat was dumping out of every pore, Newton advanced patiently and cautiously. God, somehow the worms were still alive, still firing off their *pfft!* fusillade. Newton figured they must be spores or eggs or something—a way for the worms to infect you from far away. On the peripheries of his vision, he could see the odd ribbon go floating past.

Don't breathe them in don't breathe in at all get out of here now now NOW NOW NOW

His toes hit the edge of the collapsed closet. The tip of Scoutmaster Tim's index finger lay beside his right foot. He flung down the sleeping bag and backpedaled madly as it settled over the Scoutmaster's body.

The *pfft!*s were muffled by the bag. The Scoutmaster's arm jutted from beneath it. Frozen at an unnatural angle, fingers like craggly bits of driftwood washed up on the beach.

Newton hustled over to his knapsack and made sure the nylon rope was still inside. His field book was a little water-fattened after the downpour, but still legible. He quickly checked to see if any of the ribbons had gotten on anything. No, he was clean. He stuffed the book in his knapsack, gave everything a final once-over, and hightailed it outside.

News item from the Montague (PEI) *Island Courier,*
October 22:

MEN ARRESTED AFTER BREACHING MILITARY'S QUARANTINE ZONE

Two men were placed under arrest following an incident that occurred several miles off the northern coast of North Point.

Reginald Kirkwood, 45, and Jeffrey Jenks, 43, both of Lower Montague County, were taken into custody by military police officers shortly after 10 a.m. this morning. Both were charged with Grand Larceny and direct contravention of a State of Emergency Order. The former charge carries a minimum sentence of five years under the Canadian Criminal Charter.

According to eyewitness accounts, Jenks—the town's police chief—and Kirkwood, its county coroner, stole a boat belonging to Mr. Calvin Walmack. Mr. Jenks piloted the boat across the 3-mile stretch separating the mainland from Falstaff Island, which remains under quarantine due to the potential presence of an unknown biological threat.

Exact details remain undisclosed, but available evidence suggests their boat experienced mechanical difficulties that hindered their progress. The boat was chased down by a pair of military patrol boats and both men were taken into custody.

Due to the proximity to the island and the potential for biological transfection, the boat was scuttled using an incendiary device.

The arrestees are the fathers of Kent Jenks and Maximilian Kirkwood, members of Scout Troop 52—which also includes Shelley Longpre, Newton Thornton, and Ephraim Elliot, all 14 years of age. They were accompanied to Falstaff Island by their Scoutmaster, Tim Riggs, 42, North Point's resident MD, last Friday evening for a weekend field trip. They have been isolated on Falstaff Island since the quarantine zone was established.

Calls to the military attaché's office went unreturned as of press time.

Chapter Twenty-Six

They set out just after noon. Three boys: Max, Ephraim, and Newton.

Max checked on Kent beforehand. Still huddled in the cellar under the tarp—his body looked like it was vanishing into the cellar wall, oozing into the hard-packed dirt, as if the wall had grown a mouth and was consuming Kent the way a spider eats a fly: injecting corrosive poison, dissolving the guts, and sucking them out with a long, needlelike proboscis.

"We'll be back soon," Max told him. He stood on the final step before the cellar floor, keeping his distance. "We'll find something to make you better, okay?"

Kent said nothing, just watched with eyes hard and dry as pebbles.

Shelley was missing. They called his name a few times, halfheartedly. No response.

"Should we go anyways?" Newton said.

"Why shouldn't we?" said Ephraim.

If the boys felt a vague uneasiness over Shelley's where-abouts—more and more it seemed best to keep him in plain sight—his disappearance gave them an easy excuse to leave without him. What harm could it bring?

Maybe he really did *walk into the sea*, Newton thought, not unhopefully, then quickly chastised himself for it.

Newton took the lead. Max and Ephraim didn't question this. After seeing him emerge from the cabin sweaty and near delirious with fear, his knapsack slung triumphantly over his shoulder . . . it was tough not to measure him a little differently.

The afternoon was bright but cool. Most of their clothing was inside the cabin, damp and unwearable. Ephraim had a Windbreaker. Newton only had one dry shirt.

They walked along the southern skirt of the island following the shore. Strands of kelp washed up on the rocks, looking like disembodied green hands clawing their way out of the sea. Ephraim peeled a strand and looked questioningly at Newton.

"Yeah, it's edible, Eef."

Ephraim nibbled an edge. "Holy crap, Newt!"

"I said it was edible," Newton said. "I didn't say it was any good."

Max peeled a strip off a flat rock. "Hey, it's not bad," he said, chewing. "Salty. Like beef jerky from the sea."

Ephraim took another crackly bite and chewed morosely. "Whatever. I'm hungry enough to eat a bear's asshole."

Soon after saying this, Ephraim lapsed into a moody silence. He kept rubbing his knuckles on his pants.

"You okay, man?" Max said.

He put a hand on his shoulder. Ephraim shivered as if a spider had crawled down his back. At first Max thought it was because of what'd happened outside the cellar—that awful *snap* between them, something Max had felt to his core. But that wasn't it, was it? A cold species of relief washed over Max, only to be replaced with dread. Was Eef . . . ? Max gave Newton a worried look as his hand slid off Ephraim's shoulder.

"Feeling real weird, man." Ephraim's voice sounded like it was coming from the bottom of a well. "I'm not really feeling like myself."

"Yeah, none of us are," Max assured him.

"Max is right, Eef. With what happened to the Scoutmaster and now Kent . . . we just got to hold it together a little while longer, is all."

Ephraim gave Newton a bemused and slightly shaken look. "Newton Thornton, professional pep-talker," he said bleakly.

They climbed a hillside that crested to a flat rise studded with boulders and hardy tufted shrubs. The air was perfumed by the salt wind that gusted across the table rock. The ground was pockmarked with holes. Each hole was dug down to a tight gooseneck bend that obscured its occupants from view.

"Prairie dogs?" Max asked.

"Are we on a prairie?" said Ephraim. "Where are the cowboys, Tex?"

"Shut up," Max said irritably. "Cowboys aren't all on the prairies anyway."

Ephraim laughed and scratched his elbows. He'd scratched through his Windbreaker. Max noticed blood dotting the torn nylon.

"Not prairie dogs," said Newton. "*Birds.* I've read about them. Instead of making nests in trees, they burrow underground."

Max said: "Can we catch one?"

Newton looked doubtful. "I've never seen a rope trap for birds—you need box traps for those, with chicken wire. I don't think it'd be worth it. They're pretty much just bones and feathers, right?"

Max thought about those dead shearwaters on his kitchen table and said: "Let's not bother, okay?"

"Whatever we do eat out here, you can bet it's going to be a bit weird," Newton said. "We ought to be prepared for that." He smiled gamely. "Just think of it all like chicken or something."

They crossed the plateau to a granite shelf overlooking the sea. The clean mineral smell of the rock hit their noses. Sunlight filled in the slack water between the waves in mellow gold. White ospreys took flight from their cliff-side nests, arcing over the water.

Ephraim kicked a stone over the edge. It clattered down the cliff and nearly crushed an osprey nest sitting on a jagged outcrop. Ephraim pointed at the trio of brown-specked eggs in the nest and said:

"You want to climb down for those? I could go for a three-egg omelet."

Newton looked dubious. "There's nowhere to tie the rope. If you slip, it's a long way down."

Ephraim picked his tongue along his upper teeth, still considering it. "I'd have to share the eggs with your fat ass, Newt—wouldn't I? I do all the work and you horn in on the reward."

"You can have them," Newton said stiffly. "I just don't think it's worth getting hurt over."

With the prospect of eggs fading, they wandered down a switchback descent that emptied into a salt marsh to the east of the cliff. The ocean water leached into a mucky terrain of buckled trees and diseased-looking hummocks. A rotten stench boiled up from the long grass, which was exactly the sort of grass Newton hated: the serrated-edge kind that raked your shins when you walked through it in shorts.

They trudged through, trying to avoid soakers. Their boots cracked through skeins of crusted bile-colored salt that looked like the scum topping a pot of boiled meat. Late-season grasshoppers flung themselves off the grass and stuck to the boys' clothes with their barbed legs. Newton flinched every time one pinged off his hips.

His gaze kept drifting to those hummocks. They looked like half-submerged rodents—giant mole rats suckled on plutonium-enriched water that had somehow quadrupled their normal size. They dotted the marsh like hairy icebergs, the worst parts hidden underwater. Newton pictured what might lurk below the surface: long, narrow faces and thin black lips studded with sharp rat-teeth that protruded at busted-glass angles . . . ringed pink tails sweeping through the filthy water waiting to wrap around an unsuspecting ankle.

They came upon a rotted tree stump. Newton dug his field book out, riffled through the pages, and skimmed a passage. He grabbed a flap of bark hanging loosely from the stump and pried it back. It snapped with a puff of dust. The boys knelt and stared inside. Things wriggled in the loose wood pulp. They wriggled just like worms.

"Grubs," Newton anounced. He opened his book and read: *"Witchetty grubs are the large, white, wood-eating larvae of moths."*

The grubs were a speckled white with a wrinkled exterior that resembled the skin of an apple that had sat in the fruit bowl too long. Their bodies were as big as a toddler's finger and crimped like beads on a necklace. Their back ends tapered to a pooched orifice. They moved in frantic wriggling paroxysms: they resembled creatures in a perpetual state of being born.

"The raw witchetty grub tastes like almonds," Newton read. *"When cooked, the skin becomes crisp like roast chicken, while the inside becomes light yellow like a fried egg."*

Max blanched. "Jesus. You're kidding, right?"

"Didn't I say that whatever we ate, it'd be weird?"

"Yeah, but . . . you can't eat a grub, man," Max replied. "You'd be depriving that young moth of its life goal of bashing into a lightbulb all night."

Newton plucked one out of the stump. It writhed in his palm like a section of intestinal tract trying to pass a stubborn lump of food.

Max said: "I *dare* you. Double dog, man."

Newton popped it into his mouth. Pulped between Newton's molars, the grub made an audible *squelch*. Watery pus-colored fluid seeped between his teeth.

"I can't believe you just did that," Ephraim said, awestruck.

"Ooh," Newton gagged. "*Bitter.* It's not almondy!" He dropkicked the book. It sailed across the marsh, pages fluttering like the wings of a crippled bird. "It's not *almondy at all!*"

Ephraim and Max doubled over laughing. Newton refused to spit it out—he seemed to hold the grub's revolting taste against it. He chewed with dour discipline, clenching his fists as he swallowed.

"Wait a sec," Max said, nervousness replacing mirth. "Did you say it tasted like bitter almonds? Isn't that like, *poison*?"

Newton rolled his eyes. A bit of the grub was still stuck to his lip. It looked like a bleached shred of tomato skin. "No, that's cyanide. This didn't taste like almonds at all. It tasted like bitter . . . *shit*. A bitter nugget of shit."

"How do you know what shit tastes like?" said Ephraim, swiping a tear off his cheek.

"How about *you* shut up," Newton said, stooping to retrieve his field book. "At least I'm trying, Eef." He held his arms out, an all-encompassing gesture. "You see a Burger King out here?"

Chapter Twenty-Seven

Shelley waited until the boys had humped around the island's southern breakwater before starting his games in earnest.

He'd hid in the high brush east of the cabin. The boys called his name without much gusto. The sun slanted through a bank of silvery knife-blade clouds, hitting his skin and buzzing unpleasantly—Shelley didn't care for the sun. His favorite time of day was twilight, that gray interregnum where the shadows drew long.

His fingers fretted with his lip, which Kent had split. Squeezing the wound, the cleaved flesh only semi-healed. Blood squirted, running down his knuckles. Shelley didn't feel it much at all.

Newton's voice had drifted over to him. "Should we go anyway?"

Yes, thought Shelley, playing with the blood. *Just go. Leave, now. Enjoy your hike.*

He'd followed Newton, Max, and Eef to the south shore, skulking through the brush on the low side of the trail. He disguised his presence well—Shelley was a natural chameleon; it was one of his more undervalued talents.

He was intrigued by Newton's belly and back flab. It spilled over the waist of his pants like soft-serve ice cream over the edges of a cone. He wondered how it would look if the fat boy got worms. He imagined the buttery folds of skin lapping up on themselves like those ugly-looking dogs—what were they called? Shar-peis. Newton would have a shar-pei body. Inside all those yards of empty skin, his bones would be left to rattle around like pennies in a jar. Boy, that would be something to see.

Once the boys were gone he backtracked to the cabin. He was *excited*. Oh so excited. It took events of precipitous magnitude to pierce the Teflon plating surrounding Shelley's emotional core and make him feel much of anything.

But there was much to hold his interest today.

The dead men in the wrecked cabin. The ships offshore and the black helicopter that swept occasionally overhead. The sheer fact that there was nobody of consequential authority around for miles. He didn't have to wear his mask so tightly. He could loosen the straps and let the things underneath twist their way into the light.

But mostly there was Kent Jenks—Johnny Football, Mr. Big Shot, the uncrowned king of North Point—locked up in the root cellar.

Oh my God, the *fun* they were going to have.

The last time Shelley could recall feeling this level of elation was the afternoon he'd killed Trixy, the kitten his mother adopted after finding her under their porch.

Shelley had been killing things for a while by then—although he didn't think of it as killing, per se. Other creatures, even people, were empty vessels. Of course, not *physically* empty: all living things were packed full of guts and bones and blood that leapt giddily into the air when it was released from a vein. But none of them had an essential . . . well, *essence*. They were just ambulatory sacks of skin. That was really it. Shelley honestly felt no more remorse tearing another living thing apart than he would ripping the limbs off a wooden marionette.

He'd gotten started with bugs. He'd found these two big stag beetles entangled in a territorial battle in the crotch of the backyard maple. He'd gathered them up and, after some preparation, pulled most of their legs and antennae off—he used his mother's tweezers for this delicate work, the same ones she plucked her eyebrows with—and put them in a matchbox. He was surprised and delighted to discover that beetles were cannibals: when he'd opened the box a few days later, he found one of them flipped helplessly on its back and the other one devouring its gooey insides.

He'd promptly filled the matchbox with his mother's nail polish remover and lit it with a match. The beetles' organs popped and crackled inside their black exoskeletons as they roasted.

He soon graduated to bigger, more impressive conquests. He caught deer mice in sticky traps and painted liquid Borax onto their eyeballs with a Q-tip—it was mesmerizing to watch their black eyes shrivel and sputter like fat in a fire.

Shelley found that animals adjusted to their physical diminishments much better than people. If you burned a man's eyes out, he would shriek and bleat, of course, and he'd need a cane and a Seeing-Eye dog the rest of his moaning, miserable days. A mouse just stumbled around in pain for a few minutes, pawed at its cored-out eye sockets, squeaked and twitched its nose, and carried on with what it was doing before. Animals were incredibly flexible that way.

Shelley had gone to work on Trixy during an evening when his parents were off at a silent auction for their church. He was at the kitchen table eating a Creamsicle. Trixy twined round his socked feet, brushing against his calves.

"Hello, kitty-kitty."

She hopped up on his lap. Her little claws pierced his sweatpants and dug lightly into his thighs. Shelley chewed on the Popsicle stick while petting the kitten. She arched her back to accept his soft strokes. Her fur was downy like the hair on a baby's head. He could feel her small, thin bones beneath her coat.

He carried her upstairs. She was purring quite loudly—such big, satisfied noises from such a small thing. Her body was a power plant, kicking off a lot of heat. Shelley's mother hadn't had her spayed yet.

He went into the bathroom and locked the door. He put Trixy on the toilet lid, where she kneaded the macramé seat cover. His mom said this was a sign of separation anxiety—kittens would knead their mothers' bellies to stimulate milk, so they could nurse. But kittens who'd been separated too early kneaded anything. Sweaters and sofa cushions and toilet seats—as if any of those had the ability to squirt milk. They were confused, according to Shelley's mother. A real heartbreaker, she said. Shelley just nodded as if he felt the same way, too. He found that if you nodded—slowly, deeply, your chin almost touching your chest to indicate sincerity—people would think you shared their feelings. It was one of the many tricks he'd learned in order to blend in; hiding in plain sight was a beneficial skill.

Shelley plugged the bathtub drain and ran the water, glancing back to the toilet. Trixy was still there, purring. Good. As the tub filled, his hand crept under the elasticized hem of his sweats to toy absently with his privates. He wasn't surprised to find that he was erect—a throbbing, urgent hardness that seemed to drain the blood out of his arms and legs and focus it all on his penis. He stood with his mouth unhinged, eyes alight with unspeakable excitement, an oily sweat breaking out over his long, milky body.

He opened the cabinet under the sink and donned the long plastic gloves draped over a canister of Ajax: his mother's cleaning gloves. His fingertips went cold while the rest of him burnt with a steady eager heat.

He sat Trixy on the edge of the tub. The kitten stared up at him with round yellow-edged eyes as her paws slipped for purchase on the porcelain. Another thing about animals: they had no conception that the creatures who fed them might be the same ones who could do them such great harm.

Scout Law number eight: *A Scout is a friend to animals . . .*

Shelley grabbed Trixy by her scruff and plunged her into the water.

It was as if raw electrical current had been pumped into Trixy's body: her limbs went rigid and scrabbled against the porcelain. She almost screwed out of his grip, but he grabbed her throat—his hand manacled easily around the furry drainpipe of her neck—and shoved her back down.

After twenty seconds, her struggles lessened. After about a minute, her struggles ceased. Shelley gave it another few seconds just to be certain.

He let go of her motionless body. A dry, dusty taste filled his mouth—it was like he'd swallowed a mouthful of the chalk they spread into white lines on a baseball diamond. But already the elation was subsiding. It was over so fast. The kitten had almost no fight in her at a—

Trixy shot straight up out of the water. She looked so damn scraggly with her fur soaked and matted to her skin. Shelley almost laughed. Trixy yowled and scrabbled up the sloped side of the bathtub. Shelley reached in and lovingly collected her four little legs into a bundle, clasping them all in one hand. She bit feebly at his gloves with her needle teeth. She let out a desperate *reeeeeooowl* and beheld him with tragically confused eyes.

He dunked her under the water. His face was expressionless, but the sweat had now soaked through his shirt. His penis was painfully hard and he felt the excruciating yet somehow pleasant need to urinate.

He pulled Trixy out of the tub. Her head lolled comically

between her shoulder blades. He dunked her once more, absentmindedly, the way an old biddy dips her bag of Earl Grey in a teacup.

She may still be alive, he thought. He considered letting her live. That could be interesting. Shelley figured Trixy might act like Johnnie Ritson, who as a boy had swum out beyond the shore markers and nearly drowned. Now Timmy spent his days in an old rocker in front of the Hasty convenience store saying "Hi! Hi! Hi!" to everything: customers, random passersby, delivery trucks, pigeons, the clear blue sky. One time Shelley put a tack on Timmy's rocker when he was using the toilet, waiting until nobody was watching. Timmy's reaction amazed and amused him: he sat heavily, gulping from a can of Yoo-hoo, just rocking and rocking, blabbing "Hi! Hi! Hi!" He didn't register it at all. Shelley had lingered, intrigued, and when Timmy got up he'd seen the brass head of the tack flush with Timmy's wide, flat ass, the surrounding fabric dark with blood.

Unfortunately, Shelley figured a stumblebum kitten might raise his mother's eyebrows. The safest option was the one that most compelled him, anyway.

When it was done, Shelley drained the tub and made sure everything was dried with a bath towel from the rack. He draped the plastic gloves back over the Ajax. Then he went downstairs and got an orange trash sack and put Trixy inside.

Before Trixy, Shelley had never killed anything that might be missed. Ultimately, he decided to burn her. He stuffed her in the pellet stove in the basement. Trixy went up in a burst of whiteness behind the grate. Shelley was fleetingly concerned that the smell of burnt fur would rise through the vents to permeate the house, but any suspicious odors were well gone by the time his parents got home.

It was here that Shelley had an epiphany: proper disposal was its own alibi. The kitten was gone. It wasn't necessarily *dead*. It may have run away. Cats did it all the time. Cats were stupid and ungrateful.

When Trixy disappeared, his mother was in a *state*. She mooned around the house, gazing forlornly into the back-yard—which made life harder for Shelley, as he conducted business in the yard and didn't want his mom to see him at work. "Isn't it *awful* about Trixy?" she asked. "The poor thing." Shelley nodded deeply, sincerely, chin touching his chest. Every so often he'd catch his mother looking at him—not accusingly, exactly, but . . . *questioningly*. As if the son she'd given birth to had been poached in the night, replaced with an exact physical duplicate. This duplicate spoke in her son's voice and aped his intellect and abilities, but there was some-thing *worrisome* about this new one. He—*it?*—was a step outside of humankind, looking in. Did it like what it saw?

But if his mother indeed felt this, she'd never given voice to it. Parents held an intrinsic need to believe in the essential goodness of their offspring—their kids were a direct reflec-tion of themselves, after all.

A week after murdering Trixy, Shelley lay in bed, a wedge of cold moonlight slanting through the curtains to plate his pasty, wasplike face. He replayed the scene in his head: Trixy, waterlogged and wild-eyed, rocketing from the tub. It brought the tingle back to his privates—the bedsheet tented at his crotch—but the sensation was pitifully diminished, a watery imitation of that galvanic rush. Shelley pondered: if he'd felt that rush with something so pathetic as a kitten, imagine how it'd feel with something bigger, stronger, more intelligent. The risk would only intensify the euphoria, wouldn't it?

Shelley walked past the remains of the campfire and cut around the side of the cabin to the cellar. He crouched and tapped gently on the cellar door.

"Kent," he called in a singsong voice. "Oh *Keeeeennnn-tah*."

Something clawed up the steps at the sound of his voice—it sounded like a huge sightless crab. There came the hollow *thip* of bone on wood. Dust sifted down from the hinges. Shelley inhaled a gust of sweet air that stunk of rotted honeycomb. For an instant, Shelley saw a creature between the cellar slats: a thing composed of famished angles and horrible bone, the raw outcroppings of its face standing out in razored points.

Fingers slipped through the gap between the doors. They did not look like anything that ought to be attached to a human being: shockingly spindly and so awfully withered, like ancient carrots that had been left in a cold, dark fridge so long that they'd lost their pigment. None of them had fingernails—just bloody sickles rimmed by shreds of torn cuticle. Shelley assumed Kent had eaten them, one after another. *This little piggy went to market, this little piggy stayed home . . .*

"I'm so hungry."

The voice was ancient, too. Shelley pictured an ineffably old man-boy crouched on the stairs: a wrinkled horror with snowy hair and incredibly ancient eyes, the corneas gone a sickly yellow like a cat's eyes—like Trixy's eyes?

Shelley said: "You're still hungry? Even after you ate all our food?" He *tsk*ed. "Do you think I should let you out?"

"I don't know," Kent said, sounding confused. A sulky child.

"I think you deserve to be there. Don't you think, Kent? You made us lock the Scoutmaster up. So we locked you up. That's fair, isn't it?"

Silence.

"I asked you a question. Isn't it fair, Kent?"

"Yes," Kent said in a petulant tone.

"Tit for tat, right?"

"Yes."

227

"The Scoutmaster's dead."

Silence again.

"Whose fault is that, Kent?"

The silence persisted.

"Hey!" Shelley chirped sunnily. "Remember the helicopter? It dropped a care package. *Food.* Juicy meat and buttery bread and candy and—"

"Please."

Shelley had never heard a word *wept* before. But that's what Kent had done. He'd actually wept the word *please.*

"Please what, Kent?"

"Please . . . feed me."

"I *could.* But first, Kent, you need to answer my question. I'll ask again: Whose fault is it that the Scoutmaster is dead?"

"It's . . . it's my fault. It's all my fault. But I didn't mean—I never meant to—"

"It doesn't matter what you *meant,* Kent. It only matters what happened." Shelley's voice was silky soft. "So think about this. He died very badly. A tree fell on his head, you know. His skull got crushed like an eggshell. So yes, Kent, it's really, truly, totally all your fault."

Faint, beautiful weeping. Shelley drank up the sound the way a succulent plant drinks up the sunlight. His jaws were strangely elongated, the lower part a half-inch longer than the upper to reveal a wet ridge of teeth. He looked like a salmon in rut.

"Thank you for answering my question, Kent. Now, what would you like to eat?"

"Anything. *Anything.*"

"I mean, there's so much. I can't carry it all back here. So you'll have to tell me. We have apple pie and chocolate-glazed doughnuts and big steaks and—"

"Meat. *Meat.*"

"You wait here," Shelley said, as if Kent had a choice. "I'll be right back."

Shelley stole through the cabin's shattered door. Early afternoon sunlight fell through the roof's broken latticework, quilting the floor in honey-colored bars.

The roof sagged down before him. He unscrewed an old glass light fixture that now sat at eye level—amazingly, it hadn't been smashed during the storm. Inside the frosted glass bowl were several dozen insect carcasses. Flies mostly, along with a few dragonflies and moths. He shook the crackly remains into his palm and went back to the cellar.

"Here's the first course, Kent. It's . . . peanut brittle."

Shelley placed a desiccated dragonfly corpse in Kent's fingers. They disappeared through the crack into the darkness. Eager crunching sounds. The fingers reappeared.

"More."

Shelley fed Kent dead bugs as if he were feeding a goat at a petting zoo. Kent made pitiful groveling sounds as he ate. Shelley couldn't believe his good fortune. This island, the isolation, this distracting illness—it was the ultimate playground.

His eyeballs felt tacky in their sockets; a dry saltlick taste lay thick on his tongue. His penis throbbed fiercely inside his trousers; he pushed it with the heel of his palm, squashing it against his thigh to achieve a dizzying, elating pleasure. *Quit playing pocket pool!* Mr. Turley would've said if he'd caught Shelley doing it in gym class. But Mr. Turley wasn't here, was he? *No* adult was here—except the dead ones in the cabin—meaning Shelley could do exactly as he wished . . . but he *must* be careful. It would be so easy to make a mistake—to "blow it," his father might say—ruining his lovely game. He mustn't get carried away.

"More," Kent whispered.

"All gone," Shelley said. "No more. You ate it all."

"Please."

229

"Tell me how it feels, Kent. Tell me and I'll give you something else."

"It feels *empty*. There's a hole and it keeps getting bigger and bigger and bigger. Forever and ever and ever. It wants me, Shel—and it wants you, too. Wants all of you."

Shelley crouched for a moment, gnawing on the inside of his cheek. Kent sounded bad—seriously bad. *Bugfuck nuts,* as the island phrase went. A pang of concern snuck into Shelley; at first he didn't know what it was, seeing as he didn't experience emotions the way others did. An uncomfortable nibbling in his belly, like hungry baby mice.

Shelley returned to the cabin. The dead man, or what was left of him, had fallen off the sofa during the storm. His limbs were ramrod-straight with rigor mortis. His legs stuck out straight with his toes pointed up. Patches of bright green fungus bloomed around his eye sockets and the edges of his mouth.

The man's nose had fallen into his face. Shelley watched a beetle crawl out of his sunken septum. It climbed to the crest of one nostril rim—just a hardened hole of cartilage like a little manhole in the man's face—and hung there unsteadily.

The interlocked halves of its exoskeleton came apart. A high pressurized hiss: it sounded like a steam valve blowing from very far away. The beetle cracked open. Shelley could see white things wriggling inside of it.

A subspecies of some raw emotion—not fear, but something hovering at its edges—spider-scuttled into Shelley's chest.

He knelt beside the big dead worm on the floor. It had hardened and toughened like an earthworm sizzled on a summer sidewalk. He scraped it up with the edge of his knife. Its insides were still mushy and gelatinous. Custardy-yellow goo squeezed through slits in its skin.

A new, wildly intriguing idea formed in Shelley's mind.

He returned to the cellar. Kent's fingers wriggled at the slit.

"Supper's on, Kent," Shelley said.

The leathery strap of the dead worm disappeared through the slit—jerked with sudden violence, it slipped between the slats with a breathless zippering hiss. Next: sucking sounds. Contented babyish coos. The fingers appeared again, streaked with yellow slime.

"I'm sorry," Shelley said, although of course he'd never been sorry for a single thing his entire life. "No more food. Kent, you went and ate it all. You greedy pig, you ate it all."

Shelley walked away. He'd become bored with Kent, whose throaty cackle followed him back to the firepit.

"You promised!" Kent shrieked. *"You promised me* meat! *Come back! Pleeeease!"*

Shelley sat beside the dead fire, stirring the ashes with a stick. He drew squiggles. Worms on the brain, must be. He felt like one of those circus performers who spun plates atop long bamboo poles. Lots of irons in the ole fire, as his dad would say.

Next up: Ephraim. Stupid, angry Eef. Eef the fatherless freak. Eef the cuckoo bird who went to Dr. Harley's office to babble about his *feelings.* When Shelley's homeroom teacher suggested that perhaps *he* could benefit from a session or two with Dr. Harley—this after she'd caught Shelley poking the class hamster, Puggins, with a pencil, the tip of which he'd scrupulously sharpened—his mother had scoffed, outraged. *My son doesn't need to see a damn headshrinker, thank-you-very-much-good-day.*

Earlier, back in the cellar, Shelley spotted Eef staring at his hands. His knuckles had broken open when he'd punched Kent—an incident Shelley had enjoyed immensely because it meant group dynamics were shifting. Changes made people unsure, especially boys his age, because routines were important. When you took away routines, things went haywire. And Shelley liked haywire, because then anything could happen.

Shelley could tell that Ephraim was afraid that whatever was in Kent had gotten into him—it'd leapt between their bodies, from Kent's lips to Ephraim's hand, swimming in on the rush of blood. Shelley knew Ephraim was scared and he foresaw a great profit in nursing that fear along. It would be easy. Ephraim was so predictable—so predictably stupid.

Of course, Shelley hadn't seen the teeny-tiny worms at that point—but he'd understood that the sickness, whatever it was, scurried inside of you, ate you from the inside out. That's what made it so scary. This wasn't a bear or a shark or a psycho axe murderer; those things were bad, sure, but you could get away from them. Hide.

How could you hide from a murderer who lived under your skin?

After the storm, when they went in the cabin and saw the Scoutmaster's rotting body, saw those threadlike worms squirming in his chest—Shelley couldn't believe it. Everything was coming up aces.

Now it was simply a matter of keeping all those plates spinning.

Shelley had a method of probing, of opening doors in people that was uncanny. He rarely used this gift—it could get him in trouble. But he was able to spy the weak spots the way a sculptor saw the seams in a block of granite; one tap in the right spot and it'd split right open.

I saw something, Eef.

That was all it had taken. The smallest seedling—he'd slit Ephraim's skin, just the thinnest cut, slipping that seed in. If Shelley did some additional work, well, maybe that seed would squirm into Ephraim's veins, surf to his heart, and bloom into something beautiful. Or horrible. It didn't matter which to Shelley.

Reaching into his pocket, he pulled out the walkie-talkie. He'd slipped the other one into Ephraim's backpack this morning, while the other boys had been busying themselves for the hike. He fiddled with the button, not quite ready to put his plan into action.

After all, how much good luck did one boy deserve?

Chapter Twenty-Eight

Sometime around midafternoon, Ephraim sat down and refused to get up.

"That's it. I'm not walking anymore."

They had come to a copse of spruce trees. The air was dense with the scent of pine: it smelled like the car air fresheners drivers hung off their rearview mirrors.

Ephraim sat on a moss-covered rock with his fingers knit together in his lap. His body position mimicked a famous Roman sculpture that Newton had seen in a history book: *The Pugilist at Rest*. Ephraim looked a bit like a statue himself. His skin had a slick alabaster hue, except for around the lips and the rims of his nostrils, where it had a bluish-gray tint. Newton had a scary premonition: if they left Ephraim here and came back years later, he was sure Eef's body would remain in this fixed position—a statue of calcified bone.

"Come on," Newt said gently. "It's gonna be okay. We're going to find food soon."

"Not hungry," Ephraim said.

"Well, that's sort of good news. It means you're not sick, right?"

"It doesn't mean anything." There was an undertone of liquid menace in Ephraim's voice. "We don't really know anything, do we?"

234

"We have to keep moving, man," said Max. "If we can find a good place to set a trap, then—"

"Then *what*, Max?" Ephraim's chin was cocked at its customary challenging jut. "We catch a skunk? Great! Wonderful! Let's all chow down on skunk burgers that'll taste like skunk ass."

Newt said: "We can't just give up."

"Hey, you guys do whatever you want. I'm not stopping you."

Newton looked at Max as if he should say something. They were best friends, after all—other than Ephraim's own mother, Max was the only person on North Point who could reliably get Eef to calm down and stop acting crazy. But more and more, even Max felt powerless to address Ephraim's mounting mania.

Ephraim kept rubbing his fingers over his knuckles. The skin around the raw wounds was inflamed.

"Do you see anything?" he asked nobody in particular.

Max said: "See what, man?"

Ephraim said: "Nothing. It's nothing."

Max and Newton exchanged a glance. Neither of them wanted to leave Ephraim, but they both knew they couldn't force him to come. If they pressed too hard he'd lash out, maybe even hurt one of them. The group was casting off all inessential members, winnowing down to an unlikely core.

"What would you rather," Max said. "Keep hiking and find some food or stay here alone, sitting on a rock—pouting?"

Ephraim shot to his feet, fists balled, chest butting into Max's; he got so close that their chins touched, their noses, too—so close that Max could smell Eef's breath, which was bad, yeah, but not sweet: just the regular bile-and-stomach-acid smell of a boy who hadn't eaten properly in days. He saw the familiar fire in Ephraim's eyes: less a flame, really, than jags of blue electricity crackling outward from his irises; it reminded Max of the plasma globe at the Science Center.

Ephraim's fist rose with sudden swiftness, knuckles striking Max's chin. It wasn't a hard punch, but hard enough to snap his teeth together with an audible *click.* It didn't hit Max's knockout button, his legs didn't even tremble—Ephraim took most of the steam off it—but it was a punch all the same.

Ephraim pushed Max away, as if their closeness might prompt him to lash out again. Max's heart shuddered in his chest. He could feel the lingering imprint of his best friend's knuckles on the underside of his chin: three perfect points still burning into his skin.

Ephraim's jaw worked, his teeth grinding side to side; it appeared he might burst into tears.

"I'm sorry. You know I didn't mean that, Max."

Max rubbed his jaw. He'd never been punched before. "I know, Eef. It's okay."

Ephraim shook his head. "No it's not. No. It's. *Not.*"

The three boys stood in the greenish, claustrophobic light. Ephraim slumped back on the rock.

"We have to go, Eef," Newton said softly. "Are you sure you don't want to—"

"I'm not going anywhere."

"But so . . . you'll stay right here?" Newt asked.

"I'm not going anywhere," Ephraim repeated.

"Okay. We'll be back soon."

"Do whatever you want."

Max and Newton left him. They slipped under the canopy of spruce fronds into the clearing beyond.

Chapter Twenty-Nine

After they were gone, Ephraim sat motionless. The wind stirred the treetops, blowing pinecones off the boughs. Reaching into his pocket, he retrieved one of the two remaining cigarettes, lighting it with the Zippo. It tasted disgustingly sweet, like the tobacco had been drenched in rancid syrup.

He tweezed obsessively at the swollen flesh edging his knuckles. He picked and twisted until fresh blood flowed. It dripped off his fingertips and pattered onto the brown needles. He scrutinized it for *wriggles*.

The pain was sharp but bearable. It felt really good. Really *necessary*. Idly, not really aware of his actions, Ephraim angled the cigarette until its burning ember drew near the flesh of his wrist. He felt the heat but wasn't alarmed by it. Touching his skin, the ember made a sizzling sound like bacon in a frying pan. The stink of burnt hair, the vaguely sugary smell of crisped skin. The ember left a blackened divot, pain radiating from it like the rays of a cartoon sun. Endorphins and adrenaline washed through Ephraim, calming him somewhat—but the feeling didn't last.

They were inside of him. Somehow he both knew and didn't know this unavoidable fact—or he *knew* and yet hoped with every ounce of belief that he was wrong.

I saw something, Eef. Under your fingernail.

Shelley's words drilled into his head, blistering his brain like a branding iron. How could Shelley see *anything*? Dark in the cellar, a storm shaking the earth. But Shelley's words had only reinforced Ephraim's own belief: they'd gotten inside.

Simple math: Kent was sick. He'd punched Kent. They'd shared blood. Ephraim may as well have thrown open a door and said: *Welcome to the party!*

At first there had only been one . . . a tiny, white, hungry guest squirming contentedly in the half-moon of his fingernail. And Ephraim would've permitted it to live in his fingernail, if it promised to stay under the nail like a pet in a glass bubble. Ephraim was generous—he could give up that much of his body. He'd even show it to his friends to gross them out: *Look, guys, I've got a new friend.* He'd let it have his whole finger, even; plenty of men back home on the island were missing fingers—they'd get pulled off on factory lines, shredded in tractor gears—so okay, no big loss.

But these *things* weren't content with a fingernail, a finger, a hand, or an arm. They wanted the whole enchilada.

Ephraim thought about those little white tubes bending toward him in the cabin. He'd stood mesmerized, swooning in fear as those shimmery strands floated toward him. Ephraim's heart-blood had seized, veins feeling like they'd been pumped full of quick-dry cement. He hadn't moved an inch. None of the other boys had stepped in to save him, either. Scout Law number two: *A Scout is loyal to the king, his country, and his fellow Scouters.* Well, fuck that. Ephraim's fellow Scouters hung him out to dry, even his so-called forever friend.

But he wasn't mad at them, really. Would *he* have stepped in if those threads had drifted toward Newton—even Max? He blamed himself for acting like a stupid stunned cow.

That inward-looking anger crystallized into rage, which then transformed quite suddenly into fear.

Ephraim was as terrified as he'd ever been in his life. Something was inside of him—he was almost positive of that now. Locked up behind his skin. Incubating. That something had become *somethings*. Multiplying and feeding and *breeding*. That was how any living entity increased its numbers, wasn't it? They were having *sex* inside of him, like those disgusting snakes in the rocks. Things were fucking inside his skin right this instant.

He'd never had sex himself. Sure, he'd gotten his hand up Becky Scott's skirt on the baseball bleachers behind the Lions Club before she'd protested about being a good Baptist girl—of course, she'd *taken* his hand and *put* it there in the first place. Ephraim realized girls couldn't be understood the way boys could be, but still, he'd been looking forward to touching a girl again, to reexperience that light-headed sensation of his heartbeat shivering every inch of his skin. But that seemed less likely now. Because of the stranger, and the Scoutmaster. And Kent. And now himself?

Their sly squirming infested his ears. The surface of his flesh trembled as they moved beneath it—or was that just the dappling of the sunlight on his arms? No: they were *there*. But they were being sneaky about it. Burrowing inside of him like rats in the walls. Chewing away at the insulation and gnawing at the foundation.

He stared at the crook of his elbow. A fat blue vein pulsed there. He put his thumb on it to stop the blood flow. The beat of blood through his vein seemed out of line with the beat of his own heart. Like something else had commandeered it.

We could share. Ephraim directed this desperate plea into his body like a phantom radio signal. *Share ME—my body. Okay? But like, you can't do to me what you did to Scoutmaster Tim. You really shouldn't have done that. Maybe you can't help yourselves? I get it. I have control issues, too. We could—what's the word? Like, live together. But you can't . . . you better not . . . don't you fucking eat me!*

Ephraim screamed—the sound of a nail levered out of a wet plank of wood. What a colossal fucking *idiot*. Trying to reason with these *things*. May as well reason with the tide, with a fucking salamander. He wondered if the Scoutmaster had resorted to that—if in the final hours and minutes he'd sobbed out an entreaty, wishing for mercy. What the fuck would it matter?

Ephraim wished they'd just go away. Could he flush them out? Could he *dig* them out?

"Eef? . . . Ephraim?"

His name, coming from his backpack. He lifted the flap and found the walkie-talkie. Dazedly he said: "Yeah?"

"You guys left without me."

"We couldn't find you, Shel."

"It's okay, I'm not angry. How's it going?"

"I'm by myself. Max and Newt left."

Silence. Then: *"Really?"*

Ephraim sniffed. His sinuses were full of snot, like when he used to cry—he couldn't remember the last time he'd cried. When he'd seen that repairman blown off his cherry picker by a burst of electricity, maybe?

"They had to get food. I was holding them back."

The air crackled, full of static. *"Real friends wouldn't leave you. Sorry, Eef, but that's the truth."*

"Would you have left, Shel?"

Silence again. Then: *"I'm not really a friend, Eef—am I?"*

Ephraim stared at his pointer finger. The milky crescent under the nail—the *lunate*, that part is called. How did he know that?

"No, Shel. I guess you're something else."

"How you feeling? You don't sound too hot."

There was something ghastly, something monstrously and soulsuckingly *awful* about Ephraim's situation: alone and full of *things*, his only confidant a brooding, toxic boy—Creepy Shel, the girls at school called him; the Creepazoid; the Toucher—on a crackly walkie-talkie. A sense of despondency settled into him, marrow-deep.

"*Eef, you still there?*"

"Uh."

"*You hungry?*"

Oh, fuck YOU, Shel. Rage boiled up Ephraim's gorge—then transmuted swiftly into a fear so profound that beads of sweat squeezed from the skin of his brow, *pop-pop-pop* like salty BBs. Hugging his arms tight across his body, chest hitching, Ephraim rocked side to side. His dearest wish was to be home, safe in bed, with his mother humming downstairs as she cooked: meatballs, sausage and peppers, or even lobster, which he thought of as sea bugs and totally loathed. But the surety and safety, the calm cadence of his mother's voice—yes, he missed that terribly.

The *things*. He felt them. Massing behind his eyeballs. Infesting his corneal vaults, twining round his ocular stems. Packing his sinuses, a wriggling white multitude, squeezing through his aqueous humors like tears. Spilling down his nose, down the back of his throat, million upon million gorging themselves, growing fat on him. Ephraim was crying now—yet he barely realized this.

"*I can help you, Eef.*"

Ephraim sucked back snot. "W-w-what?"

"*I said—are you listening? Really, really listening? I said I can help.*"

"H-how?"

In the still tranquillity of the island woods, wind stirring gently in the treetops, Shelley began to speak. His words were soft, honeyed, washing over Ephraim like a tropical zephyr. It all made so much *sense.*

Ephraim pulled his Swiss Army knife out of his pocket. His mother had bought it for him. It hadn't been his birthday or Christmas—she got it for him just because. She *never* did that. Never enough money in the kitty. He'd sat on his bed, gazing at it in disbelief. He'd slipped his thumbnail into the crescent divot in each attachment and pulled them out. He'd loved the crisp *snick* they made clicking into place.

"*Are you doing it?*" Shelley asked. His voice sounded far away, ignorable.

"Yeah," Ephraim snapped irritably. "Shut up, just shut *up* for a sec."

Carefully, he unfolded the can-opener blade. He sat poised, the wickedly curved blade hovering a quarter inch above his skin, a few inches from the cigarette burn. His skin seemed to jump and shiver—as if things were tunneling beneath his flesh like roaches under a blanket. *Bastards.*

He dug the sharp silver sickle into the puffy flesh of his knuckles and drew it along the phalange bone on the back of his hand. The blade opened his skin up rather easily, leaving a dully sizzling line of pain. For a moment, the incision shone pale white like the flesh of a deboned trout. Next it turned pink before running red with blood.

The anger racing through his veins dissipated with the appearance of that blood, and with it went some of the fear—just like Shelley said it would. Which was good. Very good.

"*Do you see it, Ephraim? You must see it, don't you?*"

Ephraim watched the blood trickle down his hand. He squinted. He was positive he'd seen something wriggle as the can opener cleaved through his flesh: a flicker of squiggling white, just like Shelley promised he'd see.

If he cut deeper next time, and faster, could he catch it?

Pinch it, tug it out? It may be very big. Not as big as the one that had come out of the strange man's gut but still, big.

He'd have to twist it around his fingers like fishing line and pull very carefully. He imagined tugging on the end coming out of his hand and feeling a dim secondary tug down by his foot, where its head was rooted. Tricky work. If it snapped before he got its head out, it would just wriggle away and respawn. He had to get the *head.* Once he got it, he'd squeeze it between his thumb and finger and squeeze. He'd shiver with delight as it burst with a meaty *sploosh.*

"Do it, Ephraim. Do it. Don't be scared. There's nothing to be scared of. You're almost there."

The squirming in his ears was maddening. He unfolded the knife's corkscrew attachment. He idly raised it to his ear, edging the tip into his ear canal. The cold metal tickled the sensitive hairs—the *cilia,* they were called; he remembered that from science class. *Lunate,* too, he realized—God bless science class.

Ephraim imagined pushing the corkscrew into his ear and giving it a good solid twist or two, like he'd seen his mother do when opening bottles of cheap Spanish red. She'd drunk a lot of those after his father stepped out. He pictured pulling the corkscrew out and finding a thick white tube threaded round the coils. *Gotcha.* But there could be other things on those coils, too.

Still, it might be worth it. The human brain didn't actually have any sensory receptors—yet another thing he'd learned in science class. You could stab a naked brain with a steak knife and the person wouldn't even feel it. They might piss their pants or forget their best friend's name all of a sudden—but they wouldn't feel any pain.

Shelley's voice, at one with the wind: *"What would you rather, Eef? Put up with a little pain or get your eyes eaten out* by worms? That's what they do, you know—they save the eyes for last."

Ephraim took the corkscrew out of his ear. He folded it back inside the knife and set it on his lap. It sat there: a long red lozenge with the insignia of the Swiss cross on it. He figured a guy could tear himself apart pretty easily with such a knife. Use its every attachment to pinch and pull and pry his own raging flesh until he fell to pieces. It would hurt like hell, except for the brain, of course—but maybe it would be worth it.

Ephraim sat under the spruces in the thinning light of afternoon. The walkie-talkie went silent. Run out of batteries? He already missed Shelley's helpful voice.

His fingers picked along his arms, plucking at the downy hairs there. A small, timid smile sat on his face. His gaze was set in a misty, vacant stare—as though his eyes themselves were not connected to his mind at all, but were just sitting loose in their sockets like a couple of green marbles.

What would you rather?

His twitching fingers set themselves to new purposes he could not discern. Slowly and without being fully aware of it, Ephraim reached again for the knife.

Chapter Thirty

Max and Newton hiked nearly an hour before coming across a patch of wild blueberries. They clung to bushes that grew in the shade of a rocky parapet. Many berries were so withered they almost looked freeze-dried; many more had rotted to hunks of bluish fuzz. But a few bushes must have bloomed late in the season—these ones were clung with overripe but edible berries.

The boys picked them with trembling fingers, not believing their luck. They gorged on berries until their lips and fingers were stained a pale blue.

Afterward they sat with their backs against the parapet. Newton belched loudly and shot Max a slightly embarrassed glance. His shirt was stretched across his stomach. His belly button peered out from the tight fabric like a sightless eye.

Newton pulled his knees up and encircled them with his arms. He closed his eyes and found himself back in the cabin where they had discovered Scoutmaster Tim. As he'd watched those worms waver back and forth making those *pfft! pfft!* sounds, he'd been sure things would only get worse. The odds were very sharply aligned against them, weren't they? But he remembered something his mother once said: *The only way you'll ever really know people is to see them in a crisis. People do the worst things to each other, Newton.*

Just the worst. *Friendships, family, love and brotherhood—toss it all out the window . . .*

And though he'd desperately wished he were home, some deeper part of his psyche recognized that rescue was not an immediate probability. Something bad had happened and they were trapped in the middle of it. All they could do was hang tight until the adults figured things out.

That was the biggest part of survival, Newton realized: maintaining a belief in the best-case scenario. It was when you started to believe the worst-case one that you were doomed.

The boys gathered an extra pint of berries to take back to Ephraim. Max rolled them up in a kerchief and stashed them in Newton's backpack.

The land dipped gradually. The gentle downslope led into a narrow valley. Pine trees bent over facing precipices, casting long shadows. The lowering sun burnt without heat behind gunmetal clouds. A cold breeze skated through the natural wind tunnel to pebble their arms with gooseflesh.

Newton crouched next to a lightning-cleaved tree. The stump was ringed with toadstools. Pale orange in color, each stem shaped like tiny moose antlers.

"Coral mushrooms," Newton said. "They're safe to eat, but also a powerful laxative."

"What's that?"

"They give you the shits."

"Not poisonous?"

"The antler-shaped ones are okay. Those *do* look like antlers, yeah?"

Max squinted. "Yeah."

Newton picked a few and put them in his pack. "When we get back to camp, we can boil them. Make a tea. Then Kent can drink it. Clear him right out."

"You think?"

"You got a better idea?"

Max smiled. "You know what? You're a real fun guy."

"What?"

"It's a joke Mr. Lowery told in science class. What did one mushroom say to the other? You're a real fungi."

A slow smile broke over Newton's face. "Oh, I get it. Fungi. Fun guy. That's funny. That's really, really funny."

Max frowned, and Newton immediately felt bad. It was just like him to suck all the funny out of a joke. He was a humor vampire. He thought about his Facebook persona, Alex Markson. Cool, handsome, suave Alex Markson. What Would Alex Markson Do—WWAMD? Not what Newton had just done, that's for sure.

Max said: "Mr. Walters told another joke that he got in trouble for."

"What?"

"How do you make a hormone?"

"How?"

"You refuse to pay her."

Newton cocked an eyebrow. "I don't get it."

"Neither do I. But Shelley repeated it to his mother. That got Mr. Walters in some deep shit for a few days."

Max squinted at an area about ten yards past the tree stump. A trail was tamped through the grass.

"Animal trail," he said.

Only a foot wide, maybe less, so it couldn't have been made by a very big animal. A fox or a marten or a porcupine.

"How did animals even get on this island?" Max wondered aloud. "You figure someone built an ark?"

"The Department of Game and Wildlife might have dropped them off," Newton said. "They would have surveyed the land and, y'know, figured out what species would live best."

"How's it feel carrying around that big-ass brain of yours all day?"

Newton's eyes darkened. "Don't make fun of me, Max. Not now."

"I wasn't—"

"Yes, you were. You were starting up on it, anyway. Just quit it, okay?"

Newton huffed back snot and raked the back of his hand over his nose. Was he about to cry? Max had never seen Newton cry. Not even after the most merciless teasing sessions. Not after an endless round of "Keepaway" with his Scout beret—a game that often ended out of pure apathy: someone would simply drop Newton's beret and the jeering circle would dissolve, leaving Newton to grope pink-faced in the dirt for his hat.

"Don't be an asshole, Max." Newton's eyes blazed from the reddened flesh of his sockets. "Not now."

Max took a step back as if Newton had physically struck him. He held his hands out in a penitent and pleading gesture.

"Really, Newt, I wasn't—"

The following words came out of Newton in a hot rush, like a bottle of soda that had been shaken so hard and for so long that the cap had finally blown off.

"I like weird stuff, okay? So what? And I'm fat. I *know* that, obviously. I wish I wasn't but it's not like I eat like a pig. I mean, yeah, I like ice cream but so do lots of guys. Mom says it's glandular. A slow metabolism. She even ordered me a pack of Deal-A-Meal cards from that guy on TV who wears those glittery short-shorts."

Max was stunned. Newton had never spoken this way to him—to *anyone*, as far as he knew.

"You know what's hilarious?" Newt said. "I was skinny as a baby. Like, *I-could've-died* skinny. I couldn't put on weight.

A total shrimp. I slipped four percentiles, Mom said. The pediatrician told her to feed me butter—pure warm butter."

Max wanted to apologize. To say, more than anything, that it wasn't really Newton's fault. Max and the other boys didn't pick on him because they despised him . . . it was more a case of boys needing someone to single out. A fatted calf to sacrifice. They had to turn *someone* into that bottom rung on the ladder if only so they didn't have to occupy it themselves. Boys weren't very inventive, either. The simplest flaw would do. A lisp. An overbite. Dental braces. Being fat. Add to it a few glaring idiosyncrasies—such as being a know-it-all bookworm who was fascinated with mushrooms—and *presto!* One made-to-order sacrificial lamb.

Max gave Newt a look of cautious empathy. "Sorry, okay? I wasn't trying to, like, be a shithead or anything."

Newton set his jaw off-kilter and touched his lip to his nose. "Okay. Forget it. It was nothing."

The trap proved a lot harder to build than they had figured.

Newton had found a diagram for a "sapling spring snare" in his field book. He claimed to have built one in his backyard—Scoutmaster Tim had come over and certified it, awarding Newton his Bushcraft badge.

But the saplings in his backyard were limber. The trees edging the game trail were old or dead: they snapped as soon as the boys bent them. When they finally found one that might do and tried to bow it down—the "spring" part of the trap—the natural tension of the wood was simply too much.

"This might make an okay wolf trap," Newton said with a shake of his head. "But a small animal would get catapulted into the sky."

They retired to the bluffs overlooking the game run. They sat with their feet dangling over the bluffs. The air smelled of creosote. The clouds lowered like a gray curtain coming down.

Newton said: "You don't feel sick, do you?"

Max said: "I don't know what sick should feel like."

"Hungry."

"Well, okay yeah, I *am* hungry."

"Yeah," said Newton, "but not *hungry*-hungry, right?"

"I guess not. I guess it's bearable."

Newton looked relieved. "Good. I mean if we were really that hungry—that crazy—we'd know it . . . right?"

Max rubbed his chin, wondering if Ephraim's knuckles would leave a bruise—wondering, more gloomily, if he'd live long enough for that bruise to heal. He gave no answer to Newt's question. What was there to say? If that particular hunger fell upon them, *crazy hunger*, nothing would really matter anymore. It'd be far too late.

Night birds sang in the trees: haunting, melancholy notes. Newton's foot went to sleep. He stood to walk the tingles out of it, wandering to the edge of the valley where the soil gave way to a flat expanse of shale. Gentle waves slapped the shore. The water was the gray of a dead tooth, liquefying into a sky of that same unvarying gray.

Newton squinted into a tide pool. Something popped up on its placid surface. Whatever it was, it had the coloring of an exotic bird's egg. It vanished again.

"Max! Come over here."

They peered down. Their breath was trapped expectantly in their lungs. *There*—whatever it was popped up again. Bubbles burst all around it. Then it was gone.

"It's a sea turtle," Newton said.

They crept down to the shore. The tide pool was hemmed by honeycombed rock. How had the turtle gotten in? Maybe there was a gap in the rocks underwater. More likely it had gotten carried in with the high tide and was trapped until the tide came in again.

"Could we eat it?" Max said. His voice was raspy with excitement.

"We could." Newton's voice held the same anxious rasp. Something about the idea of *meat*—even turtle meat—was insanely appealing.

They doffed their boots and socks and rolled their pant legs up past their knees. A light wind scalloped the water, spitting salt water at their naked legs.

The tide pool sloped steeply to a bottom of indeterminate depth. The turtle's shell was the size of a serving platter—they could just make out its contours when the turtle poked itself above the surface. Its head was a vibrant yellow shaded with dark octagon-shaped markings. Its eyes were dark like a bird's eyes. It had a wise and thoughtful look about it, which was pretty typical of turtles.

The boys patted their knives in their pockets. Max had a Swiss Army knife. Newton had a frame-lock Gerber with a three-inch blade.

"How should we do it?" Newton whispered with a giddy, queasy smile.

"We have to do it fast. Grab it and drag it out and kill it, I guess. Fast as we can."

"Do they bite?"

"I don't know. Do they?"

Newton pursed his lips. "It might if we aren't careful."

They waded gingerly into the pool. The water was so cold it sapped the air from their lungs. The water rose to the nubs of their kneecaps.

The turtle was a darker shape in the already dark water. It swung around lazily, unconcerned. As it rose up the boys caught sight of its shell: a mellow green patina flecked with streaks of magenta. Strands of sea moss drifted off it like streamers on a parade float.

It swam right up to them, totally unperturbed. Maybe it

was curious—or maybe it was hungry, too, and thought the boys might make an easy meal. It swam between Newton's split legs. He trembled from the cold and from the fear that the turtle might snap at his thighs. But it swam through serenely enough.

It had four flippers. The two at the front were long sickles, sort of like the wings on a plane. The two at the back looked like bird talons, except with webs of tough connective tissue. The skin on all four flippers was iridescent yellow overlaid with dark scaling. It was a beautiful creature.

Max gritted his teeth and plunged his hands into the water. His fingers closed around the edge of the turtle's shell, which was as slimy as an algae-covered rock. The turtle kicked forcefully—its strength was incredible. Suddenly Max was on his knees in the freezing surf. The rocks raked his shins. The turtle's small ebony claws dug into his thighs. He opened his lips to cry out and when he did the sea washed in, leaving him choking and sputtering.

The turtle slipped out of his grip. He splashed after it blindly.

"Newt! Get it before it gets away!"

Newton hobble-walked to where the turtle was throwing itself against the tide pool barrier. He grabbed one of its rear flippers. It was slippery and tough like a radial tire slicked in dish soap. The turtle swung around and snapped wildly at Newton. Its head telescoped out on its wrinkled neck farther than he'd thought possible: it reminded him of that game Hungry Hungry Hippos. Newton let out a fearful holler as its jaws went *snack-snack-snack* inches from his face. He caught the briny smell of the turtle's breath and another, more profound scent: something hormonal and raw.

He reeled back and nearly tumbled face-first into the water. The turtle went back to flinging itself at the rock.

Max was breathing heavily through gritted teeth. Water hissed between the chinks with harsh *hsst!* sounds. The bitter tang of fear washed through Newton's mouth. This situation had developed horrible potential, though he wasn't quite sure how that had happened.

"You grab one flipper," Max said, his eyes squeezed down to slits. "I'll grab the other. We'll get it up on shore. It won't be so tough on land."

They took hold of its back flippers and dragged it out. The turtle's front flippers paddled in useless oarlike circles. Its head thrashed, sending up fine droplets of water. Max's whitened lips were skinned back from his teeth—more a funhouse leer than a smile. A look of horrible triumph had come into his eyes.

They heaved the turtle up onto the sickle of rain-pitted sand. It tried to scuttle up the beachhead but it was hemmed in by steep shale. The boys hunched over with their hands on their knees—their kneecaps chapped red with cold—to collect their breath. The sky had gone dark: an icy vault pricked with isolated stars. A fingernail slice of the moon cast a razored edge of brightness over the sea.

"We should build a fuh-fuh-fire," Newton said, his teeth chattering.

"First we have to kill it."

A painful tension had sunk into Max's chest: the pressure of a huge spring coiled to maximum compression. He was angry at the turtle for its mute will to survive and for its defiance of his own needs. He was frustrated that the turtle had scared him. He'd have to kill it for that transgression alone.

The turtle turned to face them. Its head was tucked defensively into its shell. It struggled forward on its front flippers, aiming to return to the tide pool.

Max stepped in front of it. The turtle's head darted out to snap at his toes. Max pulled his foot away with a strangled squawk. The turtle had taken a V-shaped bite: the wound went a quarter inch into his toe, almost to the nail.

Max felt very little—his toes were still numb and his system was awash with adrenaline—but as his blood pissed into the sand he sensed all the threads inside his body gathering up, tightening, and committing themselves to a steely purpose.

He'd kill this thing. He wanted it dead.

Max found a bit of driftwood and hooked it under the turtle's shell. It wheeled and snapped off three inches of bleached wood. Max jammed the remaining portion under its front flipper and levered it up savagely.

The turtle flipped onto its back. It uttered a pitiful squall that sounded too much like the cry of a human infant for Newton's ears.

"*There.*" Max's chest heaved. "*There,* you fucking tough guy—*there you go.*"

With one trembling finger, he flicked open the largest blade of his Swiss Army knife. Moonlight lay trapped along its honed edge. His anger and fear helixed into each other. Things were speeding up and yet everything was held in a bubble of crystalline clarity: the tide swelling over the rain-pitted sand and smoothing everything with a layer of silver; the shriek of gulls overhead that seemed to urge him toward an act of savagery he'd already settled his mind around.

Max pressed the knife to the turtle's stomach, which was the off-beige color of the rubberized mat in his bathtub at home. The tip slipped into one of the grooves in the turtle's shell as if guided by its own inner voice.

Max had never killed anything. Oh, maybe bugs—but did they really count? He'd never stabbed anything, that was for sure. Newton stared at him with eyes that shone like cold phosphorus. Max wished he'd look away.

He bore down, unsure at first but steadily applying more force. The blade slipped and skittered along the turtle's belly, leaving a milky scratch on its shell. The turtle mewled. Its flippers oared in crazy circles. Its helplessness made it look stupid, comical. Max could do whatever he wanted to it.

He refolded the knife and pulled out the leather awl: just a simple metal spike. He held the knife in both hands as if it were the T-handle on a TNT detonator box. He took a rough guess at where the turtle's heart might lie, then hunched his shoulders and bore down with all his weight.

The spike pierced the turtle with the sound of a three-hole punch going through a thick sheaf of paper. Blood poured from the perfectly round hole, darker than Max had ever imagined. The turtle's back flippers clenched and unclenched spastically. Something dribbled out between those flippers: pearlescent roe that had the look of delicate soap bubbles.

Max punched the leather tool through a second time. The turtle's body compressed under Max's weight, its chest buckling like when you press down on a plastic garbage can lid. Its flippers beat helplessly at the air. Blood burst out of the wound in a startling syrupy gout. The smell was profoundly briny, as if the turtle's organs were encrusted with salt.

Max punched the spike through again, again . . . again. The turtle gurgled, then made a fretful stuttering sound: *icka-icka-icka*, as if it had a bad case of the hiccups.

Max moaned and sawed his arm across his eyes—he'd begun to cry without being aware of it—and stared at the turtle with eyes gone swimmy with tears. Blood was coming out of it all over. It rocked side to side frantically. A low venomous *hiss* came out of the punctures; it was as if the turtle's organs had vaporized into steam that was now venting through those fresh holes.

"Please," Max said. He punched the spike through again. It went in so goddamn *easy* now, as if the turtle's skin had relinquished its prior rights of refusal. "Please won't you just *die.*"

But it would not. Stubbornly, agonizingly, it clung to life. Its head craned up to take in the bloody wreckage of its own body. Its eyes were set in nets of wrinkles, inexpressive of any emotion Max could name. Its will to live was terrifying, as it rejected the notion of an easy death.

Why had he done this—*why?* Jesus, oh Jesus.

On TV it was always so quick and easy, almost bloodless: the detective shot the murderer and he collapsed, clutching his heart. Or the knife slid in soundlessly and some guy went down clutching his stomach, venting a sad sighing note—"*Eeoooogh . . .*"—before he died. But it didn't work that way in real life. Suddenly Max understood those awful stories he'd seen on the national news, the ones where a reporter grimly intoned some poor person had been stabbed forty times or whatever. Maybe the stabber would have stopped after a single stab if that was all it took. But most living things don't *want* to die. It took a lot to kill them. Events take on a vicious momentum. All of a sudden you're stabbing as a matter of necessity. You're hoping that if you just put enough holes into a body, the life will drain out and death will rapidly flow in . . .

"Newt," he pleaded. "Newt, *please.*"

The boys knelt in the sand, wet and shivering. Sand stuck to the pads of their feet. Max was shaking and sobbing. He could never, ever be hungry enough to kill something if this was what it meant. The turtle was still hiccuping, but now those sounds were interspersed with frantic *peeps*, like a baby bird calling from its nest.

Newton grabbed blindly for the turtle's head. He slashed wildly with his knife, trying to hack through its throat. But the turtle withdrew into its shell and Newton's knife only cut a deep trench around its jawbone. WWAMD? Not this. Alex would never have done this. Newton burst into a freshet of tears.

"I'm sorry," he said, his chest hitching uncontrollably. "I thought that might be the quickest way. Y'know, cut its head off. Like a guillotine. A terrible thing to do but still better than . . ."

The turtle peered out from the leathery cave where its head now resided. Its eyes blinked slowly. Its mouth opened and closed like a man at the end of a long run. Blood filled the lower hub of its shell and dripped onto the sand. It kept peeping and peeping.

The boys knelt with their shoulders bowed as the turtle bled to death. It took so, so long.

At one point, its head poked out of its shell. Its blood-slicked eyes stared around as if in hopes that its tormentors had grown bored of their sport and left it alone. Maybe it thought it could still return to the tide pool and be carried back into the ocean. Animals never gave up hope, did they? But its glazed eyes found them, blinked once, and resignedly returned to the darkness of its shell.

The great wave of the tide moved farther inland. The water lifted. The surf sucked at the boys' bare feet. The turtle's flippers went stiff all at once, then relaxed. Tiny translucent creatures that looked like earwigs crawled out from the deep folds of its skin to trundle over its cooling body. Aquatic parasites looking for a new host.

"I'm not huh-huh-hungry anymore," Newton said.

"Me neither."

"My muh-muh . . . my muh-muh . . . my *mother* says you can't really love yourself if you hurt animals."

"I didn't mean to. Not like this. If I'd known—"

"I know. It's over now anyway."

The water lapped at their feet with a dreadful languidness. The gulls hurled down shrill shrieks from high above. The wind whispered in a language they could not name.

They buried the turtle in the forgetting sand of the beach.

"DEVOURER VERSUS CONQUEROR WORMS: THE DUAL NATURE OF THE MODIFIED HYDATID"

Excerpt from a paper given by Dr. Cynthia Preston, MD, Microbiology and Immunology, at the 27th International Papillomavirus Conference and Clinical Workshop at the University of Boston, Massachusetts.

The second breed of worm, the "conqueror," is more interesting than the "devourer." It is, for lack of a better term, a "smart" worm.

As we know, the ability to manipulate the physical makeup of their host is a trait of some tapeworms. Take the African worm, *H. diminuta.* Their primary hosts are beetles, who frequently ingest rat droppings infected with tapeworm eggs. The first thing *H. diminuta* does upon entering a host is to locate the reproductive organs and release a powerful enzyme, sterilizing the beetle.

Why? So that the beetle does not waste any more energy on its reproductive system, allowing *H. diminuta* to further exploit the beetle's metabolic resources.

This is one such display of the manipulative "intellect" of tapeworms.

Dr. Edgerton's conqueror worms work in concert with the devourer worms—or, more accurately, they abet the devourer's massive appetite.

Once the mutated hydatid enters a host, it forms a colony in the host's intestinal tract. Once situated, a single conqueror worm emerges. The exact biology behind this is unknown; theoretically it may be similar to the method by which a bee colony selects its queen.

The conqueror worm is significantly larger than its devourer brethren. It perforates the intestinal wall and makes its way to the spinal column. From there it ascends to the base of the brainstem. Some conquerors twine around the host's spine, climbing it in the manner of creeping ivy climbing a parapet; others infiltrate the column itself by easing through a gap in the vertebral discs and entering the host's cerebrospinal fluid.

As it ascends, the conqueror lays eggs. These are reserve conquerors, one might say, in the event the queen expires. The conqueror larvae swim through the host's bloodstream and infest the strata of muscle tissue in the host's extremities; they are what account for the "bee-stung" look on several of Dr. Edgerton's test subjects: these are nesting conquerors. This is also a sign of a full-blown, late-stage infestation.

Once the conqueror worm enters the cranial vault, it injects a powerful neurotransmitter into the host's basal ganglia. The purpose is simple: it puts the host's appetite into overdrive. Imagine a car with a brick wedged on the gas pedal: that's the runaway hunger drive that a conqueror kindles in its host.

All the host wants to do is *eat*. In time, what it eats ceases to matter. Whether it is nutrient-rich or even properly "food" isn't something the host takes into account.

Anecdotal evidence taken from Edgerton's lab indicates that the conqueror worm's neurotransmitter may have several other hallucinogenic or psychotropic effects. Edgerton's videos show animal subjects behaving incredibly oddly; at times they appear to be unaware what is happening to them. Perhaps there is a "masking" effect: the host views itself as healthy—even healthier than before—while the devourer worms destroy it. This may enable the hosts to maintain a positive outlook, making them more productive, therefore gathering more food, therefore prolonging the lives of the worms. Otherwise they may have simply given up and died.

The conqueror worm's primary value to its colony may be

the propagation of a positive mind-set of its host—the longer the host believes it can survive, the more the colony can feast upon it.

Testimony given by the lone survivor of the Falstaff Island tragedy seems to justify this hypothesis. The boy stated that his infected troop-mates seemed, and I quote, "stronger . . . happier, even when they were falling apart. They couldn't see themselves for what they really were."

Chapter Thirty-One

"*Eef . . . eef, you still there?*"

The knife slipped from Ephraim's hands. It kept on slipping. He couldn't get a good grip. It was all the blood. His hands were greasy with it. It shone on his fingers like motor oil in the moonlight.

He'd seen it.

He'd cut a satisfyingly deep crescent around the knob of his ankle bone—he'd glimpsed sly movement there. A faint pulsation that on any other day he might have dismissed as the heavy beat of his heart through a surface vein—but now, today, *no*.

And he'd cut too deeply. He knew this immediately. His hands had been shaking too hard in his excitement—in his *need* to find it. His skin opened up with a silky sigh, as if it had been waiting all his life to split and bleed. The inner flesh was a frosty white, as if the blood had momentarily leapt clear of the wound.

In that instant, he'd seen it.

Terror had seized his heart in a cold fist. Undeniably, it was inside him. Feasting on him. Coiling round his bones like barbed wire around a baseball bat.

But on the heels of terror came a strange species of relief. He was *right*. It was just like Shelley promised. He wasn't crazy.

"Shel?" He coughed. A carbolic taste slimed his tongue, in his sinuses and lungs, burrowing into his bones to infuse the marrow with the flavor of tar. "Where did you go?"

"I've been here all along, friend. Don't you remember?"

"Ug," was all Ephraim said. A warm, sluglike blob passed over his lips, falling to the carpet of pine needles with a wet plop. Ephraim couldn't see what it was—didn't want to.

"Did you see it, Eef?"

"Ub."

"What did it look like?"

He'd seen only a flash. It was thicker than Ephraim ever thought possible. Fat as a Shanghai noodle. Its head—he'd found the *head*—split into four separate appendages. They looked spongy but predatory, too, like the petals of a lotus blossom or a snake's head primed to strike. It'd flinched like an earthworm when you ripped back a patch of grass to find it squirming in the dark loam; its body had whipped madly about as it withdrew into the sheltering layers of his muscle tissue.

"Oh no you don't," Ephraim had hissed.

He'd dug his fingers into the wound and tweezed with his fingertips. He felt the bare nub of his ankle bone—cold as an ice cube. His fingers closed around the worm, he was sure of that . . . almost sure. The parted lips of his flesh were rubbery and slick, gummed with the blood that was still flowing quite freely.

He'd gotten hold of it, just barely. A strand of spaghetti cooked perfectly al dente ("to the tooth," as his mother would say): a mushy exterior with the thinnest braid of solidity running through it. Did worms have spines? Maybe this one did.

Squeezing his fingers, he'd tried to pinch his nails together, praying he could decapitate the horrible thing. Afterward, he figured he could pull the rest of its limp body out using the Swiss Army knife tweezers. If he was unsuccessful, he guessed it would just rot inside of him. It might create internal sepsis. His innards could be riddled with ulcerated boils and pus-filled lesions. He might die screaming, but at least he'd die *empty* rather than infested.

He'd die totally alone.

In that moment, he'd thought: *Do I really want that, to die alone?* Where were Max and Newt? It was nearly dark by then and they'd promised to return. Instead they'd abandoned him. Max, his best friend, had left him alone. *Friends until the end?* Bullshit. Ephraim only had one friend left in the whole world.

He'd gripped it—the tips of his fingers pincering the hateful thing. For an instant it had thrashed fretfully between his fingertips . . . Ephraim was pretty sure, anyway. But he'd pulled too quickly. It squirted through his fingers. He'd reached again, desperately. Gone. He'd had his opportunity and lost it. It was safe inside him again.

"It gob abay, Shel," Ephraim said with despondent, child-like petulancy—marble-mouthing his words on account of the warm syrup in his mouth.

"You have to keep trying. Or are you weak . . . a sucky-baby, like everyone says?"

What? Who'd have the balls to—*nobody* said that. Did they? He pictured them on the school yard—a gaggle of boys casting glances over their shoulders, sneering and laughing. He saw *Max* laughing at him. Rage tightened the flesh of his forehead. Something thorny and superheated surged against his skull, threatening to shatter through.

"I hear it all the time, friend. At school, behind the utility shed where the big boys smoke cigarettes. They say Ephraim Elliot acts tough, but he's a pussy. He's a cuckoo—his mommy makes him see a shrink because his head's all messed up . . ."

Ephraim's gaze fell upon his stomach. His shirt had

ridden up to expose a slip of taut flesh. It rippled as something surged beneath it.

Maddening, mocking, playing peek-a-boo.

Ephraim picked the knife up. The blade was still keen. How deep could he cut?

It all depended. How deep did his enemy lie?

What would you rather?

From *Troop 52:*
Legacy of the Modified Hydatid

AS PUBLISHED IN *GQ* MAGAZINE) BY CHRIS PACKER:

"**B**IG" JEFF JENKS, as the locals call him, isn't so big anymore.

The events on Falstaff Island shrunk him. He admits as much himself—and from a man like Jenks, still possessed of a larger-than-life self-image, this is a big admission indeed.

"I stopped eating for a while there," he tells me as we take a spin in his cruiser down the sedate streets of North Point. "The appetite just wasn't there. Used to be before a shift I'd head down to Sparky's Diner and mow through their breakfast platter: eggs, rashers of bacon, pancakes, toast, plenty of coffee. And this was *after* my wife had made breakfast at home."

Nowadays Jenks's frame might be charitably described as utilitarian—although the word *threadbare* comes to mind. He floats inside his old police uniform. His arms sticking out of the XXL shirtsleeves put me in the mind of a child trying on his father's clothing. When he leans over to hawk phlegm out the window I see the fresh holes he's punched into his old belt so that it cinches his dwarfed waistline.

"It was the toughest thing I ever had to do," he says distantly. "Just sit on my hands and wait. That's not *me*, right? When something needs doing I'd always stepped up to get it done. Around here my word is *law*. But now here were these MPs and high army muckety-mucks saying I couldn't go get my own damn kid." He lapses into silence before saying: "My love can't save him. I remember thinking that. I think all of us—the parents, y'know?—were thinking the same. All the love in your body, every ounce of will you possess . . . matters nothing at all."

Though he admits the decision to steal Calvin Walmack's boat was a foolish one, he stands by it.

"You're telling me that most every responsible, loving father on God's green acre wouldn't have done the same? Now what the military won't admit and never will, I'll bet, is that those MPs beat me and Reggie pretty bad after they ran us down."

He pulls up his shirt to show me a long roping scar running up his hips to the bottom of his rib cage.

"They beat me so hard with batons that they busted the skin wide open. Right there on the deck of the boat. They didn't say nothing while they were at it, either. Just a long, silent beating. Reg got it just about as bad. We didn't think to fight back. The MPs all had guns." His voice drops to an agonized whisper. "Fact is, I'd never been beat anything near that. Not by *anyone*, *ever*. I was always the one doling that kind of stuff out . . . but only if you forced my hand."

We drive up rows of old Cape Cods, their exteriors permanently whitened by the salt spray that blows over the bluffs. It's a beautiful town. *Anne of Green Gables* pretty. The sort of place Norman Rockwell would paint.

"The official report is, nobody knows exactly what happened to my son," Jenks says. "But I'll tell you, that boy was a survivor. That's the way I raised him. You can't be Jeff Jenks's kid and not be a tough sonofabitch. But then, what you're talking about—the enemy, I guess you'd call it. *Them*. I mean, how can you fight something like that?"

He drums his fingers on the wheel. A big vein ticks up the side of his neck.

"They never found him. Never could bring my son's body home for us to bury. Just to give me and my wife some closure, right? Kent's still technically considered 'missing'—that's how it is in the books. And I'll tell you, man, missing can be worse than dead. Missing is like a book with the last few pages torn out or a movie missing the final reel. Missing means you'll never really know how it ends."

He looks as though he might break down but pulls himself back together.

"So I guess I'll never really know," he says after a while. "There's not a lot of evidence to go by, is there? But I'll tell you this: my boy wouldn't go down without a fight. I'd bet everything I own on that."

Chapter Thirty-Two

Kent was a beast. He could kill at will.

For a while there, he'd thought differently. When the other boys had left him in the cellar—*abandoned* him like a whipped dog—he'd been scared. So, so scared.

He'd felt his strength seeping away like the air from a leaky tire.

The things that lived in him now were awesomely hungry.

He knew they were there. He'd lain on the dirt floor and felt them sliding around inside him. A soft whisper came to his ears: a million snakes slithering across frictionless sand.

The thought occurred to him: he could die here. It didn't quite seem possible. He was only fourteen. Didn't God look out for drunks and children? That's what his father always said.

At some point, Shelley had come to the cellar doors to feed him. The peanut brittle did nothing to kill his appetite. But whatever Shelley had given him next—tough and rubbery on the exterior, bursting with warm softness within—now *that* made him feel great.

Still, Shelley had been a bad boy. Shelley had promised *meat*. And Kent would soon get what he was owed.

Fresh energy percolated through him. His blood zitsed

with adrenaline. He felt as though he'd eaten a raw steak—*Shelley should have brought me steak; you should never go back on your word, Shelley you scumbag*—as he inhaled the scent of blood that was not his own.

Kent was powerful. *Oh yes.*

He stood in the cellar, shoulders hunched. He could feel new bones growing up his back. They clawed through muscle and tendon before breaking through the skin on both shoulders. It was perfectly painless: he imagined this was what a caterpillar felt like when it emerged from its chrysalis as a beautiful butterfly.

Brand-new strength shot through him. Pounds of fresh muscle were slabbed onto his arms and legs. His chest cracked apart and widened as his shoulders grew broader and thicker. He did not feel pain or fear anymore. Was this how a superhero felt—or a god? Was that what he was now?

Weak light streamed through chinks in the floor, falling across his new contours. His body was a mass of fast-twitch muscle fibers and vein-riven flesh. He laughed: a low baritone. He could smash through the cellar door if he wanted to. He could find the boys who'd locked him up and tear their bodies apart like paper dolls. Find Ephraim, son of the no-good jailbird, and crush his skull to splinters.

Perhaps he would. Or perhaps he would be merciful.

But for now he'd wait. They would see him soon enough. Although their tepid hearts might burst at the sight of him.

When the other boys didn't return by nightfall, Shelley decided to kill Kent.

That was the thing about spinning so many plates—inevitably, one would topple off the pole. But the prospect of watching those plates shatter excited Shelley enormously.

He'd found a dead sheepshead on the beach. It had washed in with the afternoon tide, rotted and picked at by sunfish. He skewered it on a sharpened stick and carried it back to the campfire.

It was near dark when he stole around to the cellar with the dead fish. His breath came heavily, like a moose in rut. A dank musk dumped out of Shelley's pores: sour adrenaline mixed with something else, something fouler.

Shelley jimmied the stick loose from the cellar doors and flung them open. The granular light of dusk sifted down the steps. Shadows twisted on the warped wood. Shelley took a cautious step forward, hunting for movement in the gloom.

"Kent?"

Shelley's prey dragged himself up the steps tortuously, a ghoul crawling out of a shattered coffin. For an instant, Shelley thought he had no skin: it was just a shambling, jerking Kent-skeleton advancing upon him. As he drew closer, Shelley realized that the thinnest stretching of skin still clad Kent's wasted frame. He was covered in bulging boils: they looked like halved golf balls under his flesh. His eyes were cored sockets: Shelley was amazed they hadn't fallen out of his head to dangle by their glistening ocular stalks . . .

. . . Kent rose from the cellar, exultant. The newly crowned king. His body shone like rippled steel in the moonlight. Power and strength coursed through him. He was unstoppable. He came slowly, savoring it. His feet echoed on the steps like distant thunder. He curled his hands into fists and watched heatless lightning crackle and pop between his knuckles. He could kill a man with a look—with a simple *thought*. He had eaten the godhead and taken its power . . .

. . . Shelley stepped back in wonderment. He couldn't believe that Kent was still able to move. The boy's eyes were yellow and diseased. His lips had receded into the gauntness of his face. He shuffled out of the cellar with sickening animation, a gleeful marionette in the hands of a spastic puppeteer. The fleshless pinworms that were his lips skinned back to disclose a dizzying grotesquerie: his gums had been eaten back from his teeth, and all but one—his left front incisor—had loosened and fallen from their gum beds; yet they remained connected by Kent's braces, gray teeth linked like charms on a gruesome bracelet, clicking and clacking in the dark vault of his mouth, all hanging by that one tenacious tooth . . . which, as Shelley watched, slid from Kent's gums with a slick sucking sound, a bracelet of teeth bouncing over his lips, his chin, tumbling to the cellar steps. Kent stepped on them, oblivious to his own teeth shattering like ribbon candy.

"Wha arr ooo loogin aaa?" the boy-thing croaked.

What are you looking at?

"Almost nothing," Shelley said in a tone of pure awe.

The Kent-thing held out its driftwood arms, fleshless fingers outstretched toward the rotted meat in Shelley's hands . . .

. . . The weakling cowered at the sight of him! Shelley had glimpsed Kent's newfound beauty and power and he was quailing in fear. As it should be. This puling wretch, Shelley, held out an offering with one quaking hand. A hunk of braised meat dripping with juices. Perhaps Kent would be merciful. Perhaps Shelley would be spared . . .

. . . Shelley led the Kent-thing past the fire. The thing shambled awkwardly, staggering and collapsing and dragging itself up. It made the sucky-drooling sounds of a revolting starved infant. Saliva dripped from its flapping gums to slick its filthy Scout uniform. Moonlight glossed the dome of its skull, which was covered in bloody patches. My God, it must have torn out its own hair and eaten it.

"Come on, Kent," Shelley cooed. "There's a good boy . . ."

The Kent-thing loosed a high gibbering cackle. Night

birds screeched from their roosts in the trees stitching the shore. They were down at the water now. Shelley waded in. The Kent-thing blundered in after, slipping on the rocks while Shelley stared with sick wonder.

"What *are* you?" he said.

Shelley tossed the dead fish into the surf. The Kent-thing shambled after it. Its bonelike fingers punctured the rotted flesh. Its toothless mouth tore a stinking strip off.

"So gooo . . . sank ooo . . . so gooooo . . ."

Shelley knelt beside the Kent-thing. He was aware of the danger but couldn't help himself: he craved this closeness. He petted its head the way you'd pet a dog. His rock-hard penis pressed urgently against the wetted fabric of his trousers. A tenacious chunk of Kent's hair came away in Shelley's hand—it pulled free with no resistance at all, like wiping cat hair off a velour cushion.

"Show me," he said softly.

Kent turned to regard him. Flecks of rotted fish clung to his jaws. His mouth hung open at a quizzical angle.

"Wha . . . ?"

Shelley gripped Kent's head and lowered it into the water. It didn't require much effort at all. He caught the stunned expression on Kent's face as he went under. His arms flailed. His legs kicked weakly. Air bubbles stormed to the surface, bursting with liquid pops. His uniform rode up his back. Shelley saw the pulsing tube running next to his spinal column—it looked like an awful second spine.

Kent's struggles weakened. Shelley hauled his head up. The Kent-thing's eyes were foggy. White worms had pierced the skin of his neck, writhing furiously.

"Show me," Shelley said anxiously. "I want to *see* . . ."

. . . The illusion shattered abruptly. The mental scaffolding fell away and Kent saw himself as he was. When that happened he prayed—a quick, fervent prayer—that the sight

274

would drive him insane. Better to be mad than to witness the devastation of his body from a sane person's perspective. To see the skin stretched like parchment over the warped sticks of his bones. His body hilled with huge lumps, white worms twisting out of them in a frenzy . . .

. . . "Show me," Shelley said again.

The Kent-thing's eyes hung at half-mast. He coughed wretchedly. Something burst from his mouth, a fine mist spraying Shelley's face. Something fluttered against his nose and lips like the beat of a moth's wings. Shelley stuck his tongue out involuntarily to clear it away—realizing, in some dim chamber of his mind, the terrible danger he was in, but the fear was washed away on the tide of his awful, powerful needs.

"Show me."

Shelley wasn't even sure what he was looking for. Did he want to watch Kent's soul depart his body? Would it slip away behind the convex curve of the Kent-thing's eyes like smoke through a glass bowl?

He dunked Kent's head underwater casually. He hummed an offkey note while Kent thrashed and bucked. Shelley felt insistent wriggles on his tongue and swallowed without quite realizing it.

The Kent-thing's limbs settled. Shelley turned him over so that he faced the sky. His eyes stared glassily through the salt water.

. . . Either Kent had been fooled or he'd fooled himself. He gazed at the airless vault of the heavens stretching above the ocean. The stars were white-hot, encircled by gauzy coronas. So lovely. The unfairness of it all came crashing down. He'd never tell a girl he loved her. Never see his parents' faces again. Never sprint across the outfield at the Lions Club Park tracking a long fly ball. This fact leapt straight out at him. The world was not a fair place. His father had lied—or he'd just been plain ignorant. He'd never see his father again to tell him just how wrong he was. Never never never . . .

. . . A look of terror and loss came across the Kent-thing's face. Shelley's heart trembled. Joy washed over him in an awesome wave. *Yes. Yes.* This was what he'd been looking for.

Shelley set a hand on Kent's chest and pushed him under, hoping to lock that expression on his face. Bubbles detached from the insides of Kent's nostrils and floated up. A bigger bubble passed over his lips and burst on the surface with a wet pop.

In the final moments, Kent's face settled into a calm and beatific expression.

The joy burst like a glass globe inside Shelley's chest. His fingers dug into Kent's waterlogged uniform while he waded deeper into the sea, pulling the grotesquely buoyant Kent-thing past the breakwater, infuriated for reasons he could not name.

Shelley grabbed the stupid thing by its hair—it was dead now, and dead things relinquished their names—dragging it into the surf. It weighed almost nothing. The salt water held it up; its heels bumped over the rocks for thirty-odd feet, but once Shelley had gotten far enough from shore it floated freely, like a piece of wood.

The tide clutched greedily at the body. Shelley hesitated, not wishing to release it just yet. He was enraged—vaporous, cresting surges of anger rocked through him.

He'd expected so much *more*. Some kind of revelation. A sign of the gears that meshed behind the serene fabric of this world—a glimpse of its seething madness. But no. In the end he'd seen only mocking resignation—and, finally, bliss.

He continued to drag the dead thing through the water. If he'd been paying closer attention—and usually he would've been; Shelley was a preternaturally *aware* boy, coolly observant of everything around him—he would have seen the thing's scalp detach from its skull. The skin had winnowed to a sheer, raglike substance that peeled as easily as the papery bark off a birch tree . . .

If he'd not been off in his own little reverie, he would have heard the sound of the dead thing's scalp tearing free of the bone: a watery sucking noise, little bubbles popping as the sea flooded in to kiss the naked skullbone . . .

If he'd not been zoned-out and oblivious, he'd surely have seen the thousands of white threads twisting out of the dead thing's head—its *skull*, which was networked in fissures where the connective plates of bone had drawn thin and detached. They came out in snowy gouts, fanning out in numberless profusion, encircling Shelley's hips in a wavering nimbus . . .

His reverie broke only once they began to touch his skin. And the moment he realized this was the moment it ceased to truly matter.

"Oh!" Shelley said.

He jumped in the water—a silly, girlish little hop. "Fishy!" he said, believing that a sunfish or saltwater eel had brushed his thigh. But then he looked down, saw the worms streaming out of Kent's skull case, wriggling and darting . . . his rubbery face settled into an unfamiliar expression: horrified revulsion.

He stared, entranced. They were so *small*. The moon played over their bodies, almost shining right through them. They moved in hypnotic, transfixing undulations. He nearly laughed—not because the sight of them was funny, but because they didn't even seem a proper part of his existence. They were funny because they weren't entirely *real* . . .

They flicked around him in playful patterns. There were just *so many*. They curled into one another, jesting and flirting. He felt something playing against his skin but it was a distant, forgettable sensation. A sting on his hand. A light, burning sensation like a wasp sting, only much less severe. It was followed by another and another and—

Shelley was rocked by an abrupt surge of adrenaline. His fingers unkinked from Kent's hair. He beat the water with his palms—frenetically, spastically. His gorge rose.

They were everywhere, clinging to him somehow. He uttered shrill, nasal, squeaky notes of violent distaste: "Eee! Eeee*EEEE!*"

The threads became more animated. They poured out of the dead thing's skull, leaving a milky contrail in the dark water—it looked like a streamer fluttering from some grisly Fourth of July float.

They wriggled down Shelley's trousers, flitting and licking against his skin.

He swept the water with his forearm, trying to propel them away. His fear was unlike any he'd ever known; it made him desperate. Water fanned up, each droplet alive with wriggling white, landing on his arms and neck and lips. He snuffled salt water up his nose, sputtering on it.

He felt them inside his underwear. Some were so thin that they passed right through the weave of the fabric, needling inside, finding the sensitive skin at the bulb of his penis, the little hole where the piss came out.

Kent's body floated out past the breakwater. Threads continued to spill from it, sifting down through the water. The stars played their metallic light upon the waves. Kent was a silver shape dressed in the brightness of the moon. Smaller shapes—inquisitive fish—darted at his appendages, fussing with his fingers and hair.

Later, Shelley dragged himself back to shore. He shambled up the beachhead in hesitant steps. His lower lip hung slackly, a globule of spit suspended from it. The glob stretched until it snapped, splashing the rocks.

Tiny white things thrashed in the wetness.

He returned to the campfire and stared into its dead embers. The walkie-talkie was there, but the game with Ephraim was a distant concern.

He could resume it when Ephraim returned . . . if.

A gray curtain draped over Shelley's thoughts—but beneath it and around its edges, things jigged and capered.

His hand kneaded his crotch anxiously. The pleasure he'd experienced earlier with Kent was gone. Now that area itched and burned. *Could be a case of crotch crickets.* Shelley had once overheard a construction worker saying that to his buddy while clawing ruefully at his groin. Shelley was pretty sure this wasn't crotch crickets—it was a burn, a painful one, inside of him now. It'd raced up his piss-pipe like lit gunpowder, a bright and lively pain that ebbed to a strange hum inside his skin. Now he felt it spreading through him in slow, sonorous waves.

He bit his lip. He'd made a mistake. A big one, this time. Gotten carried away with his games. Lost sight of the danger.

It was only for a second, though, an internal voice whined. *Just a heartbeat.*

He sat cross-legged on the dirt. The burn receded. As the moments passed, it didn't feel so bad at all. A comforting numbness coursed through his limbs, his veins filling with some wondrous warm nectar.

His stomach, though. *That* was grumbling, revving up—*roaring.*

Shelley's hands clenched, tearing up clumps of dirt. Without realizing or truly caring, he filled his mouth with the contents of his hands. He chewed methodically. Grit and shell shards ground between his teeth. It sounded like he was eating handfuls of tiny bones.

"Bleh," he said, letting the half-chewed mess fall out of his mouth. His tongue was a blackened root. He looked like a ghoul who'd been eating his way down to a coffin.

"Noooooobody loves me, everybody hates me, I'm going to the garden to eat worms—to eat worms . . ."

Shelley began to laugh. A high, piercing sound like the scream of a gull. It stripped out over the water, touching not one pair of human ears.

Shelley sat that way for a few hours. He did not speak. He was motionless—except for a brief spell where he shook uncontrollably, unable to control his limbs.

When the sky reached its deepest ebony, Shelley began to feed in earnest.

Chapter Thirty-Three

Newton built a fire on the beach using the driftwood he and Max gathered. It took quite a while to get it lit: his fingers were shivering badly.

After it was going, they huddled on the sand with their shoulders touching lightly. Both of them had stripped to their skivvies—Newton's field book advised against staying in wet clothes. The water dried on their naked flesh, leaving a whitened sheen of salt. Their internal temperatures inched back up.

They hadn't spoken since burying the turtle, which they'd done before building the fire. Every so often, their gazes drifted to the spot on the beach where the sand had been smoothed by their trembling palms.

Newton's eyes found Max's above the fire. "Do you think it will go to Heaven?"

"The turtle?" Max's shoulders lifted imperceptibly. "I really don't know. It could. If there is a Heaven, I guess it ought to—I mean, right? What would that turtle ever have done to deserve *not* to go to Heaven?"

Newton's shoulders relaxed, then stiffened again as a worried cast came over his face.

"What about the Scoutmaster?"

Max frowned. "Why are you asking me?"

"Your dad's the county coroner. He works with the priests and pastors, yeah? I figured he'd know."

For all of Newton's smarts, he could be incredibly thick-headed. "I don't *know*, Newt. I'm not the one who makes those choices, am I? Nobody really knows. Not my dad or the priests or anyone. I guess when we die, we'll know who was right about everything."

"But Scoutmaster Tim was a good person."

Max blew a lock of damp hair off his forehead. "Sure he was. He was a doctor. He helped people. I guess . . . yeah. He'd go to Heaven."

"Do you think he's there now? Looking down?"

"Depends how long it took him to get there. Maybe he had a few stopovers." Max saw the look of dread on Newton's face and said: "Yes. He's up there. He's happy now."

"I never saw a dead person before, Max."

"I never saw a dead person like that, either."

"Were you scared?"

Max nodded.

"You didn't look scared."

"Well, I was."

The night's silence stretched over the immensity of the ocean—an impossibly quiet vista that stirred fear in Max's heart. Would death be like that: endless liquid silence?

Newton grabbed a piece of wood from the pile, inspecting it by the fire's glow. A black spider picked its way across it. Newton let it crawl onto his fingers.

"Careful," Max said. "What if it's poisonous?"

"Poisonous ones have red bells on their abdomens. This one is pure black."

It climbed off his fingertip. Newton watched it go with a dreamy look. "A spider used to live inside Mom's car," he said. "She parked it under the oak in our driveway. Every time she took the car out, she'd see a web hanging between the side-view mirror and the windshield. She would snap it. The next time she looked it'd be back. Finally she tilted the side-view mirror as far as it would go and looked into the compartment behind. A little white spider was living in there. Every night it came out and strung a web. Mom would come out and snap it. So it would just build it again."

"Did she kill it?" Max said.

"Absolutely not," Newton said fiercely. "Who was it hurting? She even left its web alone from then on. But then one day we were driving and I spotted the spider on the windshield. We were doing, like, eighty, tooling down the highway to Charlottetown. It was trying to build another web—*on* the windshield while the car was ripping down the road. I thought it would blow away. I could see the sunlight glinting on the web it had managed to lay down. Crazy, right? Mom pulled over. We took the spider and put her in an apple tree along the road. Her new home."

Newton smiled. Max figured he was reliving the memory: on the roadside on a wet spring day, the *cree-cree* of crickets in the long grass as his mother let the little spider slip off her finger onto the branch of an apple tree clung with pink blossoms. It was a nice image.

"After we got back on the road, Mom said, 'Insects can make a home for themselves almost anywhere. They say that about cockroaches: if there's ever a global Armageddon, they'll be the only things left. You can't beat a bug for adaptability.' I think humans can be the same, too—don't you think, Max? If we really need to, we can survive almost anywhere."

Knotholes popped in the fire. Max's ears became attuned to another sound: febrile cracking noises coming from the darkness where the rocks met the beach, near the spot where they had buried the turtle.

"You hear that, Max?"

"Hear what?"

Newton got up and crept toward the noises. His mind conjured up an absurd image that was nonetheless chilling: the reanimated sea turtle clawing itself up from its sandy grave, blood dripping from its puncture wounds, its bone-like mouth snap-snapping.

The fire threw wandering sheets of light upon the rock. The cracking noises grew louder. They were joined by other sounds overhead: the rustle of wings in the cliffs.

"Oh my God."

A clutch of pale green eggs—the patina of the sea—were buried in the sand. Each about half the size of a chicken egg. They had been covered in a fine carpet of sand. The boys had totally missed them.

Each egg was struggling with minute hectic life. Shards of shell broke off. The tiny limbs of unknown creatures were pushing themselves out.

"What *are* they?" Max said.

They didn't have to wait long to find out. When the first flipper appeared, Newton whispered: "They're turtles."

The scenario played out in Max's mind: a mama turtle swims in with the high tide to lay her eggs. She gets stuck in a tide pool. Next a pair of horrible two-legged things blunder into the pool, heave her onto the sand, and . . .

The baby turtles didn't even look like turtles, the same way those baby shearwaters on the kitchen table hadn't really looked like birds. They had no real shell, only a trans-lucent carapace draping their grape-size bodies. You could see through their skin as if through a greasy fast-food bag: the dark pinbone of their spines, the weird movement of their organs. For all their newborn freshness, they still looked ineffably old. Max reached to touch one. Newton grabbed his wrist.

284

"You can't. If it gets human smell on it, its mom won't take it back."

It took a moment for it to sink in.

"Let's just get them into the water," Max said softly.

Newton nodded. "I guess it's okay to touch them for that."

With infinite care, the boys picked up the baby turtles and carried them across the sand. They tenderly picked the shards of eggshell off their bodies. They knelt at the shore and let them go. Their flippers paddled as they made a beeline for the open sea.

The air above was alive with harried wing beats and livid screeches, the bats and gulls having been thwarted in their attempt to poach an easy meal.

The boys made sure every turtle made it safely into the water. The birds made crazed dive-bombs: their wings pelted the ocean, desperate to snag the babies before they submerged.

"No, you bastards!"

Max stumbled into the water, waving his arms. He shadowed the turtles into deeper waters, wading out as they skimmed through the sea, coaxing them lightly with his hands.

"Go on, now. Swim, swim. Fast as you can."

The water rose to his stomach. The riptide sucked at his legs. Only then did he reluctantly return to shore, dripping and shivering.

They returned to the fire. Newton smiled wanly and made a check-mark in the night air.

"That's our good deed for the day."

From *Troop 52:*
Legacy of the Modified Hydatid

(AS PUBLISHED IN *GQ* MAGAZINE) BY CHRIS PACKER:

L IKE TOM PADGETT, Dr. Clive Edgerton has earned his fair share of nicknames.

Dr. Mengele 2.0.

Dr. Death.

Then there are the garden-variety appellants that society as a whole tends to apply to men like him.

Megalomaniac.

Mad scientist.

Psychopath.

Then there is the sobriquet that Edgerton himself insists you call him by—it was, in fact, one of the conditions of our interview—the title he's rightfully earned, having graduated with top honors from the finest medical learning institute on the east coast:

Doctor.

"Dr. Edgerton is most likely pathologically insane," says his administering physician, Dr.

Loretta Hughes. "If you look at the things he has done—compounded by his near total lack of remorse regarding them—you can't help but draw that conclusion."

She leads me down an austere hallway inside the Kingston Penitentiary, her crepe-soled shoes whispering on the pea-green tiles. Edgerton has been incarcerated here, in the mental health wing, since his arrest. The ensuing trial became a sensation; Edgerton had sat defiantly in the middle of the media storm. His shaven head and outrageous courtroom antics—the grandstanding, the fulminating—gave him the air of a revivalist preacher. The talking heads and pundits dined out for months on Edgerton's daily servings of bloody red meat.

"But perhaps he's *not* insane," Hughes tells me. "The fact may be that his brain is simply unmappable. He is incredibly intelligent. I hate to use a cliché like 'off the charts,' but . . . the fact is that modern science has no real means to judge an intellect like his. It would have been the same with Leonardo da Vinci. The dividing line between genius and insanity is very thin and quite permeable—which is why so many geniuses descend into madness."

When I remark that Edgerton's genius was

incredibly destructive, Hughes matter-of-factly says: "Da Vinci drew up the blueprint for the first land mine. There's plenty of blood on his hands, too."

Edgerton's cell is 18-by-18, gray brick, with a single cot and a stainless steel commode. As the prison's marquee prisoner, he doesn't share his cell. The walls are festooned with charts and formulae and an oversize poster of da Vinci's *Vitruvian Man*.

"Da Vinci came up with the idea for the land mine," I tell him by way of introduction. "Did you know that?"

"Of course," he tells me in the bristly manner that would be familiar to anyone who saw his televised trial.

Up close it is shocking just how *un*-academic Edgerton looks. He's big. Tall. Muscular. Thick across the shoulders, which taper down to a trim waist. Twice during our interview he will drop without warning and pump out exactly fifty push-ups before returning to our conversation. He's got a Joe Namath quality: Broadway Joe a few years past his prime, going a little to seed but still possessed of the grace and quickness from his playing days.

There are two concessions to the scientist stereotype. The first is his head: he prefers to keep it shaven; it is bulbous, venous, ovoid, vaguely alien in appearance. The second is his glasses: thick lensed, black and boxy. The lenses are stuck with an accretion of grit and eye crust: it's as though Edgerton can't be bothered to wipe them. His chilly green eyes seem to be staring at me through a grease-streaked window.

Those eyes. They are not normal eyes. They seem to stare through me as though I were glass, focusing on the dead brick behind me.

"Do you know anything about Asian killer wasps?" he asks abruptly. "The Asian killer wasp is the only insect on earth that kills for fun. They're just *gigantic*. A full two inches long. They love killing honeybees. They'll destroy entire colonies. Only takes a few minutes. They grab a bee and lop its head off with their giant mandibles, like popping the head off a dandelion. It would be like a giant mutant running loose in a nursery, stomping babies to death. No reason. They just enjoy doing it."

I ask if wasps are as fascinating to him as worms.

"Oh no," he says. "Worms are much more interesting. Worms are indiscriminate, you see. They will eat anything from a hippopotamus to an aphid. They are the ultimate piggybackers:

invite one inside and it's there for good. They're nightmare houseguests: once they're in, you'll never get rid of them. They're one of the oldest species on earth. Right after the crust cooled there were worms swimming in the primordial soup. The first creature to flop out of a tide pool onto land had a worm inside of it, I guarantee you."

He smiles vacantly. "They say cockroaches will be the last things left on earth after a nuclear holocaust. Don't believe it. The last thing on earth will be a *worm* in the guts of those cockroaches, sucking them dry."

He pauses as if to regroup. Our conversation has this tenor: elliptical, backtracking, dead-ending.

"They say dolphins and pigs are the only animals that fuck for fun," he tells me. "Other than us, of course. Worms fuck *themselves*. They lay eggs in their own skin. Once a worm gets long enough, a segment detaches to become its own worm. They really are motherfuckers, pardon the pun. There's no joy in it for them at all. No satisfaction of creation, only endless self-creation."

As Hughes said, Edgerton appears to feel no remorse for the events on Falstaff Island. If anything, his abstract theorizing on the fate of the boys of Troop 52 is deeply chilling.

"How would you rather die," he asks himself, "from a chopping axe or a little blade? A *tiny* blade that makes the thinnest ribbon of a cut. Only enough to draw a single bead of blood from the skin. But it cuts and cuts and cuts and *cuts*. It doesn't stop cutting. It takes days. It is relentless. It doesn't matter how big or strong or resourceful you are: sooner or later that tiny blade will shred right through you. And it's not one blade but a million blades inside you, cutting their way out, replicating themselves, slicing and gashing and mincing you up—or slowly whittling you down like a scalpel taking delicate curls off a giant redwood. You'll get to see yourself change. It's that slow progression. You'll see your strength get sapped, see your body take on terrifying new parameters. Your mind will probably snap well before your body caves in. Personally? I'd take the axe."

Ultimately the question of whether or not Edgerton is insane becomes a moot point. He is a sociopath. It doesn't take a clinical degree to understand that. He is as remorseless and unthinking as his beloved worms.

"Do you want to know the best, most effective transmitter of contagion known to man?"

Edgerton asks me this with a pinprick of mad light dancing in each iris.

"It's *love*. Love is the absolute killer. Care. The milk of human kindness. People try so hard to save the people they love that they end up catching the contagion themselves. They give comfort, deliver aid, and in doing so they acquire the infection. Then those people are cared for by others and *they* get infected. On and on it goes." He shrugs. "But that's people. People care too much. They love at all costs. And so they pay the ultimate price."

Part Three

CONTAGION

EVIDENCE LOG, CASE 518C
PIECE F-44 (Personal Effects)
Preliminary Advertising copy for Thestomax
  (internal document only; never published)
Recovered from SITE F (Ariadne Advertising,
  364 Bay Street, Toronto, ON) by Officer
  Stacey LaPierre, badge #992

Chapter Thirty-Four

"*Fire's burning, fire's burning; draw nearer, draw nearer; in the gloaming, in the gloaming; come sing and be meeeer-rrrrry . . .*"

Shelley had moved back to the cabin, where he curled up under the shattered bed frames. He'd heaped the soaked mattresses into a sloppy teepee and lay in the mildewy darkness, singing. Anyone within earshot would have noted his lovely voice. It hit each register purely.

"*Kumbaya, my Lord, kumbaya; kumbaya, my Lord, kumbaya; kumbaya, my Lord, kumbaya . . . O Lord, kumbaya . . .*"

His voice dipped to a weak warbling note. He went silent. His body tensed. He loosed a tortured moan—the sound of a sick animal. His hands rose to his face. His nails dug into the creases of his forehead. Slowly, he dragged them downwards. His ragged fingernails tore trenches through his flesh. Blood wept from the wounds, though not very much. The sluggish trickles stopped quickly, like spigots being shut off.

In the silence, he could hear it. *Them.*

A tight, slippery sound like a Vaseline-coated rope pulled through a tightened fist. Coming from inside of him.

Things had turned out very bad for Shelley.

More than the other boys, Shelley was a realist. He understood how the world worked—bad things happened to good people, bad people died happy in their beds. It happened every

297

day. So why bother being good? The word itself was attached to a series of behaviors that was, at best, an abstraction.

A person profited nothing from being *good*.

It wasn't as if Shelley had a choice. Ever since he could remember, he'd seen the world this way. People were things to be used, peeled back, opened up, roughly dissected and dismissed. All creatures on earth fell under the same cold scrutiny.

The boy in the moon. That had been Shelley's nickname; he'd overheard the teachers calling him that one afternoon as he'd lingered around their lounge. Although for a while it had been *the Toucher.*

He'd earned this moniker for his behavior during recess, which he spent haunting the edges of the school yard. He watched the girls play. Sometimes he'd sidle up alongside one of them—Trudy Dennison was a favorite—and reach out his arm to gather up her long, soft hair, letting it fall tricklingly between his fingers.

He did not find this arousing. Shelley was rarely aroused by anything. Girls did not excite him as they did most boys his age. Boys didn't excite Shelley either. Not in the traditional manner, anyway.

When girls felt Shelley's fingers passing through their hair, a look of teeming disgust came into their eyes. That disgust often shaded into an unease that held a gasping edge of fear: as if they were thinking that the world might be a better and safer place were he, Shelley Longpre, not a part of it.

Shelley was aware of their revulsion, but it did not trouble him. He enjoyed it, actually—as much as he enjoyed anything at all. Last year, Trudy Dennison squealed on him. He had to sit down with the principal, Mr. Levesque. Shelley's father, a tire salesman, was also there. And his mother in her watered silk dress.

Shelley had been sternly warned that touching anyone without that person's permission was *bad*. Shelley nodded and smiled his sullen, empty smile. On the way out of the office, he heard his father tell the principal: "It won't happen again. Shelley's just . . . he's *slow*."

Nobody made too big a deal of it. Touching was just Shelley's *thing*, the way eating boogers was Neil Caruso's *thing* or filching cigarettes behind the utility shed was Ephraim's *thing* or playing pocket pool under the trampoline was Benjamin Rimmer's *thing*. Every boy had his thing and on the grand spectrum Shelley's wasn't so bad—it indicated a future badness, perhaps, a "signpost" as that quack Dr. Harley might say, but right now it was harmless, if slightly troubling. His fellow Scouts didn't give Shelley grief over it. For one, many of them probably wanted to touch Trudy Dennison's flowing honey-scented hair, too—they simply didn't take the next logical step. And two, the boys avoided picking on Shelley out of the sense, inexpressible yet tangible, that he might do something very *wrong* in retaliation. The worst they'd ever called Shelley was dumb. *A real dumb bunny*, as Eef would say . . . well, used to say, anyway.

Shelley was happy as a person such as himself could be with this perception. Let everyone think he was dull. Let their eyes fall on his beanpole body and sluggish limbs and feel nothing but a vague revulsion that they were unable to properly account for. Revulsion mixed with an odd sense of disquiet.

"Someone's laughing, my Lord, kumbaya; someone's laughing, my Lord, kumbaya; someone's laughing, my Lord, kumbaya; O Lord, kumbaya . . ."

Without his being consciously aware of it, Shelley's mouth dipped to the raw pine floor. He gnawed on it. His teeth *skriiiitch*ed on the wood. Splinters drove deep into his gums. Blood flowed.

299

Shelley used to be the Toucher. Now he was the *touched*, thanks to the twitchy-squirmy things inside him now. Making a home.

"*Hear me crying and laughing, my Lord, kumbaya,*" Shelley warbled. "*Hear me crying, my Lord, kumbaya; hear me crying, my Lord, kumbaya . . . O Lord, kumbaya . . .*"

And Shelley had begun to cry. Tears squeezed from the sides of his eyes—but they ceased quickly. His body was dehydrated as a banana chip. Yesterday he'd urinated against the side of the cabin. What came was just a thin dribble, clear as spring water. Not even the slightest yellow tinge—the yellow color was from the extra vitamins and minerals he usually pissed away. But now he understood the things inside of him were helping themselves to all that extra—and more.

The feeble light of the moon cast through the shattered roof, through the sodden mattresses making up Shelley's awful nest, falling upon his body. His trousers hung low, divulging a half inch of ass crack. His shirt was rucked up. The knobs of his spine were visible.

Had anyone been watching, that person would have seen the flesh ringing Shelley's spine begin to lift. Something was tunneling its way through—through and *up*. Climbing the drainpipe of his spine, corkscrewing higher and higher.

There came a series of dim pops, like weak firecrackers going off: trapped air popping between Shelley's vertebrae. The tunneling thing looped round the spine, tightening, burrowing through the lacework of tissue and muscle, around again, and again, and again.

Shelley did not scream. Did not move. At one point, he did reach around and scratch at his back, as if under the belief he'd been bitten by a mosquito.

"Ug," he said—a Neanderthal note. "Ug . . . uh-*ug*."

The tube threaded up his spine, between the sharp wings

of Shelley's scapula. Upon reaching his neck, it thinned out, appearing to struggle—then it flexed convulsively, fattening into a bulging cord up the nape of Shelley's neck, its scolex fat at his hairline . . .

"*UG*," Shelley said breathlessly. His mouth opened. A clotted rope of blood jetted between his teeth.

It entered his cranial vault. Shelley was immediately suffused with comforting warmth. He sighed, curling deeper into himself. He shut his eyes.

Later that night, Shelley would awake from a familiar dream—they all shared the same palette: shifting browns and blacks and olive greens, half-formed shapes melting into one another—shivering and feverish with a hammer-hard erection tepeeing his shorts. A booming voice followed him out of his dreamscape:

Rock and roll, Shelley m'man—THAT'S how it eats.
That's the ONLY way it eats.

Chapter Thirty-Five

Max and Newton rose with the drowsy half-light of dawn. The sun hummed over the sea, an orange sine wave radiating heat-shimmers against the leavening dark.

Max hadn't slept well. He'd kept sensing strange, vaguely menacing shapes darting at the edges of the fire's light. His skin was rubbed raw around his waist, which had shrunk somewhat over the past few days. He took a swig from his canteen and winced at the stale, ironlike taste of the water. He fingered his clothes, which he'd hung up last night. Dry enough.

Newton got up soon afterward. They tugged on their pants and socks and boots in silence. They squinted across the sea into the new sun. The dark hulls of those strange ships dotted the water toward North Point.

"We have to get Eef," Max said.

"He may have gone back to camp," Newt said. "Y'think?"

"We'd better check."

They retraced their route, passing through a glade where the light hung in brilliant icicles and thousands of green silkworms hung from the tree branches.

"Is this what they make silk shirts out of?" Newt said. "How do they even stay together? It'd be like trying to sew with spider's thread."

The day was bright and warm, the air shot with dazzling light. A deep-seated fear picked along the edges of their thoughts. They were frightened, but that emotion rested with easy familiarity in their chests by now.

They located yesterday's footsteps in the grass and followed them into the spruces and found Ephraim on the ground surrounded by spiky smears of blood.

"Eef, what . . . ?" Max said, unable to understand what he was seeing.

When the carnival came to Charlottetown last year, Max and Ephraim had gone. Max's father had driven them and bought ride tickets for both boys—a nicety Ephraim's mother accepted with stoic gratefulness. They rode the Zipper and had their spines delightfully rearranged on the Comet, an ancient wooden roller coaster operated by a carnie with a spiderweb tattooed on his forehead—a tiny black spider descended to the tip of his nose on a strand so blue, so pale, you might mistake it for a vein. After gorging on waffle cones and funnel cake, they'd come across a freak show operating out of a small blue-and-white-striped tent at the back of the fairground. Three tickets apiece granted them entry to a cramped, dark space smelling of horse manure and another scent beyond naming. The freaks took the stage to the slightly awed, mainly disgusted *ooh*s of the hick crowd.

Freaks, Max remembered thinking. *But why would they let themselves be called that?* They weren't that freakish looking. Tattooed and pierced, sure, but nothing that'd raise your eyebrow if you passed them on the street. But what the performers *did* to their bodies was truly freakish. One guy guided a power drill with a six-inch bit deep into his septum, so deep the tip must've tickled the brainstem, then skewered a metal hook—a meat hook, same as plucked hens hung in the butcher's window—through the hole, drawing the hook out through his mouth. Another guy chewed lightbulbs and stuck long steel needles through his arms, skewering himself like a bug on a pin.

Max was horrified—which, he assumed, was the sought-for reaction. Ephraim, however, was mesmerized. Max had seen that look before; Ephraim was the daredevil, after all. The boy who'd jumped his bike off the seawall, mistiming it badly and fracturing his leg. Max had sat with him in the ER afterward; Ephraim's leg hung at a crazy cockeyed angle—it hurt Max's eyes to look at it. Ephraim, however, was fascinated. *Check it out, Max*, he kept saying, a weird smile on his face. *Check it . . . owwwt.* As soon as the cast came off, Ephraim was back at the seawall for another try. His mom must've had a constant conniption fit, but Eef had always been that way.

Max figured the crazy stunts must've bled away Eef's rage—the theory of displacement, like he'd seen demonstrated in science class. Problem was, God gave you one body. What you did with it was your own business, but the truth as Max saw it was this: You throw your body at the world. The world hits back. The world wins. So you had to take great care of what God gave you. Eef had never gotten that message.

When they rounded into the sunlit clearing, Max initially thought Ephraim had been murdered.

Somebody or something had found him here all alone and set upon him in a fury. But then he saw the wounds—hacks and gouges, not stabs—and the Swiss Army knife still clutched in Ephraim's hands. He thought: *How could anyone do this to himself?* But he knew Ephraim very well. He knew him better than anyone else on earth, maybe. So he knew.

The two boys hunched beside their troop-mate. Newton touched Ephraim's chest, which rose and fell weakly. There were large, clumsy, gashing wounds in Ephraim's hand and leg. Blood was gummed in a five-inch half-moon hacked into his side. The cut was jittery but progressively deeper, as if the person who'd done it had grown bolder after the blood started to flow. Worst of all was the long twisting slash on his face: it began near his temple where the bone sunk into a shallow divot and hacked straight down around his orbital bone, cleaving so deep through the skin of his cheek that the knife tip must have poked through into his mouth, then out again, tracing the line of his jaw before petering out in the middle of his chin. The trajectory alone was a brutal and terrifying thing to look at. A mark of madness.

Newton was breathing hard, set to hyperventilate. "Who did this?"

"He did it," Max said, near breathless. "Eef did. To himself."

". . . Why?"

Ephraim's eyelids fluttered. He coughed weakly and said: "They're inside me. Or . . . maybe it's just one. But it's *there*. Sneeeeaky . . ."

Max gave Newton a helpless look. "There's nothing inside you, Eef."

"*Wrong.*" Eef's breath stunk like sun-spoiled liver. "I've seen it. It's . . ." He licked his lips. Horrifyingly, Max could see the root of his tongue moving through the slit in his cheek. "It's smart. It lets me see *just* enough, even touch it, before it slips away. But if I make enough holes, guess what? Nowhere for it to hide."

The mad certainty in his voice iced the sweat up Max's spine. His eyes fell upon the walkie-talkie—its plastic casing was slicked with blood. He looked back at Ephraim, who'd followed the movement of his eyes and now turned away, refusing to meet Max's gaze. His eyes swarmed with an emotion Max couldn't intuit: a mixture of grief and shame and something else—something much darker.

"Who were you talking to?" Max said. When Ephraim didn't answer, Max said: "You're not any skinnier. You still look the *same*, Eef."

Mostly the same, he thought queasily.

Fact was, Ephraim appeared more or less as he had when the boat first dropped them off. He'd lost a few pounds, but so had Newton and Max.

"It's inside of me," Ephraim said.

Newt said: "How do you know for sure?"

"A little birdie told me, okay?" Ephraim spat pure red. "I *know*."

There was a tone of Stage 5 acceptance in Ephraim's voice; he could have been telling them he had inoperable brain cancer. Max figured it wasn't worth fighting. As his father said: *You can't argue with someone who's already made up his mind.* He exchanged a knowing look with Newton; a silent pact was settled upon. If this was what Eef believed— that he had a worm inside of him—okay, they'd accept it for now. Anything to stop him from cutting himself.

Newton rummaged the first aid kit from his pack. Swabs of peroxide and iodine no bigger than the Sani-Cloth wipes you get after a messy meal, butterfly bandages, a spool of gauze no bigger than a roll of quarters. Pitiful, really, when facing bodily devastation like this.

Max attempted to paste a bandage over the gash in Ephraim's cheek. Eef screamed—a shocked bleat—so loud that Max's hands fled from his face.

"What do you *want*, Eef?"

Ephraim fixed Max with a pleading look. "Get it out of me."

"How?"

"Newt, you've got a better knife than mine. It's burrowed deep. It'll take a longer blade."

Newton covered his mouth with his hand. He couldn't

imagine hacking into Eef in search of something he knew he'd never find—not after the turtle. Not ever, at all.

"I can't do that, Eef."

"Pussy." Ephraim spat the word out like poison. "Max—your dad cuts people, right? You helped the Scoutmaster. You could do it."

The best tactic was the one that stopped Ephraim from doing more damage to himself, Max figured. He'd tell him anything he wanted to hear.

"I can do it, Eef. But not here. We need a cleaner site. You could get infected."

"I already *am* infected."

"Yeah, but if I cut really deep and get it, we'll still need to patch you up. There's a medical kit back at camp."

"I found some mushrooms, too," said Newt. "They should make you throw up and . . . poop your pants. Maybe we can get it out without having to cut."

Ephraim closed one eye as if he were squinting through a telescope. "Y'think?"

Max slipped Ephraim's Swiss Army knife into his pocket. "We get you back to camp and try the mushrooms. If that doesn't work, I'll use the knife. Deal?"

Ephraim squeezed his eyes shut. Long, thick veins pulsed at his temples. *My God*, Max thought, *they really do look like worms.*

Chapter Thirty-Six

They returned to camp to find Kent gone.

It had taken nearly three hours to half carry, half drag Ephraim back. His wounds kept tearing apart and bleeding. The rusty smell of blood clung to their clothes—could he infect them that way? Only if he was infected, which both Max and Newton couldn't quite believe.

By the time they got back, ashy afternoon light was already hanging between the trees. They laid Ephraim on the picnic table by the cabin. Newton went round to check on Kent. The cellar doors were flung open.

"Kent?" Newton called down. *"Kent!"*

He inspected the doors. They didn't look to have been busted open. Maybe the stick Ephraim jammed between the handles had snapped or rattled free in the wind? Which could mean that Kent had escaped. He could be out there in the woods.

And no sign of Shelley either—a fact that was not a concern because it was a relief not to have him around, yet deeply concerning, seeing as neither boy wanted to contemplate what Shelley might get up to out of sight.

"You see Shel?" Newton asked Max back at the picnic table.

Max shook his head. "You think something happened?"

"Something *must've* happened, right?"

Mercifully, Ephraim had passed out. Blood loss, shock. They left him temporarily, unease gripping their postures—the boys walked with a slight stoop, shoulders hunched against a phantom breeze—as they made their way down to the shore.

"What if Kent's gone?" Newton said quietly.

"Gone where, Newt? What do you mean?"

In truth, Newton didn't know. A shape sat in the dead center of his mind—only a notion, really. Its outline was nebulous but he could make out its heart: a dark and sinister silhouette within the larger blackness that winked and writhed and wanted to play.

"Do you think he might've tried to swim back?"

Max kicked a pebble. "He'd be crazy to try . . . that doesn't mean I can't picture him doing it."

"Do you think he'd make it?"

If he'd actually done it, Max was sure Kent was dead by now. The water was freezing, the undertow deadly—plus he had a strong suspicion Kent might not be welcomed with open arms even if he'd managed to reach shore.

Max put Kent out of his mind for now. A merciless strain of expediency had settled over his thoughts. Ephraim needed help and was right here to receive it. Kent was gone and therefore beyond immediate help.

Max wondered how he and Newton had managed to stay sane these last few days. This thought arrowed out of the clear blue. They were still okay, seeing what they'd seen, where Ephraim and Kent and Scoutmaster Tim and maybe Shelley had cracked. He couldn't say why that was, exactly . . . it wasn't that he didn't feel the same fear. Human beings couldn't function in a state of perfect ongoing terror, could they? Their bodies would seize like a car with sugar in its gas tank, minds fusing shut as paralysis leeched into their bones. Constant, unending terror warped minds; brains thinned and went brittle and then snapped—that's exactly how Max pictured it: a singing *snap!* like an icicle coming off a February eaves trough. It could happen to anyone. It'd happened to Eef, hadn't it? But everyone's built to different tolerances, and you didn't know your breaking point until the instant you hit it.

How had Max kept that crushing fear at bay? He didn't really know—maybe that was the trick? Maybe it was that he'd found a way to bleed it away in the quiet moments. Breathing deep, feeling it slipping from him in almost imperceptible degrees.

Maybe Newton had his own strategies—or maybe it wasn't anything you could strategize. It came down to that flexibility of a person's mind. An ability to withstand horrors and snap back, like a fresh elastic band. A flinty mind shattered. In this way, he was glad not to be an adult. A grown-up's mind—even one belonging to a decent man like Scoutmaster Tim—lacked that elasticity. The world had been robbed of all its mysteries, and with those mysteries went the horror. Adults didn't believe in old wives' tales. You didn't see adults stepping over sidewalk cracks out of the fear that they might somehow, some way, break their mothers' backs. They didn't wish on stars: not with the squinty-eyed fierceness of kids, anyway. You'll never find an adult who believes that saying "Bloody Mary" three times in front of a mirror in a dark room will summon a dark, blood-hungry entity.

Adults were scared of different things: their jobs, their mortgages, whether they hung out with the "right people," whether they would die unloved. These were pallid compared to the fears of a child—leering clowns under the bed and slimy monsters capering beyond the basement's light and faceless sucking horrors from beyond the stars.

There's no 12-step or self-help group for dealing with those fears.

Or maybe there *is:* you just grow up.

And when you do, you surrender the nimbleness of mind required to believe in such things—but also to cope with them. And so when adults find themselves in a situation where that nimbleness is needed . . . well, they can't summon it. So they fall to pieces: go insane, panic, suffer heart attacks and aneurysms brought on by fright. Why? They simply don't *believe* it could be happening.

That's what's different about kids: they believe *everything* can happen, and fully expect it to.

Max knew he was at that age where disbelief began to set in. The erosion was constant. Santa Claus had gone first, then the monster in the closet. Soon he'd believe the way his folks did. Rationally.

But for now he still believed *enough*, and maybe that had kept him sane.

He was idly working all of this over in his mind when the screams started.

From the sworn testimony of Nathan Erikson, given before the Federal Investigatory Board in connection with the events occurring on Falstaff Island, Prince Edward Island:

Q: Please clarify something for the court, Dr. Erikson: So far as you were aware, you and Dr. Edgerton were working on a diet pill?

A: What do you mean?

Q: I'm asking specifically about the grant Dr. Edgerton received.

A: From the pharmaceutical concern, yes.

Q: And it was the only funding the Edgerton lab was receiving?

A: Yes.

Q: No.

A: Excuse me?

Q: No, it wasn't the only funding the lab was receiving, Dr. Erikson.

A: I'm sorry, what . . . ?

Q: Dr. Erikson, for someone who claimed to have a higher IQ than most everyone assembled at this hearing today, is it possible that you were unaware of the end goal of the very experiments you were administering?

A: Of course I know. I told you. A diet pill.

Q: Dr. Erikson, I'd like to show you something.

[Dr. Erikson is handed a piece of paper]

Q: Can you tell me what that is?

A: It's a bank statement.

Q: It's Dr. Edgerton's bank statement. For the account that administers the operating costs of his lab.

A: Yes, all right.

Q: Now if you scan down, you will see the deposits made by the pharmaceutical company.

A: They're here, yes.

Q: Now can you see the other single deposit—the one made on January second?

A: Yes.

Q: Can you tell me how much that one is for?

A: Three million dollars.

Q: Exactly?

A: Three million, fifty thousand, five hundred dollars. And forty-two cents.

Q: Can you tell me who made the deposit?

A: Is this a spelling test now? T. N. O. Printz Mauritz.

Q: Do you know what that company does, Dr. Erikson?

A: I have no idea.

Q: They are a military research firm.

A: Okay.

Q: Three years ago, they were subjected to a grand jury investigation. The company was indicted on charges of industrial espionage and selling goods to foreign despots for the purposes of cementing various puppet regimes.

A: I don't keep up on any of that.

Q: As a company, they do not have the cleanest of hands.

A: If you say so.

Q: Dr. Erikson, may I ask you this: If Dr. Edgerton is the genius you claim he is, why couldn't he keep the worms where they belonged—in a subject's intestinal tract?

A: As I said, even worms are complex organisms. Terribly complex.

Q: But—and please forgive my ignorance—isn't it the baseline nature of *most* tapeworms to remain in the gut?

A: Generally so, yes.

Q: Dr. Erikson, I will cut to the chase: Were you aware that Dr. Edgerton was in fact receiving *competing* grants? One

from a biopharmaceutical company and the other from a military research firm? One of those companies was anticipating a diet pill. The other, Dr. Erikson, was anticipating a biological weapon.

A: No.

Q: Would it shock you, Dr. Erikson, to discover that I have in my possession correspondence between Dr. Edgerton and the CEO of T. N. O. Printz Mauritz discussing this very thing?

A: That would shock me a great deal, sir.

Q: Do you see how such a creature could, in certain engagements, be an ideal method of warfare? Setting ethics and humanity aside, of course?

A: I . . . I suppose I do.

Q: It would be traceless. It would spread rapidly: An eyedropperful into a public reservoir would do it, yes?

A: Oh, Jesus. Oh, God.

Q: It could tear a country apart in short order, yes? Cause mass hysteria, destabilization, rampant infection, riots, fear, rage, secondary bloodshed in any order. It would defy both the letter and intent of the Geneva Convention—but it's just a hypervirulent worm, yes? Nobody knows how it came to be. **Mother Nature once again works her many strange wonders to behold, yes?**

A: I had no idea. You *have* to believe me.

Q: Dr. Erikson, I am under no obligation to do any such thing. That particular question of belief is up to this court to decide.

Chapter Thirty-Seven

Shelley waited until Max and Newton went down to the beach before climbing out of the cellar. The gauzy afternoon light stabbed his eyes like cocktail swords. The dark suited him now.

Last night, he'd lain in the cellar and dreamed of darkness slipping over the world. A forgiving dark: you could do things in that kind of blackness and get away with it. Nobody would ever see you. They would only *feel* you, and you could feel them.

Shelley found Ephraim lying on the picnic table. The sight was a pleasant one. It meant his game was progressing nicely. In fact, it appeared to have entered endgame stage.

Shelley swayed lightly on his feet with a dreamy look on his face. "Nobody loves me," he warbled, "everybody *haaaates* me . . ."

He ran a finger down the gash on Ephraim's face. When the boy didn't stir, he pushed the tip of his finger into it. His nail broke the gummy glue of blood. His finger moved inside the wound. He pushed harder, grunting lightly. His fingertip went through Ephraim's cheek into his mouth— for a thrilling instant he felt the smooth enamel of his teeth.

Ephraim's eyelids cracked open. Shelley withdrew his

317

finger. It came out with a gooey sound, like pulling your finger out of a pot of wallpaper paste.

"Shel? You don't look so hot."

Shelley supposed he didn't. At some point last night, he'd crept out of the cellar to eat the long timothy grass growing around the cabin. Down on all fours like a cow at its cud. This morning, he'd chased a plump pigeon along the beach, screaming and frothing at the mouth. The foam falling from his lips was white, tinted with green from the grass; it looked like the spume that washed up at the North Point jetty.

He hadn't caught the pigeon, but later he'd fallen asleep and dreamed that he had. In the dream, he'd torn its feathered head off—but not before eating the black jewels of its eyes as it struggled frantically in his hands—laughing and hissing as the bird's head separated from its body. He'd awoken to find his belly swollen to match his dream. The skin was pocked with lumps that looked like fledgling anthills.

"You saw it, didn't you?" Shelley asked dully. "The worm."

Shelley noticed the yellowish tinge to Ephraim's eyes. It was as if the oily madness in his brain had leeched into his corneas.

Ephraim's upper lip quivered. His chin went dimply as a golf ball. "It's still inside me, Shel."

"Is that so?"

"Can't you fuckin' *see*, man? Can't you *see it*?"

The pleading note in Ephraim's voice was auditory honey sliding into Shelley's ears. He furrowed his brow and stared intently at Ephraim—then he drew back suddenly. His head swept side to side, a sad and solemn gesture.

"I'm afraid so. It's still there. Didn't you do as I said?"

Ephraim's mouth twisted into a furious snarl; it was

quickly replaced by a scrawl of breathless panic. "I tried! I did exactly what you said. *You* got to get it out."

"Why couldn't you do that?" Twisting the knife in a person's psyche was nearly as much fun as twisting it in living flesh, Shelley had found. "Is it because you're weak, like everyone says?"

Ephraim wept silently, clutching at Shelley. "I can't do it. It's sneaky." Leaning to one side, he spat a reeking sack of blood onto the grass. "Can't . . . I can't . . ."

Shelley's expression remained placid—hesitant even— but a mad light capered behind his eyes.

"Want me to get it for you?"

"Do you have a knife?"

Shelley nodded. "Of course." He had a Buck knife with a five-inch blade, an inch and a half longer than the Scouts' official limit.

"Do you really see it, Shel? The worm?"

After a beat, Shelley said: "I saw it, Eef. It was in back of your eyes for a moment. A ripply thread behind the whites."

Ephraim made the most wretched, delightful sound Shelley had ever heard.

"You've got to get it out of me. I can't *stand* it."

"Okay, Eef." Shelley smiled, a happy camper. His teeth looked much bigger now with the gums peeling back. "But first, you have to say one thing."

"What?"

"You have to say *please*."

"Please." Ephraim clutched at the hem of Shelley's pants, squealing. *"Please."*

Shelley stifled his giggles—they built in his stomach like effervescent soda bubbles, rising up his throat in a hysterical wave. He didn't find any of this genuinely funny; not at all. Ephraim had offered him a rare gift. The rarest. It took so much to penetrate the senseless jelly that enrobed Shelley's brain—took so much to make him *feel*. But now he was feeling so, so much—needles of light streamed across his vision, unearthly and pure like a rift into Heaven.

He snapped the blade of his Buck knife into position. "I'll do it, but only because we're friends."

A look of pitiful gratefulness came over Ephraim's face. "Yes," he breathed. "Get it out."

Shelley's eyes cut down to the beach. No sign of Newt or Max. He'd sharpened the knife the night before their trip. He was scrupulous about such matters. You could split a doll's hair with the blade—split it into *thirds*.

He brought it down to Ephraim's face. He circled the tip around his earlobe and up around the teacup handle of his ear. The skin broke easily, just the first layer of epidermis. Blood teared up along the cut.

"Did you see it there?" Ephraim asked.

Shelley said: "In your ear, yes. It poked out for a second. I saw it wriggling."

Ephraim's fingers whitened around the table's edges. "Oh *God*. Please, Shel. I can't stand to have it in me."

"Mm-hmm," Shelley said, casually flirting the blade around the basin of Ephraim's ear. The steel tip brushed the microscopic hairs guarding his inner ear.

"Turn your head," he said sternly. "I need to see down."

Ephraim shifted onto his side. His eyes stared glassily at Shelley's swollen belly. A few buttons had popped off Shelley's shirt. Ephraim could see his lumped-up flesh through the vent. The inflamed anthills seemed to be twitching and breathing.

Shelley gripped Ephraim's jaw with his free hand. How would it feel to sink the knife into Ephraim's ear? Would he encounter resistance or would it be like stabbing a brick of cold butter? He pictured Ephraim staggering up with the

320

knife hilt protruding from his ear, his smile beatific as he screamed: *Did you get it? Did you? DID YOU?*

Instead, he idly slid the knife up Ephraim's head into his thick hairline. The flesh opened up as if by magic. A pair of red lips cut through the dark mane. Shelley thought of Moses parting the Red Sea. In the middle of the incision, he could see a vein-threaded rift of skull bone. Endorphins rushed through Shelley's system, lighting his neurons up like a pinball machine.

Ephraim didn't cry out. Instead he trembled with an outrush of powerful emotion and whispered: "Thank you. Thank you so much."

Shelley hacked a half-moon into Ephraim's head. Blood of a shockingly vibrant red sheeted down the boy's face.

"Thank you," he kept mumbling with pathetic gratefulness as the blood bubbled over his lips. "Do you see it? Oh please find it. Thank you thank you thank you . . ."

Shelley was remotely disgusted by Ephraim's behavior, but also fascinated. Ephraim's psychosis had some weird narcotizing effect. He wondered: If he cut around Ephraim's head until he hit the initial incision, could he tear his scalp off? Just like the Indians used to do. If so, would Ephraim even care?

The notion that he could be here for hours, hacking into a willing victim, sectioning Ephraim apart piece by piece, was thrilling in the extreme . . . and if things kept swinging his way, he wouldn't have to dispose of the body as he'd done with Trixy. Once he'd relished Ephraim's death, extracted from him the secrets Kent had withheld—and once Max and Newton were dead, too, a task he foresaw as daunting but still achievable—once they were all dead, Shelley would have their bodies all to himself. He could arrange them around the fire, posing their limbs and thumbing their stiffening faces into expressions he couldn't quite comprehend, playing with the blood that wept like treacle from their wounds . . . or he could cut them to pieces and reorganize them—different heads on different bodies—insulting them in death by disgracing their corpses, which would be funny, *terribly* funny, so funny that the giggles started to rise in his throat again. Afterward he could leave them to the insects: their bodies would become shelter and nourishment for beetles and slugs and worms. Yes, they'd be worm food.

But Shelley had to be careful—the other two would soon return. Shelley thought he could hear their voices near the fire pit. He bit his lip, thinking.

Finally he said: "Wait here, Eef. I'll be right back."

He shambled around to the generator, rocking it to see if any gas was left. There was. He descended into the cellar and found an empty mason jar. Then he popped the valve on the generator and drained gasoline into the jar.

He returned to Ephraim and said: "I can't cut it out, Eef. It's too sneaky. The only way to get it is to burn it out."

Ephraim's eyes were very white and wide in the bloody mask of his face. Shelley's words came to him as a revelation. They were the most sensible words anyone had ever spoken. Fire purifies all.

Shelley set the jar next to him.

"Burn it out, Ephraim. It's the only way, my friend." Shelley touched Ephraim's twitching face with great tenderness. "You know that, don't you? You're my very best friend."

Ephraim swallowed. For a moment it seemed he would bat Shelley's grublike fingers away—but they dropped of their own accord. Shelley handed Ephraim his barbecue lighter.

"That's okay," Ephraim said, pulling out his Zippo. "I've got my own."

Ephraim picked up the jar and held it over his head. It hung there a moment. His face shuddered as if under the pressure of deep internal forces, then it went slack.

"Thank you, Shelley," he said. "You're the only one who gets it."

Ephraim's hand tipped downward to saturate his flesh with gasoline.

Chapter Thirty-Eight

By the time Newton and Max ran back to the cabin, Ephraim was on fire.

A towering cone of flame enveloped the body of a boy who suddenly looked small, shrunken, and trapped within it.

They bolted into the clearing only to check up by degrees: their feet lagging like cars rolling to an awkward stall. Their horror inspired inertness.

Ephraim was on fire.

A swiftly charring effigy. Their minds collectively yammered at them to do something but dear God, what could they *do*? The idea of shouting at him to stop, drop, and roll seemed quaintly absurd.

The flames swept up from Ephraim's shoulders in orange wings. He was glowing and ephemeral: he might lift off the ground like an ember swirling up from an open fire. His flame-robed arms oared in lopsided circles. The sound of his legs scissoring the air was like sheets of very fine silk being ripped apart. Horribly, Max could see that he was *inhaling* the fire: flames were crawling down into his lungs, igniting them.

Ephraim crumpled to the ground. His legs kept kicking as if he were trying to step over a low obstacle.

When they finally acted, it was too late—had it ever *not* been too late? Max dashed into the cabin, heedless of the men lying dead inside, grabbed a sleeping bag, ran back, and dropped it over Ephraim, where he lay curled in a thatch of crabgrass. Plumes of meaty smoke drifted around the bag's edges. One of Ephraim's feet jutted from under the bag. The soles of his boots had fused into a smooth black sheen that resembled a slick drag-racing tire. A single point of flame danced on the tip of his boot.

When Max pulled the sleeping bag back, it was obvious at first glance that Ephraim was dead. The heat had curled his body up like when you toss a cellophane packet into a fire: his thighs were tucked tight to his chest like a child in the fetal position. His kneecaps appeared to be heat-welded to his forehead. His clothes were either burned off or fused through grisly alchemical processes to his skin. He was charred all over like something left too long in the oven. His features were erased the same way a mannequin's would be if someone had taken a blowtorch to its head.

"Oh, Jesus," Newton said. "Oh, Eef, Eef . . ."

Merciless bands of iron clapped around Max's chest. His breath came in shallow jaggedy bursts. The shock was such that he could only stare at the body, coring a hole into it with his eyes.

"Where the hell's Shelley?" Max said.

Max's left eyelid developed a weird tic: the muscles kept clenching and releasing; it looked like he was trying to wink but couldn't quite get his face to cooperate. He felt the anger boiling out of him—which was how he figured it must always happen. Pressure turned fear into rage as surely as pressure turns coal into a diamond. Fear was an internal emotion: it got trapped inside of you. You had to let it out. For that you turned to rage, the ultimate external emotion.

All rage ever needed was something to focus on—was

this how Eef had gone through life, fighting this rage that was a kissing cousin to pure madness?

Shelley rounded the cabin. Seeing him, Max's chest hitched in sudden shock—*hic!*

Max thought Shelley looked as if someone had located a hidden zipper down his back, tugged it down, and skinned thirty-odd pounds of meat from his bones before zippering the sagging shell back up again. He couldn't help but notice the blood on his hands.

"Hey, guys." Shelley waved chummily. The tone of his voice was faintly mocking.

"You." Max leveled a finger at Shelley. "Where *were* you?"

"No place special."

Shelley's gaze fell upon Ephraim. If he exhibited any emotion at all, it was dry revulsion: the look a passing motorist might give roadkill.

"Where the *fuck* . . ." Max said, his words coming out in great livid gasps, ". . . were you?"

Shelley shrugged with his hands in his pockets: a carefree, maddening gesture. Huge boils the size of cherry bombs throbbed on his neck where his adenoids should've been.

"Stay away from him," Newt whispered to Max. "He's sick with it."

But Max's rage was all-consuming. The reek of gasoline wafted off Shelley. He'd *done* something.

"What did you do, Shel?"

Max thought: What did any of them really *know* about Shelley? He was a lanky, furtive boy who kept to himself with an inner intensity of evasion and secrecy. The other boys tolerated him but nobody would call him a friend. They didn't make sport of him—not because he wasn't mockable, with his thick-lipped vacancy and stunned inability to comprehend the simplest jokes.

"Stay away from him," Newt told Max, a little louder.

Max continued to advance. He'd never really been in a fight. Eef got into scraps all the time. He was good at it, too. He was fearless—*had been fearless*. Ah, Jesus. This felt like more than a fight to Max; the acid boiling through his veins told him so.

He reached for Shelley. He'd wrap his hands round his throat and squeeze until his windpipe collapsed. There were no adults to tell him no—besides, who says an adult wouldn't act just the same?

One of Shelley's hands released from his pocket. A quicksilver flash. Next, pain was sizzling along Max's sternum just above his hipbones.

Both boys stared down. An inch of Shelley's Buck knife was inserted into Max's abdomen.

Max stared at it quizzically, his dizzied mind thinking: *Now*, that *doesn't belong there.* The strangest thing in the world, being stabbed. Had he even *been* stabbed—or had Shelley simply held the knife out defensively and let Max impale himself on the blade?

He glanced at Shelley with a panicky grin that showed too many teeth. It was a grin that said: *This was an accident, right? Things haven't gotten this bad, have they?* But Max saw the rancid emptiness in Shelley's eyes and saw his own cheese-white reflection in Shelley's dilated pupils and knew that yes, yes, things had gotten this bad.

Shelley's arm flexed stealthily. Max pulled away but still a half inch of the blade divided the red sheets of muscle. Shelley's expression was impassive, marginally curious. He could have been carving a roast or dissecting a pickled pig in science class.

A stick of wood whistled down and struck Shelley on the back of his skull. It landed with a solid *whock!*—the sound of a baseball struck with the sweet spot of a bat.

The knife slipped from Shelley's hands. His knees

327

buckled. His eyes rolled back so far in his skull that Max saw the quivering whites.

The wood slipped from Newton's trembling hands.

"I had to," he said. "He was gonna kill you, Max."

Chapter Thirty-Nine

Shelley staggered up. A goose egg swelled on the back of his head: it was so huge that it stretched the hairs on his scalp apart to reveal the vein-snaked skin. A crazed, curdled light shone in the pit of each iris. He took a step forward, swooned like a man on the deck of a storm-tossed ship before falling down on his ass. He laughed—a thin, warbling titter that tapered to a drone.

"I'll k-kill you," he said between volleys of laughter. There was no real menace in his voice. He could have been stating a matter of his daily agenda. "Kill you both . . ."

A flash pot of rage exploded in Max's chest. Blood was running from the stab wound to soak the hem of his underwear.

"You'll kill us, huh? Is that what you'll do, you crazy fuck?" He stepped toward Shelley. "What if I kill you first, huh, Shel? What if *I* kill *you*?"

Shelley cocked his head at Max. A predatory gesture— was he baiting Max? Shelley sucked back snot and hocked up phlegm. He opened his mouth and showed them the oyster of thick mucus on his tongue.

Max saw things wriggling in it.

Shelley's mouth curved into a smile as he diddled the oyster around on his tongue.

"You're sick, Shelley," Newton said. Max figured he wasn't just talking about the worms, either. "We found these mushrooms. You could take them. They might flush them out."

Shelley's head swung side to side like a pendulum—then he spat. Max dodged; the spit sailed past his leg. It hit the dirt and picked up dust. *It's squirming, Jesus his spit is squirming.* Max's first urge was to stamp on it like he would a revolting bug, but he resisted the impulse.

They backed away as Shelley struggled to stand. Max was sure he'd just keep hocking until he hit the mark—that, or bite them or even lick them. He'd infect them for the pure sport of it.

Max's heels hit the edge of the campfire. The rocks forming the ring weren't all that big. Some of them were fist-size, some smaller. He picked one up, testing its weight. It felt good in his hand. It felt *mean.*

Shelley was coming. Max pegged the rock. The muscles flexed over his rib cage and caused the cut on his belly to tear even wider. The stone whanged off Shelley's knee. Max thought he saw something crumple and sag under his pants and wondered if he'd shattered Shelley's kneecap—and in that moment he was so hopeful that he had.

Shelley squawked and fell, clutching at his leg. Max picked up another rock.

"The next one you'll catch with your face, Shel," he said. His voice was coolly businesslike, but his bloody hands were trembling.

Shelley hissed at them—actually *hissed*, like a vampire who'd had a cross jammed in his face. He scrambled away, retreating up the dirt path behind the cabin.

Max pursued, following Shelley until the path tracked into the pines. He paused—could Shel be waiting in ambush? Turning reluctantly, he doubled back to Newton.

"Where is he?"

"In the woods," Max said. "He was limping bad. I might have broken something." He considered this possibility, his lips forming a hard, thin line. "Good. I hope so."

"What if he comes back?"

"I don't know, Newt. I just don't know."

They turned their attention to Ephraim. The wind had blown the sleeping bag back over his body, which was a small mercy.

Max said: "We got to bury him, Newt."

"Yes," Newton said. "We ought to do that. It's the only way he'll get to Heaven."

It was dark by the time they put Ephraim in the ground.

But first Newton bandaged Max's wound. The edges of the cut were clotted with dirt—Newton debrided them as best he could with salt water fetched up from the beach and dressed it with bandages from the medical kit. Blood seeped through the gauze almost as soon as he applied it. It would have to do. The medical kit was almost empty.

They buried Ephraim in the ground south of the campfire. It was softer, almost sandy. They used a collapsible shovel Newton had bought at the Army Surplus. When its handle snapped off, they used their hands.

When the grave was finished, they dragged Ephraim to it. The sleeping bag's neoprene shell slid over the ground with effortless ease. At first, they were terrified the hole wouldn't be deep enough and that they'd have to dig deeper while Ephraim's body sat right next to them.

It was deep enough. They scooped dirt over and patted it down to discourage animals from digging the body up. Newton recited a short prayer that his mother often said. He didn't know that it really applied, but it was the only one he knew by heart.

God in Heaven hear my prayer,
Keep me in thy loving care.
Be my guide in all I do,
Bless all those who love me, too. Amen.

Afterward their eyes were hot and dry. Max wanted to cry if only to release the tension in his chest. But his body wouldn't release the tears because his mind wouldn't allow it. It seemed inconceivable that Eef could be in a hole in the ground. Just last week Max had raced him across the monkey bars at recess. Eef won. Afterward they'd sat in the shade by the baseball diamond and ate their lunches. Eef's mom had packed some crackers for him; they'd stuffed their mouths with the dry squares and seen who could recite the alphabet fastest. They were spitting out shards of cracker and laughing like mad. Eef had won that game, too. Eef won just about everything where Kent wasn't involved.

Max and Ephraim would never hike to the bluffs behind his house, staring up at the stars as the shearwaters called from the cliffs; they'd never talk about girls and candy and their dreams and who'd win in a fight, Batman or James Bond. They'd made a pact to be friends forever, but forever could be so, so brief.

Max curled into a wretched ball beside the grave. Eef *was* dead. *Everyone* was dead or missing or insane. The cabin was in splinters and things were falling apart.

Which seemed so *unfair.*

Where were the adults? Max couldn't believe *someone* hadn't come for them yet. His parents were always nagging him to be on time, to be responsible and to think of others. Well then, what the *fuck*? His folks were full of shit. Or else they'd be here. And Kent's parents—including his hot-shit policeman dad—and Newt's and Eef's, too. Didn't they give a shit about them? Maybe they were all complicit in it. A plot. They'd all bought into it. Get them out to the island and cut off their escape route. Let nature take its course.

No. That was idiot talk. Their parents would never do that. The fact that they weren't here actually spoke to how dire the situation must be. Because this wasn't *nature*, was it?

This was something else.

Those things. The way they spread infection—the way they *spread*.

Newton got a fire going. The warmth helped the anger and confusion melt out of Max's brain; they were replaced by exhaustion. He felt as if he were wearing one of those heavy lead coats the dental hygienist draped over his shoulders before taking X-rays.

He lay beside the fire. Almost instantly, he was fast asleep.

Chapter Forty

Eat eat eat eat . . .

Shelley rose in the dead of night to hunt.

He'd found a cool, dark place to hide. He'd limped into the woods, clutching at his hurt knee. He eventually came upon a cavern burrowed into the island's bedrock. It was deep and narrow and it held the tang of salt. Perhaps it was fed by an aquifer that led out to sea.

He lay in the sheltering dark, listening to the water trickle on the rock. This place suited him. It would be a wonderful place to give birth.

The *boys.* Max and Newton. Skinny and fat. Jack Sprat and his wife. They thought he was sick. They couldn't be more wrong.

He *wasn't* sick. He was simply changing into something entirely new.

He could feel it inside of him: a vast darkness, itchy-black, unfurling like the petals of a night-blooming flower. It would hurt. Oh yes. But then change always did.

The hateful boys had wounded him. They may have hurt his babies—but no, he could feel them squirming contentedly inside of him. Thank goodness.

The boys needed to die.

Shelley had been planning on killing them, anyway. He wasn't sure it'd be much fun at this point, although it might provide the same fleeting thrill he'd experienced while drowning Kent: a fizzy, sudsy bath-bubble feeling in his veins. But now he'd kill them as a simple matter of principle. They had harmed him, which meant—inadvertently or otherwise—they had harmed his babies. And a father always defended his children.

Shelley exited the cave. The night enveloped him. He was part of it, dark just like it.

EAT EAT EAT

Oh my, weren't they so needy? So hungry. They asked so much of him, as all children must . . . but Shelley was only too happy to give.

He came upon a diseased elm. Its trunk was pocked with tiny bore holes. He tore away a chunk of bark—his strength was immense!—and clawed inside the rotted tree. When he withdrew it, his hand was teeming with woodlice. He crunched them into paste. They fidgeted on his tongue and tickled his throat when he swallowed. He giggled hoarsely while sucking the last few lice off his fingers.

GOOD GOOD EAT MORE MORE MORE

Shelley caught his reflection in a pool of moonlight-sheened water. He was horribly wrinkled. It looked as if spiders with legs of thin steel wire had battened onto his flesh, curling and tightening, trenching deep lines into his face.

His stomach was a swollen gourd. It bulged through his shirt and over the band of his trousers. Its pale circumference was strung with blue veins and sloshed with a dangerous, exciting weight . . .

. . . in the dank wastes of his brain—his undermind, you could say—a species of mute fear twined into his thoughts. *This isn't right*, a voice said. *You're being eaten alive.*

. . . a wave of acidic warmth washed through those thoughts, burning them away.

Oh, they asked so much of him! It was tiring, feeding all those hungry mouths. And the mouths just beget more mouths and more mouths and more and more and—

Shelley slid down the incline to the campsite. Firelight crept around the cabin's shattered angles. He snuck around the far side and surveyed the fire pit. Max was sleeping. He imagined grabbing his hair and jamming him face-first into the white-hot coals. He pictured the silly boy's face melting like a latex Halloween mask.

The fat one, Newton, was staring right at him.

His heart jogged in his chest: ba-*dump*. Newton sat on the far side of the fire. The flames played over his eyes, which seemed to be staring directly at him.

EAT EAT EAT EAT

In a moment, he thought. *First I have to kill them. Then I'll be alone. Then I can give birth in peace. Then we can all play.*

But how would he do it? He'd lost his knife. Was Newton *really* looking at him?

"I see you, Shelley."

Newton pulled a knife out of his pocket. *His* knife. He unfolded it carefully and stabbed the tip into a log. The knife quivered in the wood. An invitation?

"Go away. Get out of here. Now," Newton whispered.

A cold, slippery eel ghosted through the ventricles of Shelley's heart, cinching itself tight. He retreated like a groveling animal. He wanted them dead so badly but . . . but . . . but he was so *hungry.*

Shelley's stomach swayed as he tripped sideways, whimpering softly as his belly brushed the edge of the cabin—for a moment he felt it might detach and burst like a water

336

balloon on the forest floor. Then he'd lose everything. His children. His precious babies.

Shelley was in the forest again. Night folded over him. The hunger was hellish, unspeakable, but one must suffer for what one loves.

He shambled through the woods, eating whatever. It came to him in flashes. In one moment, he was hunched under a log devouring eggs, maybe—termite eggs whose sacs burst between his teeth like albino jellybeans . . .

. . . next he was along the shoreline ankle-deep in the freezing surf, gorging himself on the decayed carapace of some creature that had once crawled in the sea. So tasty. It slipped between his numbed fingers and he collapsed into the surf, squealing like a piglet, clutching at his stinking prize . . .

. . . later, much later, Shelley lay in the darkness with the cool trickle of the rock. He was screaming or maybe crying, he couldn't tell. There was a watery echo down there that did funny things to his voice.

None of that really mattered anymore, anyway. His home, his foolish parents, his teachers, the many jars buried in the backyard full of his playthings, all in various states of decomposition. That was his old life; his silly, forgettable life.

He was going to be a great daddy.

The *best*.

From the sworn testimony of Stonewall Brewer, given before the Federal Investigatory Board in connection with the events occurring on Falstaff Island, Prince Edward Island:

Q: Please state your name and rank, sir.

A: Stonewall Brewer, admiral, Canadian navy.

Q: Stonewall?

A: I always tell people that my mother must have had a premonition.

Q: Very prescient of her. Admiral, when were you made aware of the events occurring on Falstaff Island?

A: About oh-three-hundred. Can't recall the exact time on the display of the clock beside my bed—although the call was tracked, so we could get you that info if need be.

Q: What were you told?

A: That a nonspecific contagion of unknown lethality had breached containment.

Q: Were you aware of the nature of this contagion?

A: At the time, no.

Q: No idea at all?

A: You will find you'll only have to ask me a question once, my friend. The first answer is the answer you'll get every time.

Q: Only seeking to clarify matters for the court, Admiral. What's your experience, if any, with the spread or neutralization of a contagion?

A: If I had no experience, I don't imagine it would've been my phone ringing in the dead of night. I spearheaded the containment efforts on the SARS outbreak that hit metropolitan Toronto back in 2002.

Q: If I recall, forty-four people died during that outbreak.

A: Could have been a lot more. That was my first rodeo.

Q: And all you knew about the contagion in North Point was—

A: I hit the ground with the intel available at the time. We had one case of infection—

Q: That would be Tom Padgett.

A: That's right, the guinea pig. Typhoid Tom. It was SOP: quarantine the area, detain all residents, set up a zone of infection. Nothing comes in and most importantly, nothing gets out. That's how we treat icebergs.

Q: Icebergs?

A: That's how threats like this are known internally. The idea is that only ten percent of an iceberg is visible. The other ninety percent is below the water. So when we've got a threat without set parameters, one that could be huge, we call it an iceberg.

Q: And containment was vital?

A: Always is, but even more so in this case. Word came down that we could be up against a three-tier bug: the virus could be carrier-borne, waterborne, or airborne. The terrible threesome.

Q: What were your orders?

A: I don't take orders as a rule. It's my duty to dole them out.

Q: What was your agenda, then?

A: It was full-scale. Total neutralization. Quarantine the island and all life-forms on it. Nothing comes or goes. I had to enact some very serious measures.

Q: Such as?

A: First off, we couldn't do anything about the kids. That was rough, no two ways about it. But we couldn't risk it.

Q: Anything else?

A: When I said *nothing comes, nothing goes,* I meant it. If a seagull took off from that island and tried to fly back to land, I had a recon sniper shoot it out of the sky. I had military personnel in hazmat suits fish the corpse out of the water. After the island was cleared, I ordered four million gallons of Anotec Blue to be dumped into the surrounding waters. We call that stuff Blue Death: it kills every-thing, indiscriminately. Marine life, plants, plankton, protozoa. The eggheads at the CDC told me I ought to make another pass just to be sure. A few earth mother types got their knickers in a twist over that. We razed the island, too. Took four separate napalm strikes—you know how hard it is to find napalm? My marching orders were to render Falstaff Island biologically sterile: not one living thing left. Maybe there's a few amoebas still swimming around. I'm constantly amazed at the tenacity of all life on this planet. But if anything's still alive, it's not for lack of trying on my part.

Chapter Forty-One

Max dreamed he was in the mortuary with his father. It's the only chance he got to see him some days. People didn't die that often in North Point, but they did like to hunt and fish, meaning his father had a backlog of taxidermy projects. The nature of taxidermy being what it is—framing the anatomies of dead animals before they begin to decay—timing is everything. Of course, the same held true for human anatomies.

His father worked in a white-tiled room beneath the city courthouse. The air held the sharp undertone of charcoal from the air purifier that pumped away in a corner. The shelves and fixtures were stainless steel. A huge steel slab dominated the room's center.

Max watched his father work. He wore a long white coat—the kind pharmacists wore—and an apron of black vulcanized rubber. His dad whistled while he worked. Today it was "The Old Gray Mare."

"The old gray mare she ain't what she used to be, ain't what she used to be, ain't what she used to be . . ."

A woman's body lay on the table. She had died at a very old age. A white sheet was draped over her hips but her chest was bare. Her breasts were long and tubular, as if something had pulled them out of shape. Her empty sockets were withered like two halves of a cored-out squash forgotten for days on a countertop.

His father worked with his back to Max. He picked up an ocular suction cup.

"What happens is," he told Max in a weird singsong voice, "the eyeballs get sucked down into your head after you die. Did you know that, Maxxy?"

His father never called him Maxxy.

He thumbed the ocular cup into the woman's socket. Tiny barbs on the cup attached to her naked eyeball. He pulled. The eyeball sucked back into its socket with the sound of a boot being pulled out of thick mud.

"All better . . ."

His father was whistling again. A sputtering, wheezing noise—it sounded as if it was being made with a different orifice altogether. Fear slammed into Max's belly.

His father turned. At first Max thought his head had been submitted to some incredible pressure: it was flattened, elongated, pancaked. It projected upward and curled over on itself like a lotus petal.

"Oh Maxxy Maxxy Maxxy . . ."

A worm's head jutted from his father's lab coat. It was the greasy white of a toadstool. Noxious fluid leaked from its ribbed exterior, dribbling down to form a pumicey crust on the collar.

"Thee ole gray mare, thee ain't what thee useth to be . . ."

The voice was coming from a pit in the middle of its head: round and ineffably dark like the air in a caved-in mine shaft. The pit was studded with translucent teeth that looked like glassine tusks.

"Thee ole gray mare . . ." his worm-father sang, swaying and burping up goo.

A pair of yellow dots glowed in the direct center of the pit, looking like the headlights of a car shining up from the bottom of the ocean. Before he woke up, Max swore he could hear another voice coming from the deepest part of the worm—the ongoing scream of his own father, trapped somewhere inside of it.

Newton was shaking him.

"Max! *Max!*"

He jerked up. The sunlight stabbed at his eyes. The dream drained thickly from his brainpan, departing his body through uncontrollable twitches and shivers.

"You okay? You were screaming in your sleep," Newton said.

"Yeah. Just a bad dream."

It was morning. He didn't know how long he'd slept. His spine was knotted and his gut kicked over sourly.

They walked to the shore. The ships still charted their distant orbits. They were like the heat-shimmer on the highway: no matter how fast you drove, it didn't get any closer or draw any farther away. Max wanted to scream at them, but why bother? A waste of his swiftly diminishing energy.

Newton rubbed the sleep-crust out of his eyes and wandered toward Oliver McCanty's boat. He hauled on the motor's rip cord. The motor went *wuh-wah*—the same discouraging sound it'd made when they'd tried a few days before. Newton pulled it again. Again. Again. He thought about the poster in science class—Albert Einstein, shock-haired with his tongue stuck out above the quote: *The definition of insanity is doing the same thing over and over again expecting different results.* Defeated, he let go of the cord, staggered back, tripped, and sat down on his ass. He cupped his hands over his eyes, lowered his head between his knees, and wept.

"Hey," Max said. "Hey, Newt, it's—"

But Newton was too far gone. The pent-up sobs ripped out of his throat. They were the most wretched noises Max had ever heard. He put an arm around Newton's shoulders and felt the tension: like grasping a railroad track in advance of the onrushing locomotive. He didn't tell Newton everything would be okay because it wasn't—it would never be as it had been. The past had a perfection that the future could never hold.

Max just let Newton cry.

His sobs trailed off. He drew a few hitching breaths and said: "Sorry, Max. That wasn't very . . ." He hiccupped twice, exhaled steadily, and said: ". . . wasn't very cuh-cool of me. WWAMD?" he said, more to himself than to Max. "He sure as hell wouldn't cry like a baby."

"I don't think being cool really matters now, do you?"

Newton let go of one more shuddery breath. "No. I guess not."

Max walked to the boat, cracked the motor casing. Inside were two small holes where the spark plugs should go. He thought of his dream—the two yellow dots glowing up from the dark pit . . .

His mind jogged. Two revelations joined in his head like puzzle pieces slotting into place.

"He must have *eaten* them."

"*What?*" Newton said. "Who did? Ate what?"

"The spark plugs," Max said softly. "The man. The stranger. He swallowed the spark plugs. Ate them."

"*Ate* them? Why would he do—?"

Newton thought about the man—how cadaverous he'd looked, skinny as a pipecleaner. Thought about Kent and Shelley, too. Yes, he decided, the man probably *was* hungry enough to eat spark plugs.

"He ate them because he was hungry, huh?"

Max shrugged. "Could be. Or maybe he didn't want to

345

be found. Without spark plugs, the boat won't start—right? Maybe he figured the best place to hide them was inside of himself."

"How do you know?"

"Because I *saw* them, Newt. When the Scoutmaster cut him open to get the worm out. I saw them shining in . . . well, his stomach, I guess."

"You're sure?"

"Positive."

Ten minutes later, they were in the cabin, standing over the dead stranger.

They tried to not pay much attention to the state of his body. It seemed wrong, somehow—desecrating him with their eyes. They tried to focus on him abstractly: as a puzzle or a riddle. They had to solve him in the easiest and safest way.

Still, they couldn't help but stare.

His elbows and knees had been eaten away by something. That was the most obvious thing. Animals, insects? How could that have happened so quickly, though? Or perhaps the skin had been so thin that the bones had worn through all on their own, the way your knees will wear through a cheap pair of jeans.

His face had fallen into itself. It was distracting—they couldn't drag their eyes away. Newton draped a dish towel over it.

"Do you think the worms are all dead?"

Max nodded. "They have to be—right? That's what the Scoutmaster said. Once the host is dead, the worms die, too."

Newton still seemed doubtful. "What about eggs? They might still be there, right? Eggs don't need food, do they?"

Max set his fingertips lightly on the man's wrist. "He's cold. He's been gone a long time."

"Okay, but put something on your hands first."

They found a pair of dishwashing gloves. Newton scrounged up two empty plastic bread bags.

"The gloves go on first. Then the bread bags overtop. Then I'm gonna tape your shirtsleeves to the bags so nothing can get in."

"Good idea."

The sun shone brightly through the cleaved roof, glossing insects that hummed over the body. Already the island was taking over the cabin. Mold edged up the walls, fungus grew in the cracks. Soon the foundations would rot and disintegrate. Maybe that was for the best, Max thought.

"Try not to breathe too deeply," Newton said.

"Okay, fine. You're creeping me out."

Newton gave him a bewildered look. "Max, jeez—you're about to reach inside a dead guy. You *better* be creeped out."

Max pushed his fingers into the pasty lips of the wound, through a thin membrane of gelatinized blood and into the dead man's abdomen. *Cold oatmeal,* he told himself. *You're just rooting around in a bowl of cold oatmeal.*

The man's insides had liquefied and turned granular; they didn't seem to have any definition anymore, no organs or intestines—his hand moved through layers of cold, chunky tissue that felt a little like mashed bananas.

Mashed bananas, then. You're looking for spark plugs in a big pile of mashed bananas.

Max's hand slipped into a squelchy pocket. A rude farting noise. The air filled with a rotted, sulfury, swamp-gas stink. Max's gut roiled but nothing came out—just a dry heave that filled his mouth with the taste of bitter bile. His hand closed upon something hard. He pulled it out.

"Holy crow," Newton said.

The spark plug lay in Max's cupped palm. It was smeared

in pinkish-gray curds, but they could clearly make out the word *Champion* down its side.

It took Max a minute to find the second one. He had to sink his hand in fairly far—almost to the elbow—ripping through some rubbery kinked hoses in the man's abdomen to get it: tubelike things that tore up like the witchgrass growing in the shallows of North Point bay.

When it was done, the spark plugs lay side by side on the floor. The boys grinned at each other. It had to be the best news they'd ever gotten. They had to grope through a dead man's insides to get it, but still.

They were both suffused with a feeling they hadn't truly experienced in days:

Hope.

Chapter Forty-Two

They carried the spark plugs down to the shore. Max was so excited that he didn't even bother to strip the wash gloves off. The sea came into view over the rocky scree. For the first time since they could recall, that vista didn't seem so vast or the distance to North Point so very daunting.

Newton popped the motor canopy. He frowned.

"Should we just screw them in like that? All covered in . . . you know."

"You think it matters?"

"It could. We should clean them first."

Max said: "Won't that ruin them?"

Newton pointed at the words running down the side of the plugs in small green type: *Marine Standard*. "That means they're waterproof."

They washed off the gray-pink curds in the frigid sea. They did so carefully, the way you'd wash oil off a baby mallard.

When they were clean, Newton put them on the big flat rock to dry. Newton chose it specifically because it was large, and flat, and flecked with pink granite. A very peculiar rock. He chose it because he wanted to be absolutely *sure* they could find the spark plugs again.

Max knocked on the motor's gas tank. His knuckles brought forth a hollow *whonk.*

"Sounds almost empty."

"What about the generator?" Newton said. "It should have gas."

They returned to the campsite. The cap had been wrenched off the generator's gas tank. The surrounding earth held the gleam of spilled gasoline. Max rocked the generator. Nothing sloshed inside.

A pall of hopelessness fell over them. The universe was aligned against them. Why? It struck Max that the universe ought to find better targets. Had to be plenty of psychopaths and deadbeats out there, right? Why pick on a couple of kids? The universe could be a stone-cold asshole sometimes.

"What about the emergency jerry can?" Newton said. "The Scoutmaster kept it in the cellar."

The steps groaned as they traced their way down the stairs. Bars of sunlight fell through cracks in the cabin floor. The cellar was eerily clean: not a single spiderweb, none of the sickly gray mushrooms Max had spied growing in the corners when he was down here the other day.

God, Kent must have eaten them, he thought queasily.

Max picked the jerry can up. It was joyously heavy.

"There's at least a gallon in here," he said.

Maybe the universe wasn't such an asshole after all. But it sure as hell made you suffer something fierce.

Case in point: when they returned to the boat, the spark plugs were gone.

The pink-flecked rock was bare except for two wet spots where they had lain. Newton actually laughed—a strangled squawk of disbelief.

"They're here," he said, shaking his head, a strained smile

on his face. "No, no, they're here somewhere, I'm sure of it. Where the hell else could they be?"

The boys waded into the frigid surf and poked doggedly around the rocks. Maybe a big wave had crashed up on shore and pulled them into the sea. But that *couldn't* be—the rocks were dry as saltines. Their ankles turned pink, then blue. Max stomped out of the water.

"Are you kidding? Where the fuck are they, Newt?"

"How should I know? I left them here."

"You should've put them in your pocket."

"So it's my fault? Are you serious? What do you think happened—a fish jumped up and swallowed them? A bird flew off with them?"

"Okay, what if a bird *did* pick them up? A pelican, like the ones perched on the buoys out at Barker Bay? My dad says they swallow soda cans."

"*God.* Don't be so stupid." Newton adopted a superior tone—as if he were talking to a preschooler who'd just claimed the Tooth Fairy was real. "Pelicans are *shore birds.*"

"So what's all this then, Newt?" Max spread his arms out. "Is this a *shore*, or are you just a big fat moron?"

"Pelicans are mainland shore birds. This is an *iiiisland*. Mainland shore birds don't fly to *iiiiislands*. Do you understand that, or do I need to draw you a map—"

Max took two steps forward, planted his palms in Newton's chest, and shoved. Newton went down with a jolt. Max expected him to stay down just as he always did—but instead Newton propelled himself off the rocks and drove his shoulder into Max's stomach, knocking the wind out of him.

They tumbled across the shore, striking at each other. Their blows didn't have much pop, but they were thrown with cruel intentions. Newton's fist collided with Max's nose, and the impact set Max's skull bone ringing like a cathedral bell.

Max rolled over, snarling, and his elbow caught Newton under the chin. Blood leapt into the air, startlingly bright in the morning sun.

They shoved away from each other, breathing hard. Max's nose was a squashed berry. Blood lay stunned across his cheeks. The wound in his abdomen had opened up again. Blood was dripping from Newton's chin. They eyed each other warily, trying to gauge whether the fight was over or this was just an interlude before hostilities commenced anew.

"Are we done?" Max mumbled.

"Yeah, we're done," Newton said with downcast eyes.

They sat in silence as the adrenaline burnt out of their systems. In its wake came dull relief. It was like tripping the release on a steam gauge: they could breathe easier and think straighter.

Max offered Newton his hand. Newton took it. Max pulled him up.

"That was a waste of time and energy," Newton said.

"Yeah."

"I don't know why guys do it. I feel sick. I taste blood between my teeth."

"Sorry."

Newton shrugged. "Don't be. I did it, too." He smiled out the side of his mouth. "Bet you didn't see that coming, did you? WWAMD!"

"What?"

"Nothing. Your nose okay?"

Max gripped the tip of his nose, wiggled it. "Hurts, but I don't think it's broken."

They looked out over the sea.

"It was Shelley," Max said.

"Yeah," Newton said. "I was thinking the same thing."

"You figure he chucked the spark plugs into the sea?"

"I don't think so."

"You think he took them with him?"

"Uh-huh."

"You figure he wants us to come find him?"

"Uh-huh. Hide and go seek. Fetch boy, fetch."

Max sighed. He felt about a hundred years old.

"Red rover, red rover, please send crazy asshole Shelley over."

"Olly olly oxen free."

"Come on," said Max. "We got to find him."

Chapter Forty-Three

They set off in pursuit of Shelley just after noon.

"I got my animal-tracking badge last year," Newton said to lighten the mood. "But, y'know, they don't give out a man-tracking badge."

They decided to search the areas off the main trail. Shelley couldn't have gone too far. Before leaving, they ate the last of the berries they'd collected—the ones for Eef. They tasted bitter, but they'd need the energy.

Newton packed his field book into his knapsack along with a map of the island, some rope, and a flashlight. Max snapped a branch off an elm tree. It was as thick and as long as a mop handle. He sharpened one end to a wicked point.

"I don't want him coming near us, Newt."

"How else are we going to get the plugs?"

"Maybe we can convince him to toss them to us."

"You think?" Newt looked dubious. "You don't figure *he'd* swallow them, do you?"

They set off on that unhopeful note. The sun was obscured behind ashy clouds. The temperature had dipped. The daylight was already starting to fade. They were bone-tired before they even took their first steps on the steep switchbacking trail.

"I saw him last night, you know," Newton said. "Shel. He came round while you were sleeping."

"Wait, *what?* What for?" Max shivered involuntarily. "What did he do?"

"Just crouched there. Watching, you know. The way Shelley does."

"So did you do anything?"

Newton shook his head. "I just watched him right back. Honestly, I figured it wouldn't be so bad if he died out here. I know that's awful, but . . ."

Newton held Max's gaze when he said it. Max glimpsed— not for the first time in the past few days—that seam of stoniness running through Newton. It was unexpected coming from someone who usually rolled over and showed his soft belly. If anyone had asked Max who'd still be standing after all this, he would have said Kent, maybe Eef. But Newton had that survivalist's outlook. It wasn't about the badges he'd earned or the fact he was best at starting a fire. Newton had inner resources that the rest of the boys simply didn't possess— even Max himself. Getting teased your whole life must force you to grow some pretty hard bark.

"I don't mean that we should hurt him," Newton said. "When we get back to the mainland, we should tell the police he's still here, and sick, and maybe they'll be able to do something."

"I know."

"I'm just saying if they don't get here in time—"

"Let's not talk about it, okay, Newt?"

"What should we talk about?"

"I don't know. Maybe food?"

Newt grinned. *"Yes."*

They covered all their favorites. The peach cobbler at Frieda's Diner that came with a scoop of just-starting-to-melt vanilla ice cream. The porterhouse steaks Max's father cooked up at the annual summer barbecue, two inches thick and marbled with rich melty fat. The pies from Sammy's

Pizza down in Tignish—you had to pay five bucks extra for delivery to North Point, but it was so worth it to scarf down one of those slightly chewy slices covered in little spicy pepperonis and mozzarella cheese.

"Oh oh oh!" Newton said excitedly. "The cannolis at Stella's Bakery. The *best*." He threw his hands up with an air of finality, as if he'd settled some hard-fought argument with a fact that was beyond dispute. "Crunchy on the outside, filled with sweet cheese and chocolate chips on the inside. They crack apart in your mouth and that filling just . . ." His tongue inched out of his mouth. ". . . *splooshes*. It *splooshes* onto your taste buds. I could eat about a million of them right now."

Max bent over, clutching his belly. Newton's rhapsody had left him a bit light-headed. "Crap. Maybe we ought to talk about something else."

They found a skunk den—it was clear by the smell—and what may have been a fox run, but no sign of Shelley. They debated where he might be hiding, or whether he was hiding at all.

"Maybe he's following *us*," Max said, a possibility that spooked the hell out of them.

"We should follow our noses," Newton said. "Like Toucan Sam, y'know? The stranger and Scoutmaster Tim and even Kent—they all started to smell sweet, right? Like, *gross* sweet."

Max nodded. "Yeah, like rottenny kinda? Like someone's puke after he ate two cones of cotton candy at the fair and got on the Zipper."

"I guess like that, yeah. So if we smell that—"

"We'll know Shelley's close. Okay."

The sun slipped lower in its western altar. Twilight piled up along the horizon in ever-darkening layers. The boys hunched their shoulders into the brisk wind.

Newton laughed and said: "You know, my mom's going to *kill me* when this is all over."

Max loved that Newton still thought that way—that he still saw a time when this would all be over. When they would be home, safe.

"Why would she, Newt? For what?"

"For all this. Getting myself into it."

"None of this is our fault, Newt. It's just some awful thing that happened."

"I know, I know. My mom's just like that sometimes. She cares too much, y'know? Makes her crazy. Remember that flour baby project we did for home ec?"

Of course Max did. Their teacher had given them each a bag of flour to take care of as if it were a baby. Some students hadn't taken it seriously. Eef tossed his flour baby off the school's supply shed and hooted as it detonated across the hopscotch court. Kent duct-taped the entire bag to avoid ruptures. Their teacher frowned on this. *You wouldn't duct-tape an actual baby, would you?* she'd asked Kent. *Are you suuuure?* Kent replied with a sly smile, earning sniggers from the rest of the class.

"I really tried to take good care of that flour," Newton said. "I drew a face on the sack and everything. But the thing is, I've got sweaty hands. It's a condition. Sweaty armpits and feet, too. Can't help it. Every time I touched it, the sack got wet. It started to come apart. I told myself to stop fussing with it, but I couldn't help it. I kept touching it just to know it was there and safe. It ripped a little and then a little more until it finally ripped right open. My flour baby . . . well, *died.* I guess I killed it."

"It was just a stupid sack of flour, Newt."

Newton made a face that said: *You don't get it, man.*

"I'm just saying that sometimes the more you care for something, the more damage you do. Not on purpose, right?

357

You end up hurting the things you love just because you're trying so hard. That's what Mom does with me sometimes. She wants me to be so safe that it ends up hurting me in a weird way. But I get it, y'know? It must be the hardest thing in the world, caring for someone. Trying to make sure that person doesn't come to harm."

The sky was the color of a bone-deep bruise when Max caught the first traces of a high sweet stink.

"You smell that?" Max whispered.

Newton nodded. "Where's it coming from?"

They held their noses up, zeroing in on the location where it seemed to emanate from: a cavern set into a shale-strewn hillside.

They retired out of earshot to formulate a plan.

Max said: "Should we yell down to him?"

"Maybe he's sleeping. Why wake him up? We can just pluck them off him."

"Right out of his pocket?"

"If that's where he's keeping them, I guess we'll have to."

"Okay, fine," Max said, expelling a few rabbity breaths. "But what if he's awake? What if he fights back?"

"Are you asking if we should hurt him?"

"I don't know. I guess so. I mean, you already cracked him over the head, so . . ."

Newton bit his lip. "Let's just hope he's asleep. Rock, paper, scissors for who goes in first?"

Newton's hand came down clenched in a fist. Max's hand came down flat. Paper covered rock.

"Forget it," Max said. "We go down side by side."

Newton shook his head. "It looks too narrow and anyway, fair's fair."

Chapter Forty-Four

The cavern floor dipped just past the cave mouth, plunging them into darkness. A sticky, coagulated darkness that coated their skin like oil. It was as if the rods and cones in their eyes had been shut off like flicking a light switch: *click!*

Newton was in the lead, clutching with both hands the crude spear Max had made. He figured this was the blackness that must exist at the bottom of the sea—a blackness prowled by sightless things whose skin was so pale and gelatinous you could see the inner workings of their bodies. Things with nightmare anatomies that would evoke cries of horror were they ever glimpsed in sunlight: blind eyes bulging atop skinny stalks, rubbery mouths big enough to swallow a Hyundai, rows of tiny needlelike teeth. Such creatures could only survive in the deeps: their bodies had no protection against the sun—their skin would roast and disintegrate to mush before they even reached the surface. But they had learned to adapt to their lack of sight. They jostled and bumped with the other creatures that lived beneath the light, occasionally lashing out with barbs or tentacles or teeth.

WWAMD? he thought. The answer came swiftly: *Alex Markson would be scared shitless. Anyone else on earth ought to be scared shitless, too.*

The boys' collective breath came hot in their ears. Their boots sent little avalanches of shale skittering down the cavern slope. Water trickled over the rocks somewhere below—a sea-seeking tributary. The air was laden with the smell of sweet corruption.

Max's hand was wrapped tightly around Newton's flashlight. He had not switched it on yet. Newton would tell him when. Darkness pushed at his eyeballs. Steady fear pulsed behind them: a monstrous pressure massing behind his eyes. With darkness pressing from the front and fear pressing from behind, he was terrified his eyeballs would burst like grapes in a vise. This was the strongest evidence yet that something must be terribly the matter with Shelley: no sane human being would want to hide out down here.

They inched their way down the incline, hands outflung so they wouldn't run face-first into the rock. The cavern walls were slick with some viscid substance: algae, maybe? Max pictured tiny albino crabs scuttling along the gluey stuff, their pincers *tik-tik-tikk*ing. He imagined millions of them forming a chittering umbrella above their heads. His cheek came into contact with a shelf of slimed rock: it felt like a giant raspy tongue. That he didn't scream out in terror had to count as a minor miracle.

The darkness was disorienting. Nothing could moor itself to it: not even their breathing, which seemed to float out only to hit some unseen barrier and rebound back at them. It could make a person go mad simply because it consumed them: creeping into their mouths and into their ears and up their noses and behind their eyes, invading every part until they were one with it.

The boys moved deeper into the silent cavern . . . and then came the sounds.

Those horrible sounds, from God only knew what.

* * *

Shelley heard them coming. His ears were very keen now. Oh yes. Very keen indeed.

He could not see the boys yet. The boys who'd come to collect their little prizes. The silly little boys who wanted to get back to their stupid homes, their stupid lives.

He couldn't see them—but he would soon be able to *feel* them.

EAT EAT EAT

Oh yes. Shelley would eat. The fat one first, then the skinny one. Eat their eyes so they couldn't see. Eat their feet next so they couldn't run away.

It would be a paradise. A beautiful new world. Everyone would be so much happier down here. It would be an adjustment, of course. But they could be useful.

They could be daddies, too. Yes, they could *all* be daddies.

What a lovely idea.

The sounds caused the ventricles of Newton's heart to seize up. He could actually *feel* them constricting with a painful squeeze.

Long, liquid noises: *sllllllrp . . . sllllllrp . . . slllllrp . . .*

"Flashlight," Newton said. The word came out as a compressed nugget of sound.

Max flicked it on. Stark whiteness washed over the cavern.

Slllllrp . . . sllllllrp . . . slllllrp . . .

The boys' faces were eggshell-white: it was as if fear had blown the blood right out of their skin. Their necks and arms were rashed with gooseflesh. The clammy rock trapped the sweet stink, making the boys dizzy with it.

They were in a small antechamber. A hollow bubble in the rock.

"There," Newton said, pointing.

The spark plugs sat in a shallow saltwater puddle in

361

the middle of the chamber. Could it really be so simple? Max scanned the puddle for white wriggles. It was clear. He picked his way over, grabbed the spark plugs, and turned to Newton with a tentative, hopeful smile. The flashlight in his hands shone on the rock behind the other boy.

He caught a sly flinching movement to the left of Newton's waist. The spark plugs slipped from his numbed hands.

Newton's forehead creased as Max's hand rose, one quivering finger pointing to the spot behind him. He wheeled suddenly, stumbling, and watched in horror as it emerged.

The thing that once went by the name of Shelley Longpre unfolded itself from a dark chalice in the rock. Crawling out like a spider, folding each of its long, pale limbs out, unpacking itself from its hiding spot with the showy grace of a contortionist.

"Yessssss . . ." it lisped, the hiss of an adder that crested and eddied.

". . . sssSSSeeeeeYeeeessssssss . . ."

It was long in its extremities and bulbous at its middle. It was naked and translucent and webbed with huge blue veins that snaked over its body. Its arms and legs were nothing but bone wrapped in a thin sheath of skin. Trapped in the eye of terror, Max found himself thinking of the Christmas just passed. His folks had bought him a trombone. They'd wrapped it and put it under the tree. Of course Max knew what it was: a trombone wrapped in shiny paper looked practically the same as a trombone not wrapped in paper.

That was how its legs looked: like bones wrapped in skin-colored Christmas paper.

"EeeeeeYYYEEEEEEESSSSSSSSSSSS . . ."

Its voice was the lonely squeal of a hermit. It scrabbled

toward them with a leer of hideous glee, hideous hunger, hideous *need*. Its left eye was completely white: something had sucked the pigment out of the eyeball the way a child sucks the red stripes off a peppermint candy. Its right eye was as shriveled as a dehydrated pea; white threads licked and lashed in the wide raw socket, making a *whish* sound, sort of like wind-swayed grain in a farmer's field.

Max noticed clearly in its nakedness that its stomach was an obscenely pendulous appendage. The size of a beach ball, it swayed between its legs with a quivering expectant weight. Its rib cage jutted in monstrous fingers. Huge knobs of flesh seeped filth all over its shoulders; a belt of ulcerated boils encircled its hips. Max's mind reeled—scant days and hours ago this *thing* had been a boy, not much different from him.

Slllrppp . . . sllllrppp . . .

Its lips hung down like the lips of an old horse. Its teeth were gone; its gums hung in whitish rags from the roof of its mouth like the pith inside a pumpkin. It reached for Newton with extremely long fingers. It had nibbled its own skin off the tips. Its voice lost its sibilance as it rose to an insane gibber.

"YEEEEEEEE!"

Snapping out of his torpor, Newton managed to lash out with the spear. He struck the thing across its face; its skin tore apart in crepey rags. It mewled piteously and crab-walked around the edge of the chamber, its gut dragging along the rocks. The skin mooring its belly to its abdomen stretched and tore in thin fissures. Max was horrified at the possibility that it would burst apart. What in God's name would spill out?

"*Go!*" Newton yelled at Max.

Max pressed his back to the wall and swung round. The Shelley-thing's tongue darted out of its mouth: a gnarled root. Max wondered if it was trying to taste his scent the way snakes do.

It scuttled toward Max with horrid speed and ferocity. He caught a glance of its back. Something was twined around its spine, like an electrical cord.

One of its bony claws manacled round his ankle, and Max's bladder let go. Warm wetness drained down his leg. The Shelley-thing seemed to sense that, too—it stared up with those alabaster eyes, keening and snuffling at Max's calves. Max screamed and kicked it off. The flashlight slipped from his hands and hit the ground, spinning in lazy circles.

Max caught hold of Newton's arm and dragged him back toward the chamber's mouth. His mind was yammering; soon the terror would weld it shut . . .

The flashlight spun to a stop. Its glow climbed Newton's madly backpedaling legs—then the Shelley-thing darted out of the darkness, squealing with the high excitement of a pig who'd found a truffle, clamping onto Newton's right leg.

"Let go!" he shrieked. *"Get off me!"*

It kept squealing and clawing up Newton's body. Newton felt the warm weight of its gigantic belly pressing between his own thighs. Beneath the sucking sounds, he could hear squirming ones—coming from the wet black hole of its mouth.

"Oh Jesus Max it's gonna—"

When the Shelley-thing's stomach ruptured, it did so with a moist ripping tear. Newton's thighs and abdomen were washed in a warm broth of desiccated organs and shrunken intestines and untold multitudes of writhing alabaster.

Newton screamed in terrified disgust as the Shelley-thing's face relaxed into an expression of extreme contentedness.

Newton kicked free and skated his heels over the slippery rock. The Shelley-thing toppled face-forward onto the cavern floor. It landed with a sickening crunch that collapsed all the tortured bones of its face.

From the sworn testimony of Stonewall Brewer, given before the Federal Investigatory Board in connection with the events occurring on Falstaff Island, Prince Edward Island:

Q: Admiral Brewer, I'd like to ask about your methods regarding Tim Riggs and the five boys who were on Falstaff Island when Tom Padgett arrived.

A: Fire away.

Q: I'd like to know why, during the entire course of the containment, you never tried to contact Mr. Riggs. Or, after his passing, why you didn't make contact with the boys.

A: For what reason?

Q: To tell them what was happening. To let them know, if nothing else, that their parents were being forcefully detained as opposed to purposefully leaving them there.

A: These points were duly considered and dismissed. We felt—*I* felt—it was best to institute a "look but don't touch" policy.

Q: You could have dropped a care package. Food and aid. Or notes written by their parents. That wouldn't be "touching," would it?

A: If you'll check the record of our conversation here today, you'll recall that I said: *Nothing comes, nothing goes.*

Q: But does that apply to *information*, Admiral? A virus cannot be borne on information.

A: But hysteria can. Information isn't always power. Information can do harm just as easily as ignorance. Say we'd told those boys what they were up against, okay? They may have gone—pardon my French—batshit.

Q: Wouldn't you concur, Admiral, that based on the evidence of the events as we now know them, that some of those boys went batshit anyway?

A: Hindsight being twenty-twenty and all, yes, I surely can. Listen, tribunals like this get held because of men like me.

Q: Define for our purposes "men like you," Admiral.

A: I'm talking about men who take a line and hold to it. Some people think that makes men like me inflexible. Hard-assed. At worst, inhuman. It's true that the decisions men like me make can seem, from an outward perspective, to be that: *inhuman*. People will always second-guess you. Why did those people have to die? Why those forty-four in the SARS outbreak? Why those kids on the island? Well, that's fine and I accept all that—the second-guessing, I mean, not the fact that every epidemic is going to have its fair share of deaths. It's my hope and goal to have zero fatalities. But the fact is that unless men like me make those decisions, the questions asked in the aftermath might be a whole lot different. Instead of why did those forty-four have to die, it's why did five million have to die?

Why did the whole eastern seaboard have to die? At that point, nobody has the luxury of a tribunal. At that point, everyone's just trying like hell not to get sick.

Q: So you're saying—

A: I'm saying that the decisive actions of men like me make second-guessing possible. We're the first-guessers. And sometimes that's all it is: educated guesswork. We don't know how bad it might get. We assess the risk, gauge what the collateral damage might be, try to minimize it, and then hold that course. I'm not saying it doesn't make for some uneasy nights. But it's what you have to do.

Q: Admiral, I'd like to change course.

A: It's your circus. You can call the tune.

Q: Wonderful. Admiral, did you know about Dr. Clive Edgerton and his experiments with the modified hydatid worm?

A: Before all this? No.

Q: Remind me: You did sit on the panel of the Board of Safety in the Fields of Communicable Diseases and Epidemiology, did you not?

A: I have, as I'm required to by duty.

Q: So then I find it odd that . . .

A: Yes?

Q: I find it odd you'd have no knowledge of Dr. Edgerton. I say so because the board—the board you sit on—is very aware of Dr. Edgerton. Two years ago, his name was brought up in conjunction with several other doctors. According to the board, the work of those doctors should be subject to a higher degree of oversight and scrutiny, seeing as their research could pose a significant risk.

A: I don't go to every meeting.

Q: But they send you the minutes?

A: Yes. I read them as thoroughly as I can, but my schedule is busy.

Q: Admiral, what are your thoughts on the effectiveness of the mutated hydatid as it applies to warfare?

A: I think it's monstrous. It's a monstrous question.

Q: Yes, I'm afraid it is, but such questions need to be posed. You say it's monstrous.

A: I do indeed.

Q: That's not the question I asked you.

A: I suppose it would be effective as a weapon. In certain, very prescribed situations.

Q: Like on an island?

A: What's your name?

Q: [name redacted]

A: Well, [name redacted], if you are suggesting that I dragged my feet and somehow used those kids as—as what? Test subjects? If you're suggesting *that*—

Q: Admiral, does the name Claude Lafleur ring a bell?

A: No. Why should it?

Q: Master Seaman Claude Lafleur was one of your men.

A: The entire navy is *my* men.

Q: Master Seaman Claude Lafleur was stationed at the same base you operated out of. Lafleur's daughter often babysat your children. You're saying you don't know Claude Lafleur?

A: That's right.

Q: Claude Lafleur was a locksmith before entering the navy.

A: You want to hurry this up?

Q: As you already noted, this is my circus, Admiral. I'll choose the pace. Some time ago, Claude Lafleur was given a four-day executive leave. That leave started the day before Tom Padgett escaped from Dr. Edgerton's facility.

A: Yes? So?

Q: Are you aware that you signed Claude Lafleur's leave papers, Admiral?

A: I sign plenty of leave papers. I spend half the day signing papers.

Q: Are you aware, Admiral, that Claude Lafleur's fingerprints were found on the rear access door of Dr. Edgerton's lab?

A: You'll have to speak to someone else about that.

Q: Are you aware that we presently have Claude Lafleur in custody? Are you also aware that Lafleur has some fairly damning things to say?

A: You'll have to talk to my superiors about that.

Q: Admiral, who *are* your superiors?

A: [Witness maintains silence]

Q: Are you saying that even admirals take orders from someone?

A: [Witness maintains silence]

Q: Admiral, just earlier you used a term I'd like to revisit. *Monstrous.* Perhaps you'd agree, Admiral Brewer, that purposefully releasing a contagion would be *monstrous*? And if Tom Padgett were that contagion, Admiral, then wouldn't it stand to reason that Falstaff Island could be seen as no less than a giant petri dish, and the events that occurred

there no less than an unsanctioned experiment—on children?

A: [Witness maintains silence]

Q: Wouldn't that just be absolutely *monstrous*, Admiral? Wouldn't that be the most inhuman thing you could ever imagine?

A: [Witness maintains silence]

Chapter Forty-Five

Nightfall greeted the boys as they stumbled out of the cavern. In the silvery fall of moonlight, Newton saw that he was soaked in gore from the waist down. Revulsion swept over him in a dizzying wave.

When Max approached with a handful of leaves—all he could find for Newton to clean himself off—Newton held his hand out.

"Don't come near. It's too late—they're all over me."

He could feel them inside his pants, prickling his skin with strange heat. They wriggled in the hairs he'd just started to grow down there.

Max said: "What can we do?"

"Get back to camp. I'll wash up in the ocean. See if that helps."

They moved through the woods without a flashlight. Chilling noises emanated from the lacework of tall trees: hoots and scufflings and a frenzied cackle that rose up and up until it dropped to an ongoing buzz like an enormous hummingbird trapped in a rain barrel. Whatever was making those sounds couldn't possibly be any worse than the Shelley-thing back in the cavern.

When they got back, Max made a fire using shingles that

had blown off the cabin roof. Newton went down to the water to wash. Max could just make him out past the moon-glossed shore. He sat cross-legged in the surf, scrubbing and scrubbing. He returned in only his underwear, which sagged wetly around his hips. There was a defeated hunch to his shoulders that freaked Max out.

"I'm hungry, Max."

"I'm hungry, too, Newt."

"I think I'm hungrier than you."

Somehow, they slept. In the witching hours, Newton sat bolt upright. His insides were alive and seething. He bit down on his lip until blood came.

An hour later, Max awoke as Newton puked into a thicket of poison sumac. He was curled up on his side, breathing in rapid little bursts.

"I took the mushrooms," he said. "They do the trick."

Newton pointed at the puddle of vomit. Nothing but a thin smear of liquid tinged purple from the berries they'd eaten. It was alive with wriggling whiteness.

"I figure one of the little buggers swum up my . . . my piss-hole."

He realized there was a better word for it, a scientific word that he probably even knew, but he was too dog-tired to think of it. Besides, *piss-hole* summed it up best. It was a *hole* that your *piss* came out of. Newton laughed to himself. Hah! For whatever reason, he found it deliciously funny. *Piss-hole*. Hil-*aaaa*-rious! WWAMD? He'd laugh at *piss-hole*, too, because it was the funniest word on earth!

Maybe he was delirious. That, or those mushrooms had mind-bending properties. He tore out a clump of poison sumac and rubbed it on his leg.

"What are you doing?" Max said.

"It'll give me something else to focus on. I can itch myself silly."

Newton ate the rest of the mushrooms and was violently, frighteningly ill. He vomited with such force that the capillaries burst in his eyes and even his nose. By the time the sun came up, he looked washed-out and haggard, as though his innards had all been wrung out like wet washcloths.

They lay together by the fire. Any time Max moved closer, Newton waved him back tiredly.

"You're going to catch it," he warned.

"I don't care anymore."

Heat kindled in Newt's eyes. "You *should* care. Don't be stupid. *You should care.*"

Max withdrew, wounded for reasons he couldn't quite process.

Sometime that morning, the black helicopter cut across the postcard-pretty sky. It dipped low, rotors throbbing, panning a circle around them. It was so close that Max could see the sunlight flashing off the pilot's visor.

"Help us!" he yelled as the blades whipped debris all around. "He's sick! Can't you see that? We need help!"

The pilot's face remained impassive. Max picked up a rock, threw it on a pitiful trajectory. It wasn't even close. The helicopter banked southward and returned toward North Point.

"Fuck you!" Max screamed as it retreated. "Go fuck yourself!"

Afterward he collapsed. The adults were supposed to act in the best interests of the children. They had to know what was happening. Yet stubbornly, they did nothing but stand idly by.

The adults were content to watch them die.

375

"I wonder who built them," Newton murmured.

Max wiped his eyes. "Built what?"

"The worms."

"I don't know what you mean."

"I mean," Newton said, "they seem too *perfect*."

"They don't seem perfect at all, Newt. They're like the worst things on earth."

"That's what I mean, I guess. Maybe they *are* the worst things on earth. But that would make them perfect, wouldn't it? Perfect at being what they are and doing what they do. Perfect killers."

"They haven't killed everyone. We don't know about Kent."

Newton's eyes pinched up at the edges. "I hope he's still alive. Really, I hope so."

"He could have swum back."

Max stared out over the slatey water and wondered if he really believed that.

"If anyone could have, it would be Big K," Newton agreed, if only for Max's sake.

"Maybe he'll talk to the adults. They'll finally come for us."

"Anything is possible."

Around noon, Newton told Max he was having a hard time seeing out of his left eye.

"It's all fuzzy around the sides." His laugh held a lacy filigree of hysteria. "It's like staring at the world from inside a peach or something."

Max leaned over and inspected Newton's eye.

"It looks okay."

Newton scratched at the purple stains on his legs from the poison sumac. He'd been scratching all morning. The flesh was raked open and bloody in spots.

"It does? Okay, well . . . jeez, it hurts. Maybe it's not my eye. I don't think there are any nerves in an eyeball. Maybe it's behind it. You think?"

Max knelt closer. Terror was building in his chest, gaining a keener edge.

"Spread your eyelids with your fingers. I'll look."

"Okay," Newton said dreamily. "Yeah. Good idea."

Max held one hand up to shield his own eyes from the sun and squinted closely. Nothing. Just bloodshot whiteness.

"It's fine, Newt. I can't see . . ." His breath caught. ". . . can't see . . ."

"What? What is it?"

It was nothing. Just a teeny-tiny quill. No bigger than an itty-bitty claw on a baby mouse's paw. It sat at the bottom of Newton's eye. It was probably just a trick of the light or a sty or something—until it moved.

"What is it, Max? I can *feel* it."

The minuscule writhing worm lashed side to side as if stretching itself out in its new digs. Max reached out to grab it. Maybe he could tease it out of Newton's eye the way his grandfather used to pull coddling worms out of a crabapple . . . until Max realized it was *inside* Newton's eye. Swimming in the jelly.

No. The word ran through his head on an endless loop. *No no no no—*

It all at once went still. Then it seemed to flex toward Max—as if it *knew,* in the single vile atom it called a brain, that it was being watched.

"What is it, Max? Tell me. *Tell me!*"

Chapter Forty-Six

An hour later, Max was back at the cavern.

Newton had asked him not to go. Begged him. *What if something happens, Max? Then we'll both be alone.*

Max simply waited until Newton fell asleep—the smallest kindness he could now afford. He'd found a signal flare in the cabin. The ones Scoutmaster Tim brought had gotten drenched in the storm, but this one—which Newton had brought personally, in a Ziploc bag—might still be okay.

Max *prayed* it would work. If not, it meant going down in the dark with the Shelley-thing still there. He'd have to paw around blindly for the spark plugs. What if he touched *it* instead?

Max had been happy enough to leave the plugs and try to figure out some other method of escape, but now, with Newt as sick as he was, he had no choice.

Listen, it'll be no big deal, he thought, bucking himself up. *Go on down, grab the plugs, and get the heck out of Dodge. It's not even that far down: it just felt that way yesterday because you were in the dark. It's probably not much farther down than the basement stairs at home.*

The sun had fallen a few degrees in the sky. It shone brightly through the tree branches and into the cavern mouth. Bright as it was, after a few yards the sunlight turned spotty and that awful darkness took over.

He tore the strike strip. The flare burst alight with a heat so unexpected that it singed the hairs on his arms. They'd been standing on end, along with those on the nape of his neck.

He nudged his foot into the cave mouth. The shadow of the overhang cleaved across his boot. He tried to take the next step—but his back leg wouldn't move. It may as well have been glued to the ground. The muscle fibers twitched down his hamstrings: antic, fluttering waves under the skin.

"Come on," he whispered. "Come *on*."

An act of profound concentration and willpower was required to budge his back leg. He finally threw it out in front of him in an awkward stagger-step that nearly sent him tumbling down the steep grade of the cave, but he checked his forward momentum in time.

"Don't be a baby," Max said to himself, though he had every legitimate reason in the world to act like one. Scout Law number three: *A Scout's duty is to be useful and help others, and he is to do his duty before anything else, even though he gives up his own pleasure, or comfort, or safety to do it.*

The temperature dipped by ten degrees as soon as he entered the cave. The air came out of his lungs in short, popping breaths—it almost sounded like he was hiccuping, or on the verge of having a good cry. The fear was as strong as ever: that disembodied ball of baby fingers relentlessly tickling his guts.

One foot in front of the other, he told himself. *You can always run. You can pelt out of here like your ass is on fire.*

It amazed him that the voice in his head—confident, jokey—could be so different from the piss-scared boy it resided within.

At least he had a flare. The journey was much less

disorienting with a light to go by. Salt sparkled on the sea-eaten rock, tinted bloodred by the flare light.

The rocky shelves were overgrown with patches of sickly yellow moss. Colonies of huge white toadstools jutted from the cave walls at lunatic angles; they hung like fleshy ears, their undersides frilled with soft gills—or in some cases, little spikelike teeth. Max's neck came in contact with one as he rounded a sharp bend in the descent, and it felt horridly clammy and bloated, like the flesh of a waterlogged body coughed up from the sea.

The air was still sweet but didn't seem as cloying. His breath came shallowly. He could hear the blood beat in his ears. The flare sputtered.

Don't you go out, Max thought—prayed. *Oh don't you* dare *go out.*

He came to the mouth of the chamber. The smell was strangely enticing: sweet plums packed in salt. The air was alive with sounds, curiously stealthy, over the drip of water. He held the flare aloft. The chamber's ceiling was clad in the same yellow moss; tendrils of witchgrass draped down. Trundling over the moss, clinging to its spongy folds, was an army of sea creatures: sand crabs and pulpy slugs and huge sightless beetles Max had never seen before. The clicking of their pincers and other appendages created a mammoth chittering above his head.

The Shelley-thing lay to the side of the chamber. Its limbs were spiked out at odd angles; it looked like a dead spider pressed flat between the pages of a dictionary. So *small*. Death did that, didn't it? Shrunk everything. It lay in the same position as it had yesterday . . . didn't it?

He wasn't so sure now. Maybe it had inched away from the cave wall—but *how* could it have done that? He pictured the things inside of Shelley doing that . . . somehow *pulling* Shelley's lifeless body along the cave floor.

Max wondered if the chamber was fed by an aquifer leading out to sea. The tide might have rolled in, flooding the chamber. That would explain the sea life on the ceiling: he didn't think they'd been there before. It would also explain the Shelley-thing's positioning: the body would've floated up with the tide, bumping around the chamber, brushing into the walls, becoming saturated with seawater before settling on the floor as the tide flowed out.

Had some of those worms flowed out with the tide? Max imagined them wriggling through the water, latching on to a codfish, which got eaten by a seal, which got eaten by a shark, which got caught in a drift net and hauled on board a trawler and slit open on the dock, billions of worms spilling out in front of the perplexed crewmen . . .

Or maybe Shelley's body was in the exact same position. It'd been dark and crazy. Yes, Max figured. It was in the same spot. *Yes.*

He squinted past the sputtering flare light. Was anything else moving? He thought he saw floating flickers in the air—but no, *no*, those were just vapor contrails from the nearby seabed. He could hear the seethe of the sea seeping through the rock.

The flare had already sputtered well down the paper tube—that shouldn't happen, should it? Maybe it was an old flare. Its glow had diminished alarmingly.

He set one foot inside the chamber. His leg appeared to stretch out as if made of flesh-toned rubber, pulling the rest of his body with it. His throat was dusty-dry, filled with the ozone taste of the rock. The peripheries of his vision were blown out huge—he could see almost around the back of his head. His pupils were so dilated that they'd overtaken his corneas, turning them black.

He inched around Shelley's body. A brittle strand of witchgrass brushed the back of Max's neck. He bit back a scream but still, a breathless little moan came out of him.

Which is when he noticed them.

They were on the stick—the long one he'd sharpened yesterday, the one Newton abandoned in the madness. It jutted from beneath Shelley's body at a weird angle. All along it, stuck to the wet wood, were tiny nodules. Clustered in white bunches that looked like tiny albino grapes. Tens of thousands of them. Others were larger. They dotted the stick like curlicues of white icing on a cake.

A sea slug fell from the ceiling, going *plop* in a puddle near the stick. The white nodules stirred in unison. The larger ones uncoiled and stood stiff.

The sea slug sucked its way out of the puddle. Its eyes swiveled lazily on stalks. The large worms jettisoned off the stick, drifting with horrible languor. They settled atop the slug and swiftly coiled around it. The smaller nodules launched next: a shimmering flotilla settling around and atop the slug. Only its stalked eyes were visible amid the banded whiteness; soon, they, too, were cocooned.

Max felt something bursting up inside him, a fearsome bubble packed with razor blades and fishhooks and shattered lightbulbs that strained against the heaving walls of his chest.

He inched around the Shelley-thing, hugging the cave wall. Several more large worms went rigid—they followed him the way a compass needle follows magnetic north, but they didn't detach from the wood.

The spark plugs weren't where he thought they'd be—he swore he'd last seen them next to the body. But then maybe the body had moved . . .

Or something had moved the body . . .

Or *something else* had moved the spark plugs.

For an instant he was seized by a terrible possibility: that *something else* was in the cave with him. An image formed in his head: something huge and pulsating-white and gently, sensuously ribbed, gliding up behind him making the soft *suck-suck* of a fat, toothless infant mewling for its mother's breast.

There. Thank God, right *there.* He spotted the plugs in a shallow pool farther into the chamber. He must've flung them there the last time he was here, when the Shelley-thing had reached for him.

He edged around carefully, his butt scraping the wet rock. His eyes hunted through the dwindling, smoky light for threats—they were all around him now. The flare was hot in his hand: the phosphorus was burning the last of its stores, heating through the cardboard tube.

The plugs lay at the bottom of a weirdly ridged pool: it looked like the fossilized remains of a giant clamshell. He reached toward them, then suddenly flinched back.

The dark, festering ooze ringing the puddle—a rotted mulch of witchgrass and kelp—was studded with white specks. They'd stirred agitatedly as his hand had reached for the spark plugs.

How had they *known* to surround this particular pool?

But as Max's eyes dodged around in the ebbing light, he realized they were everywhere.

They coalesced around him: specks of white nestled in the ooze, clustered in the rocks, above him, to the sides of him.

Everywhere.

A deep vein of terror threatened to cleave him in half. He felt that tickle inside his skull now, those little fingers trying to unmoor his sanity.

Almost absently, Max brought the flare down, singeing the edges of the puddle. The ooze sizzled; the worms exploded with little pops.

He reached into the puddle, grabbed one spark plug—

The flare went out. Max's heart seized.

It sputtered alight again. The top was wet now; water dripped down into the tube, dousing the phosphorus. He reached for the other plug, wrapped his fingers around it—

The flare went out again.

Something dropped from the cave ceiling, crawling and clacking on the nape of his neck. Max let out a choked sound of disgust before the flare caught again. He knocked the thing off his neck. One of those huge black beetles. As soon as it hit the floor, it was lit upon by white strands. Max looked for the chamber mouth and—

The flare went out. *Jesus oh Jesus no*—he stood blindly, tripping, slipping on a patch of slime in the dark. He stumbled back and nearly fell—his arm reached out for balance and collided with something that felt like waterlogged fatback . . .

The flare sputtered alight. In the bloodlike luminescence, he saw he'd touched the Shelley-thing. His fingers had sunk into the flesh of his back. Its skin was flabby, greasy, seeping nameless noxious fluid.

The skin cracked slightly down the Shelley-thing's spine. Max saw something flex underneath.

He turned to flee. The air was alive with floating strands. He waved the flare desperately, catching a few: they sizzled up like ghost fuses.

He heard a hideous skin-crawling sound. A splitting, rending sound. He froze. He pictured it being made by the Shelley-thing as it pulled itself up. It was the sound of its body disconnecting from the rocks, its burst-open chest cavity dangling syrupy strings of ichor, twisting with worms while it lisped *Yeeeeeesssssss* . . .

Max couldn't bear to turn around. He feared if he turned and saw *that*, all would be lost. The terror would crystallize into a hot barbed nut in his brain. Maybe it would just be better to go mad and have done with it for good and all.

With the greatest courage he'd ever summon, Max wrenched his head slowly around.

The Shelley-thing's body *was* moving, but the movement was coming from inside.

One foot in front of the other, Max.

It wasn't Max's own voice in his head now: it was Newton's.

It's just five steps. Four maybe, if you take long strides. Go on now. It's okay.

Max obeyed, moving quickly and silently. Every nerve ending was on fire and every synapse in his brain was on the brink of rupture, but he managed to slip around the chamber walls until his ass hit the tunnel mouth.

The last thing Max saw in the glow of the sputtering flare before racing up the incline was the skin cracking and splitting down the Shelley-thing's back. A huge white tube, just like the one that ripped out of the stranger a lifetime ago, was twisted round the gleaming spine bone: it looked like a flag that had gotten blown round a pole in a high wind.

Max watched it unfurl with slow elegance and rise into the dark air. It stood stiff as a bloodhound's tail with the hunt running hot in its blood.

Chapter Forty-Seven

When Max got back, Newton was awake. A patch of gauze was taped clumsily over his eye. The other eye stared at Max balefully.

"You left," he said reproachfully.

"I got the spark plugs."

"That's good, I guess."

Newton looked thinner already. A jarring sight: Newton Thornton, the pudgiest boy in school, with winnowed cheekbones that looked as if they'd been carved out of basalt. The wind blew his loose clothes around his body.

"Who needs Deal-A-Meal cards," he said, catching Max's look. "Richard Simmons is a . . ." Newt managed to smile. ". . . a fucking *pussy*."

He sat on a rock, humming a tuneless song, while Max fiddled with the boat's motor. Night was already coming down; the cold seeped under their collars and iced the skin cladding their spines.

"I'm hungry like you wouldn't believe, Max."

"You should try sucking on a pebble. My mom says that's how the Indians used to control their hunger. When they were on a vision quest or whatever."

Newton plucked a pebble off the shore and popped it into his mouth.

"Salty," he said. "And *stony*."

They laughed a little. Max turned back to the motor. He screwed the spark plugs into their holes and snapped the covers shut.

"I swallowed the pebble," Newton said. "*Ooooops.*"

"Suck on another one," Max said, struggling to maintain a casual tone of voice.

The jerry can of gasoline was where he'd dropped it yesterday. He unscrewed the motor's gas cap and let the gasoline *glug-glug* down, making sure he didn't spill any. He could hear grinding sounds over his shoulder. He was very worried they were being made by Newton chewing on a pebble.

"You should gather whatever you need," he said, not daring to look. "We should leave soon."

"You don't even know that the motor will start," Newton said tiredly. "It probably won't."

"Why would you say that, Newt? Why wouldn't it start— why wouldn't you *hope* it'll start?"

Max turned and saw Newton regarding him with tragic eyes.

"All I mean is," Newton said, dropping his chin and staring down, "even if it *does* start, you should go alone."

"What a stupid— Why would I do that?"

"Because I'm sick, Max. And if I'm sick, maybe they won't let you go back home. Because they'll think you're sick, too."

"*They* meaning who?"

Newton shrugged. "Come on, don't be dumb. Whoever's out there. The police. The army. The guys in the helicopter. Whoever is making sure nobody comes to rescue us."

"Well, maybe I'm sick already too. Who cares? They can cure us."

Newton shook his head knowingly. "If you were sick, you'd feel it."

Max came over and set a hand on Newton's shoulder. The heat radiated through his clothes. That awful sweetness wasn't so bad coming off Newton. It smelled a little like Toll House cookies.

"I'm scared, Max," Newton said softly.

"So am I, Newt."

Max was afraid that if he left without Newt, they—whoever *they* were—wouldn't allow him to come back. Which meant Newton would die here. Curled up inside the cabin, perhaps, or in the cellar, like an animal that sought the darkness to die. He would die in pain, but more important and much worse, he would die alone. Newt didn't deserve that. Newt was a good person. He should live a long time. Marry and have kids. Teach them all the nerdy things he knew. Be happy. That was the only fair outcome.

But if Max left without Newt, he was positive he'd never see him again.

This fear of abandoning Newt was more profound, if less visceral, than that which he'd experienced back in the cavern: if Newton died, it meant all the terror and frustration and rage they'd both experienced had been for nothing.

If they couldn't leave together, what had they done any of it for?

Max said: "You sit at the front of the boat, okay? I'll sit at the back. We won't touch. They won't have any reason not to take me."

Newton smiled gratefully. "That sounds like a very good plan, Max."

Chapter Forty-Eight

It was dark by the time Max eased the boat off the beach into the slack tide.

It took a few hard cranks to get the motor going. Smoke belched from the engine housing. For one heart-stopping instant, it seemed the bearings would fry and the motor might seize . . . but after a few rough revolutions, it settled into an even cadence.

Max goosed the throttle and piloted toward the distant lights of North Point. He'd driven boats before: his uncle was an oysterman and he'd often let Max take the helm of his boat while he dragged in the lines. *It's a lot easier than driving a car,* he'd told Max. *The ocean's just one big lane, plenty of room for everyone.*

Newton sat at the bow. He was wearing his Scouts sash adorned with the badges he'd earned. He wasn't sure why he'd put it on—maybe he wanted to show whoever was waiting for them that he was a responsible person. An individual of value.

"Hey, Max?" Newt called out over the motor.

"Yeah?"

"I had this dream today. While you were gone. It was pretty weird."

"Okay, so spill it."

Wind whipped off the water. Newton nearly had to shout to be heard—the effort drained him.

"So, well, I was with my mom. We were on this trip. I didn't know the city. We were in this hotel lobby. Very swanky, which is weird because we don't have enough money to stay at swanky hotels. But we come through those rotating doors—those doors always kind of scare me, actually; I think they're going to suck me between the glass and squash me—through those doors and there's a couple arguing outside. A man and a woman."

The swells grew larger as the shore receded. The boat skipped over the waves, salt spray licking up over the gunwales. Max squinted over the night water. Shapes loomed against the horizon.

"The man started hitting the woman. Right there on the street. Her head was snapping back. Blood was painted on her cheeks. Then this van stops on the sidewalk. These guys get out and start yelling at the other guy, saying he can't do that. The guy says he wasn't really hurting her, only teaching her something. So he wraps his hands around her neck as if to demonstrate, he wraps his hands round her neck and starts choking her right in front of these guys . . ."

The shapes were beginning to coalesce. A loose group clustered where the water met the night sky, blocking out the lights of home.

"One of the guys from the van puts the guy in a headlock. They drag him away from the woman and over to the van, like they're going to throw him into it. Suddenly people are pouring out of doorways and out of office buildings. Carpenters and lawyers and deliverymen. The woman who was being choked starts screaming at the guys from the van, telling them to leave the guy who was choking her alone. Then one of the guys from the van punches the choker guy in the face. He goes down in a tangle, unconscious before he even hits the ground. He was wearing loose pants, I remember, and they fell down so I saw his underwear, which were blue and droopy with holes like mice had chewed them."

Boats. Squat ones that had chased down Calvin Walmack's cigarette boat. They were painted with some kind of special black paint that prevented the moonlight and starlight from reflecting off them. They floated silently, motionlessly.

"Things sped up. Everyone was getting punched or punching. Fights were spilling all over the street. I remember a tricycle getting crushed under the wheels of a speeding car. Then the choker guy who got punched out gets up and looks around all embarrassed and says, 'Oh *hell* no!' and he wades into this big huge fight—which was everywhere by then—hitching up his pants. And there were fires burning at the tops of the skyscrapers and sirens everywhere and I could tell, in that weird way dreams have of telling you things, that the violence was everywhere. Like a virus, Max. *Everywhere.*"

The boat drew nearer to the floating vessels. Max cut the motor and drifted with the current. Figures were massed along the decks.

Newt's voice dropped as the wind dipped. "My mom got her hand on my shoulder. I shrugged it off. I didn't want her touching me. And if she put her hand back on my shoulder—and I was thinking she might do that, Max, for the same reason that I wanted to shrug it off—then I might *shove* it off. Or bite her fingers. Violence was in the air, Max. We were all *breathing* it."

A searchlight snapped on, pinning them in its cool glare.

The boys raised their hands slowly, like robbers who'd gotten caught inside a bank vault.

"We need help!" Max yelled.

Nobody answered.

"We're okay!" He tried to smile. His filthy clothes flapped in the wind. "We made it. Tell them, Newt. Tell them we're okay!"

Newton seemed unsure of where he was. One eye stared without recognition. He laughed—a weird, jittery laugh that bounced off the water and fled into the empty vault of sky.

Max thought: *Oh no oh please don't laugh like that, Newt . . .*

Newton stood up in the boat. He held his hands out toward the light: a gesture of supplication.

"I'm fine! I'm *aces*! But there is one thing."

No Newt—

"I am very . . ."

No Newt no Newt—

". . . so very very . . ."

No no nononono—

The wind rose to a shriek that sucked that final word out of Newton's mouth.

A hole appeared in the back of Newton's neck. A small hole that appeared as if by magic. *Presto!* The torn edges of his flesh blew back, creating a perfect little starfish.

Newton pitched over the side. He lay on the sea's surface for an instant—like a water skimmer, those bugs that danced across the water's skin—before the sea claimed him; Newt's body went headfirst, bubbles trailing up from the new hole in his throat as he sank swiftly beneath the boat.

Max barely had time to cry out. He was staring down at the bright red dot hovering on his own chest.

From the sworn testimony of Lance Corporal Frank Ellis, given before the Federal Investigatory Board in connection with the events occurring on Falstaff Island, Prince Edward Island:

Q: "Hungry."

A: Yes, sir.

Q: That's the word you heard Newton Thornton say before you shot him?

A: Yes, sir, it was. He said he was hungry.

Q: He said it just like that?

A: No, sir. I suppose he said it more quietly. And there were some pauses in his speech. He said something like: *I'm very very . . . hungry.*

Q: If he said it so quietly, are you certain he said it at all? It was night, on the ocean. The weather reports for that evening indicated high winds.

A: That's all true, sir. It was windy and choppy. But the Big Ears picked his voice up loud and clear.

Q: I'm sorry?

A: The Big Ears is what we call it. It's a parabolic listening device: a big dish, basically. Looks like a satellite dish. It's for long-range acoustical assessment, which is really just a prissy way of saying it helps us hear what we wouldn't be able to hear naturally.

Q: And the Big Ears told you that Newton Thornton said:
I'm hungry?

A: Correct.

Q: So what?

A: Repeat that, sir?

Q: I said, *so what*? He was hungry. He'd been on an island for days. Nothing to eat. Wasn't it reasonable that the boy might be hungry?

A: Yes, sir, he may have been. I suppose it was the way he said it.

Q: The *way*?

A: Yes, sir. He said it in a way that sounded like he was somehow *more* than just hungry. Hungry as you or I would know it, anyway. Maybe those starving kids you see on TV pledge drives might know that kind of hunger. But even them, I'm not sure. He sounded like he'd eat his own arm off if he could just bring himself to cross that line.

Q: Pardon me, Lance Corporal Ellis, but that sounds paranoid.

A: I suppose it does. I think a lot of us were jumpy. We kept hearing things.

Q: Out on the boat?

A: No, I mean internally. Rumors. Stuff was starting to leak out about that psycho doctor's lab. They'd found some of those awful videos. The one with the poor gorilla or whatever. We were jumpy. That sort of stuff you can't just aim a gun at and eliminate.

Q: But you did.
A: I did, yes. But the boy said one of our trigger words.

Q: Explain that.
A: We'd been given orders. The chief petty officer came into the snipers' bunks and told us if anybody came off that island and spoke one of those trigger words, we had authority to open fire. *Hungry* was one of them.

Q: Any others?
A: I can't entirely remember. *Worm,* I'm sure was one. *Infected.*

Q: And so because a very hungry boy on a boat *said* he was hungry, he got himself shot.
A: He was infected, sir. That much was made clear in the aftermath. And from what I've heard about some of the others, a bullet was an easy way to go.

Q: You didn't answer my question.
A: With all due respect, you didn't *ask* a question, sir. You made a statement, sir. I'll tell you this: I never trained as a combat sniper thinking one day I'd shoot a young boy on a boat. That's not why

men join up. We're supposed to be doing it for God and country and . . . Jesus. It haunts me. I heard people use that phrase and I never quite understood. Honestly, I thought it was a bit histrionic. But I get it now. I know what it is to be haunted. That boy's face haunts me, sir, and it will until the day I depart this world for whatever's waiting for me.

From *Troop 52: Legacy of the Modified Hydatid*

(AS PUBLISHED IN *GQ* MAGAZINE) BY CHRIS PACKER:

MAX KIRKWOOD IS the oldest-looking fifteen-year-old you'll ever see.

His eyes fade into his head and their edges are knitted with wrinkles. His hair has a stripped-out, mousy aspect. There is a pronounced stoop when he sits down: his shoulders are rounded and hunched in a gait one associates with the elderly. He looks like someone who has been subjected to unimaginable pressures and now, that pressure withdrawn, his body still bears the weight.

You have to remind yourself that Max is still a boy. But he's a boy who has seen far more than most others his age.

We speak through an impermeable barrier at the clinic. It is not unlike the way inmates speak to their spouses in jail. There are phones on each side of the Plexiglas. After I finish, an orderly will wipe down the earpiece with a powerful germ-killer. The clinic operates at the highest levels of precaution. It took months of wrangling and compromise to secure a brief interview with Max.

The clinic itself is a gargantuan boxy structure far removed from any population center. The things inside the clinic are potentially lethal to humankind. The humans who reside in the clinic aren't dangerous—what may be thriving inside of them, though, are very dangerous. The viruses and contagions and parasites. The worms.

Max is in good spirits today. He's wearing a paper gown and slippers. He tells me that everything is burned after he wears it, as a precaution.

"When you get a whole new wardrobe every day, I guess it's best that they're made out of paper," he says with a wry smile.

Max Kirkwood was spared. His fellow troopmate Newton Thornton was not. Why? That is as yet unknown. Recent revelations at the tribunal trial of Admiral Stonewall Brewer—chief tactical commander of the Falstaff Island event—indicate that the thinking may've been that Max would be a good candidate for study. There is a possibility he was spared because if not, there would have been nobody left to gauge the effectiveness of the worm. It is shocking to believe such thinking may prevail at the upper echelons of the military establishment.

Max is well clear of that now. In fact he seems to remember little of his experience on Falstaff Island. It is entirely possible, of course, that he doesn't *want* to remember—that his mind, seeking peace, has simply jettisoned these memories. Who could blame him if that is the case?

He speaks about the others in clipped, jagged sentences. They are the only aspects of the ordeal that he claims to truly recall, and by and large he recalls them with great fondness and care.

Of Tim Riggs, his Scoutmaster: "Dr. Riggs was the coolest adult I ever knew. But he didn't try hard to be cool. He was actually sort of not-cool, with the way he dressed and his fussiness. But he was cool because he treated us the way he'd treat grown-ups."

Of Ephraim Elliot: "Eef was my best friend. You could count on Eef. He always stuck up for you. He had a really big heart. I just think that, on the island, something crawled into his head and he couldn't get rid of it."

Of Kent Jenks: "I still have a hard time believing he's gone. I mean, he was like

Superman—really, he was. If anyone could have swum back to North Point, it was Big K."

Of Shelley Longpre: "There was something the matter with him. I'm not so sad about Shel, to be honest. That's a shitty thing to say, but whatever."

Of Newton: "Newt would have been a great dad. The *best*, I just know it. He knew so much. The strongest of any of us. I really wish we hadn't ragged on him so bad."

When I ask him what else he can remember, his face grows distant, as if his mind is sprinting away from my question.

"There was a turtle," he says finally.

He grows silent. Then the words pour out in a shocking flood.

"Do you know how *hard* it is to kill something? Nothing wants to die. Things cling to their lives against all hope, even when it's hopeless. It's like the end is always there, you can't escape it, but things try so, *so* hard not to cross that finish line. So when they finally do, everything's been stripped away. Their bodies and happiness and hope. Things just don't know when to die. I wish they did. I wish my friends had known that. Sort of, anyway. But I'm glad they tried. That's part of being human, right? Part of being any living thing. You hold on to life until it gets ripped away from you. Even if it gets ripped away in pieces. You just *hold on*."

He grows silent. His head dips. When he looks up again his eyes are red at their edges and he's near tears.

"I killed a turtle," he says simply.

It seems the most wretched admission he's ever made. I want to reach out and hug him— but I can't because a thick barrier prevents it and anyway, there may still be something inside of Max that could kill me.

An orderly leads me away shortly after this. Max has been overstimulated. He needs to cool down.

I walk out to my car. The sky is gray with the threat of rain. I try to put myself in Max's shoes on that island. I picture being confronted with a faceless hungering threat that he never truly understood. And it amazes me that he—that all the boys—hung tough together. They didn't abandon each other—maybe it never entered their minds that they *could*. Those ideas come with the dawn of adulthood, and all the cruelties implicit in that stage of life.

To: Alex Markson

Subject: Hi . . .

Message:

Hey Alex,

We don't even know each other really, so maybe this is weird. But I don't know what's happened to you—you vanished off Facebook! I hope you're not gone for good. :(I'd miss all your great posts. So weird, I know, because you're a stranger. But it doesn't feel that way. I guess I was just thinking about you, maybe even a little worried, because of what's been happening lately in my little town. It's been crazy. Not good crazy. Scary-crazy. Anyway, this is silly. I'm sure you're just taking a break. But still, I hope you're OK. Sincerely (is that weird?), Trudy Dennison.

Chapter Forty-Nine

Some nights, Max Kirkwood would climb the bluffs on the outskirts of North Point and stare out over the water toward Falstaff Island.

This was after it had all happened. After the arrival of the hungry man; the madness of the island. After he'd stood at the prow of Oliver McCanty's boat with the glowing red dot—a sniper's laser sight—pinned to his chest.

After the military decontamination, they had transferred him to an isolated clinic. He was toxic, after all. *Infected.*

Or maybe not.

They had poked and prodded, drawn pints of blood, endoscoped him, X-rayed him, done MRIs and cranial maps, dosed him with every vaccination known to mankind.

After all that, they adjudged him to be clean.

It felt strange returning to North Point. Everything was the same, but everything was different. His Scouting friends were gone. Those who'd been his friends before now kept their distance. People treated him differently. Most of them pitied him. Some, though, felt that he must have done horrible things on the island to have survived. Others crossed to the opposite side of the street when he came walking down it.

At irregular intervals, a black van would show up at his house. Men in hazmat suits would get out. More tests. More needles. They collected his blood and fluids and solids in sterile pouches. It made Max laugh to think that some scientist in a white lab coat would be picking apart his shit with tweezers, frowning and tutting as he searched for clues—well, it *almost* made him laugh.

Max had bad dreams. Those were the only dreams he had anymore—most nights it was just blackness. He closed his eyes and *bang!* Black. Eight hours later, the black went away. He woke up. Those were the good nights.

On the bad nights, his dreams were still black. But the blackness was infested with sounds. Squirming. Always this squirmy-squirmy noise in the blackness. And when he woke up, Max would be drooling like a baby.

His mom kissed him good night on the forehead now. Used to be on the lips.

He tried to return to the life he'd known, but that simply didn't exist anymore.

He wasn't allowed to go to school. The parents of many students didn't feel right having Max in the same airspace with their kids. Nothing against Max personally. He was a good kid. A survivor.

But the things Max had encountered on the island were survivors, too. The parents had read the newspapers. One of Dr. Edgerton's videotaped experiments had leaked online. Everyone knew what those things could do—objectively they did, anyhow. Everyone had *seen* things, clinically, but those things hadn't touched them. Not in any tangible way. So people knew in their brains but not inside their skin, and there *was* a difference.

Everybody thought they knew what had happened on that island. Everyone was an expert. But they didn't *really* know. What they thought was bad. What really happened was a lot worse.

Max studied at home. The teachers sent assignments to him in paper envelopes. He had to send his answers back via e-mail, as the teachers expressed concern over actually *handling* the papers he'd touched.

One morning he found a poster tacked to his front door. It was supposed to look like a carnival poster—like, for the Freak Tent.

The Amazing Worm Boy, read the blood-dripping type underneath.

His mother made sweet-and-sour pork for dinner one night. The smell was so familiar to Max—that high stinking sweetness—that he started to scream. He didn't stop until his father tossed the pan of pork outside in a snowbank. It took him a while, on account of the fact he limped real bad; the MPs had shattered his right kneecap after he and Kent's dad stole Calvin Walmack's cigarette boat.

Max kept to himself. No choice, really. He wandered the woods and down by the sea.

He thought about his friends: Kent and Eef and Newt, especially. He'd recall the strangest, most trivial things, like Cub Kar rally night. One year, his car had lost to Kent's car in the finals—except everyone thought Kent's dad helped him build the car. Its wheels were thin as pizza cutters. Eef's mom had said it was cheating. Newt's mom agreed. Things got pretty heated. Kent's dad kicked over the canteen of McDonald's orange drink and stormed out. Eef's mom's eyes had popped out and she'd said: *And that man is our police chief.*

Max missed them all so much.

It was weird. They'd all had other friends. But now, Max couldn't think of any friends who'd mattered as much.

He'd give anything to have one more day with them. Even one of those piss-away ones they used to have in Scouts: roaming the woods on a fall day with the smoky smell of dead leaves crunching under their boots. Playing King of the Mountain and Would You Rather? while nerdy Newt collected samples for some dumb merit badge or another. Stealing away with Ephraim to stare at the stars and dream their crazy dreams. And they would all be just like they were before. Not skinny or hungry or trying to hurt one another.

There was nothing Max wouldn't give to have that again. Just one more day.

And Shelley? Well, Shel wasn't in these daydreams. If Shel popped up at all, it was in his nightmares.

Max had a shrink now—the same one Newton and Ephraim used to visit. When he'd told Dr. Harley about wishing for one more day with his old friends, he'd been advised against wishing for things that couldn't happen. Harley called this negative projection. Max thought Harley was an idiot.

If there was one thing he wanted to tell his lost friends, it was that *lots* of adults didn't have a goddamn clue. It was one of the sadder facts he'd had to come to grips with. Adults could be just as stupid as kids. Stupider even, because often they didn't have to answer to anybody.

Of course, Harley wore a face mask during their sessions, same as a doctor would wear when he's operating—same as Scoutmaster Tim had worn, probably.

Sometimes Max wanted to rip it off and cough into his stupid sucker-fish face. The Amazing Worm Boy strikes again!

406

Chapter Fifty

One evening, Max borrowed his uncle's boat and piloted it toward Falstaff Island.

His heart jogged faster as the island came into view, rising against the horizon like the hump of a breaching whale. It was charred black. Nothing but the odd burnt tree spiking up from the earth. The water had the sterile chlorine smell of a public pool. It was the most desolate place he'd ever seen. It echoed the desolation inside of him.

The emptiness . . .

The emptiness?

Max leaned both hands on the gunwale. A nameless hunger was building inside of him. It gnawed at his guts with teeth that called his name.

Acknowledgments

Thank you to my father, who read the rough manuscript and said: "Son, you may have something here. I don't know what that something is, to be honest, but something." To my agent, the kick-ass Kirby Kim, who wasn't repelled enough by the subject matter to dismiss it out of hand. He may have even said something like: "We could actually have something here . . . possibly." To my editor, Ed Schlesinger, who put the manuscript through the proverbial wood chipper, gathered the shreds, and helped me put them back together, then said: "Hell, we just may have something here." To Scott Smith, who kindly read the manuscript and offered some fantastic suggestions, all since implemented.

Thank you, Ian Rogers, who proofed the typeset pages and caught all of my goof-ups. And to Derek Hounsell for creating the Thestomax ad.

I'd like to thank Stephen King, whose first novel, *Carrie*, was a great inspiration to me while I was writing. The use of newspaper clippings, interviews, and magazine profiles seemed a perfect way to tell not only *Carrie* but also *The Troop*, where so much information is unknown to the main characters yet must be related to readers. Seeing how artfully Mr. King employed these devices, I figured I'd . . . uh, *borrow* . . . that structure. Steal? Lord, I hope not. Let's just say I found the narrative chassis of *Carrie* to be perfect for my uses, and grafted my own story on it. If you've read this book and are now reading this, hopefully you'll agree that the plot of *Carrie*—a story about a telekinetic girl with a really bad mom who rains death and destruction on her small-minded hometown—and the plot of *The Troop* are about as dissimilar as any two books could be. That said, I want to honor the master. So, honor paid.

Finally, I want to thank Colleen, the love of my life (corny, sure, but it also happens to be the literal truth) and Nicholas, our son. There was a time when I wrote almost solely for myself. I don't anymore. I write for our family, and I'm deeply grateful to be able to do so.